Frederi

The House of Elmore

SALZWASSER
VERLAG

Frederick William Robinson

The House of Elmore

Reprint of the original, first published in 1865.

1st Edition 2022 | ISBN: 978-3-75259-026-5

Verlag (Publisher): Salzwasser Verlag GmbH, Zeilweg 44, 60439 Frankfurt, Deutschland
Vertretungsberechtigt (Authorized to represent): E. Roepke, Zeilweg 44, 60439 Frankfurt, Deutschland
Druck (Print): Books on Demand GmbH, In de Tarpen 42, 22848 Norderstedt, Deutschland

THE
HOUSE OF ELMORE.

A Family History.

BY THE AUTHOR OF

"GRANDMOTHER'S MONEY," "WOODLEIGH," ETC.

"When will the ancient curse be still'd, that weighs
Upon our house? Some mocking demon sports
With every new-formed hope, nor envious leaves
One hour of joy. So near the haven smiled—
So smooth the treacherous main—secure I deem'd
My happiness; the storm was lulled; and bright
In evening's lustre gleamed the sunny shore:
Then through the placid air the tempest sweeps,
And bears me to the roaring surge again!"

SCHILLER.

LONDON:

1865.

THE HOUSE OF ELMORE.

INTRODUCTION.

Reminiscences of the past seldom bring bitterness to our wandering memories. With most men there is allied with suchlike recollections, a sad, sweet, holy calmness, that teaches the lessons of content and love; that hallows forms over which the dark curtain has long since dropped; that passes over bygone griefs, misfortunes, and regrets so lightly, that they become fair mental resting-places; that reconciles us to the great home-losses, the household gaps for ever blank and void, pointing at the same time to the doctrine of resignation from the pages of the Book. Such men I can envy.

My father was a rich man and a proud one. At the time of which I write, he had scarcely reached his nine-and-thirtieth year, and his wife, and my mother, was twelve years his junior. He had led her to the altar a bride of sixteen summers, and time had not blunted the first romance of his attachment, nor made him less of a worshipper.

The remembrance of the home in which he lived (a mansion overlooking the West-end parks), would not be so strongly engraven on my mind, were it not for the shame that fell upon the name of Elmore there. The ban and interdict laid upon recurrence to that home, served but the more indelibly to fix its lasting impression on me; strengthened as it was by the great blot on my father's honour—the lasting change in my father's life.

From the time that my parents set forth upon their marriage pilgrimage, they lived for society and pleasure, and the present was the sole study—the single idol at which the knee was bent. There was no future in their anticipations; the world was before them, and they could enjoy it with their riches—there was little bound to them, for my father was ranked as one of the wealthiest commoners in England.

There were four children to bless my father's marriage. Gilbert, the eldest born, a tall, pale boy, of ten years old, with thoughtful dark eyes and long black hair; myself, two years his junior; Edward, a blue-eyed, golden-ringleted child, of some six years; and my sister Agnes, twin sister of my younger brother, and the flower of the flock.

We saw but little of our parents; strict devotees to fashion, and ever with the glittering crowd, they left us to our nurses and our governess, and, assured of our comfort, looked for content beyond the hearth. A few light words, some stray kisses and endearments now and then, sufficed to assure us that we had father and mother living, and that was all.

But the dawning of a great change came upon this unprofitable existence, and dimmed the brilliant vista on which my father's gaze was ever fixed.

By and by, my father came more often to our rooms, and sat longer with us, and took greater interest in our studies and occupations. Sometimes he would gather us round his knees, and teach us from the great storehouse of his own learning, and linger with us till the servants came to summon him. But he was changed. There was not that free, careless look upon his handsome face—the colour had faded somewhat from it, and was, even to our childish observation, lined with anxiety, and often haggard.

Amongst the frequent guests at our house, one was particularly remarkable—a Sir William Ashford—a fine-looking man of about thirty years of age. My father had had only one friend, to whom he was particularly attached, and he had lately gone abroad; therefore, Sir William Ashford came more prominently into view, and the house seemed never free from him.

With all but my father he was a great favourite. He brought me and my brothers costly books and expensive toys, and Agnes articles of more delicate workmanship; and took an interest in us, and paid us considerably more attention than is due from the man to the child.

In those quiet evenings, of which we had so few, we looked forward to the arrival of Sir William with some anxiety, and watched from the windows for his coming carriage.

To my mother—my beautiful and graceful mother—he was the soul of chivalrous gallantry; and it was this rapt devotion that, beginning by slow degrees, and gaining ground, had attracted the notice of my father.

There was nothing to cause a decided suspicion, or to afford a pretext to break off his acquaintance, and yet there was a marked attention which did not seem to displease my mother, and which began to prey upon her husband.

Then there was a quarrel—the first quarrel—between our parents; and I stole down, with my brother Gilbert, to the door of the room, and stood tremblingly there, listening to the deep voice of my father, and the softly reproachful answers from my mother, and afraid to enter. The storm passed over, and they were friends again; and my father came less to our rooms for a few weeks, and Sir William Ashford was more attentive than ever to my mother, and more kind to her children. Then there were more quarrels, and more reconciliations, and still *he* came, and still my mother received him graciously, as if in gentle defiance to my father's wish.

There came a December night, when there were more guests, more music, feasting, dancing in the house, than I had ever known. It was after one of those reconciliations before alluded to, and also the anniversary of my parents' wedding-day. Upon such occasions as these—and on these alone—my father had a peculiar wish to see his children mingling with the guests. At no other time were we suffered to know anything of the great people that came to the house to join in fête and ball, save what we could learn by ourselves from the servants, or by stolen observations taken at half-open doors. But each anniversary of the day he married pretty Agnes Witherby, he set aside all rules of fashion, and courted and treated his boys and girls as principal guests. "Surely, they have a right to participate in the festivities of the occasion," he would say with a laugh, "and my heart cannot deny the little rogues." We counted the days and weeks that intervened between his first promise and the realisation of the event, which, in itself, was indeed a golden night.

On this particular evening it was a grander night than usual; there were more guests—an ambassador or two—a sprinkling of members of Parliament and their wives, and more than one peer of the realm. Sir William Ashford had been invited, but had not accepted the invitation, neither had he responded to it; but there was my Aunt Witherby, a sister of my mother, and a very important personage indeed.

I can remember the sensation which my doll of a sister Agnes created, as, perfectly self-possessed, she paraded the rooms like a queen of the fairies, at the least.

There were many covert smiles at pretty Aggy exchanged between the guests, and my aunt rounded her eyes in mute astonishment, when she clambered to the vacant seat by her side, and puzzled the woman of the world (a woman not easily puzzled either) with her questions and replies. They were not childish questions, neither were they suggested by a premature oldness of thought; they were satirical, and critical, and bold; and my aunt shuddered once or twice, and sniffed at her bouquet, to hide her embarrassment.

I sketch this scene and these characters in mere outline—parts are to me, of course, faint and indistinct; but many of these guests—figures passing dimly behind the screen—may come into the daylight with the future record of my life.

The fête was in its full glory, when my mother was observed to leave her partner abruptly, and sink upon a chair, faint and exhausted. Ere my father could reach her side she was in a swoon.

The dance was abruptly broken off, and the guests crowded round her, and came flying towards the point of interest with glasses of water, wine, and smelling salts. She soon recovered, but complaining still of faintness, was led by my father from the room, he tenderly solicitous of every step.

"Continue the dancing," she murmured; "I will return presently; this oppressive feeling will soon be gone. It is the heat, I think."

In less than a quarter of an hour my father returned, with the tidings that she was better, but too faint to make her reappearance so quickly after her nervous attack.

Agnes glided from the ball-room, and came back again, and sat beside me on a couch.

"I have been to see mamma."

"I hope she is better, Aggy?"

"Oh! much better; but her head aches so, she tells me. I wonder why she kissed me to-night, when I went up to her room, and why she cried so bitterly?"

"Did she *cry*, Agnes?"

"Yes, Luke."

"That's strange."

"Well—perhaps it is—but let us sit here and watch the

dancers. I wish we could dance, Luke. Mamma says we are too young to learn, but shall when we are old enough. I am sure I am quite old enough to dance—don't you think so, Luke?"

But I was thinking of my mother.

My father went out again, and came back apologising for Mrs. Elmore, who was still suffering from a violent headache, which, he regretted to say, would incapacitate her from rejoining the party. My father did not quit his guests for some hours, and strove to make amends for the absence of the hostess by the polite attention of the host.

It was nearly one o'clock, when, watching his opportunity, he stole away to see after the health of his dear Agnes, and left the company waltzing gaily round.

The hour was late, and the carriages were locked in masses without, and the torches of linkboys were flaring to and fro in the dark night.

"This is my favourite waltz," said Agnes to Gilbert and Edward, who came toward us arm-in-arm; "now sit still and listen. This is the 'Honeymoon Waltz,' Gilbert."

The waltz proceeded, the dance seemed to grow more furious rather than to flag, the music crashed from the further end of the room, the waltzers spun rapidly past, when the door opened, and my father stood on the threshold.

He was not remarked at first save by ourselves; and we looked from one to the other inquiringly, and held our breath in mute suspense and horror. There he stood, so ghastly white, with eyes so fixed and vacant, and mouth unnaturally distorted, making no effort to approach further into the room. A young officer and his partner were first caught by his wild appearance, and stopped suddenly; another pair, attracted by the intensity of their gaze, halted abruptly also; then another and another; then a scream from more than one lady; then the whole mass of dancers still and terrified. The band ceased playing, and all eyes were turned towards the door.

"What is the matter, Elmore?" cried a dozen friendly voices.

"Matter?" he answered, vaguely.

"What is it—what is it?" inquired others; and more than one shrieked out, "Don't go near him!"

My father walked slowly into the room, the guests shrinking back and making way.

"Pray continue the dance; I disturb you!" he said, hurriedly; "nothing has happened; I am well—very well Where is Sir William? Let us have some more lights! Nothing has happened—nothing has happened," he repeated, looking wildly round; "continue the dance, for God's sake! Don't mind me, I am well—only my head—my head keeps swelling so. Mrs. Witherby, will you favour me with your hand for the next dance?—nothing has hap——"

He stopped, and, pressing his hands to his temples, gave vent to such a prolonged yell of madness, that on each face came the pallor of the dead. Another instant, and he was surrounded by his friends, and borne shrieking from the room, and all was tumult and confusion in the house.

He was carried to his bed a maniac, and we four children were left in the deserted ball-room, strewn with music leaves, stray gloves and ribbons, motherless and disgraced.

* * * * *

If the fable wonders of the Eastern Magi were not all creations of a subtle brain, and we could look into their magic crystals, and witness—standing within enchanted circles, or girded by belts, the power of which is illimitable and potent—the lives we might have followed, the pursuits we might have led, the faces that might have been bent over us;—gazing at the ambition of a life hanging by a single hair, waiting a word, a glance, a movement of our own; looking at the future as it might have been mapped out to us, and which we, groping onwards with the blind, pass by in search of darkness; watching the quicksands in our path, and following no meteors that lead to ignorance and follies; preparing for the sorrows that are to come, the friends we are to shake hands with and pass by on the road; meeting the enemies that are to thwart those projects on which we build our hopes and prayed for their fulfilment;—if we could do this, we might learn many a lesson of content, for what is marked out for us *must* be good.

Still, with the knowledge of what my life has been, and what incidents, shifting as the coloured glasses of the schoolboy's toy, have mingled with it, and with the careers of those I loved, the thought is ever with me what would have been my progress—what friends should I have had, destinies to meet, difficulties to encounter, and hopes to strive for—had I lived as my childhood began—had my guilty mother never left the blight upon the hearth, or my father never fled that society which once he lived for and made his study of, but with his riches braved the world in that home where his fond heart was wrecked?

CHAPTER I.

A MAN OF IMPULSE.

THERE is a pleasant sea-side town called Wharnby, on the English coast. One mile from Wharnby—which was in itself, at the time I write, but a nest of houses buried between white, giant-like cliffs, that flanked it right and left—stood my father's house, a dark red-brick mansion, embosomed within a thick plantation leading to the very verge of the cliff. There was not a habitation between it and Wharnby; it stood alone, exposed to the howling winds that came rushing and roaring from the sea on tempestuous nights, making every window rattle in its casement. There were extensive garden grounds, a miniature lake, a large park well stocked with deer, shrubberies, preserves, everything indicative of the taste of an English gentleman; and yet standing perched on the summit of the white crag, with the black trees nodding over its roof, it presented a gloomy, desolate appearance. There were some lovely views from the top windows of the house: looking inland there was to be seen a fine undulating country of wood and dale, and broad field golden with corn, green with meadow pasture, purple with the clover, which stretched for miles on either side, and was intersected here and there by a winding chalky road. Looking seaward, there was one vast expanse of green waves, over which occasionally glided a solitary fishing-smack or row-boat. The coast was a dangerous one; and ships of heavy burden and deep draught were warned from the hidden rocks and quicksands lurking near the tempting land, and by lighthouse and floating beacons were shown that Wharnby was no resting-place by night. Despite these precautions, many a shipwreck in the fierce winter months occurred off the coast, many a gun of distress caused me and my brothers to look up with meaning and terrified looks from our studies, and watch the pale face of our father as he sat reading by the fire. Many a time have we gone down to the cliff's edge, and gazed over at the battered vessel, struggling with the surging waves, like a living thing, for life.

It was only a scene of danger like a wreck that could tempt my father out of his usual cold demeanour—an icy kind of sternness and immobility of visage which stood ever in contrast to his black, restless eyes that shifted from one object to another—from sons to daughter, and daughter to sons—fifty times within the hour. So terribly impassive was his accustomed manner, so little interest did he take in any passing thing or any childish action we might do, that there was a relief in even the sound of the minute guns booming over the great waste, for then *he* was interested, anxious, and more natural. He was the only teacher of myself and brothers, a severe yet good preceptor, and we learned of him rapidly and well. It was a curious sight to witness our studies every morning, in a long, low-ceilinged room, commanding a partial glimpse of the sea from a corner window. My brother Gilbert was as grave and sedate as his sire; whilst Edward and I, less considerate and reflective, were constantly meeting with harsh reproofs for our inattention. So partial was my father to his teachings—his only occupation—that he often prolonged them beyond the allotted period of time, much to the dissatisfaction of his children, which was expressed on the part of my younger brother and myself by restless motions on our seats, and loud whispers to each other.

One day, after being detained fully two hours over our usual time, we were reluctantly dismissed—a detention the more annoying to me, as I had been anticipating the launch of a toy-boat from the sands, and the tide had risen during the delay. I gave vent to my displeasure by muttering discontent, as I sauntered through the park with Gilbert and Edward.

"Never mind, Luke," said Edward, as he ran by my side, with his light ringlets dancing over his shoulders; "to-morrow will do, won't it?"

"We must make it do, it seems," I grumbled.

Gilbert walked by my side for several minutes without speaking; then he laid his hand on my arm, and, giving me an impressive look, said—

"You would wish to have more play-time, Luke?"

"Of course I would."

"But our work-time is the happiest period of our father's life, Luke," said he; "I am only eleven years old, but I can see that. He is fond of teaching us; it is his only pleasure. More play-time do you wish now, brother?"

"I—I—why, no."

"That's right; I feel tired myself very often, especially over the Latin and Greek; but I do not show it; it pains him."

Profiting by the hint, I never attempted a sign of rebellion again; and my father expounded and elaborated without a dissentient look.

About this time our household was enlivened by a fresh face—a rosy-cheeked, motherly-looking woman, who came in answer to an advertisement for housekeeper, and on whom my father immediately decided. She was about fifty years of age, and had two sons out at sea, concerning whom she was continually narrating anecdotes, to which we boys sometimes listened, my sister paid but little attention, and my father heard with a stoical gravity, never disturbed by any astonishing turn the narrative might take.

Mrs. Higson was a very chatty lady, full of ghost stories, and gifted with a keen appreciation of the marvellous; exceedingly nervous after dark, and subject to spasmodic jumps at nothing; but, withal, she was a valuable addition to the household—an honest, trustworthy old soul, and a godsend to the sons of Elmore. My father required no fashionable attendants now. There was a governess, who called every day, and took Agnes under her especial care—a short, prim lady of forty, very learned in the sciences, deep in the mysteries of grammar, and rules for chaste deportment, and an accomplished pianiste, under whose tuition Agnes profited and progressed, despite the repeated reports of Miss Berncastle to the parent, on divers subjects connected with Miss Elmore's conduct.

We had no guests at "The Rest," as my father had christened his retreat, upon our first arrival at Wharnby. Numerous letters came daily, to all which my father replied not; then they grew scarce, and more scarce, and finally dropped altogether.

There were many letters, written evidently by one person, that were the last to cease. The address, the only portion that came beneath our vision, was in a fine, small hand as clear and sharp as if it had been engraved. These letters followed one another, day after day, pertinaciously. My father would read them, appear agitated, and, after a re-perusal, tear them into the smallest fragments before he trusted the pieces from his hand; but he never hazarded a comment concerning them, and they finally ceased, after lingering some time beyond the others. When they came no more, my father used to stand at the window looking on the drive, till the post-hour had gone by. It was evident that he missed the epistles to which he had never returned a single line.

Having attempted to give a picture of my father's home,

and of his pursuits and ours, I commence my story four years from the date which made my father a changed man, and altered the whole tenor of our lives.

One evening, early in December, we formed a family group in the dark wainscoted sitting-room, the panels glowing with the roaring fire, to which Mrs. Higson had given a final stir, and departed. My father's favourite seat was an old-fashioned leathern chair, studded thickly with brass nails; and therein he was ensconced on the evening mentioned, pale, silent, thoughtful, with his long black hair (he wore it nearly touching his shoulders) hanging over his white, but puckered forehead; his thin hand, marked with dark veins of unusual thickness, buried within its masses, and affording a support to his weary, aching head. Thus would my father sit for hours, with his shifting restless gaze, so peculiar to him now, with his finely cut lips unnaturally compressed, and full of those bitter thoughts which he took a wild, morbid pleasure in recalling and in fostering, and yet which made him draw in his breath and writhe as with sudden pain. My brothers and myself were employed in diligently working at our tasks for the morrow, by the light of two wax candles, in massive silver candlesticks which my father particularly prized as the work of a great artist, whose name is a household word amongst us. Agnes was not with us at the time, and the light music of the piano from an adjoining room told of her employment.

"Is that wind?" asked my father, suddenly breaking in upon a silence of above an hour's duration.

We listened, and the heavy, smothered roll of the tempest was heard sounding in the distance.

"It sounds seaward," said Gilbert.

"God help those at sea, then!" said my father, "for there will be a heavy storm to-night."

In a few minutes there were signs of his prediction being shortly verified: the wind increased in sound, and roared and plunged, and made strange noises round the house, whilst, with every lull, the lively music from the next room came in as an accompaniment.

"What a curious child!" he half muttered to himself; "had I been alone at that age, upon such a night as this, I should have died with fright."

"Aggy is no coward, is she, father?" asked Gilbert, looking up, and glad of a pretext to engage him in conversation.

"Too brave!" he murmured; "I wish she were more like a child; but, then, you are all strange children."

"Strange!" cried I, attempting a laugh; "how do you make us out strange, papa?"

He did not answer; he had resumed his old, brooding demeanour, and neither our voices, nor the music in the house, nor the increasing fury of the wind, had more effect upon him than if he had been a marble image.

The storm gathered—the wind howled—the casements rattled, like peals of musketry—and the whole house seemed rocking in the tempest. Suddenly, across his pallid features passed a remarkable change; a crimson flush mounted to his cheeks—his teeth ground together—his hands clenched—and he leaped from the chair, crying, "Tell her to stop! Tell her to stop, in the name of God! Agnes! Agnes! Agnes!"

The music suddenly ceased—little feet came pattering along the passage—the door opened, and my sister, white with fright, ran into the room.

"Oh! what has happened, papa?" she cried; "what is it?"

"Agnes Elmore," said my father, grasping her fiercely by the wrist, "where did you learn that music?"

"Which, papa?"

"The last—the—the——"

"The waltz, father?" she inquired.

"Ay, the waltz," with a shudder.

"It has been in my music-book a long while—a very long while, papa," said she. "I played it over with Miss Berncastle this morning."

"Go and fetch it."

As she went out of the room, he flung himself back in the chair, griping one hand within the other.

Edward sat still, with his blue eyes fixed upon him; but Gilbert crossed to his side, and cried, "Are you ill, papa? are you ill?"

"No, my boy; there, go on with your tasks. Well?"

Agnes re-entered with the music-book.

"This is it."

It was a handsome book—its leaves radiant with gold, and its covers richly gilt morocco; but my father tore ruthlessly from it about half a dozen leaves, and thrust them on the fire.

"'Honeymoon Waltz!'—mocking words, coined by a devil," he cried; "there is your fitting place! Agnes, as you love your father, or his word, never play that waltz again; even when I am away from here, or dead. It is an insult to my memory; it is a curse—it is a brand—a burning iron on his soul!"

"Because——" began Agnes, shrinking from him in his vehemence, but keeping her large eyes fixed upon his face.

"Because it was played on a night about four years ago, when a guilty woman broke my heart, and crushed all hope and love. Because everything associated with that woman is accursed to me in my disgrace. Because you have never had a mother worthy of the name—a name which if even one of you muttered in your sleep, would make me hate you all my life. You will understand me better when you grow older, children. Understand me sufficiently enough now to know that her name is lost, her home is gone, and such things as that waltz belong but to the past, and madden me by recollection."

He had hardly ceased speaking, when the bell at the lodge was heard to ring loudly.

We listened; a furious gust of wind followed, and then the bell rang again.

"Where's Johnson?" asked my father. "Is he not down at the lodge?"

Johnson, our lodge-keeper, a feeble old man, whose office was a sinecure—there being but few calls upon his attention at "The Rest"—knocked without.

"Come in."

"There's—there's a ring, Mr. Elmore."

"I know it," said my father, briefly; "that is the third peal. Listen!"

The bell rang for the third time.

"Who can it be?" said Johnson, with an anxious look at my father.

"Go and see," was the laconic rejoinder.

Johnson—whose nerves had been somewhat shaken by a wild legend of Mrs. Higson's, concerning a wandering spirit, supposed to have been formerly in the corporeal possession of an old fisherman who was found drowned on the sands many years ago, and which spirit was addicted to nocturnal meanderings with a net and top-boots—slowly took his departure, not at all reconciled in mind to a walk down the long avenue, as far as the lodge gates, in the darkness and the wind.

"There must be some mistake," said I, hazarding a conjecture.

"Probably," replied my father; "there are few visitors—and we want few. We have no friends, and I know none worth the having."

It was some time before Johnson made his re-appearance, which he did with an important air and a bustling manner, indicative of news.

"If you please, Mr. Elmore, it's Mr. Silvernot."

"I do not know Mr. Silvernot; send him away."

"But—but—Mr. Elmore—sir——"

"But what?"

"Mr. Silvernot's the rector of the parish."

"What of that?"

"You don't mean to send *him* away, sir!"

"I am busy—I am ill; another time."

Johnson, very ill at ease, shuffled towards the door, halted on the threshold, and scratched his head.

"I made sure on your seeing him, Mr. Elmore," he stuttered, "and so he's in the parlour, along with the globes."

"Blunderer!" cried my parent, his eyebrows lowering, "show the man in."

"It may be something of importance, papa," I said.

"Importance, Luke!" said my father, with a half bitter laugh, that told how little importance the world and its doings had for his deadened mind.

"Mr. Silvernot!"

Holding the door wide to admit the rector, Johnson announced the coming of the stranger, whose peculiar appearance took us all by surprise, and even half roused my father from his apathy. He was a little, dwarfish man, hardly five feet in height, perfectly well made, and of good figure, with a pale, wrinkled face, little grey eyes shining through the glasses of gold-mounted spectacles, and black, stubbly hair that stood on end and looked implacably wiry. His white cravat had experienced the effects of the fierce wind, and the neat tie was close under his ear, whilst his black coat, being fastened to the throat by the wrong button and the right buttonhole, made this little personage present a figure more fit for a farce, than for the representative of the church of Wharnby. His age at this period did not exceed two-and-thirty years; but the first impressions made upon us by his deeply lined face, was that he was a venerable son of the clergy, whose years were verging upon two score and ten at least.

He advanced towards my father with a very graceful bow, and extended his hand.

Appearing not to observe the friendly gesture, my father, pointing to a chair, said—

"Be seated, Mr. Silvernot. If your business be of that importance that my children——"

"Not at all," hastily said the diminutive rector, persisting in standing before my sire with outstretched hand; "not at all. I hope I see you well, sir."

My father, forced to place his hand in that of the stranger, did so with a marked coldness that apparently had no effect upon him.

"Mr. Elmore," said he, coolly taking off a pair of india-rubber over-shoes, and standing them in the fender at a remote distance from the fire, "you are, perhaps, slightly astonished at my visit?"

"Truly I did not anticipate so unexpected a *pleasure*," with a marked emphasis on the last word.

"Mr. Elmore," said the rector, seating himself, "I am a child of impulse. Throughout my life I have been actuated by impulse, subjected by it to commit actions which I have sometimes bitterly regretted; but, truly, I have no strong command or control over myself. I became a rector through impulse, sir. I was intended for the army,"—drawing himself up stiffly,—'or the navy, or the bar. I liked the army—intended to choose the army, sir, when one day impulse mastered me. Why not the church? I asked myself. The next day, sir, I was at Cambridge."

He paused, but my father made no comment.

"Impulse has brought me hither to-night. When you first settled at this retreat, many friends—my parents amongst the rest—called. You did not see them. I did not consider that strictly courteous; however, no matter. I grieved to see that neither yourself nor children attended divine service at Wharnby Church, and I felt for you, sir. To-night, I was sitting alone at my vicarage (for I am a bachelor), when I thought of 'The Rest' on the cliff. Impulse immediately laid a fierce hold upon me. 'I'll go and see Mr. Elmore,' I said. I started off, lost my umbrella, and nearly went over the cliff; but here I am."

He looked up with a complaisant smile at my father, and commenced warming his hands before the fire. For the first time since his great loss, I detected the twitching at the corners of the mouth—the half-parted lips—the effort to repress a smile.

"Mr. Silvernot," said my father, "impulse has led you to a strange action, indeed, when it prompted you to visit a solitary like me. I am a Timon of Athens, and would shun society. This is 'The Rest'—a rest from a busy, lying world—my first step to the grave."

Ere he had finished, the heavy, callous look, habitual to him, was darkening his face.

"Mr. Elmore, you have met with a misfortune?" said the rector, changing his tone of voice into one more kind and gentle, as if he were speaking to a child.

"I have."

"May I inquire——?" he began.

"You may not," sternly interrupted my father.

"Your pardon. I imagined myself a spiritual adviser to you. I am so used to offering all the consolation I can to those of my own flock, that, for the moment, I forgot my place. It was not a paltry curiosity that suggested the crude inquiry, believe me. Suffice it to be, then, a misfortune. Do you know that all misfortunes are sent as trials for us by One who, with a breath, can make them vanish in His time?"

"I have learned to doubt it. I have no belief in any power, be it Divine or human, that can cancel the injury I suffer from."

"With such doubts, it is my place to aid you with my counsel," said he.

"You are not an old man?" asked my father, suddenly.

"I am thirty-two."

"*I* am forty-four—that is a difference of twelve years between us; and yet you would attempt to school your senior in years, your superior in education, your master in philosophy."

"You know nothing of the extent of my education, or the depth of my philosophy," said the dwarf, warmly. "My education has taught me the wisdom and mercy of the God you doubt, and my philosophy how to profit by it. You are in a dangerous state, sir," talking louder; "you are not fit to be left here and brood upon such thoughts. I shall not leave you so long again; no, sir; I shall call very often, so I tell you. There!"

For the second time that night, a faint smile flitted across my father's face. After a pause, my father said—

"I said I doubted that Divine power could wholly make me forget my misery. As I feel now, I must believe it. God can turn my brain, or take my soul, and do it that way—no other, sir—no other."

"Yes, sir, by prayer. By true and earnest prayer, He can make you a changed man."

"I *have* prayed."

"With bitterness at your heart, then—with hatred of some object—with the world you affect to despise festering in your thoughts. Have you prayed with your whole heart?"

"My heart is broken, or become a stone, I know not which."

"You are a misanthrope."

"Perhaps so."

"You abuse your power of reason."

"Very likely."

"You abuse that trust reposed in you, when God gave you these children for a blessing to your life. Such children as these should make no man's existence so full of utter gloom, if he have a father's love. These children should be your care and——"

"They *are* my care," he interrupted.

"Care!" cried the little man, very hot and flushed with enthusiasm. "You may teach them, sir, a few sciences, a few hard names, a few abstract ideas; but can you teach them a true love of God,—the lessons of patience—self-enduring patience,—fortitude and resignation, knowing what you are yourself?"

"I teach them all I know—all that I believe."

"Boy!" cried the clergyman, beckoning to Gilbert, "come hither."

Gilbert rose from his seat, and walked with a fearless step towards him.

"What is your name?"

"Gilbert Elmore."

"And age?"

"Fourteen."

"Is that book you are studying the Bible?

"No, my Greek Lexicon."

"Where is your Bible?"

Gilbert coloured, and made no reply. Mr. Silvernot repeated the question.

"I have not got one. There *is* a Bible somewhere about, though," added Gilbert, in extenuation.

"Mr. Elmore," said the rector, sternly, "here is your eldest son. Are you training him up to sting you when he grows a man, and when, to all your reproofs, he will say, 'Father, you should have taught me better?' You are incurring a heavy responsibility, sir, in these four children. Good God! sir' it is fearful! These children will be a curse to you, instead of a blessing. Is there no memory of a dead wife, who loved them, to school your unruly mind?"

"Peace, peace!" groaned my father.

"Is there no memory of a father or a mother, who taught you in the days of *your* youth,—nothing to make you turn and cry to God for pardon? Mr. Elmore," suddenly snatching his hand, "you will let me call and see you again? You will not close your doors upon me, till we have seen each other once more?—you will give me that poor promise?"

"Well, well—yes. When will you come?"

"I cannot say," he said, releasing my father's hand, and relapsing into his first odd manner; "it all depends upon impulse. When that attacks me, I shall be here. Don't be alarmed if I knock you up in the middle of the night; I am a strange man when the humour seizes me. I will wish you a good night, now," drawing on his shoes carefully, and rising. "Boys, I trust we shall be better acquainted; I've got a nice little villa, and hope to see you in it some day;—and my pretty miss," stooping to kiss Agnes, "there's a little sister at my father's house, and you must see her too. I hope I have not been too severe," said he, turning to my father; "but it is a good cause I fight for, and I am a zealous man."

My father slightly inclined his head, and sat looking at the fire long after the rector had withdrawn, and the wind had risen to a hurricane.

Long, long after, when the grate was a blackened void, and we sat wondering when my father would speak or make a movement, he still remained in his chair, dreaming. Mrs. Higson, knocking at the door, made him and us start, at a late hour.

"Let me have my night-lamp, Higson," he said, in a low voice.

When it was given him, he bade us all "good night," and went out of the room, saying, half aloud, "A strange man! a strange man!"

Presently he came back, and laid his hand lightly on the head of my elder brother.

"Gilbert," said he, in a voice he vainly endeavoured to render firm—"Never say to me, 'Father, you should have taught me better!'"

With the same grave face and thoughtful air, he went slowly up the broad oaken stairs to his room.

CHAPTER II.

THE SILVERNOTS OF WHARNBY.

Mr. Silvernot came again to "The Rest," and extorted from my father the promise for a fresh interview. He came a third, a fourth time—then once a week, then twice, then thrice a week, then nearly every day.

My father began to look forward to his coming, and, although he endeavoured to assume an indifference which he did not feel, it was evident that the visits of Mr. Silvernot were gradually having a salutary effect upon him, weaning him from the bitterness of his present life, and softening the heart which he had thought for ever hardened. All this was done, tôo, with so unassuming an air—with so evident a desire to do good, merely for the sake or the pleasure of it alone—done in the little rector's odd, whimsical, and impulsive manner, that it won into the better nature of my father by imperceptible degrees, and gradually began to work a change.

Alas! as there will be good and evil angels—good and evil genius—good and evil thoughts, warring against each other in unceasing conflict, in unremitting struggle, till time shall be no more, and eternity shall end all mystery—so are there (although every man is not capable of distinguishing the face beneath the vizard) good and evil friends marching side by side with every traveller to the goal, crossing each other's path, and making life a great enigma.

What a crude misnomer—"The Rest!" Is there any rest but the grave for the descendants of Adam? Is not peace—peace of mind and body—a fabled invisible on this side the mysterious mark drawn by the Great Hand? Go not, O man, to the wildest solitude where no other human footstep but thine own has trodden, and say, "Here will I rest"—for life is not rest, not peace, not content—and they abide not on the earth where thou dwellest! Mr. Silvernot was of that happy disposition which seldom resents an affront, and also a man who was never abashed by a first refusal; so after he had become more intimate with the Elmore family, he broached the subject of Divine worship at Wharnby Church, expressing a wish to see the faces of his new friends beneath its roof. To this hint my father broke out in his impetuous way—"Church! No, no, you will never work so great a miracle as that.

What good has church ever done me that I should go dogging to and fro like a great baby of a girl? I went to church once, and no result followed, save that of misery. Can I not pray in my home, with my children, and feel myself as good a Christian?"

"I think not," said Mr. Silvernot, running his hands through his hair, each single one of which seemed bristling up with argument; "such peculiar notions I look upon as excuses, a trifle stronger than ordinary, but still palpable excuses. Besides, *do* you pray with your children? Remember the Bible, Mr. Elmore."

"My children can find their Bible now, sir," said my father; "they read in class to me every day."

"That's well, that's very well," said the little rector, his eyes sparkling through the spectacles, and his hands rubbing violently together in his exhilaration; "there's reason in you. I shall make something of you after all."

I am not writing a theological work, or I would give the whole of the elaborate argument that ensued between my father and the rector, concerning private and public worship; suffice it to say that it ended as arguments generally do—in neither party giving way, in my father snatching up his light and abruptly putting an end to the interview, by retiring to his chamber, and in Mr. Silvernot strutting out of the house in the mildest of rages, exclaiming, "The ground is untenable, Mr. Elmore; your last premise—irrational. Good night, children, God bless you;" then in a lower tone, not intended for our ears, "and your fool of a father too. Good night, dears."

Mr. Silvernot returned to the charge night after night, and my father began to flinch. He would think of it. How far was it to Wharnby Church across the cliffs? He would not promise what Sunday—he had never said he *would* go decisively—well, some day—well, a month's time—well, next Sunday morning—*there.*

Happy time, short happy time, the few months that followed, one bright blue spot amidst the thunder-clouds, one gleam of sunshine on us all. Oh! that first going to church along the path near the cliff, with the green sea glistening in the light of heaven, the richer green of the landscape bathed in sunlight, the winding road, the tall stone tower, from which rung out the merry clashing bells, peering over the tops of the grove of elms in the distance; the churchyard with its old gravestones telling of centuries past, and its new sepulchres speaking of a few days gone! There were many curious glances at us as we mingled with the flock of our friend the rector; my father, with his tall, wiry form, his pale face and long black hair, presenting an object worthy of attention and a matter for considerable speculation; not to mention my brothers, my sister, and myself, the design for whose costumes was invariably furnished by Mrs. Higson and Miss Berncastle, whose united genius had enveloped us in garments of a peculiar cut indeed, but which we were confidently informed by those respective ladies were models of artistic taste and fashion.

It was a fine old church, that of Wharnby, with a stained glass window of almost fabulous worth—the work of some cunning master in his art, well versed in mysterious pigments and marvellous tints—occupying the eastern side of the interior, and casting its coloured shades upon the stone pavement and broad massive columns, giving the place the air and solemnity of a cathedral. There were high pews lined with a dark drab cloth; and I felt relieved when we were ensconced within a pew near the pulpit, and hidden from intrusive gaze. My father rested his head between his arms, and leaned forward, with a heavy sigh.

What memories the resumption of an old practice will call up!—not always of the gentlest, for the countenance of my father was deeply agitated, as he rose with the rest of the congregation, and the deep rich tones of the organ swelled forth, and the service began.

I found courage to observe when the standing part of the ceremony brought my eyes an inch above the top of the pew, and in this I was assisted by a very large and dropsical hassock, which I invariably surmounted. I had a slight recollection of a fashionable church in London, and of a seat in a corner of a crimson-padded pew, by Aggy's wide straw hat; but this was entirely different. There was very little fashion at Wharnby, and every pew within my range of vision was carefully made a study of. I felt I was "seeing life" for the first time, and I rather liked it. It was such a change from the eternal dreariness of "The Rest."

I took a peculiar interest in the pew adjoining our own, originally promoted by detecting a portion of its denizens taking a peculiar interest in us; chiefly in myself, I remarked, for my father hung back; Gilbert, abashed by so many faces, imitated his example; and Edward and Agnes were invisible to mortal eye, and cast envying looks at my tower of observation, perched upon which, I surveyed human nature in infinite variety.

The pew before me contained five inmates: a portly gentleman, with a highly-polished bald head, who read from a prayer-book of immense size, adorned with great brass hinges and twisted metal work, like some frightfully mechanical cash-box; a thin, little woman, bending beneath the weight of a white satin bonnet, and half a bushel of flowers on the top of it; a pretty girl, of about Agnes's age, with a myriad of glossy black ringlets showering round her face; a very tall young lady, something like her, on a plain scale, with a wisp of a curl straying on each cheek; and another tall young woman of an uncertain age, but certainly not under forty for all that.

The young lady with the black ringlets and her elder sister occasionally fixing me with their eyes, caused my immediate disappearance upon a kind of trap-door principle, and it was only at uncertain intervals, when I had recovered sufficient confidence and strength of mind, that I slowly re-emerged. For all this, I was very particular over my prayer-book, with a slight drawback in being a trifle bewildered between morning and evening service, with the churching of women occasionally intervening and totally confounding me. I could not help admiring the family group, the black ringlets, the stupendous bonnet, and the prayer-book of the cash-box pattern; once I detected a smile on the little girl's face, and was venturing to simper in return, when, being detected by the bonnet, which suddenly jerked up and disclosed a pointed visage very much powdered, I descended from the hassock, and appeared no more. I did not like Mr. Silvernot in his pulpit so well as I did sitting before our winter fire at home; he made me sleepy over the sermon, and then startled me out of an incipient doze, by a terrible bang on the cushion as he clinched some irresistible argument. He was very energetic in the pulpit; he bounced to the right and the left, stood upon tiptoe, and leaned over, vociferating at the top of his voice at the miserable sinners beneath him, crumpled his manuscript (which he seldom glanced at) between his hands in his vehemence, and in fact, although a little boisterous, preached as I wish a few of the holy order of reverends that I could name would preach—as if he meant it.

The service was concluded, and my father lingered in his pew, declining to mingle with the retiring crowd, and preferring to wait till the church was empty. We sat there till every pew was vacant, till the clerk had arranged the book marks for the evening, and the organist had come tripping down the aisle with some leaves of music in his hand, and passed into the sunlight, and the pew-opener—an old white-headed man with the palsy—had got fidgety and nervous, and wanted us to be gone, that he might lock up the church and go home to his dinner.

"We can go now, I think," whispered Gilbert to my father, who still lingered.

"They have all gone?" looking round.

"All gone."

"Very well. I am ready."

He rose, and we followed him along the aisle, which was so silent yet so full of echoes, so great a contrast to a few minutes since when it was so full of life.

As we entered the churchyard, my father started and halted abruptly, as if with the intention of returning into the church, for at a short distance from us, and evidently awaiting our approach, was Mr. Silvernot, accompanied by the late occupants of the pew into which I had so frequently bestowed my obtrusive gaze.

"My dear Mr. Elmore," said the rector, advancing and speaking in a low voice; "you will suffer me to take advantage of this happy day (happy for you and for me), and to celebrate it by an introduction to my parents and my family. I would not press you—I would not have waited for you, had I thought my waiting would have been considered distasteful or repugnant; but I think you have lived too long alone, and that a little society will be essentially good."

"You are very kind, Mr. Silvernot," said my father, shrinking back; "but—but you pain me. I have lived too long alone to have any desire for new faces meeting mine. I am no companion for——"

"Stuff!" exclaimed the eccentric rector; "excuse me, my dear sir; but —— stuff! A solitary life will make you a madman or a fanatic, and a parcel of savages of your children. I must have no denial."

He snatched my father by the sleeve, and dragged him forward.

"Father, mother, sisters, I have the pleasure to introduce to you my very esteemed friend, Mr. Elmore. Mr. Elmore, my father, my mother, my sisters."

"Happy to have the pleasure, my dear sir. I hope I see you well, sir. How *do* you do, sir?" said the portly gentleman, in a thick, rolling voice, as he extended a fat hand to my father.

My father shook hands with Mr. Silvernot, senior, raised his hat courteously to Mrs. Silvernot and eldest daughter, who were executing a complicated kind of *salaam* with impressive gravity, smiled faintly at the pretty little girl in the black ringlets, and catching the glance of the lady of ambiguous age, again raised his hat.

"I beg ten thousand pardons, Miss Wigginton," said Mr. Silvernot the younger. "Mr. Elmore, Miss Wigginton. There," with a sigh of relief, "I have seen the accomplishment of a long-considered project—the introduction of my family to Mr. Elmore. These pretty boys, and this pretty girl, are Mr. Elmore's children," calling attention to us by a wave of the hand in our direction.

"How do *you* do, my dears?" said Mr. Silvernot, senior, creasing his broad face into a hundred smiles.

We looked sheepishly at the group as they acknowledged our presence. Gilbert murmured something in a husky voice, and Agnes, ever self-possessed and cool, and at her ease, advanced, like a diminutive woman as she was, and extended her tiny hand, as she had seen her father. There was a quivering lip in one of the group, a sigh almost of pain as she did so, kindly inquiring at the same time after the family's health.

"Your only daughter?" asked Mrs. Silvernot of my father, as we sauntered though the churchyard and along the country road.

"My only one, madam," was my father's reply.

"What self-possession!" she chirped, looking up at him with one eye, and fixing the other on Agnes as she tripped along with the younger daughter of the Silvernots, quite a dear friend. "I often wish I could bring my Celia up self-possessed. There is such a charm about a quiet little girl, don't you think so, Mr. Elmore?"

"I would rather see my Agnes like—like a child. Although I am a grave and quiet man myself, yet a grave and quiet girl, never at all put out, never showing a child's affection, or a child's curiosity, is painfully unnatural."

This was a long speech for my father, but he said it with his eyes fixed upon the dusty road, as if he were reading it thereon.

"Well, I don't know. Now, Arabella, that is, *the* Miss Silvernot, Mr. Elmore," explained she, "was a self-possessed child; and there she is now, a calm young lady with no nerves. Oh! those dreadful things, the nerves; I suffer from them myself, terribly. You cannot imagine the state of my nerves, Mr. Elmore."

"Indeed, I rejo—— I am sorry to hear so sad an account," said my father.

"That cool development of—of—of—bless the word! what is it?—but you understand me—is only demonstrated in one of our family, and that is in Arabella. My husband is nervous, and very irritable; and George—that is my son—is so impulsive, that he is really at some times quite alarming."

She paused; and Mr. Silvernot, senior, who had been anxiously waiting to get in a word, rolled out—

"You must be considered a fortunate man, in having such quiet children, my dear sir, for all your opinions on that subject. Really, I never saw such quiet children in my life! Your eldest son, and that black-eyed gipsy of a boy," pointing to me, "look quite philosophers; and that pretty boy with the ringlets, who has got hold of George's hand, is almost as grave."

"They are quiet children—too quiet."

Mr. Silvernot, the rector, had sharp ears, for he caught the words, as he strolled on in advance with Edward; and after stopping till they came up with them, said—"I agree with you, Mr. Elmore; they are too quiet. But I'm going to have a change; I'll set the rogues alive. This is the beginning of a new life, sir. Mr. Elmore," suddenly, "you must come home with us to-day."

My father turned ghastly at the thought.

"Not to my rookery, understand," pointing to a pretty white villa in the distance; "that is as bad—that is as *dull* as 'The Rest;' but to the house—Wharnby House—of father. Celia will be a capital companion for Agnes; and there's Master Redwin, a playmate for the boys—he only lives at the next house, across the fields; and I'm quite a boy myself when I like. If it was not Sunday, we would have such games, my lads! But, at all events, you must come home with us to-day, Mr. Elmore?"

My father shook his head.

"No denial; the Silvernots never take denial," said the senior of that race. "Come, you must."

"We should feel it quite an honour," said Arabella, breaking in for the first time.

"And the boys would like it," said the rector. "Boys, how should you like to go to Wharnby House?"

"If papa will go," said Gilbert, quietly.

"And Master Luke?"

"I should like to go," I stammered.

The mere idea of a fresh house, a new scene—almost a new life—made my heart leap.

"And Master Edward?"

"Oh, very much, if you please."

We were all in a group now.

"And Miss Agnes?"

"Oh, I should be delighted."

My father looked at her. Her eyes were sparkling, her lips parted, and her light but rich ringlets dancing again as she tossed her head gaily. She seemed more of a child than ever she had been yet.

Was the secret of her premature oldness of thought but the want of companionship with those of her own age? He had never dreamt of that.

"Mr. Silvernot," said my father, after a long deliberation, "the invitation is so sudden that—that I cannot accept it for myself; but if the children like to go, it would be a change for them, perhaps, and do them good. *I* will not come," he said, decisively; "another time—another time, I may. But I will be at Wharnby Church to-night, and they can meet me in the evening."

The rector checked any further entreaty of his family by a look, and said—

"Well, a change will do the boys and Agnes good, I'm sure, and so I shall confiscate them; but remember, Mr. Elmore, you have made a promise to come and see us; we have you there, sir, we have you there."

"Then I will leave them with you," said he, with a sigh, as he stopped at the winding path that led round to the cliffs and "The Rest;" "I am much obliged to you for the kind invitation; I fear you will find them very troublesome."

"Not at all, not at all," said the head of the family.

"Aggy, be a good girl," said my father, kissing her; "and boys"—aside to us—"be good boys. God bless you! A pleasant day!"

He bowed to the Silvernots, and struck off towards the cliff, walking very slowly and very thoughtfully.

We had gone some hundred yards, and had looked back once or twice at the tall, receding form of my father, when Gilbert stopped.

"I beg your pardons, all, but"—with a wistful look behind—"I must go back."

"Go back!" everybody exclaimed.

"If you please," said Gilbert; "father will be very lonely by himself, I'm sure he will. I should have liked to have gone with you, but—but—I *must* go back."

He slid away his arm from the light touch of the rector, and ran along the road, and down the winding path, never turning round or looking back till he had reached his father's side, and held his father's hand. We stood watching them; we saw my father stop and speak for several minutes, looking towards us all the time; then they turned and walked towards "The Rest."

"God bless me!" said the rector, blowing his nose violently; "what a singular boy! what a faithful—what a *remarkable* boy! Dear me!—dear me!—dear me!"

We resumed our journey towards Wharnby House; I, with some scruples of conscience as to whether it were not advisable and filial to bide my opportunity, and desert from the main body, on my eldest brother's principle.

Wharnby House was a large house, of Gothic build, receding some hundreds of yards from the road, but with a sloping garden, full of choice flowers and rare shrubs, reaching to the lodge gates. The perfume of the spring flowers was a pleasant welcome to our new friend's home as we entered upon the broad gravel walk.

"You have a garden, Master Elmore?" asked Miss Silvernot, by whose side I chanced to be walking.

"Yes, miss."

"Quite as large as this, is it not?"

"Larger, but not so pretty; we have more shrubs, and less of these nice flowers."

"Are you fond of flowers?"

"I don't know,"

"I am," chimed in Edward, thinking it a favourable opportunity to say something.

"That's a sensible boy," said Arabella; "never say you don't know."

I coloured, and began to dislike Miss Silvernot; indeed, from that moment I formed the resolution of transferring those affections to Miss Celia which heretofore had been hovering and vacillating between that young lady and her sister. Miss Silvernot was only a year or two behind the age of the rector, but that made her more imposing. A broad green lawn, in the centre of which a fountain was playing, stretched before the house; and as we crossed it, and moved towards a flight of stone steps leading to the central door, the figure of a youth, about the age of Gilbert, came running towards us.

"Why, where have you been?" he cried, panting for breath; "I have been waiting for ten minutes at least. Ten minutes!" drawing a tiny gold watch from his embroidered waistcoat: "if it is not nearer a quarter of an hour, I'm considerably out of my calculations."

This young gentleman was received with smiles, and shaking of hands, and friendly greetings, indicative of a well-known visitor; and whilst these were being exchanged, the children of Elmore were lost in admiration. There was something particularly attractive in this young stranger, something which we had never seen before, and which made us feel a kind of inferior being in his sight. I have said he was about fourteen years of age; tall as Gilbert; with chestnut hair, curling closely to his head; large brown eyes of a peculiar softness; a straight Grecian nose; and lips red, full, and half-parted, as if it were too great a sin to hide the perfect row of small, white teeth beneath. But it was not his face that struck upon us children at the moment; children are not so much attracted by the features of a new comer, as by the dress, and in this particular he had arrested our entire attention.

He wore a full jacket, elaborately braided, and from an outer pocket on the left side, peeped the whitest of handkerchiefs; a grey, satin waistcoat embroidered with the same colour in fanciful devices, and across which meandered a tiny-linked gold chain; a cambric shirt, with glistening studs, that Edward could not take his eyes from; a loose, black neckerchief carelessly, yet artistically, tied; and black trousers strapped over the smallest of patent boots, completed the costume of this juvenile dandy. We say completed, for he was bare-headed, and had evidently not stayed to snatch up his hat when he had caught sight of his friends from the window looking and opening on the lawn.

"Master Redwin," said the rector, "I have brought you some new friends, and I think you will all get on together capitally. Masters Elmore and Miss Elmore; dear me, I am very ungallant—Miss Elmore and Masters Elmore, my young friend, Master Redwin."

"How do you do?" said he with a careless nod to Edward and me, and somewhat more of a bow to Agnes. We both hazarded it as our opinion that we were very well, and hoped he was the same, at which expression of our interest in his health he gave us another friendly nod, and said, half-laughing, he hoped so too.

"But, Paul, go in directly—you will catch your death of cold!" cried Mrs. Silvernot.

"Not I," shaking his curly head; "it's so precious hot now, I hardly know what to do. Pooh!"

"Where's your grandmother?" asked Mr. Silvernot.

"Why, there she is, to be sure," he cried, pointing to the open window; "you don't think I have been out of her sight all this time—do you?"

Following the direction indicated, we observed, at the open window, a tall, slim old lady, with white hair, who was keeping us in view, by shading her eyes with a hand on which several rings were glittering in the sun.

We ascended the steps, and entered the house. Greetings were exchanged between Mrs. Redwin and the Silvernots, and we went through a feeble ceremony of introduction to the aristocratical old lady, which she appeared to receive in a half supercilious manner, and in a way I hardly approved of on my part, and therefore mentally resolved to give it further consideration when the bewildering effect of these fresh scenes and characters which, with my younger brother and sister, I had made acquaintance with, had been fully recovered from and got over.

With the exception of Agnes, who was perfectly at home, and at her ease, we felt rather out of place. Everything was so new and strange—and we wondered how our sister managed it. Agnes was not an eccentric child, nor particularly old-fashioned; but she seemed never to feel abashed, or appear confounded, no matter in what society she became suddenly placed. She took no great interest in anything, or anybody, at this age; there was a want of affection in her nature which I have never witnessed in any other child, and never read of in any book or story—a cold, unsympathetic way, which seemed to have been born with her—a sluggishness in her blood, that prompted her to shrink from all evidence of affection in father or brothers, and shunned their kisses and embrace as if there were something in them antipathetic to her own mysterious nature.

I might have written all this at another time—have chosen a more fitting period in the course of the wild tale I have to relate; I might have left that which I have penned in this lonely chamber, in my still lonelier solitude, to the further progress of my life; but thinking of her more this night than is my usual wont, and recollecting events that have long gone before, and that have to be chronicled herein, I partly draw aside the heavy curtain that enshrouds her.

To my story.

I began to like Wharnby House. I began to think that the occupants of Wharnby House and I would get on very well together. With the exception of a slight drawback in my incipient dislike to Miss Silvernot, which, I regret to say, did not decrease upon further acquaintance with that estimable spinster, my opinion of the family in general was rather favourable. Mr. Silvernot, senior, was imposing, but good-humoured; Mrs. Silvernot unpleasantly fidgety, but attentive and considerate; the rector I had liked long ago; and Celia—ah! there I was a worshipper. I thought of the prince who died for love, in one of Mrs. Higson's stories; and I felt that matters must shortly be arranged between Celia's papa and mine, or serious consequences must infallibly ensue.

Master Redwin became a pretty good sort of a fellow after a while; he had given himself a few airs of superiority at first, but they wore away as our acquaintance improved, and he finally condescended to devote his entire attention to myself, as we strolled through the grounds, after an early dinner of cold meats, for the Silvernots kept strictly their Sunday.

"I say, Elmore," remarked this youth to me, "why don't you go to school?"

"My father is my teacher."

"Egad! what a droll idea. You live at 'The Rest,' they tell me?"

"Yes."

I felt half inclined to add, "sir;" he looked such an important young gentleman, with his smart hat jauntily set on one side of his head, and a small cane, with a gold mounting, in his right hand, which he twirled close to my eyes in a very reckless manner.

"What profession is your father?"

"Nothing;—what's yours?"

He coloured at this counter inquiry, and said, "My father's dead; so is my mother. They were wrecked in the Hope coming home to England. I live with my grandmother. I go to school at Hornwell Hall, fifty miles away. I shall be a rich man when I am twenty-one years old. What a time to wait!"

Having relieved himself of these particulars, he glanced at me, to note the effect they had produced, but, being naturally of a phlegmatic temperament, I received his narrative with a cool "Indeed!"

The gardens pertaining to Wharnby House were of considerable extent, and Master Redwin and I, deep in conversation, had lost sight of the remainder of the party.

"Why, we have lost them!" I remarked.

"What of it?" he said, carelessly cutting a rose off its stalk with a switch of his cane; "they're not particularly good company to young fellows like us. The Silvernots are old-fashioned, you see, with the exception of Celia. I like little Cely."

"Indeed!" I said for the second time, but not with quite such an amount of complete indifference.

"You've a nice sister yourself, though,"—with the air of a connoisseur in matters of beauty;—"it's a pity you all dress so exceedingly droll."

"Is it?" replied I, with burning cheeks.

"Upon my honour, it is. Who can be *your* tailor, now?"

"Mrs. Higson," I answered, with all the confidence of twelve years old, for I had great faith in Mrs. Higson.

"Mrs. Higson!" he cried, exploding into a fit of laughter; "and who on earth is Mother—Mrs. Higson?"

"Our housekeeper."

"By Jove! this is droll," he said, wiping the tears of mirth from his eyes with a laced pocket-handkerchief (evidently one of his grandmother's treasures). "Mrs. Higson, tailor to 'The Rest!' Does she sit cross-legged, like the Great Mogul, Elmore? All crack tailors do."

I began to feel heartily ashamed of Mrs. Higson, and to consider what a difference in dress there was between my new-found friend's artistically cut, braided and embroidered habiliments, and my own shabby brown clothes, of so indifferent a fit. A bright excuse suggested itself to me.

"Ah! but then you have a grandmother, and she is very clever, and, perhaps, understands these things better than Mrs. Higson."

"What!" he shouted.

I repeated the surmise.

"You don't mean to say that you think my grandmother makes *my* clothes?" he exclaimed, with a look of horror in his face.

"I understood—that is, I thought so."

I felt I had got completely out of my depth. Where was Gilbert—kind, thoughtful Gilbert—to rescue me from this dilemma, and assert the dignity of Elmore, and the honour of "The Rest?" Why did he run away, and leave me the sole defender of the family?

"What a perfectly *astounding* idea!" he ejaculated, after an examination of my features for several consecutive minutes—an operation which particularly embarrassed me; "why, my grandmother is a lady. She make my clothes! Well, you are an extraordinary young fellow! My tailor comes up from London to attend to *me!* When I want anything new, I drop him a line. That's the way, Elmore!"

This constant designation of "Elmore" had an overwhelming effect upon me; there was no getting over it, or offering resistance to it. Once I attempted to return the compliment, by addressing the superior being by my side as "Redwin," but sticking fast at the first syllable, necessity compelled an immediate and ignominious apology. I was just the gentleman for Master Redwin; he could not have had a better listener, one more quickly dazzled and impressed by his assumptive manner, or more inclined to do him reverence. Acting upon these grounds, he paid great attention to me; and highly flattered by his marks of almost royal favour—a youth as old as Gilbert, and such a gentleman!—I felt Paul Redwin must be my bosom friend and confidant.

"How I should like to go to Hornwell Hall," I remarked, as we continued our promenade.

"Should you?" he answered, quickly. "There's good blood in you, Elmore. That's true spirit, friend! Not home-tied, eh? Well, your father could afford it, I suppose, or he wouldn't live in such a precious large house."

"Afford it! Of course, he could."

"Then, just put the question to him, Elmore. Candidly enter into an explanation of your wishes. Think what a polish old Milvertree would put upon you; besides, you would see me every day."

I felt this to be a great inducement, and said so.

"I don't go back for three weeks, so it could all be arranged by that time—couldn't it? Do you think, if I ran over to 'The Rest' to-morrow or next day, and mentioned this to your father, he'd think of it, now?"

Good heaven, what a boy this was! Run over to "The Rest"—the dark, gloomy "Rest," whose gates were locked and guarded jealously—like giants' castles in old fairy tales—and mention it to father, as stern, and grim, and fierce as any tenant of those fabulous creations! Why, this boy must be a man of iron nerve, with nothing appertaining to juvenescence but the boy's look about him.

"I—I don't know, I'm sure," I said, with some hesitation; "I—I really do *not* know."

"Well, there's no harm in trying. I should very much like you to come to my school. Didn't I hear your curly-headed brother mention another of you—Gilbert, I think? Who's he?"

"My elder brother," I answered, proudly; "about your age. I wish you knew him!"

"Oh! I shall know him by-and-by. Is he like you?"

"I believe he is something like me."

"Dress in the same style—antediluvian?—ha, ha!"

"Ye—es," I replied, echoing his laugh, although extremely doubtful if I fully appreciated the point of his joke; which appeared to tickle his imagination so much, that, during the remainder of our stroll, he was continually indulging in suppressed inward merriment, that kept his complexion of a fine shade of purple.

It was a pleasant day, take it for all in all; and I regretted that it went so soon, and that the time for going back to church seemed to have come with such full spread-wings of haste.

We bade Master Redwin good-bye before we started with the rector and his family. Master Redwin's health was not considered sufficiently good by his careful grandmother to allow of his accompanying us to church, and risking the ill effects of the night air, although the rosy hue of his cheeks, and the elasticity of his spirits, did not bear particular evidence as to the delicate constitution of my new friend.

"Good evening, Elmore," he said to me. "I shall certainly take 'The Rest' by surprise before I start for Hornwell. What day is most convenient to you?"

"Oh! any day, thank you," I feebly replied.

"No engagements for the present week?" he inquired; "because if you have, state the days. I don't want my ride for nothing, Elmore."

"No engagements at all. I'm sure."

"Very well, one day in the week you will expect me, and I will broach that little matter to your father. We should make capital chums. Good evening."

He shook hands with me, elevated his hat to Agnes, nodded carelessly to Edward, who had been regarding him with open mouth and distended eyes for the last five minutes, spoke a few words of farewell to the Silvernots, and then ran back to his grandmother.

The rector, his father, mother, and elder sister, led the van along the chalky road towards the church, and from the old tower rang out the evening bells. Miss Wigginton, with a watchful eye upon the remainder of the party, followed in the distance.

Miss Wigginton was such a bony female, with such protruding, fishy eyes, that I felt my position by her side to be particularly uncomfortable. I imbibed a dread of Miss Wigginton; she was infinitely more terrible in appearance than Miss Berncastle, and I felt awed before her, and wondered how Agnes and Celia (what a lovely name, Celia, to be sure!) had the courage to keep chatting in her awful presence, unmindful of a repeated "hush!" from that stately guardian.

We found my father and Gilbert waiting for our approach beneath the church porch.

"Well, children, have you spent a pleasant day?"

"Oh! very pleasant indeed, thank you, papa," cried Edward, and Agnes and I responded with equal fervour.

"I am glad of that."

We entered the church, and took our seats in the same pew into which we had been formerly ushered, and the Silvernots filed into the one contiguous, and the rector went round to the vestry. My father was more moody and thoughtful than ever

The church, by night, with its numerous wax-candles burning (gas was unknown at Wharnby), the repose that seemed to dwell within, as if night lay hidden behind the pillars waiting patiently for darkness, the scanty congregation, the number of empty pews, the shuffling tread of the pew-opener, all had a soothing effect upon my nerves; for a few minutes after our estimable friend, the rector, had peeped over the red cushion of the pulpit, I was enjoying the luxury of a peaceful sleep, undisturbed by my parent, who sat stiffly in his pew by my side, with his dark, sunken eyes shifting restlessly to and fro—from the minister to the floor—from the floor round the church, and looking up at the carved rafters, and glancing over his shoulder —but never for a moment still.

CHAPTER III.

MASTER REDWIN'S RECEPTION AT "THE REST."

"Mr. Paul Redwin!" said my father, turning the glazed card over in his hand, and looking from it to the portly form of Mrs. Higson (we had no male attendants in the interior of "The Rest"). "What is the meaning of this? I have no knowledge of Mr. Paul Redwin."

My father was standing before a desk, on which reposed a large book of history, and his sons were ranged beneath, and had been listening attentively to a lecture on the reign of the first Henry.

Edward and I exchanged a meaning glance, but neither of us felt inclined to throw a brighter light upon a subject so evidently mysterious to my father; we had not the courage.

"Who is this gentleman, Mrs. Higson?" inquired he tapping his finger on the card.

"Really, I don't know, upon my word, Mr. Elmore," replied our housekeeper, crossing her fat hands; "Johnson sent the card up to the house by the under-gardener."

"Have I not given orders at the lodge that I am never at

home to strangers?" said my father, sharply. "There is no object for this man's coming—Not at home!"

He tossed the card to Mrs. Higson, and arranged the book upon the desk.

Mrs. Higson was taking her departure, when I ventured to speak.

"If you please, father, it is a—a—*gentleman* I saw at Wharnby House, and who promised to call——"

"Promised!"

"That is, who—who—said he would call and see me, and you, and—and———all of us."

Gilbert opened his great black eyes to their fullest extent, and stared at me with profound astonishment.

My father, as perplexed as his eldest son, looked irresolute.

"Stay, Higson, a moment," he said; then, looking at me fixedly, he added, "And did you not tell him in return, this officious gentleman, that his visit would be uncalled-for, that my house is called 'The Rest,' and that I *would* rest, child?"

"No, I did not, papa; I did not like."

"Silenee gave consent, it seems. Admit him, Higson."

Mrs. Higson departed, and my father said—

"This is the result of your visit to Wharnby House. One incident, trivial as it may be, brings up another, and another, till the turning of a single yard out of one's path may be the means of many years of bitterness. Had you never gone to the Silvernots, I should not have been pestered by this fresh face."

My father was evidently angry, and I trembled for the reception of my new friend; I wished to make perfectly clear to my father the juvenility of the visitor, but had not the heart to enter into explanations with that lowering brow.

"Understand me this, once for all," said he, speaking in a loud voice, as a premonitory hint to the gentleman advancing up the passage; "ask no one to 'The Rest;' and if a man thrust himself upon your notice, actuated by a paltry curiosity —for he can have no other motive—tell him that the Elmores are of sterner stuff than most men, and would shun the artificial life called society, in which most men fritter out their vain existence."

"Mr. Redwin," cried Mrs. Higson, who had considerately waited outside for the conclusion of the speech, and as Paul Redwin advanced, insinuated her round rosy face into the room, to watch the effect of my friend's entrance upon my father

My father, who had wheeled round with an imperious look at the mention of the name, was completely dumb-founded by the appearance of the visitor, who advanced with a gracious smile, his hat and cane in his left hand, and his right extended, with a frank, easy, unembarrassed air.

"I have much pleasure in making the acquaintance of Mr. Elmore," he said, shaking my father by the hand, which he had, almost unconsciously, extended in return; "and this is Mr. Gilbert Elmore, of course," turning to him. "I am very glad to see you, friend."

My father had looked forward to the entrance of an elderly gentleman, or a young man, at least, and the coming of a youth not older than his eldest son perplexed him how to act. Coldness, or an arrogant demeanour, would be but a burlesque towards this boy, who had had the confidence, or the temerity, to enter the dull precincts of "The Rest."

"Miss Elmore is well, I trust, sir?" again turning to my father.

"Miss Elmore is very well, I thank you," replied my father. "Will you be seated?"

"Thanks," said Redwin, taking a chair indicated by a wave of my father's hand, and, placing his hat and cane at his feet, he proceeded to withdraw his gloves.

"Don't let me disturb your class, sir," said he politely, almost regally, as if he were according permission to proceed. "Pray complete the lesson—I am in no hurry."

My father turned away his head; one of those smiles, more frequent since he had known the rector of Wharnby, crossed his deep-lined face.

"The lesson is not of grave importance, *Mr.* Redwin," said my father, with a strong emphasis on the title by which he addressed him. "You are a playfellow—a new little friend of my son Luke's, I understand."

"I saw your son Luke at Mr. Silvernot's last Sunday, and we had some conversation together," said Master Redwin with dignity. "I told him I should give a look-in during the week. How are you, Elmore?"

"Quite well, thank you."

"And Master Edward?"

Master Edward murmured something respecting a perfect state of health.

"I suppose, Mr. Elmore," said my friend, turning to my

father, "your son Luke has mentioned the subject which I have come hither to-day to urge upon your attention?"

"I cannot say he has."

"I am purely disinterested in this affair, of course," said Paul; "but it suggested itself to me that these boys," with a careless look in our direction, "would get on better at a school —a first-rate school, such as mine—than under the tuition of a parent. Eh, now?"

There was a gathering gloom on my father's face that I did not like the appearance of: it was ominous of evil.

"It suggested itself to *you?*"

"To me, sir."

"I should feel flattered by the reasons for your inter—— your suggestion."

"Oh! they would strike any one," said Redwin, rattling on perfectly unconscious of a coming storm. "The reason for the suggestion was, of course, my introduction. The reasons for leaving home are numerous."

"The introduction of my children—that is to say, their general appearance and behaviour at first sight—inclined you to think that they would get on better at school, sir?"

"That is it, Mr. Elmore."

"Were they so cubbish and so ignorant, and did such little justice, or such strict justice, to their father's teaching, then?"

"No, no!" stammered Master Redwin; "but they, they know nothing of—of—in fact—what boys generally know."

"Now the 'numerous reasons' for leaving home, *Mr.* Redwin."

Master Redwin, with a vague idea of something wrong, but still unconscious of giving offence, boldly went on.

"Why there is," he said, "more scope for energy, more desire for distinction, more change, more pleasure, more life on their side. On yours there is the annoyance of teaching dispensed with, and you could find something better to set your mind to—something more suitable. That's how *I* put it."

Now nine men out of ten would have been amused by my friend Redwin's *nonchalant* manner, and have drawn him out accordingly; but my father, having overcome the first novelty of his appearance, and never being in a vein for jesting at another's weakness or another's folly, but, on the contrary, extremely irritable and impatient, took this grotesque assumption of the child in a light that few other men would have done or thought of. My father leant across his desk, and fixed Master Redwin with his eyes, till that young gentleman, despite his habitual composure, reddened, then turned pale.

"I hardly comprehend the latter part of the argument, Mr. Paul Redwin," observed my father, quietly.

"Why, you *must* find teaching dry work—irksome work, I mean," said Master Paul, with an effort to maintain his cool deportment.

"Wherefore?"

"Because a gentleman must feel out of place at it."

"You say you go to school?"

"Yes, sir."

"Boarding-school?"

"Of course."

"A school, where hard teaching for five months gives a letter of credit for the sixth to be passed at home, free of all restraint—passed in impudence, and sometimes in affectation—very often both."

"Sir, I hardly comprehend you."

"Impudence, in intruding upon a neighbour's house unsolicited and uncalled for; affectation, in aspiring to be thought a fine gentleman, quite a man—a reasoning man, too!—when but a child in years and experience. I hope you comprehend me now."

The bitterness with which my father made the above speech was not worthy of its object; it was too harsh a severity, and I felt the blood burning in my cheeks and on my brow.

Looking towards Gilbert, I saw that his face was scarlet, too; evidently the same idea had suggested itself to him, and he blushed, like myself, for the treatment of my friend, who, totally unprepared for such a ferocious onslaught of words, sat on his chair, with heaving chest and twitching hands. irresolved how to take it.

My father was turning over the leaves of the History of England, when Paul Redwin jumped to his feet, white with passion.

"Sir, I wish, for your sake, I were an older man."

"Why so, *Mr.* Paul Redwin?" calmly looking up from the book.

"Because, sir, I should be entitled to call you out for so cowardly an insult. I do not know whom you may be, but I would have you to know, that I shall be as rich as you are at twenty-one, sir, and that I have a claim to be called a gentleman even now—which you have not, and which you cannot have. You dared not have uttered to any other than a child the uncalled-for aspersions you have thrown on me. You remind me well I am but a boy, sir; some day I will remind you I have become a man."

He stayed to hear no more, but, snatching up his hat and cane, tore out of the room.

"John—my pony!"

We could hear the grinding of horses' hoofs on the gravel outside, and then a rapid galloping away told of Paul Redwin's departure from "The Rest."

"We will proceed with the lesson," said my father, over whose features I thought I could detect a passing shade of remorse. "Stay!"—shutting the book—"what was Henry the First surnamed, Gilbert? Let me see that you all have remembrance of my recent lecture. Surnamed——?"

"Beauclerc."

"Date, Luke?"

"1745."

"What?"

"1745"—with lesser confidence.

The remainder of the day Luke Elmore was in disgrace.

CHAPTER IV.

THE EVIL NIGHT.

THE unceremonious manner in which Master Redwin and my father had taken leave of each other, was the cause of great mental distress to me for several days. I had a great respect for Master Redwin, and a great ambition to hold a respectable place in his opinion; and now, what could he think of me? And that stately grandmother, too, who had awed me into reverence—what was her opinion of the Elmores? and my dear friends, the Silvernots—why, it was enough to break off all friendship between us.

But our friend, the rector, came as usual, in impulsive moments, and chatted away as briskly as ever, and brought invitations for us, which my father, with a lively remembrance of the result of our first visit to Wharnby House, invariably declined. It was evident Master Redwin had not mentioned the incident at "The Rest," and my father studiously avoided any recapitulation of the same.

But my father could not wholly sink back to the old frigidity of his life, and close the doors of "The Rest" against the world. My father had been introduced to the Silvernot family, and could not refuse admission to them when the carriage brought the senior members to the house on morning visits. That he hated these morning calls I was convinced, by his nervous, impassioned manner after they had come to a conclusion; but in the presence of Mr. and Mrs. Silvernot, the rector, and his sister, Arabella, he was calm, grave, and courteous, and bowed them to the carriage with the chivalrous attention of that old time when he was a man of fashion, and Beau Elmore at his club.

He continued his visits to Wharnby Church of a Sunday morning (the evening service he had altogether eschewed), when the weather was sufficiently fine to allow of his taking us the customary walk along the cliffs: ride, or let us ride, he never would. There was a stately old carriage, with his crest emblazoned on the panels of the doors, dusty and mud-bespattered, shut up in the stables, of which he kept the key locked within his desk; but there was no coachman, no horses—nothing of the past grandeur, which would have been, at that time, but an aggravation of his misery. "The Rest" was sufficient for him, and for all his wants and pleasures; why should it not be for the children growing up around him? Could he not carry out the plan he had been so long building up in his busy brain—to be isolated with his family, and in that isolation to feel happiness, by seeing content on the faces round about his table? He had dreamed so. It was a wild dream, and he had better have died before the waking came upon him!

There was no particular restraint put upon the actions of myself and brothers, although we felt it—felt it the more for the lack of tangible evidence to the contrary. With my sister Agnes, Miss Berncastle had evidently received some secret orders; for that respected lady never left her charge half an hour at a time—accompanied her in all her walks, and often followed her from room to room of the house, like a trusty guardian. My father could not have told of what he was afraid, and yet he had a lurking distrust of her being lost or stolen, or of her meeting chance acquaintances that might tell her of the pleasures of society—of the gaieties of the world around her, and make her sigh for that brilliant apple—fashionable knowledge. It was certain, all talk of amusements were strictly interdicted—on dancing was laid a fearful prohibition—and it was only at Miss Berncastle's express solicitation and with a reluctant groan that he had consented to her learning the pianoforte. And yet, he wondered she was not more a child—wondered why, with all his kindness and affection—for he loved her very dearly—she gave so poor and forced a return—why, with her brothers for playfellows, she preferred her solitary studies in the music-room.

Agnes had a spirit of opposition in her, too, which she disclosed at times, much to the disquietude of Miss Berncastle. When that latter lady was more than particularly watchful, Agnes was more particularly capricious—wandering about the house in search of some piece of music which she had carefully concealed beforehand, and leading the lady, who was short of breath, and rather stout, a long, rambling journey to the roof of the house and back again, taking in as many stairs as it was possible to find. Miss Berncastle's chief reason for pertinaciously following Agnes, was the inclination my sister had to absent herself on any trifling errand, and descend to Mrs. Higson's room, where she would remain, if allowed, the entire day, listening to the housekeeper's bloodthirsty legends with breathless attention. This erratic propensity, combined with a trying calmness of demeanour when Miss Berncastle was most excited, and a love of opposition and contrary views to her governess on almost every subject connected with her education, made that lady's place far from the most agreeable. There was but one thing had effect on Agnes Elmore, and that was Miss Berncastle's threat of stating her conduct to her father, when, in most cases, she gave in, and resigned herself to her studies with a great effort at attention.

I have said that there was no particular restraint exercised upon the actions of my brothers and myself, so that it often happened, upon our Wednesday and Saturday afternoons—our half-holidays—we stole out of "The Rest," and made for the sea-side.

About a mile from our house was a rude cutting in the cliff, said to have been made by smugglers many years ago, which, by a sloping, gradual descent, opened upon the sands beneath.

Down this cutting, well known at Wharnby by the name of "Freeman's Gate" (Freeman having been a desperate smuggler in his time), we regularly descended on the afternoon I have specified, and amused ourselves by launching miniature ships and boats. Sometimes, but very seldom, our father accompanied us in these expeditions, and would sit on some rough seat, formed by the white cliff, gazing at the sea, or vacantly staring at an open book upon his knees, too absorbed to read. It was as lonely on the sands as at "The Rest"—there were no visitors at Wharnby, and, with the exception of a shrimp-dredger at times, or a boatman struggling to get off a sand-drift, on which he had run aground, it was as gloomy a place as any round the coast.

One Wednesday afternoon, about a week succeeding the event chronicled in Chapter III., Gilbert, Edward, and I (the latter young gentleman staggering under the weight of an enormous ship, with real canvas sails, and ropes tarred in the most natural style), descended the stony path of Freeman's Gate, and made their appearance on the sands. The tide was very low, and the new vessel, which had been a study of mine for months, refused to be launched upon any principle whatever, but ungracefully stuck fast at every attempt we made.

"The tide runs very low to-day, Gilbert," I said; "let us go farther round the cliffs."

We sauntered along till we were stopped by a well-known mass of low rock, rugged and heaped in the wildest shapes, and overgrown with brown sea-weed, rendering a firm footing an impossibility. Over this, when the tide rose, the sea dashed, and foamed, and roared, with a noise that could be heard in the rooms of "The Rest."

"Then we shall not see the ship in the water to-day," said Edward, after an ineffectual attempt for the last time, in which I had fallen upon my hands and knees, and nearly crushed it beneath me.

"Yes, we will," I said, resolutely, as I gathered myself up—"oh! yes, we will, though."

"Why, how can we?"

"I've heard Mrs. Higson say, about half a mile over the rock there's a bay. Don't you remember that story she told us of the Dark Man of the Bay, who was brought from over sea by French pirates and murdered there?"

"And whose ghost walks there every day and every night," said Edward. "Oh, yes! I'm going there, I am."

"*I* shall go," I said, decisively.

"Are you so foolish, brother Luke?" said Gilbert. "Why, it would be madness to cross over this treacherous rock, I tell you. You shan't go, Luke!"

"But I will go," said I, fiercely (for with my brothers, I am sorry to confess, I was impetuous and headstrong). "If I'm alive, I'll cross the shingle to the bay before an hour is gone, and launch my ship."

"Go on," said Edward, tauntingly; "let's see, Gilbert, how far he'll go, before he comes sneaking back again, like old Johnson's terrier after a sound whipping. Go on, Luke."

My brother Edward was rather a favourite of mine, but I had great difficulty in restraining myself from flinging the ship at his curly head. Gilbert began to urge me to return, but I had already clambered up the rock, and stood with my ship in my arm, ready to advance.

"Am I to go alone? You, Gilbert, too!"

"It is the height of folly! You cannot launch the ship, if you reach the bay alive."

"Yes, I can. The declivity breaks off suddenly, and there's deep water. Are you coming?"

Gilbert, who had not expected such firmness in my nature, and had still his misgivings of my resolute appearance being but a bombastic pretension which would soon fail me, shook his head, and said—

"I shall go home with Edward. Come, Ned."

"Cowards!" I yelled. I was foaming with rage—my teeth gnashed together with passion, as I saw them turn and move off in the direction of home. I went on—I felt I would have gone on to spite them, had I been sure of death upon the rocks, and that the tide would have been dashing over me, and made my grave there before the hour had passed.

A bend of the cliff soon hid me from my brothers' view; and, firmly resolved upon fulfilling my promise, I staggered over the slippery rock, clutching my ship tightly to my breast. I was alone, with the giant, ghost-like cliffs frowning down upon me on my left, the broad green ocean leaping and tossing on my right, and the waves breaking into spray with a murmuring ominous noise, as they dashed against the breakers. The tide was still running down; I had plenty of time to spare, and, disguising to myself the sense of loneliness allied to fear, I kept on towards the bay where, years ago, the French pirates brought their living victim, and stole away again, leaving a white, upturned face upon the sand. Harassed by the latter thought, and excited by the novelty of my position (for I could scarcely remember five consecutive minutes spent alone during my short career), I forgot the precarious nature of my path, and suddenly fell with violence amongst the sunken rocks, splitting into twenty pieces the ship, which, in conjunction with my brothers, I had expended so much time upon.

For five minutes I remained in a dreamy, half-conscious state, huddled, with the fragments of my ship, amongst the chalky heaps and wet sea-weed, gazing out of my half-closed eyes at the waves rolling and plunging in the distance.

With a vast amount of courage shaken out of me by my fall, I got upon my feet, and stood meditating as to my future progress, with a rueful look at the ship, which not the finest water in the world could have sustained, or been of assistance to, from that time forth.

Should I return? I looked in the direction of home. I had a vague hope that Gilbert had not deserted me, and that I should see his figure in the distance coming towards me, in which case I might have given a more attentive ear to his expostulations, and returned with him. But he was not to be seen.

"Yes, I will go on," I said, with a frown at the prospect far ahead of me. "I said I would reach the bay, and reach it I must. I cannot launch my ship—but go I will."

I shouted the last words in fierce defiance, as if I had a host of living witnesses to my intention standing round me, and then obstinately persisted in continuing my dangerous journey. Leaving the broken ship on the rock, a landmark where I fell, I, with more precaution than had been taken heretofore, made towards the bay, slipping at every second step I took, but in most cases saving myself from a fall by grasping at the jutting points of the cliff with my left hand.

What will they say at home, Luke Elmore of "The Rest?" But Luke Elmore was deaf to any remonstrance—every wavering step towards his object rendered him more determined in it, and the landmark on the rocky beach was soon far behind and lost.

It became still more precipitous as I proceeded—immense masses of cliff, that had fallen from above, blocked up the way in some places, but I clambered over them, and kept on in my fixed resolution : here and there were patches of half mud, half sand, into which I sank to my knees, and waded through to the sea-stained crags beyond.

Surely I had gone more than half a mile. It was an hour since I had left my brothers, and yet nothing in sight but rock on rock, with the sea-weed, in green, brown, and red masses, thick upon them, or hanging round fresh-fallen portions of the cliff, in slimy filaments, like hair must hang on drowned sailors' heads, or round that face of the foreigner immortalised in my memory by Mrs. Higson, who was murdered in the bay. Horrid thought! How cold it made the wind blow from the sea.

Still onwards. Two more falls, the last a crasher, from a rough mass of chalk, which seemed immovable as Fate, but which gracefully revolved as I reached the top, and shot me forcibly some three or four feet amongst my old companions. Five minutes' calm deliberation of the sea again, with the shingle before me brilliantly illuminated with coloured lights, and then I continued my way, with a very manly-looking gash meandering across the forehead, and descending to the bridge of my nose in a serpentine course. I stopped once more for serious reflection. I had to return the same way; there were all these difficulties to be again encountered; I felt faint and exhausted. Should I go on? I deliberated. Yes, I would go round that great overhanging cliff, that seemed to be dashing forward to meet and breast the sea; that cliff, on which the friendly lighthouse gave its nightly warning signal to ships far out upon the deep—I would go round that, and then think again.

It was farther than I had calculated on, and I could hear some church-bell striking five very faintly in the distance, as I reached the jutting point. Five o'clock! It would be seven, and nearly dark, before I reached Freeman's Gate again. What *would* they say at home? I stood beneath the cliff; I looked round; there was the bay a hundred yards from me. With a wild hurrah that startled even myself after I had given voice to it, I ran towards the bay, leaping from rock to rock, staggering, reeling, plunging—till with a dash I sprang from the last crag into the deep, soft, welcome sand. "I said I would do it!" It was a bay of considerable extent, and lighted by the sun, which another three-quarters of an hour would behold sinking into that great dreary sea, it had a bold, imposing effect, flanked as it was by the irregular curving cliffs, their white expanse dotted here and there by samphire.

There was no deep water. Whoever asserted that statement as a fact must have been a man without the slightest grain of consideration for his species in his whole composition. Had my ship been sound, and had I borne it safely, my chance would have been equally the same as at the spot so far away, where I had left Gilbert and the twin brother of sister Agnes. The water was about the same distance from the cliff—so far as I could judge—but it was coming up, instead of going down. Making allowance for a moderate quantity of falls, I had time enough for a safe return; so I flung myself full length on the sand, and lay panting from my recent exertion, looking at the sea.

I thought of Edward's taunts; of Gilbert—that bold brother Gilbert—whom I would have followed through fifty times such danger, and yet who deserted me! I could hardly keep the tears back when I thought of it. I had such trust in him—such belief in his love for all of us—such an instinctive knowledge that he loved me more than all the rest; and yet he had left me to go my way alone.

"It is not cowardice," I murmured to myself; "look at his dark, unflinching eyes, and his great, white forehead, and his bold, lion-like look! No, no; it was spite. He would not give in to me, he does not care for me!"

I buried my hands in the sand, as deep as I could thrust them, and tore them out again, to dash their contents wildly around me. I did not take into consideration the reverse side of the medal; I did not ask myself if I gave in to his wishes, or had not a little selfish spite to gratify, when I so obstinately set forth upon my journey. But my thoughts precipitately took another direction—a subject a trifle less pleasing than my brother Gilbert's ingratitude even; for, chancing to alter my position, I beheld a tall figure, with a white face, and black moustache and beard, standing by my side and gazing down upon me.

The French stranger (I believe Mrs. Higson said a French noble) flashed to my startled recollection, and, with a half-suppressed shout of horror, I scrambled to my feet, and reeled several paces backward. The figure stood regarding me with a calm, fixed look of attention, but uttered not a word.

He was very tall—evidently some inches above my father's height—and standing there before me, with a horseman's cloak draping his form, and no contrast to his stature, save my diminutive self a few yards distant, he had all the appearance of some giant of a past age, who had returned for a few minutes to life, with the intention of looking about him, and seeing how the present world was progressing.

I felt transfixed with horror; he was evidently the Frenchman; and Mrs. Higson was, for the future, to be implicitly believed—that is, if I were ever lucky enough to see that round, ruddy face again.

"Well, my extraordinary specimen of juvenility, are you dumb?" he said, at last, in a clear, deep voice; a ringing kind of voice, as if his throat was lined with bell-metal.

"I—I beg your pardon, sir; I took you for——"

"For what, my 'raw head and bloody bones' looking youth; for what?" he said, quietly observing me.

"For a man that was—that was murdered on these sands, one moonlight night, by—by French pirates."

There was a slight flickering kind of smile upon the thin, red lips beneath the black moustache; a sinister kind of smile, that had no merriment in it, and that revealed, for a moment, white, even, gleaming teeth.

"Are you frightened at ghosts, and spectres, and mystic characters, in shrouds and grave-clothes, born of wild legends and rambling story-books, boy?" he asked.

"I am—a little, sir."

"And yet you lie on the sand in this desolate and cut-throat-looking spot, coolly dreaming of the past. Was it the past or future, boy?"

"The past."

"Then henceforth, dirty and disfigured-looking child, remember the past is but for fools; the future, but for dreamers; the present, fit alone for men."

This observation I had nothing to reply to, so stood shuffling the sand in a heap at my feet.

"And now, boy, attention. I *am* the Frenchman."

I gave a sudden and spasmodic jump, and gasped out—"Who was murdered?"

"Were there *two*, then?" he inquired.

"No; not that I was aware of, sir."

"Then I can be no other than the one, can I, boy?"

I thought not.

"Attention, lad," said the stranger; "where does that infernally uneven road, or beach, lead to?"

"To Wharnby."

"What an ass, not to keep the path on the cliffs," he said; "surely I must have had a romantic fit on me, for a sea-side walk, like a maudlin boarding-school girl, at the fourth teen, to come crawling down that path instead of progressing direct. Humph!" said he, musingly; "it must be three miles back. Which way have you come hither, lad?"

"That way," pointing towards Wharnby.

"Then that way goes Jacques Vaudon."

He strode a few paces forward, then stopped.

"Follow me, boy," he said; "and here, take this—my arm has ached enough with it in good truth. Forward."

When he tendered me a portmantcau, which had not been observed for the cloak that partially conccaled it from my view, my doubts concerning the authenticity of his fearful statement were dispelled, and convincing proofs as to his identity with the rest of creation were fully established, for I had never heard or read of any respectable ghost travelling about with heavy luggage; so, reconciled to his mortality, I took the portmanteau from his hands, and prepared to follow him, not a little interested as to how his ghostship would get over the more difficult portions of the journey between the Frenchman's bay and Wharnby.

"Upon my word, boy," said the stranger, pausing before the steep and slimy crag that formed the bend of the cliff, "this is choice walking. Do you indulge yourself in this way often, *mon enfant?*"

"This is my first journey to the bay, sir."

"May your journey in life be as smooth, you little wretch," said he; "if I get to Wharnby without a compound fracture, I shall be a happy man."

We rounded the point, and in a few minutes were too deeply engaged crossing perilous gaps, and stepping from rock to rock, for further conversation. I could not help smiling at my companion's gingerly tread across the rock, his sudden leaps over doubtful heaps of sea-weed which seemed covering some pitfall, his calm, unmoved face when he turned to see if I were following in his track, so white and corpse-like, in contrast to the black beard and moustache, which gave so majestic a look to his peculiar cast of features.

He fell twice before he reached the spot where I had finally prostrated myself in reverence, but gathered himself up again in a cool, unimpassioned manner, solacing himself with a few oaths in French and English, uttered without elevating his voice above the usual tone, as if it was his duty to swear in such a position, but to swear in a cool and gentlemanlike manner—quite in a business kind of way.

"I'll take my portmanteau, boy," said he, stopping to witness my recovery from a sudden slip and fall, in which I had come with no light weight upon the article in question. "Thank you. Straight on, I suppose."

"As straight on as you can go," I said, with a grim smile.

"Through this, my infant maniac?" he said, calmly pointing to the mud and sand before-mentioned, and which bore the imprints of my late journey through them.

"There's no other way."

"Droll!"

He sank a considerable depth, and, with no slight exertion, finally gained the other side. Suffering with intense pain from bruises and cuts in various parts of my arms and legs, and heartily sick of my adventurous exploit, I, despite of all, burst into a fit of laughter at the efforts of the gentleman to force his way towards the opposite and uninviting bank.

A peculiarly expressive scowl rewarded me for my unseasonable merriment when I had joined him and was by his side. It was a scowl that totally expelled all inclination to laugh; the eyes seemed to retreat into the head, and yet to concentrate a flashing fire within them; the thick eyebrows seemed dropping over them like a curtain; and as he stood before me, fixing me with that annihilating glance, vague fears of being in the presence of the Evil One himself came across my excited imagination.

"Ill time for jesting, my lad," he said, in his mild voice, "and a mocking laugh is to me especially, at all times, distasteful. Understand me—the place is a desolation. Who would be the wiser if I went on to Wharnby alone and unaccompanied?"

I felt my heart collapsing with dread. Oh, that frightfully meaning glance! Was he jesting with me, or did he threaten me in sober earnest? I trembled in every limb.

Satisfied with the impression he had produced, he continued his way, and I, with some suspicions as to the good intentions of my companion, kept a few steps in the rear.

One of the mountainous heaps of chalk occasioned by the

fall of a portion of the cliff overhead, brought him again to an abrupt halt. He stood waiting for my approach, and I, chary of advancing within arms' reach, stopped about twenty yards from him. The sun was going down—the tide was coming in with a roaring noise—the night would soon be deepening.

"Have we to climb this ?" he asked.

"Yes—and some three others."

"And you came this way ?"

"I did."

"For what purpose ?"

"To launch my ship."

"Indeed !—I see no ship."

"I fell with it, and broke it."

"Why did you go on to the bay, then ?"

"I said I would go—I had made up my mind."

Leaning his back against the chalk, and placing the portmanteau at his feet, he folded his arms and looked full at me.

"All this is a lie, or you are mad. A boy like you, for no object in the world, to come a path that would deter ninety-nine men out of a hundred. To whom do you belong ?"

"The Elmores, of 'The Rest.'"

"Indeed !"

For the first time, his voice, usually so calm, changed into a low, deep tone, and for a moment or two he breathed hard, like a man who had been running.

"Has your father so little care for you—so little heed for a son, as to let you come so dangerous a way as this ?"

"My father never dreamed of such an action on my part."

"Possibly," said he. "Let us proceed."

We struggled up the mound, and descended on the other side, displacing huge fragments at every step that went rolling over the rocks with a crushing noise.

"Hark !" said he, raising a gloved hand—"some one calls."

I stopped and listened.

"Luke ! Luke ! Luke !"

"It is Gilbert—it is my dear brother Gilbert," I shouted, dashing forward ; "he has come to seek me."

In a minute more he was holding me in his arms.

"Thank God, you are alive !" he said, in a tremulous voice.

"I had almost given you up for dead. Have you been hurt at all ?"

"Not much, dear Gilbert—I have a gash across the forehead. I am very glad you have come after me. I thought you were at home."

"I only went to the gates of 'The Rest,' and saw Edward safe; then I returned."

"Where have you been all the time, then?"

"Full length on the rocks an hour or more—the sun was shining when I fell," he said.

"Are you hurt?"

"Not much. A sprained ancle, I believe. But what's a sprain, Luke? I have found *you.*"

"Quick, quick!" cried the stranger in our ears; "do you not see it is getting pitch dark, and we need a bright noon-day to save our lives in such a place as this? Come along."

"Who is this?" said Gilbert.

"I do not know—I met him at the bay. Let us follow him."

I moved quickly forward; but Gilbert, after one or two ineffectual attempts to keep up with me, hung back.

"I cannot go quite so fast, Luke," he said, with a suppressed groan of pain—"my hip is hurt, I think—but you make haste, and——"

"Lean on me, Gilbert," I said. "Oh! I am so sorry I came this dreadful way. It is all my fault—it is all my wicked obstinacy of temper. You are hurt very badly. I know it—I know it!"

"Nonsense, Luke, nonsense," he said, with a forced laugh. "Let me lean on you, then, and we shall get back all right enough. Come, Luke."

But my assistance was of very little service to him, and we slipped at every step. The tide was rising rapidly, too—it was but a few feet from us, and the crested heads of the waves seemed rearing towards us as if they claimed a lawful prey.

A thought struck me. The stranger was some distance ahead. "Wait here a minute, Gilbert," I said; "I will ask that man's help. One minute."

I flew along with unerring feet, and reached his side.

"Stay, stay!" I gasped forth; "you must come back. You are a strong man—my brother is hurt; help me to carry him home. For God's sake, do not hesitate! Are you a man, are you a man?" I shrieked, wringing my hands.

"Do you see the tide? Do you see the night coming on?

Do you see this hell's-own pavement stretches on—on—on, without a break? I can do nothing. Each one for himself."

"You shall not go!" I screamed, clinging to his cloak; "you are not so base a coward, so great a villain, as to leave us. By your fear of God's vengeance, come back with me, sir. I am but a boy, but *I* am not afraid."

He hesitated—he stood with a brooding gaze upon the wet rocks, as if he were calculating some chances in his brain. He looked up—

"I will return with you. It was but a momentary pang of fear, and yet I am considered a brave man, too," he said. "Well, well, brave men have a twinge of dread once in their lives—mine has gone, I think. I must relinquish the portmanteau. Can I put it anywhere out of harm's way?"

"Impossible! Quick—quick!"

"Then, ho! there," he cried, with a ringing laugh; "if there be any friend floating ahead—a distressed mariner, whose ship has foundered, here's dry clothing for you. Ho, there."

He swung the portmanteau round his head, and relinquished his grasp. It whirled through the air, and then fell with a heavy splash into the water.

"Now I am ready," loosening his cloak. "Now, mad offspring of the Elmores—quick, yourself!"

He hurried after me, folding his cloak upon his arm as he did so. I gave a wild cry, as I reached Gilbert—he lay cold, pale, and senseless against the cliff.

"He is dead!—he is dead!"

"Tush! but a swoon, child," said the stranger, covering him with the cloak. "Now, help me to carry him. Stay," he added; "I will carry him alone, and you lead the way. Are there any more of those d——d chalk banks?"

"I do not know—I think so. Follow me, sir—follow me."

We hurried on, occasionally slipping right and left, crunching the sea-weed beneath our feet, and sending showers of water splashing in the air—past the rocks, which looked overgrown with green, lank hair—by coloured weeds, all one dark brown to us in the night fast coming on—over the high mounds of fallen cliff, and chalk, and earth—through mud and sand, and fast accumulating water. Shall we never see Freeman's Gate again? I kept on at a rapid pace; my footing seemed more secure in the darkness, and I seldom swerved from a sure tread upon the treacherous breakers. It was dark night now, with the stars shining over head.

"How is Gilbert?" I asked.

"I do not know. He is still insensible, but an hour will set him right enough. The fellow's plaguey heavy. Quick! there, boy—haste!"

We were a foot deep in the sea, and the waves dashed over us as they came rushing in. I could hear the subdued oaths of my strange acquaintance behind, as he stumbled in my track.

A glare of lights attracted my attention in the distance. My companion observed it at the same time.

"What is that, young Elmore?"

"I do not know, but I think—I hope it is Freeman's Gate, and that they are looking for us. Yes, hark! they are calling."

The loud halloo rang through the silence of the night. Friends were at hand with help, if needed.

"Halloo! Halloo!"

We were treading the sand again; the servants of "The Rest"—the gardeners, the lodge-keeper, and my father, were grouped together on the sand with flaring torches in their hands. Some boatmen, a few yards from them, were preparing to set forth in search of us.

"Saved! God, I thank Thee!" cried my father, rushing forward to meet us. "My son Gilbert!" he cried, with a stifled cry, as the stranger advanced with his burden, "what has happened? Man, for the love of mercy, say he is alive!"

He tore the cloak away that covered him, and gazed at the white face of his son. The dark eyes of Gilbert opened, then, meeting the sudden light of the torches, closed again.

"Here, you men," cried the late companion of my perilous adventure, "take this young fellow: I've had him long enough, in my opinion—he's no light weight."

Gilbert was transferred to the careful arms of two of the servants; another was instantly dispatched for the surgeon, and slowly we ascended Freeman's Gate.

"Are you hurt, Luke?"

"Not much, father," said I, meekly, and with an inward dread as to future results accruing from this expedition.

"And Gilbert?"

"Has sprained his ankle, father."

"No more than that?" he asked, sternly.

"I hope not."

My father's hand, which held the torch, shook with agitation—his whole frame trembled violently; the reaction from the past terror and excitement was coming on.

"Your children are well enough, Gilbert Elmore," said the stranger, placing a hand upon his arm; "of their deliverer you ask no questions, or give one thank to. And yet so old a friend did not build upon so cold a welcome, even from one whose genial heart has hardened with the world's ingratitude!"

My father started and turned to the stranger. The torch he held shed its red glare upon the features of the speaker, who stood with an extended hand and smiling face.

"Good God!" said my father. "Jacques Vaudon!"

"An old friend and a true one."

Their hands met, and I could see my father press his convulsively, and ring it with an iron grip.

They had met once more. Fit meeting in the dark night, with the rugged cliff and angry sea around them, and the treacherous sand beneath their feet! Oh, night! ominous of evil, on which those disunited links of a Past, whose memory was madness, joined hands together once again.

CHAPTER V.

THE EVIL NIGHT COMES TO AN END.

My father and Jacques Vaudon walked side by side towards "The Rest." Unobserved and unnoticed, I kept close to my father, listening to their conversation. My will was to fly to Gilbert's side, but an undefinable motive compelled me to remain with these re-united friends.

Vaudon, after recapitulating his adventure with myself, and the meeting with Gilbert, changed the conversation, by remarking, "I had no belief, Elmore, in Time working so great a change as I have found in you. It was mere guess-work—a chance, afterwards confirmed by your agitated manner, that made me claim you as the brave friend of other days. You are strangely altered, indeed."

"I cannot say the same, Vaudon," said my father, with a sad smile; "the years that have intervened between us sit as lightly on you as——your cares."

"Ay," said Vaudon, in reply, "'my cares!' Well—why

should we mourn, and grow prematurely old, over unavailing sorrow. Has not Time wrinkles enough in store for us? May I ask a question, Elmore?"

"I guess its purport. Still—ask it."

"Have you heard from her since that night?"

"Never!" in a hollow tone.

They were speaking of my mother; my lost and almost unknown mother. I held my breath, and listened.

"I saw her three years ago, in Paris."

"Enough!" said my father, sternly. "I care not with whom, or how. There is but one fate for that false woman—the fate of all her sex who fall. Its history can be read on myriads of faces, whose haggardness is hidden by the lying paint—yea, myriads of myriads, swarming the streets of every great city. There is but one solace for the dishonoured man left behind—utter forgetfulness. If that becomes an impossibility, silence, deep as the grave, at least spares many a pang."

"I understand you," replied Vaudon. "But is not this lonely spot which you have chosen more apt to suggest deep and painful thoughts?"

"At least, it is better than meeting faces on which you read your secret—faces, full of hidden sneers, or false sympathy, or an affected interest put on whilst you are standing by. I have come to this spot not to forget, but to rest."

"But forgetfulness is to be found amongst the crowd—in the giddy pursuit of pleasure—in the struggle with that which interests the world; not in solitude," said Vaudon.

"Ah! but in the whirl of those pursuits there is always a recoil; and then a deadly horror follows the false excitement you have entered into. No, no—I have chosen 'The Rest' on a lonely cliff, looking over a desert sea, and I am content. I have only known entire forgetfulness once since that time which we allude to."

"And that?"

"The three months that followed my disgrace."

"How! those three months——?" began Vaudon.

"I was a raving madman!" interrupted my father; "that time was a blank, and I was happy. Had it not been for my children, my waking into reason would not have been God's blessing, but his curse!"

"It is not every man bears his misfortune so heavily, friend

Elmore," said Vaudon; "and so much the better for fair England."

We were before the gates of "The Rest."

"Enter, Vaudon," said my father; "not only as an old friend, but, as the deliverer of my son, you are welcome. 'Welcome!' It is the first time I have uttered that word for years."

We entered—walked slowly along the gravelled walks, with the dark shrubbery on either side, and arrived at "The Rest."

"Where is Gilbert?" asked my father of Mrs. Higson, who came hurriedly down stairs to hear the full particulars of the evening's adventure.

"We are putting him to bed, Mr. Elmore," said Mrs. Higson. "He groans a good deal. How could it have happened?"

"Excuse me a moment, Vaudon," said my father. "Luke, show this gentleman to the parlour."

"Had I not better show him to a room where he can change his things, papa. He's wet."

"Wet!" cried Vaudon. "My dear youth, you are growing considerate. I should scarcely have dreamed of *that*, now. Elmore," to my father, "can you offer me a few clothes? Mine are at the bottom of the sea."

"Take Mr. Vaudon to my room, Luke."

Followed by Jacques Vaudon, I led the way to the bed-room of my father. It was a large apartment, with three windows, heavily hung with drapery.

"This is like a chamber in one of those haunted castles we read so much about," observed Vaudon, as he entered; "and these windows look upon the sea."

"Yes," I said, holding the candlestick high in my hand; "how did you know that?"

"I thought your father would choose some such cheerful prospect, my young believer in murdered Frenchmen's spirits," said he, flinging his coat on a chair; "that will do. Put the light down and leave me, Master Luke."

Eager to be gone, I gladly complied with his request, and flew along the passages, and up the second flight of stairs, and into our bed-room—a spacious dormitory, containing three small bedsteads for my father's sons. It was empty. I heard voices talking in the adjoining room, and repaired thither.

It was a room occasionally used by Miss Berncastle, when a sudden change in the weather prevented her customary departure at five o'clock in the afternoon; and in that great bed, thick with snowy hangings, lay my brother Gilbert, whiter than them all.

His great black eyes were opened, and fixed in a dreamy unconsciousness upon the figure of my father, sitting by the bedside, and holding one hand with nervous clutch. Agnes and Edward stood at a little distance from the bed, gazing on him, and Mrs. Higson and one of the maids were walking on tiptoe about the room, and whispering together concerning sundry matters connected with the domestic arrangements required.

"Why do you keep up this incessant talk?" cried my father, turning hastily to them.

"Bless my soul, Mr. Elmore!" cried Mrs. Higson, with a nervous start, "we must prepare a bit for Mr. Whittaker's coming. Jane, stand that shepherd on the mantel-shelf a little straighter, please!"

"Do nothing," cried my father; "leave the room—it excites Gilbert."

Mrs. Higson, after swelling to an enormous extent with silent indignation, made a signal to Jane, and left the room, followed by the aide-de-camp.

I advanced.

"Is he very ill?" I asked, in a husky whisper. "Why does he keep so quiet, and look so strange?"

"Hush!"

"But, father, tell me, is he very ill?"

"I do not know." His eyes caught my wild and disordered appearance for the first time, and he said, "Go to your room and change your dress, wilful and wicked boy! Had it not been for you, your brother would not have been lying here."

I knew that fearful truth too well; I needed no severe reminder of my headstrong folly to tell me that. I moved towards the door, still looking at my brother Gilbert; I went out on the dark landing, and closed the door silently behind me. I walked to my room, with something choking in my throat, and stifling of my voice, and had hardly reached it, when Agnes and Edward joined me.

"I knew how it would be, Luke," said Edward, half reproachfully, and half tauntingly; "you'll go to Frenchman's Bay again, I think. Gilbert's hurt himself very much—I'm sure of that. There'll be no leaving 'The Rest' again, and all through you."

Selfish as the speech of Edward was, I took each word as a reproof, and stood silently before the dressing-table, with my hand upon it.

"It wouldn't so much have mattered if it had been you, Luke," added Agnes; "but Gilbert was so handy, poor fellow!"

"Go away—go away," I cried; "I know all this. I feel all this. Go down stairs, and leave me here, alone."

Edward, after staring with his full blue eyes, and mentally wondering at my impetuous manner, whispered Agnes to accompany him to the parlour.

"But I want Luke to tell me how it all happened," said Agnes.

"Not now—not now, Aggy. Do go away, please."

"Come along, Agnes, do," cried Edward; "you know I never can bear going down all those stairs without a light."

They left me, and I immediately secured the door. I walked about the room—I tried to cry, to call the bitterest imprecations on my head, but my throat was too parched to utter one sound, and my eyes seemed burning into my brain. I sat before the table, and gazed at my smeared and bloody face in the dressing-glass; I leant my head upon my arms and tried to think, but a restless inquietude pervaded me. I wanted to be walking about the house, to be running along the cliffs for help, to be going to and fro from my own room to my brother's, and learning how he felt and looked each moment. Taking off my shoes, lest their creaking sound should give warning of my presence, I crept back to the room I had a few moments since been expelled from, and listened eagerly at the door.

All was still. The door was ajar, and I pushed it slightly inward, and peered round. My father was sitting in the old posture, by the bed-side, still clinging to the hand and gazing at the face. I ran noiselessly down stairs, and looked through the hall-windows, along the dark vista of shrubbery, and of country beyond. There was a light at the lodge—I could see it glimmering through the trees; but no one was coming yet, and all was silent. I walked up and down the marble flags, heedless of the icy coldness that struck to me, and then looked out again. No one was coming yet. I passed the parlour door; it was wide open. There was a fire burning in the grate, and the stranger guest, wrapped in my father's dressing-gown, was sitting before it, fast asleep, with Agnes and Edward crouching at his feet, and looking with childish interest and wonder at his pale face, and black moustache and beard. Before Gilbert's room again, and standing motionless in the shadow of the door-way—an unseen and watchful sentinel of "The Rest." A few minutes in that attitude, and then I leant forward in a listening posture. A faint voice was speaking—

"Where is Luke?"

It was Gilbert's voice. Changed by pain as it was, I felt relieved. I had had a vague horror of never hearing it again, and that the foreshadowing of death was hovering by him. Thank God! it was his voice, and asking for me.

"Keep still," said my father, in a low tone; "he is in his room, my dear child."

"Is he unhurt?"

"I believe so."

"How did I——"

"Don't speak, my dear son; don't speak," said my father. "You are getting feverish with every word. You will keep still, to please me, will you not, Gilbert?"

"Yes."

They were silent. I went down into the hall again, and looked into the darkness of the night. The light still burning at the lodge, but no one coming yet. Past the parlour, where the stranger sat upright now, talking to the children at his feet, and where Mrs. Higson was particularly busy in looking for nothing in a work-box, and glancing suspiciously over the lid, from time to time, at the intruder. Before my brother's sick-room door again, and waiting patiently. Mrs. Higson came creeping up the stairs, and arrived, panting for breath, on that landing, into the remotest corner of which I had crept, to elude detection.

Tap, tap.

My father, in a whisper, asked from within, "Well, what now?"

"Mr. Vaudon's compliments, and shall you be long?"

"I will rejoin him presently, and—Higson!"

"Yes, sir."

"Get Mr. Vaudon some dinner."

"Dinner, sir!"

"Yes, yes. He is fatigued. Get him something. Do you hear?"

"Yes, sir."

Our hours were very unfashionable at "The Rest," and

hence the surprise of our housekeeper at my father's order for so late a meal.

Mrs. Higson was three stairs in her descent when my father called again.

"Higson!"

"Yes, sir."

I crouched further back, as my father emerged from the room and stood in the doorway.

"Has he not come yet?"

"No, sir."

"Send off another servant. Let him get a horse at the first inn. Quick!"

Mrs. Higson hastened down-stairs, and my father re-entered the room, and closed the door.

Five minutes more, I was half way in my third descent, when the lodge bell rang. I ran to the staircase window looking on the drive, and gazed out. A horseman was galloping towards the house, and two servants with lanterns were flitting about the path and lighting the surgeon's way. My heart leaped again with joy. I ran back to the door of the room, and knocked.

"The surgeon is come, papa," I cried; "he will be here directly. I have seen him coming along the drive."

My father opened the door. He started when he saw me.

"What are you doing here? Where have you been? Why still with that stained face, and torn and muddy dress? Go to your room at once!"

"But, Gilbert——"

"You shall know all directly Whittaker takes his leave. Go now, go now!"

Before I could reply, lights shone upon the stairs, and the surgeon, a stout, middle-aged man, came slowly up them, followed by Mrs. Higson and a maid.

My father had never met the surgeon before, but in his agitation he grasped him by the hand as if he were an old friend.

"Come, sir; come, Mr. Whittaker, tell me what is the matter with my son."

He almost dragged him into the room with his vehemence. Mrs. Higson following immediately behind, and coming suddenly upon my ghastly figure, jumped a surprising height, and fell heavily against Jane, who, totally unprepared for so sudden a retreat, slipped three stairs with a frightful howl.

My father furiously darted forth.

"A curse upon you!" cried he, savagely. "Why do you women make this hideous riot before the very door? Begone! If you are wanted, you will be sent for; I will ring."

"It's—it's Master Luke in that—that awful mess, that alarmed me so dreadfully sudden, like," cried Mrs. Higson, not yet fully recovered from the effects of my appearance.

My father turned to me. His livid face, his fiery eyes, his long dark hair disarranged, his set teeth, and his clenched fists, terrified me, but I did not flinch.

"Again I say, Go!" he screamed, in a suppressed voice of smothered rage. "Are you not satisfied with the devil's work you have done?"

"I will not go till I know how Gilbert is," I answered, boldly. "I *must* know, or I shall die!"

My father glared from me to the women on the stairs, then went back into the room.

"Stay, then."

The door closed, and was locked on the inside. Mrs. Higson and the servant-maid, muttering discontent, took their departure. I crept close to the door, listening to the footsteps across the room—the low voices—the sharp, quick queries of the surgeon—the faint voice of my brother in reply.

Quarter of an hour—half an hour—nearly three-quarters of an hour—then the bell rang.

Mrs. Higson came up-stairs, kept back a strong desire to jump again on finding me still there, and knocked. The door was unlocked, and Mrs. Higson passed in slowly.

I crouched still closer to the door, wondering what every frequent sound and so much shuffling of feet could mean. I held my breath, and listened eagerly. I could hardly restrain myself from beating at the panels with my clenched hands, and screaming for admittance.

At last, my father and the doctor came forth together, in close consultation. In my hasty glance into the chamber I saw Mrs. Higson sitting by the bedside in the attitude of a resigned watcher.

"Why—why, who is this?" exclaimed Mr. Whittaker, starting, as I sprang towards them.

"Tell me how my brother is. What is the matter with him? Is he going to die? Good God! is he going to die?" I screamed.

"Back! back!" cried my father.

"I will know! You shall tell me all!" I shrieked forth, as I darted before them, and intercepted their passage down the stairs; "you shall not go down, or pass me, till I am told all that has occurred. I am his brother—his dear brother—and I have a right to know."

I had no fear of my father's anger; I thought of nothing but the mysterious silence which they kept towards me, and maddened by it, I stood arresting their progress, and with flashing eyes, and heaving chest, called upon them for an explanation.

"Is this Luke?" asked Mr. Whittaker of my father.

"It is."

"The child is very ill, excited, and wild; he is in a——"

"Tell me! Tell me!"

My father, who appeared to have no sympathy for me, in lieu of being alarmed at my unnatural manner, lost all command of his fierce temper, and cried out—

"If you will know all, know it. It is your right, and part and parcel of your folly. It is your inheritance of care, if you have any brotherly love for that poor sufferer lying in yon room. He may recover health, or he may die. If God spare his life, every time that poor cripple comes before you, it will recall to you the bitterness of this evil night, making of a loved brother a living reproach, and lasting shame to you! Now, are you satisfied?"

With the last word, I dropped, like a stone, senseless at their feet.

It was the last red mark on the evil night—the *third* misfortune to "The Rest." Luke Elmore, in his raging fever, yelling from his restless and disordered couch, with many faces hovering over him—a white and ghastly one—a frightened girl's and boy's—one dark and foreign-looking, with black beard and thick moustache—a throng of servants—all clinging to each other, ever shifting, varying, never with a look alike, but passing from fear to hate, from hate to laughing scorn—a crowd of gibbering figures now close beside me—now whirling round—now vanishing in mist!

CHAPTER VI.

GILBERT.

I HAVE but a faint recollection of the many weeks that I lay in my fevered bed, delirious, and standing with one foot advanced towards the valley of death, my life upon a chance, and every hour an uncertainty.

I can remember the faces ever changing, receding, and advancing; the heat that seemed to concentrate within my burning brain; the music, wild and unearthly, now playing softly in the distance, now clashing loudly in my ears; the heavy stupors; the dull, listless feeling of inanimation; a burning mass of heavy metal, pillowed carefully, and watched night and day.

After many weeks, the fever left me prostrate and dizzy on my bed, and consciousness came back. Conscious that it was summer time, and many birds were singing in the garden, outside the window; that it was my father's face looked through the curtains at me in the early morning; that Mrs. Higson was the night-watcher at my bedside, who made such strange gurgling noises in her sleep as she lay coiled up in the arm-chair by the fire-place; that the portly man, with the large diamond ring burning on his little finger, was Mr. Whittaker, the surgeon; conscious that Gilbert never came to see me, and that Agnes and Edward were led in half reluctantly, and, after a trembling look at my pale face, led out again—conscious of all this, and yet too weak to speak.

I grew stronger day by day; I murmured feebly, "Better, papa!" to my father's anxious "How are you, Luke?" I took an interest in the doctor's coming, and sat up pillowed in the bed, and traced likenesses of Mrs. Higson, the gardener, and the Silvernots, in the straggling pattern on the wall.

Stronger still, and my mind troubled about Gilbert more and more. They never spoke of him; they never mentioned to me his name, or anything concerning him. I trembled violently, and lay sick at heart, with dread imaginings of Death having stolen in the house whilst I lay ill, and taken him far away across the cliff to Wharnby's green churchyard, and set a white stone over him.

"What is the matter, Luke?" asked my father, as he

detected the agitated look upon my face; "do you not feel so well?"

"I want to know about—Gilbert."

"He is getting better."

"I thank God!"

A pause; then I asked, "Where is he?"

"In his room."

"Can he get up yet?"

"Yes."

"Can he come to see me?" I asked, eagerly.

"Not yet; it is better not yet."

"When can he come?"

"I cannot say—soon, soon."

"Father."

"Yes, Luke."

"How long have I been ill?"

"Ten weeks."

"So long as that!"

While I mused upon the time, passed like a distorted vision, my father, watching his opportunity, stole out of the room and left me. The sparkling light in my eyes had warned him of my increasing excitement. There was great care needed yet.

Another week, and I could sit up in my bed half the day.

I waited anxiously for Mr. Whittaker's coming, and fixed him one day with the question—

"When may my brother Gilbert come to see me?"

"Are you strong enough to see him, my dear boy?" he asked.

"Oh, yes. It would do me so much good."

"To-morrow, then. Yes, I think we will say to-morrow. You must keep very calm, and then, in a few days, you can return his visit."

"Thank you, sir."

"And in a few days after that, if you take your medicine like a man, you may go down-stairs and see them all; your little brother and sister, too. You forget them!"

"Ah! true; but I see them every day. And Gilbert may come down, too?"

"Um! Yes."

In the evening, my father came to bid me his usual good night. I had been thinking of something all the day, and, when he entered, the question leapt to my lips—

"Is *he* here still?"

"Who, my child?"

"The man with the beard and black moustache, and thick eyebrows—like a—like a bravo."

My father smiled.

"He is here," he said; "he saved your brother's life; he is a very, very old friend."

"I thought all old friends were dead!"

"And I! Yet——" he paused.

"When does he go away?"

"Go away?"

"Yes; will he stop at 'The Rest' much longer?"

"I have asked him to stop; I have offered him the shelter of my home, Luke. He will be a companion to you—to all of us."

"Does he stop here for ever?" I asked, alarmed.

"For ever, Luke? That is a long date."

"But—but why does he stop at all?"

"Luke, do you begrudge me one friend?"

"No, no."

"This one friend, my son, was a schoolfellow and a fellow-collegian; till—till a certain night, our friendship had known no diminution. We were inseparables; we had the same thoughts, the same wishes and ambitions. I loved him with a brother's love."

I thought of Gilbert, and said, "Then let him stop. I am so glad, so very glad he has come."

"Do you remember the letters that came so constantly; that came so long after I had taken up my 'Rest' upon the cliff?"

"Were they his?"

"They were. He was a rich man then. Since then he has speculated and been ruined. For the love of an old time, I could not bid him go from my home friendless and penniless—this man I had known so well in better days."

My father appeared more than usually anxious to account for the presence of Jacques Vaudon to his son. He had broken through his resolution of the utter abandonment of past friends; he had gone one step backward; he had given up the solitude of home. The gloomy, brooding look was, even in so short a time, less apparent on his face, and yet he seemed haunted as by an accusing conscience—he was so prolific of plausible excuse. I said no more about Jacques Vaudon to him; and he stooped and kissed my forehead, bidding me "Good night."

I thought of the new addition to our home long after he had gone, and wondered what changes his coming would bring upon "The Rest." If, stretched upon my weary, weary bed, I could but have seen all the changes pre-destined for it, I could have closed my eyes and died, saying, "It is best for me!"

Early the following morning, Agnes and Edward came to my room.

"You are looking better now, Luke," said Edward, glancing askancely at me.

"Oh, you'll soon be better again, now," said Agnes; "and then that hateful doctor will be gone, and we shall be so happy," clapping her hands, "and so merry—so merry!"

"You were never of a particularly merry disposition, Aggy," I said.

"Oh, I don't know what I am, at times."

"Have you been to Wharnby House since I have been ill?"

"No," said Agnes. "I should like to see Cely again. I think I shall persuade Mr. Vaudon to let me go."

"Persuade Mr. Vaudon?"

"Yes," said Agnes; "if he were to ask papa, I think he would let me go. Papa is fond of Mr. Vaudon."

"Yes, that he is," added Edward; "they sit and talk about this and that, and 'don't you remember?' all the night."

"Do you like Mr. Vaudon?"

"Yes," said Edward; "like him! to be sure I do. He's going to teach me chess, and draughts, and backgammon, and I don't know what!"

"And he tells stories better than Mrs. Higson," said Agnes; "such pretty stories. I was frightened at his great beard, when he first came, but now I love him."

My sister Agnes' enthusiastic admiration of Vaudon was so different from the usual phlegmatic indifference to everything and everybody round her, that I began to think I should like Jacques Vaudon myself, when I was strong enough to join them in the sitting-room, and see more of him. They gave place to Dr. Whittaker, who somewhat hesitatingly accorded his full consent that Gilbert should come in a few hours; but I must promise to be very good.

"If you get excited, or cry, or give way to any nonsense,

you'll throw yourself back ; and then I shall have all my work to do again, and more, perhaps. So be a good boy, and he shall come."

Every minute was an hour, counted by my affection for him, before he came. I had had no conception that there was so great an amount of love in my whole being as I felt I had for Gilbert.

How I longed to see him! We had exchanged many a little verbal message the last week or two, Mrs. Higson or my father being generally the medium. "Gilbert's love to Luke," and "Luke's love to brother Gilbert," passed to and fro twenty times within the day. How would he look? Was he much altered? Was he a cripple?

Mrs. Higson was the bearer of the message, that set my heart plunging in my bosom—"Gilbert was coming!" My father had given strict orders that our meeting should be unwitnessed ; and, accordingly, the housekeeper, with another warning not to be distressed about it, left me.

He was coming. I could hear a faltering step, an uncertain footfall, accompanied by an ominous sound which I guessed too well. The door opened ; I sprang up in bed, and tore back the hangings. Two white faces met each other. It was Gilbert—but, O God! how altered.

The face, destitute of a single particle of colour, rendering the black hair blacker by the contrast ; the tall figure (he seemed to have grown, since his misfortune, several inches) ; the two crutches on which he supported himself, and with which he advanced towards me with that old gentle, mournful smile—I took them all in at a glance, and stretched my arms towards him yearningly, crying out his name.

He dropped the crutches, and fell upon my neck ; and we wept long and silently together, he clinging round me—a frail support to him, indeed!

"Oh, Gilbert—dear Gilbert!" I sobbed ; "what a wreck I have made of you! What a punishment and retribution is this day to me!"

He climbed upon the bed, and sat beside me, his hot hand in mine.

"Dear Luke," he said, brushing away a shower of sparkling tears from his eyes, "I am not crying because I am a cripple ; I do not care for that. Why should I? We shall soon get used to it—look at it as a thing of course, and be as happy as the day is long. Why, Luke, since my misfortune, I think you love me better."

"I should be a wretch indeed, if I did not."

"Then what have *I* to mourn for? With such a storehouse full of affection for me in your heart, I shall not grieve much over these poor crutches. Besides, I am not doomed to *two* all my life; Whittaker says, I am to have only one when I get stronger. Think of that, Luke—only one."

Poor Gilbert! It was the height of his ambition *now!*

"I shall miss the long runs through the garden, and the jumps over the bushes, Luke," he said, half laughingly; "but, after all, what is it? If I had lost my sight, and could not read or see you—if I had lost an arm, and could not write, or do a thing without a valet's help, then I might grumble; but because I limp about the house, I am to tear my hair, and think my life is to be all cloudy weather—why, that would be like a baby, Luke!"

"And can you ever forgive me, brother?"

"Forgive!" with another laugh: "there is so little to forgive, that it seems a playhouse farce to talk of such a thing. I should have been more careful—not gone running on as if I were on smooth ground, or Turkey carpet. Forgive you! yes, Luke, with all my heart and soul, I do."

My very weakness made me cry again, as he stooped and kissed me on the cheek.

"Tears again! Cheer up. If I journey at a slower pace down the pathway of life, I shall have you to help me—your kind hand to guide me. A brother's love unites us in a bond that no misfortune now will ever separate. God bless you, brother Luke!"

My father entering the room, an hour later in the day, found us both asleep upon the bed, the sun shining on us, as we lay with arms round each other's neck.

* * * *

I pause. The days of childhood, and of the love naturally belonging to it, fade like snow from mountain side; and the rugged rock of manhood peers forth through the spotless covering, fast melting into water, and vanishing into unknown depths below, from which Echo cries, like Fate,—"No more return—no more return! The past for ever melts into the present, on the mountain side of life, whose summit points to heaven, telling of the future!"

In the recollections of my fevered dreams, one white-faced figure, with a tall, shrouded form, is ever prominent. From that time of sickness unto this, the calm, grave face, inflexible as an Egyptian idol's, has ever at strange times met mine. So often in my sleep, so often in my waking moments—dim, but yet palpable to me, it has stood before me like a spectre. It may have been born of fever, but it died not with it. Bred of my wild imagination, and fostered in that fever age, it glided silently into reality, and took its stand before me, defying all resistance and mental conjuration. Shunning the morning of life, and the youth of the heart, it waited for me—choosing its own time, selecting its own night, and pointing out my track. Standing now upon that mountain side, from which the snow—fair type of purity—is melting, this genius, or shadow of my life, leads silently the way, and with many backward looks and yearnings of my heart, I follow.

CHAPTER VII.

THE CHANGES OF SIX YEARS.

SIX years—so interminable a time to look forward to—so short a journey, when we stand upon the hill, and they are gone for ever—have passed over "The Rest" upon the cliffs, near Wharnby; and there have been changes, and lights and shades upon it, as there have been seasons of spring flowers and autumn leaves, since Luke Elmore recovered from his fever, in the beginning of one summer-time. Let me look upon "The Rest" as present to me in that spring-time of my manhood, and chronicle the changes that six years have brought upon it, and those who live beneath the shelter of its roof-tree.

I am eighteen years of age—more, I am four months past, and my nineteenth birthday is within eight months' stride. I am tall for that important age, and very manly in appearance. I have a small moustache fringing my upper lip. I have wrestled in the spirit concerning that hirsute appendage ever since it exhibited signs of coming greatness. I have given way more than once or twice, and passed the razor ruthlessly across it—I have relented for a week—I have even gone a fortnight and three days, and then remorse has touched me, and the budding darkness has disappeared again—I have studied Mr. Vaudon's with admiring glance—I try to look into futurity by forestalling Nature's growth, and experimentalise with burnt cork, in the early morning, before the dressing-glass—I resolve, at last; it grows and grows, and I am a moustached young man, with incipient whiskers budding forth on either cheek. I have a very fair allowance of pocket-money; and, needlessly to say, I wear patent boots in imitation of a young gentleman that rode away in high dudgeon from "The Rest" some years ago, and on whom I have never since set eyes. I inquire sometimes of Mr. Silvernot, who tells me he is finishing his education at a Parisian school of the highest polish, and is quite a man—which assertion I consider to be an uncalled-for remark of extreme significance, as implying I am not, and giving rise within myself to a difference of opinion with the worthy rector. I have a horse, and an especial groom, named Tom. I believe Tom has no other name, or if blessed with one, must have forgotten it with long disuse, for he is Tom to all the world. I have changed my tailor, and patronise a fashionable gentleman in a large town, twelve miles away, whose cut of cloth and diversity of pattern I prefer to Mrs. Higson's of old time.

I say of old time, for Mrs. Higson has departed—she was one of the first changes at "The Rest."

Yes, ere a year had passed since Jacques Vaudon accepted the situation of my father's secretary (secretary to what?), my father listened to that strange gentleman's proposals with singular complacency.

"What freak of fortune brought that uncultivated woman to 'The Rest,' Elmore?" said Vaudon, one day.

"I answered her advertisement," said my father. "I certainly did not expect quite so crude a specimen of humanity, but she was honest, homely, and good-tempered. I was in no vein for a fashionable housekeeper—that ghost of a departed lady!"

"I would have rather had a ghost in your place," said Vaudon, quietly; "if it be merely a vision of gentility, it is better than a personal embodiment of vulgarity in the shape of a shop-woman, or a fish fag."

"She will do," said my father, curtly.

"Then I am content," returned Vaudon; "I have no voice in the matter. Let us to the school-room."

From that time forth my father looked with prejudiced eyes

at Mrs. Higson; her clumsy movements irritated him. What a difference to the past. He was clinging to the past still!

Mrs. Higson left "The Rest." She had become attached to the place, and many of its inmates had become attached to her, amongst whom I might assuredly reckon my humble self. She cried when she went away; kissed the children all round, and wished us a life's happiness as she started on the road to meet the London coach; Johnson, the lodge-keeper, wheeling a heavy pile of luggage at her heels, and regretting the future winter evenings, when let him steal to "The Rest" as often as it pleased him, he would find no Mrs. Higson there, with a roaring fire and a good ghost story to while away the frozen nights.

Jacques Vaudon was a man of considerable talent, and had a keen eye for the weak points—the foibles of his fellow-creatures: he found out a man's secret, a man's hobby, in half an hour's acquaintance with him, and won his heart through it, fascinating him like any snake-charmer. Yet there was no sycophancy in Jacques Vaudon's composition: he was sharp, satirical, and very often bitter; he spared no one in his peculiar way, and yet he became a general favourite—although to all he was an enigma. There was no reading his true character—he seemed to keep it back and live in an artificial existence as if it were his own; with the gay and sparkling he was light and brilliantly witty; with the children of "The Rest" he had a particular character for each, and won us all by a trait distinct in itself; with my father he was gloomily philosophical; with the rector of Wharnby he was argumentative; with the Silvernot family quite a chatty, matter-of-fact gentleman, with a little vein of acrimony, as if his temper were naturally sour, running through all his characteristic impersonations. He was the son of French parents, who had settled in England a few years before his birth; he had been a friend of my father's at Oxford, and a fellow-collegian; and there were many reports of the gay life he had led in the days of his youth, and the money he had squandered recklessly and the fair hearts he had broken. Closest of friends as he had been to my father, it was frigid courtesy to the strength of the renewed intimacy between them. It seemed as if my father had concentrated all his old love for the world in the friend he had met upon the sea-shore on the evil night.

I have known and seen changes like this. Men that have

seemed ever hardened and incapable of diversity of action—that have gone on in one continued plodding round for a score or more of years—led at last by some master-hand, who has found the key to the buried sympathies that appeared for ever lost, and unlocks the rusty casket at his will.

It was so with Jacques Vaudon and my father; and the former's powers worked greater wonders at "The Rest" with a few light words than all his children on their bended knees in prayer to him could have effected. For instance, "The Rest," in the present—that is the present which I have with a few words summoned up—(would I were potent magician enough to cancel all that followed, and begin the life again from the time I write of—begin it with a knowledge of the sunken rocks, the pitfalls, and the snares, and with lights across the dreary waste, as guides to the erring wanderers on the track of destiny)—behold the change! It is a change, worked by such slow degrees in the six years that have passed, that my father is hardly conscious of it, and dreams not that the shadow of the old time partly rests upon him as of yore. There are many servants at "The Rest"—liveried menials flitting to and fro, bedizened in the old state of servile grandeur, as in the fatal house that looked upon the park. The carriage is no longer locked within its stable, but glossy with its paint, and glowing with its silver mountings and its emblazoned crest upon the panels. There are horses in the stalls to draw it—there are horses for us—for all but Gilbert—poor, crippled Gilbert!—and I ride with sister Agnes, looking so bright and pretty in her long habit and her golden ringlets, and so graceful on her chestnut mare; and Tom, with the Elmore crest on every shining button, trots behind us in good style.

But it is not the old love of display that brings so splendid a scene upon the stage on which my father plays his part; it is the old pride that has come back—the pride of his wealth—of his supposed station in the world.

Neither Jacques Vaudon nor my father is a great lover of society; they are used up to its charms, and the attractions that it had for them when they were younger men. "The Rest" is almost as free from visitors as ever. My father occasionally rides over to Wharnby House; but solitude has every charm for him, though that solitude is more gilded, and has lighter shadings. The change that has come should have taught its lessons, and have made him eagerly press back. With his distorted view of human nature—his want of faith in human love—it were better for him to retreat. More irritable than ever, and, combined with that irritability, an overbearing pride, that was old to him but new to us, it mingled with the master's authority, the friend's welcome, and the father's affection, and made of him a mystery.

Agnes is quite a young woman in manners and appearance. The oldness of thought peculiar to her when a child, has ripened her into the woman at sixteen years of age. She is tall, of graceful figure, and singularly beautiful. Six years have so greatly changed her, that a stranger to her for that period might look in vain for any trait of resemblance in her to the little, old-fashioned Aggy Elmore. Miss Berncastle, tottering with the weight of six more years comes still regularly, and goes through some formula of teaching, with an evident fear of her accomplished pupil, whom she treats with great respect, and to whom she gives in with a mechanical kind of helplessness to all propositions Agnes makes, and has degenerated into the toady by slow and imperceptible degrees.

It is "Shall we have the pleasure of reading together that interesting history?" or "Will you oblige me, Miss Elmore, with that delightful set of quadrilles you play so enchantingly?" or "Well, how becoming that lilac satin is to your complexion, to be sure!"

Patience, Miss Berncastle! The new character you have assumed—the airs of humility you have adopted to win the pupil's heart, and remain her sage preceptor, will avail you very little. The eye of Jacques Vaudon rests upon you, and reads your policy as thoroughly as though you had printed every word of it in Roman capitals on your wrinkled forehead.

Agnes had given promise of being somewhat pretty, but we had not anticipated her being a "beauty" (ominous word!); and so like the mother that won my father's heart! I have said it was a singular kind of beauty—a most striking beauty—that dazzled the first sight. The features, at the time I write, are small; if there be any imperfection, it is the slightest disproportion of her face to her commanding height; her hair is of that silvery brown—that tinge which, catching the light, seems of a metallic lustre; her eyes are of large almond shape, and of the brightest blue, and she has great command of them, and can make them speak any language; the nose and mouth are Venus's own; and yet, with each feature perfect, and the entire face as lovely a one as I have ever seen, there is an indescribable expression on it. It is attractive—but what is it? It is more apparent at one time than another: it is now a faint outline, very dim and indistinct; then it is strongly marked, and lines the features till they wholly change; it comes across her when she sits in reverie, and stronger still when anything opposes her or thwarts her; and then, mingled with a defiant look, it blazes forth; it is something unallied to calmness, something in which the soul speaks not; it is deep as the sea that bounds the garden of "The Rest," it is full of calculation. Women that have risen to power, or have been very famous, or ambitious, or great intriguers, or meddlers in politics and treason, or wholly bad, like Faustina and Messalina, of the City of Dead Rome—all must have had a look like unto this. Women, who have gone out of their sphere, and thought with their head instead of heart, must have had my sister's strange expression on their countenances when they were young, and have had it deepened on them as they progressed on in life.

I dwell too much upon this look. I was not observer enough to think much about it at the time—the look was only dawning on the face, To the present—this false present, that my wandering pen swerves from so often. I again attempt the picturing.

My brother Edward is more of the child than any of us, and somewhat of a capricious child, too. He has still a resemblance to his twin sister, and not alone in feature. There is a tolerable amount of selfishness in brother Ned, and he is a little envious at my sudden start away from him in the race to manhood. He thinks of shaving every day, and makes satirical jests upon my hairy lip, without success. He endeavours, with strenuous effort, to keep up with me: he has banished jackets from his sight, and walks about, extremely ill at ease, in frock coat and stand-up collar. He is somewhat of a tyrant to the domestics at "The Rest;" and I have heard his name commingled with muttered complaints in the servants' hall, more than once or twice. Edward and I have our matters of dispute; and they occur very frequently, and are not got over in a hurry, owing to an attribute peculiar to Edward Elmore. There is a sulkiness about my brother Edward that has often vexed my father equally with the other members of the family: a proneness to dwell upon a fancied slight received, and to maintain a rigid silence for hours, or days or weeks, according to the extent of his imagined injury. Not even his father can influence him when subjected to these brooding fits of sullenness, and so we have given him up incurable; and, as they affect us little, we take little heed accordingly.

And Gilbert. I have left him to the last, that I might speak of him at greater length, and more at ease before I resume the thread of my biography. He is not so tall as he gave promise; for his injury has put a check upon his growth, and he is a good two inches beneath his brother Luke in height, but how much more manly-looking!

The features are calm, placid, and commanding; the eyes full of thought; the forehead lofty and broad; the lips firm and seldom parted; the hair long and thick, and giving an appearance of heaviness to his bold head that a second look soon cancels. He has one crutch, and walks remarkably quickly and hardly ungracefully with it; he is a deep reader and an earnest student, and there is not a book in the great library of "The Rest" he has not pondered over. He is very reserved in his manner to strangers, but his misfortune has not depressed his spirits or made him a despondent youth, by any means. There are few heartier laughs at "The Rest," when there is anything worth laughing at, than his. And the affection between us, though never spoken of since the day he paid me a visit to my sick couch, is very deep and true, and is never lessened by an angry word. We have never quarrelled, our tastes or wishes when they jarred have accommodated one another's, we have tried to forestall each other's wishes—we are truly brothers. If he feel a pang of regret—a secret, inward pain when he sees me return to "The Rest," flushed by horse exercise, and full of recitals of friends I have met, or minor adventures I have encountered—he hides it so well beneath his open smile and genial look that I know nothing of it. The story of the Frenchman's Bay is a dead topic between us—we never speak of it or make comment concerning it; it is remarked upon by my father and others to him and me, but between ourselves we hold it sacred. My father's words ring ever in my ears—"It is your inheritance of care, if you have any brotherly love for that poor sufferer lying in yon room."

If I have any brotherly love! as if my love for him were to be doubted or made light of, that brother of my heart!

My father spoke of the lasting reproach Gilbert would ever be to me—a reproach unto myself every time he came before me; but, true prophecy as it was, the reproach is in my own breast: there is nothing but affection in his generous welcome of my coming, though I come fifty times a day.

What a great heart he has! What a love for the father he had been so considerate of, and so fondly attached to, as a boy! It does not waste; it increases, and commands respect and reverence. I do not know if he likes or dislikes Jacques Vaudon; he evades the question, and speaks little of him to me. They converse together a great deal, and argue strenuously, one on each side the fire; and perhaps there is a half-attachment between them. Vaudon, who has a greater flow of language, and has seen more of the world, generally comes off victorious in argument, at which Gilbert shakes his head and laughs, saying, "Wait a while: I shall recollect the subject, and pose you some fine day." And, sure enough, when the topic has been entirely forgotten, Gilbert, who has slowly built up his facts, and taken counsel with himself, returns suddenly to the charge, and confounds him utterly with a fresh series of ideas. Gilbert writes a great deal, too, but we know not on what subject, as the papers are carefully secured in a cabinet he has had fitted up in a pretty study on the ground-floor, with a window opening on the garden, and he refuses, jestingly, to state the purport for which he labours on so perseveringly.

I am a second favourite with the members of the household, Gilbert, undoubtedly, being the first—there is nothing can be done well enough, or quickly enough amongst the servants, for Mr. Gilbert Elmore; he is so gentle, so kind-spoken, and so quiet—a dear young man indeed, they say.

I do not know what he would be if fairly roused; but gentle and quiet as he is, I believe there are latent energies which would battle against any obstacle, if they were called into being for a purpose. There is no craven look in him—no lamb-like resignation to a wrong, I feel assured, about him—there is power written in his face—power and an honest pride.

(I write as I thought at the time—whether future events will bear me out, time will show.)

Even Edward never sulks with Gilbert; but then Gilbert readily gives in to all his whims, and puts aside any task to help him, at a moment's notice; and Agnes's capriciousness stops short at my brother's study-door: his look disarms them, and his unselfish nature completes the conquest. But this is the youth of the children of Elmore—what is to come? what is to come?

The Silvernots are only visiting friends—the rector, more impulsive than ever, is continually calling at odd times, and sits chuckling over the surprise his sudden appearance has created for several minutes after his arrival. He is very chatty, very communicative, and when any argument occurs, and he and my father join in with Vaudon and Gilbert, the noise is absolutely terrific. He looks very old; the six years that have passed, score twelve with him, but his heart is younger than ever. He regrets we are all running up so terribly fast, and that he shall have no excuse to play and romp any more.

"And as for you, Miss Agnes," he says, with his odd, good-tempered smirk, "it must be 'my dear Miss' soon, or plain 'Miss Elmore'—you have grown such a lady. All alike—all alike! There is little Cely at the Minerva House, Hammersmith, grown like a May-pole, and is coming home for good. Why, let me see, how long is it, Luke, since you have seen Cely?"

I don't like his picking me out from all the family—it looks suspicious; I redden and reply—

"Two years."

"Two years! Why, how is that? Oh! I recollect, the last holidays—(holidays once a year, that is all—capital plan!)—were spent at a relative's—true. Well, she *has* altered. As much as —Agnes here. So tall! 'pon my honour, when I called upon her three months back, I hardly liked to kiss her—she seemed somebody else."

"Time is a tyrant only to the old, Mr. Silvernot," says Vaudon, as he looks round from a reverie, at the open window (it is summer time); "the young find him a friend, that adds a fresh grace every day."

"Ay, but he turns traitor after thirty. Fickle as Dame Fortune," says Mr. Silvernot.

"Time *must* be a lady, I think then," adds Vaudon, his hand dallying with moustache and beard—a constant habit of his when engaged in conversation—"and a lady of *uncertain* age. Volatile, and full of whims, with some especial favourite in train, why, Time must be a woman—eh, Agnes?"

"No; Time is of the rough mould in which you men are fashioned," says Agnes; "Time is too severe and resolute for us."

"Leave the subject for another day, observes my father from his seat. "It is a difficult one. So Celia has improved, Mr. Silvernot?"

"Well, I really think she has," says the rector; "she is quite a young woman. Bless my soul! how girls melt to womanhood in one imperceptible stage!—and how the boy struggles and flounders between his satchel and his first razor!"

Edward, taking the rector's observation as a personal allusion, leaves the room immediately.

"I used to consider you, Luke, as Cely's little sweetheart," says Mr. Silvernot; "but, ha! ha! she'll frighten you—she will, indeed! In fact," says he, in a lower tone of voice to my father, but which is not inaudible to me, "there's a fast young scamp, whose father's in the Treasury, sneaking about the exterior of the school, who's touched in the heart, or"—correcting himself—"in the head, and," very sternly, "I'll have none of that nonsense."

I have a lively remembrance of the pretty, fresh face of Celia Silvernot, and admire the rector's principle accordingly. I wonder he did not call on the father in the Treasury, and point out to him the flagrant conduct of his offspring; and I wonder more at what he means by Cely frightening me—frightening, indeed!

So, the summer-time is green and young—"The Rest" is brightening a little from the gloom—its children are shaking childhood from their backs and marching onward, and Cely Silvernot is coming home.

CHAPTER VIII.

A MORNING CALL.

THE successor to worthy old Mrs. Higson had not yet been determined upon, and the shadow of her presence, like many shadows of her legendary histories, hovered about well-known passages, and came stealing up the stairs after sunset, and lurked in the darkest corners of "The Rest."

My father had resorted to the newspapers, and had answered several advertisements he had seen therein; but the replies were not satisfactory, and Jacques Vaudon read, or feigned to read, the characters of the writers with the skill of any modern chirologist; and the result arrived at was far from complimentary to the ladies out of place. Vaudon appeared to have my father's interest and that of his children greatly at heart, he studied our wants and our pursuits so well. If he had a motive for every new suggestion, I am at a loss to what to attribute it. Here and there I can fathom one, but some were too deep, or had no meaning.

Miss Berncastle progressed on in her sage policy, and, winning favour in her young mistress's eyes, took extra importance upon herself for the same, and became quite majestic, and, when in good humour (which was not always), condescending and sublimely gracious.

First favourite with Agnes Elmore, what was there to fear? If Agnes were pleased, the family must be, of course. Why, even Mr. Jacques Vaudon, who so courteously and invariably raised his hat from his head when he met her coming towards the house from Wharnby, and smiled so heavenly, was full of the praises of her management!

One morning, the Elmore family were seated at the breakfast-table, Agnes Elmore presiding.

"Papa," said that young lady, as she handed him his large cup of chocolate (his favourite morning beverage), "I am going to make a request, and I want you to promise me something."

"I shall have no difficulty in acceding to it, I dare say, Aggy," said my father, dubiously.

"But will you promise?" with a winning smile, which my father could not withstand.

"Well, well. Yes."

"I wish I could manage father in that cool style," said Edward, bluntly; "you must let me into the trick, Ag."

"Don't call me 'Ag,' if you please," said my sister, with freezing dignity; "any one would think you are speaking of a witch; especially"—with a sharp twinkle of her bright eyes—"as the 'h' drops in unconsciously, my little ploughboy."

Edward, with a stifled grunt, looked daggers, and swallowed half a roll.

"Now, the promise, Aggy," said I. "What can it be, I wonder? A new bonnet or a book of the fashions—the last number—I'll wager."

"More serious—more serious than that," said Gilbert "Agnes advances too cautiously for so slight a matter."

"Not so slight a matter!" cried Vaudon; "a new bonnet is an affair of great importance to the daughters of Eve: there are colours to choose, complexion to suit—as much study as they use in Parliament to pass a reform bill; and a book of fashions, it is priceless! It is a pity that, like the ladies it is written for, it is so continually on the change."

Agnes, with no heed to the three last speakers, said, "I have been thinking, papa, that as my studies have nearly reached a conclusion, Miss Berncastle, a lady I greatly esteem, should not be ungratefully set aside upon their termination."

"I have never purposed so *ungrateful* an expedient," my father remarked, curtly.

"Therefore, I should like you to install Miss Berncastle as housekeeper in Mrs. Higson's place. Miss B. is more of a lady, naturally so, and is not averse—I am sure she will not be averse—to accepting the same. I am very much attached to Miss Berncastle."

"If Miss Berncastle considers——"

"One moment, Elmore," said Vaudon, placing his hand quickly on my father's arm. "This would be a rash promise to fulfil."

"My father never breaks a promise, Mr. Vaudon," said Agnes, with an imperious look.

"Nor would I have him, Miss Elmore," was the respectful reply of Vaudon; "but the subject interests us all, and should not hastily be concluded."

"What have you to say against it, Mr. Vaudon?" asked Agnes; "let us hear the objections you can urge, sir."

Vaudon stroked his beard and commenced.

"I will place a few statements before you all. I will leave it to you all to reflect upon. I do not pronounce them law," he added, as he caught sight of a peculiar smile on Agnes's face, "neither have I a right, nor hold a place to do so."

My father, very little interested, sipped his chocolate, and half listened and half thought of other matters.

"In the first place, Agnes Elmore, your studies have *not* reached a conclusion: Miss Berncastle may be a learned lady, but she is one of an old school, and goes an old-fashioned way to work. You have learned all that she can teach; but is it enough to bestow upon you that easy grace and calmness characteristic of the high-born? has she even given you tact enough to steer your way through a crowded ball-room or a brilliant party?"

"A crowded ball-room or a brilliant party! Good God! Jacques Vaudon, have you gone mad?" cried my father, leaping up from his leathern chair in his amazement.

My sister's face wore the strange look upon it I have before spoken of, mingling with a flush of pleasure at some suggested picture of the future. Jacques Vaudon, catching the expression, smiled, and then turned to my father.

"I exaggerate and alarm," said he; "your pardon, Elmore; supposing even parties and balls set aside."

"As they will be," stiffly said my father.

"As in all probability they will be," continued Vaudon, "yet in the meeting of even our Wharnby friends on social evenings—for I am prophet enough to foretell we shall have more of them than we ever had——"

"Why?" interrupted my father once more.

"I am coming to it, Elmore," said Vaudon, impatiently; "give me breath enough to speak, and room enough to breathe, if you have a Christian spirit in you! Let me see—where was I bewildered last?"

"In social evenings," reminded Edward.

"Yet in the meeting of our Wharnby friends on social evenings, as I said before," continued Vaudon, "you will carry your crude manner—or Miss Berncastle's manner—into the room with you. It will be seen less on you than on others of the same teaching, perhaps; but still it will be plain enough, Miss Agnes. You would not have disparaging inferences drawn, Mr. Elmore," said he, turning to him, "between your daughter and the fascinating Miss Silvernot, brilliant with London polish? You have more pride."

"He would be a bold man who hazarded the remark in my presence," said my father.

"Still it will be hazarded," said Vaudon, coolly; "and you cannot enter the lists and run a tilt with fat old dowagers, and bony spinsters of many years standing—can you, *mon brave*? No; but this you can do. Get an accomplished governess, one who has mixed in first-class society herself, and a week will work great wonders. Let that same lady, if she be willing, enter upon the housekeeping management of 'The Rest.' I take it there is no one deeply indebted to Miss Berncastle; she has been paid well enough for the duties she has performed; and she is but a country governess, after all."

"We will think of this more," said my father, "another time; what say you, Aggy?"

"Another time, then, papa," said Agnes, very thoughtful; "the promise was a rash one—the thought that suggested it, but ill-considered at the best. Yes, we will think of it—we will think of it."

And before the week passed, the father and daughter had arrived at the same conclusion. The father's pride, that Agnes, *his* daughter, should stand a mark for comment even to the Silvernots, and a foil, to enhance the good breeding of the young lady so shortly expected home, revolted within him, and asserted its supremacy. And Agnes, calculating, perhaps, on one step leading to another, looked forward on many a fête at Wharnby House, and even many a ball. It was true that there was still a great objection—she could not dance. But her father had changed his mind in many things of late, and she would wait patiently for the turning of events.

Miss Berncastle had held a long conference with my father in the library, and had been apprised of the intended change. Miss Berncastle had gone through a series of complicated manœuvres with a pocket-handkerchief and a bottle of smelling-salts, and sobbed, and choked, and sniffed, and gave little guttural sentences between whiles, which she invariably left half finished in her mental anguish and emotion. Miss Berncastle had been treated with great gentleness, and had received a gold watch from my father's hands, as a token of respect, which she kissed spasmodically as she retired, backing with great gravity out of the room, and curtseying to the ground in reverence.

A few more days were to complete Miss Berncastle's dominion at "The Rest," when the answers to my father's advertisement in a London paper came pouring in at Wharnby's diminutive post-office, at which place all applications were directed to be addressed.

Tom, laden with the missives, came into the room.

Gilbert and Edward were walking in the garden, Agnes and Miss Berncastle doing nothing in the music-room, and I sat reading at the window alone.

"Here be the letters from the post-*orfice*," said Tom, dropping a leathern bag with a bang upon the table; "may I be bold enough to ask, Mr. Luke, what they *air* all about?"

Tom was of an inquisitive turn of mind, and, as I had favoured him of late, he had become quite a familiar gentleman.

"Nothing particular," said I; "you can go."

"Oh!"

Tom reluctantly withdrew, and my father shortly after entered the room.

"Has Tom been to the post-office to inquire for letters, Luke?" asked he.

I pointed to the bag of letters on the table.

My father seated himself, and poured out the contents of the bag before him.

"What a sad reflection, Luke," he said, pointing to them, "that to three or four lines, almost lost amongst a mass of print, should come some hundreds—ay, hundreds—of urgent applications: women of talent—women who have known better days—women struggling for an honest living. Now, out of this mass, I can choose but one—save but one from the stern thoughts poverty may bring. And which one, from all these epistles—some of which have been prayed over—some written with a heaviness of heart akin to despair—some, unconscious of the crowd of rivals, full of hope and confidence—is it to be?"

He spread the letters over the table with his hand, and gazed mournfully at them.

"The first post has arrived, I see," said the deep voice of Vaudon, as he entered; "by my faith, a goodly muster!"

"I was thinking, Vaudon," said my father, looking up, "of the many broken hearts these letters are a type of. I would wager a goodly sum that every one of these notes could tell a sad story."

"Sad enough!" replied Vaudon; "but there are plenty of missives here, not written by those to whom your advertisement was addressed. For instance," snatching two or three up in his hand, "here are Mrs. Higson's class—the heavy, illiterate old ladies who can hardly spell their own names."

"And there are many representatives of Miss Berncastle amongst them, or I am much mistaken," I remarked.

"Representatives of all classes upon earth," said Vaudon, flinging the red-wafered epistles he had snatched up to their places again; "a few fitting for the office—the greater number ignorant as asses. Now, which epistle strikes the eye amongst the number here collected?"

I went to the table, and looked observantly at the chaos of letters. There was one letter sealed with black, which particularly attracted me; the address was evidently written in haste, but it was written gracefully, and contrasted with the more studious efforts that surrounded it.

My father leant forward and took it up from the rest.

"The very one that struck me!" I exclaimed.

"The very one I should have chosen last," said Vaudon; "a black seal, ominous of death. Some gloomy maiden, cold as an icicle, without doubt."

"The envelope is not black bordered; the loss is a minor one, or has not recently occurred," said my father; "and Death may have taught a lesson that she can teach again."

"A lesson!" I exclaimed.

"The lesson that the world is not to be worshipped like the heaven that shines over it," said my father, in a hollow tone of voice.

"Does Agnes Elmore require telling that wise truth?" asked Vaudon.

"It is never out of place to teach it, Vaudon," he answered. "We may all learn it with good grace."

"But the letter?"

My father broke the seal, and, after reading the contents in silence, passed it to Vaudon.

"Humph!" mused Jacques, with his hand almost buried in his flowing beard; "there may be something in it, after all. It is, at least, worth some attention."

"I like this letter for two reasons," said my father. "In the first place, she has been a governess in a high family; in the second, she is not a lady who has ranked high once, and so there is little room for airs of vanished greatness; she has no pretension to be anything more than the daughter of a late lieutenant in the navy. Her letter has no assumption about it, yet it tells of an accomplished woman."

"She mentions no age," mused Vaudon; "she may be as old-fashioned as Miss Berncastle. Yet," looking at the letter closely, "the handwriting is too firm for a nervous dame over thirty. Suppose you take care of Miss Osborne's letter, Elmore, for the time."

"I will do so," replied my father. "Now, Luke, help us to open some of these letters. If you come to anything worthy of note, let me know."

Before I had broken the first seal, there bounced into the room, with the freedom of an old friend, the little rector of Wharnby.

"Ha! ha!" he cried, shaking hands with all of us—"taken you by surprise—I thought I should. I've walked—that is, run—all the way. Couldn't wait for my horse being saddled to bring you such news! Impulse was not to be resisted."

"Good news, I trust?" said my father.

"Why, that's as it may turn out in the end—eh, Mr. Vaudon?" said the good-tempered clergyman.

"True, Mr. Silvernot," replied he, "'news' is a better word. He is a bold man, who makes a statement, and calls it 'good news.' In a year he may curse the hour he ever learnt the tidings."

"True—true enough," murmured my father.

"A man may consider the news '*good*' that conveys to him the offer of a marriage from a rich man to his daughter," continued Vaudon, who was evidently in a ruminative mood; "but a few hours can make a change to the contrary, rather startling. If you accept Miss Osborne, she will account it the luckiest of news, whereas it may be the harbinger of ill fortune —the pioneer of distress."

"Accept Miss Osborne!" cried the rector—"who is Miss Osborne? Why, why—you're never going to marry again, Mr. Elmore?"

"Marry!"—with a half groan—"no, not marry."

"My father has advertised for a governess," said I, in explanation.

"Indeed!"

"A finishing governess," added Vaudon—"neither a Miss Berncastle nor a Miss Wigginton."

Miss Wigginton, by the way, was still a resident beneath the roof of Wharnby House, acting as companion to Mrs. and Miss Silvernot.

"Ha! ha! Miss Wigginton!" repeated Mr. Silvernot. "I suppose not. In fact, I proposed Cely's change from Wharnby to Minerva Academy, Hammersmith, solely on account of Miss Wigginton. This is in confidence, you understand. Not that I dislike Miss Wigginton—merely Miss Wigginton's teaching. And so Miss Berncastle is going?"

"Yes."

"And if I may ask the question, Mr. Elmore, who is Miss Osborne?"

"A lady who has offered to become the resident governess at 'The Rest.'"

"But why not send Miss Agnes to a London school—or, in my opinion a better course still, a Parisian academy?" asked Mr. Silvernot.

"Too much society—too many faces—too much gossip and wild romantic fancy, Mr. Silvernot."

"Well, it may be so," said he; "but my news—good gracious, they'll be here before me! How very silly I am, to be sure!"

"Who will be here?" ejaculated my father, with more vehemence than was, perhaps, consistent with politeness.

"Why, my sister Cely, to be sure."

"Cely Silvernot!" I exclaimed, with all the vehemence that characterised my father's manner.

"To be sure," said the bustling rector, rubbing his hands; "she's coming with her sister Arabella, and my respected father—you'll never know her—you'll never know her."

In the rector's delight at his sister's return, he had imagined that all the inmates of "The Rest" would be imbued with the same feelings of exhilaration, and now looked wistfully at the grave, unmoved features of my father.

"I shall be happy to welcome her at 'The Rest,'" said the head of the house; "she was quite a child when I saw her last."

"Oh! quite," said he; "and now—but, Lord bless me! you'll never know her—you will not, indeed."

He seated himself at the table, jumped up again, and ran across the room, took his hat off the chair, and put it on his head, snatched it off again with a hasty apology, and then launched into a full account of every incident in Celia's life, from the day of her birth, with a face glowing with fraternal pride.

Watching my opportunity, I slipped from the room, and ran up-stairs three steps at a time.

"Hollo! Luke!" cried Edward, meeting me on the first landing, "where are you going—what's the matter? Gilbert's been asking for you—we've just come out of the garden. Some one has been at the peaches since yesterday—I'll swear they have."

"Nothing's the matter," I said, confusedly—"that is, nothing worth mentioning. When I say not mentioning, I mean—upon my soul, Ned, I don't know what I mean."

"And upon *my* soul, I think you're about right," said he, amazed.

"Tell Gilbert I'll be with him in a minute or two," I rattled on, "and, oh! I forgot to tell you, Ned, the Silvernots are coming."

"What of it?"

"Nothing," I answered, "except Celia—you remember Cely—is coming with them. She's home from boarding-school."

"What of it?" for the second time.

"I thought you'd like to see her—that's all," I stammered.

"Oh! I shall see her often enough," was the callous answer; "but who could have taken those peaches?—my favourite tree, too!"

Disgusted with such a base indifference to the Silvernots, I passed my unfeeling brother, and entered the room.

There were separate rooms for the children of Elmore now; the little cribs were gone, and we each slept in stately loneliness.

I hardly knew what motive had brought me to my dressing-room save a desire to shine and appear manly in the eyes of Celia Silvernot, who had grown so much of a woman since we last met. Remembering her but as a child, I could have no other reason, and yet I was as agitated and perplexed in choice of dress, as if I had been in love. Did I want to make an impression on Celia Silvernot? Really, I could not answer. I wanted to look well, that was my only satisfactory excuse—a vain one enough, perhaps, but I was contented with it.

Before I was half ready to descend, I heard the grating wheels of a chaise along the drive, and the door open, and voices in the hall.

I had been perplexed in the choice of waistcoats; had been vacillating between a snowy white and a black embroidered, when the arrival of Celia led me to dash at the former, and, after a few minor arrangements of hair and moustache, to dart from the room. My hand ready to open the parlour door, when the fearful thought of appearing in a white waistcoat of attractive spotlessness in the early morning, entirely unmanned me. I flew back again, like a madman, exchanged my costume with the rapidity of any harlequin, gave another brush to my hair, with which I was exceedingly displeased—half a dozen attractive wavy curls over the forehead, which had been there for years, having entirely disappeared—and descended.

I met Gilbert at the bottom of the stairs.

"What, Luke! I should hardly have known you," with a smile. "Are you going anywhere?"

"No, no," I replied, with an effort to be cool, although I felt assured I was considerably redder than a fire-engine; "but I had on an old morning-coat, and it was hardly respectful enough—was it now?"

"I will tell you when I've seen the coat, Luke," said he, with an odd, comical look. "How soon you wear your clothes out, to be sure!"

Gilbert had a capital memory: my morning-coat had only been brought home last week.

We entered. God forgive me! but it was a foolish vanity —a refined selfishness—that made me draw myself up to my full height, and walk with a proud step, as if to afford a contrast to the lesser stature and limping gait of my poor brother. The Silvernots were there. Mr. Silvernot senior was talking to my father in a very voluble manner, with two fingers inserted in his button-hole; Vaudon was leaning over Miss Arabella's chair, and quite gallant in his attentions; the rector was contemplating the scene, all smiles; a sylph-like creature, not quite so tall as Agnes, was by Agnes' side, at the open window, looking on the garden. Edward, very much out of place, and looking vacantly abstracted, sat biting his nails in a sheepish kind of manner.

I heard the roll-roll of Mr. Silvernot's "How d'ye do, my dear boys?" the "Good morning, sirs," of stately Arabella. I had an undefined impression on me of feeling their hands in mine; and then I was lost in the blaze of effulgence beaming from the prettiest of pink silk bonnets.

"What, Mr. Gilbert! Mr. Luke! I am very glad to see you, after so many years of separation."

It was such a tiny hand, encased in light brown kid, extended to me. There were such myriads of black ringlets on either side her face; her eyes were so bright and sparkling; her cheeks of such a roseate blushing tint. She was very, very pretty, and I was—yes, the rector was quite right, after all—very, very frightened.

Gilbert was perfectly at home, and not in the least embarrassed or awe-struck. Whilst I was stuttering through my expressions of pleasure at our meeting, he said, so coolly too—

"I am very glad to see you at 'The Rest.' Now there is to be no more going back to London, may Wharnby House and this retreat be almost one!"

Not so bad, Gilbert! I wish I could have said that, and been rewarded with so sweet a smile for the expression.

"What a change there is in everybody," said Celia, with a merry laugh. "Mamma said I should find you all very much altered; and she was right, indeed. Why, Mr. Luke, time has worked wonders with you."

"Yes, Ce—— I beg pardon, miss, what did you say?"

"Time has worked wonders with you," she repeated.

"Yes, miss," was my sapient reply, made with cheeks of a vivid scarlet.

"Miss!" she echoed; "I used to be Cely once, Luke, when we were playfellows, and you used to run over to Wharnby House on Wednesday afternoons with Agnes or Edward. If we have grown older, are we to grow frigidly courteous, and become so particularly formal? You speak as if you had never seen Celia Silvernot before."

"I can hardly believe it is the same little girl that used to race me across the lawn three years ago," I said, plucking up more confidence; "I am doubtful, even now."

I drew a chair between her and my sister, and Gilbert leant across the back of it, and completed a group of which Celia was the centre ornament.

So we chatted of old times, those childhood's days so dear to every memory, and drew pictures of the pursuits and whims that had interested us, and that, in the recalling of, made us again old friends and dear companions.

I could not help contrasting Celia Silvernot with my sister Agnes, as they sat together. They were a great contrast to each other, both beautiful in their particular style. Celia's dark hair and eyes were so opposite to Agnes' light-brown locks and large, blue, searching orbs. Their complexions were both of a brilliant white and red; but there was an air of frankness in Celia's face that was more than ordinarily apparent after looking at my sister. Agnes was a beauty of a more patrician order, of a more wavering expression—perhaps, to strangers, of a more attractive potency; features more regular and classical (I have often traced resemblance, more or less faint, in the marble heads of famous heathen goddesses to Agnes); but there was the whole heart in her friend's face—one could read it like a book.

How the time had flown! Why they were going, and apologising for their long stay, when it appeared to me to be scarcely but a minute since the chaise came winding round the drive.

"And now no more of your snail-like practices, Mr. Elmore," said the bustling rector; "no keeping in your own shell. One large happy family—eh! my dear sir—eh?"

"If you will promise me a quiet day at Wharnby House

and keep your friends for other occasions more important, I will call and see you now and then," said my father.

"That's a bargain, sir," said the senior member of the Silvernot family. "I rely upon that promise, sir—I rely upon that promise. Well, well—when is it to be? Run over this evening, all of you. Suppose we say this evening, Mr. Vaudon. I trust in you to help me."

"I will use my best endeavours, Mr. Silvernot," said Vaudon, in reply.

My father did not relish anything half so precipitate; and, firmly declining so early an invitation, he promised that a week should see him, God willing, at Wharnby House.

I took a long walk in the park appertaining to "The Rest," after the chaise had rolled away, and borne a fairy face away with it. I was clean gone—shot neatly through the heart. I had almost expected it. First sight had never worked so sure a result in matters of love as this first meeting after two years' absence.

So beautiful, so accomplished—was there hope?

I would keep my passion such a secret in my own breast; I would hide it deep beneath the superficial manners of society; I would strive to win her; I would slowly and by degrees gain that love, without which my boy's heart said happiness could never be. We should be much together. There were no such aids to love as constant companionship and kindred pursuits—I knew that for true philosophy. And by-and-by, I thought, as I walked on at a pace as rapid as the emotion in my breast, when my close intimacy would warrant me to tell her how I loved her, and how long that love had nurtured every aspiration of my soul, I should win her timid "Yes," and, like the sequel to the fairy tales, live happy ever afterwards.

Dream on, Luke Elmore! Your happiest times will ever be your dreams; your fairest hopes will bloom and die in rosy visions. Dream on, Luke Elmore, of "The Rest!"

CHAPTER IX.

SYMPTOMS OF MANY THINGS.

I FOUND many excuses to my family for visits at Wharnby House. I began to fraternise with the warm-hearted rector, in his pretty villa, near the church, and called many times thereat; more especially when I made the important discovery that Celia was very fond of riding thither also—sometimes to disarrange his papers, sometimes to listen, with patient gravity, to his last concocted sermon.

I detected in Celia Silvernot a love for flowers, too; and, although perfectly aware of the immense green and hot-houses in the Wharnby grounds, made choice bouquets from my own flower-beds, and presented them with trembling reverence. I became particularly studious of my personal adornment, and ran up extensive bills with my tailor at Cliverton, and astonished my father, beyond all measure, with the elaborate costumes of the period.

I reached to a pitch of excellence in the cultivation of the moustache, and became absorbed in the study of whiskers, and made deep experiments on my own straggling tufts, so unworthy of the usual cognomen bestowed upon them. I discovered I had a taste for poetry, too—and copied many lackadaisical effusions from the "Poet's Corner" of our county paper, and attempted, more than once, to compose odes and sonnets of a fiery nature and extreme significance, but universally failed in lines deserving of the glorious subject I had chosen.

That was a happy time, too, when we all rode over to Wharnby House, one summer evening, and made our promised visit. I do not know what occurred, or what topics were discussed, or anything, save that our family was there, and Jacques Vaudon there, and all the Silvernots, and Celia. I know all concerning Celia; how very pretty she looked in white, with a red rose in her hair—how angelically she sang—what a merry, ringing laugh she had—what a lady-like grace in everything she did—what happiness was in her beaming looks—what a heart without a care, *then*—what a suffocating kind of pleasure I felt about the region of the chest—what a hoarse voice I had every time I spoke to her—what a love un-akin to a boy's in my boy's heart!

Yes, I believe—nay, I know—that mine was not a child's

first fantasy—the day-dream of an affection that shrivels up before the burning heat of a true passion ; no, it was deep and pure, and there was not a selfish thought alloyed with it. The solitude of "The Rest" had kept me from the world ; I had been brought up differently from other boys, and I was a young man, at eighteen, very different from other men. I had learned love from the books of my father's library ; I had been imbued with something of their romantic nature. I looked upon the passion as something holy, and felt within my glowing breast a gratitude to God for it.

And the picturings of my imagination ! The golden future, when we were married, and had some charming villa near my father's house, and passed a life away without a cloud.

I returned home that night wrapt in ecstacy. Vaudon and I rode on horseback a few yards before the carriage that contained my father, his daughter, his eldest and his youngest son ; and Vaudon endeavoured to draw me from the dream-land into which my thoughts had plunged, failing, and looked with penetrating gaze at me from the corners of his eyes.

I remember it was a bright moonlight night, and the dark firs and full-leaved elms of "The Rest" could be seen—a black mass near the edge of the cliff—from the moment we left Wharnby House. I remember the rippling, shining sea on our left hand, and one distant ship, with full-spread sails—a silver spot—on the murmuring waters.

Vaudon roused me, at last, with a home question, "What do you think, Luke, of Celia Silvernot ?"

"I—I think she is very pretty," I replied, with burning cheeks.

Feeling conscious that his eyes were on me, I turned my head and looked towards the sea.

"She will be a fine young woman," mused Vaudon ; "quite a star in the family ; for"—with a short laugh—"the other Silvernot constellations sparkle not very brilliantly in contrast."

We trotted briskly home.

"Why, faith, Luke !" cried Vaudon , "I verily believe you have not come from the house at Wharnby heart proof."

I ventured to indulge in the weakest of ironical laughs.

"There would be nothing very remarkable in Luke Elmore marrying Celia Silvernot !" he exclaimed ; "it is natural enough, if you make haste."

"Make haste! Mr. Vaudon."

"Haste, of course," said he. "When I was a young man, I always struck whilst the iron was hot. 'More haste, worse speed,' is not a wise truth in matters of love."

"I should have thought your example contradictory to that precept," I remarked, "for you are still a single man."

"True," with a peculiar expression flitting over his face; "I may have had reasons for remaining blessed in my singleness. Take my advice, and make haste, my young lover."

"I have never owned to the influence of the blind god's passion, Mr. Vaudon," said I, somewhat vexed at the transparent manner in which my young secret had been hidden; "you misapply clever counsel."

"Then, it will do for the time that will come one day," said he, lightly; "you have the recipe. Profit by it, Luke, whenever occasion serves."

"Why do you recommend such haste?" I asked, with some curiosity.

"Because, where a beauty is concerned, or an heiress, or, in fact, any girl one may be deeply interested in," said Vaudon, "it is as well to make sure by a speedy proposal. The very suddenness of the onslaught takes by surprise, and then capitulation follows. If you vacillate, and hang back, and wait for opportunities, in lieu of making them, a fresh actor steps in, a more accomplished rival intercepts your progress, and, with a few compliments, half a dozen sighs, and three or four whisperings in the ear, walks gaily off with the prize you have dallied with so long, and leaves you a fine prospect of blue sky with no sun in it—a dead blank, Luke—a dead blank!"

"What, a blank with moon and stars?" I asked, laughingly, as I followed up his simile.

"The moon may be a second love, a false light borrowed from the first; and the stars are weak and frail, and sometimes fall from heaven."

"True." I was thinking of my mother.

"No happiness in moon or stars. But," suddenly said Vaudon, "men are often ignorant of the sunrise. First-loves are very often comets, blazing past, and dazzling the eye. Woe to the man who pursues them for his sun!"

"Woe indeed!"—still thinking of my mother.

"So there's my advice," said he; "find a storehouse for it in your memory."

"It is advice that will do me little good," I replied; "I may believe in comets. Give me a touch-stone to detect the truth."

"There you puzzle me," cried Vaudon; "the truth is beyond 'plummet's sound.' Watch for it. I can advise no better—some men are blind all their lives."

He left me to my reverie after that statement, and waited for the carriage to come up with him, and rode by its side, talking to its inmates, the remainder of the journey. I had soon forgotten all the philosophy of Vaudon, and was thinking of Cely in white muslin, with a red rose in her hair.

Agnes was very dull all the ride home, and very silent and meditative on the following morning, so much so that my father asked if she were ill.

"No, I am well enough," she answered, peevishly; "but where is the new governess, that is to make a lady of me? To make me sing those Italian and German songs of Celia's, and not the odious Scotch airs and maudlin ballads, a century old at least. To give me something to talk about—of new books, new music, new fashions—to talk about France, and to give me the true French accent—why, Miss Berncastle gabbles it like Irish!—and Mr. Vaudon studiously keeps it to himself."

"You would be a fashionable lady?"

Agnes looked penetratingly at him.

"Why, hardly fashionable," said she, evasively; "but still not a female 'Robinson Crusoe.' Oh! how I would learn!" she cried, excitedly, "how I would learn!"

When my father left the room, which he did with an agitated face, she said, passionately, "Oh! Luke, what an hideous guy I am, compared with Celia Silvernot. We are both of the same age, too. She knows so much of the world, has such high-bred manners, such a fashionable air; and I, who could do all these things better, more gracefully, more winningly, am as ignorant as our gardener's red-faced daughter, Kitty."

She breathed quick and short—I stared with wonder.

"And she will go to the Cliverton balls, and the Yeomanry balls, and the parties given by all those great neighbours we shut ourselves away from, and keep our doors closed to," she cried, her white hands clenching; "and I, Agnes Elmore, must stick here like a hermit in a cell, and hear of her at third-hand, and see her name in that *Cliverton Herald* day after day, and have her praises ringing in my ears eternally."

"Do you think she will be so fond of all these pleasures?" I asked, rather alarmed.

"Fond of them!" she answered; "who would not be? Why, there's a grand ball coming off in two or three months, at the Town Hall, Clivertou—a ball given by the officers of the —— Regiment, quartered there, and she is already thinking of her dress; and only my age, Luke—but sixteen!—only a few months past sixteen!"

"Is she going alone?" with a look of intense horror.

"Alone, you simpleton?" she said, with a compassionate glance, expressive of her pity for my helpless ignorance; "she is going with all the family, except the rector, and with a host of friends. All Wharnby is going, save those who should be head of Wharnby—the dead-and-alive Elmores."

"But we are not children, now; father is less stern and less exacting; he does not treat us like children, Aggy. We may go. I believe we have but to ask."

"Ask, and see," said she, with a scornful laugh; "and even gain his consent—gain it, if it be possible—and then stalk about the room to be sneered at and commented upon. Fancy me being asked to dance a quadrille, and stammering out, 'I do not dance.' Sixteen, at the Cliverton ball, and don't dance!" She unconsciously snatched a handful of flowers from a vase, and strewed them about the carpet in her vehemence. "Why, Luke, what are we but one degree above the savages?"

My father re-entered with a sealed letter.

"Luke, if you intend to ride to-day, I will entrust you with this letter; if not, I will send it by one of the servants."

"I am going out directly."

He gave me the letter. I glanced at the address, and read—

"MISS OSBORNE,
"Merner's Library,
"Knightsbridge."

In the left-hand corner of the letter my father had written 'Immediate,' and underlined it with a thick black stroke.

He smiled grimly as he detected my eyes resting on the word, and said—

"It is a pressing case! I have delayed and delayed—for what reason, it is difficult to say. I have decided now. God send, Agnes, she may be *fashionable* enough for you!"

Agnes flushed scarlet, but said nothing.

"I shall not want you, Tom," I said to my groom, as he stood holding my horse at the door; "I am merely off to the post-office. We'll drop ceremony, Tom, for once."

"Very well, sir," with a downcast look.

The truth was that, since I had become a victim to the tender passion, I had imbibed a preference for riding alone—the clatter of the horse of my attendant in the rear disturbing my meditations; not to mention the attendant himself, who was very partial to a little conversation, and rode closer at my heels than necessary, for that ostensible purpose.

So I rode to Wharnby village alone, and harassed myself about the great Cliverton ball, and the coming parties, and the society in which Celia was to mingle and be made so much of. I had thought to have her all to myself, it seemed. I should have rivals, probably. I must make haste and profit by the counsel of Jacques Vaudon.

As I passed through the village, there were two old women—one in a red cloak and peaked hat, like a witch—talking together very attentively in the middle of the road, and a curly-headed boy was playing with a dog, and gambolling round them.

"Grandmother!" he cried, as I advanced, "come out of the road; here's one of the Elmores from 'The Rest.'"

"So that's a young Mr. Elmore, is it?" said the red-cloaked witch, shading her eyes with a brown, wrinkled hand, and looking full at me as I rode by; "well, he's a handsome young fellow, anyhow—eh!—Mrs. Clover?"

I did not hear Mrs. Clover's corroborative testimony, but I rode on with a pleasurable feeling, notwithstanding. She was an old woman, and, perhaps, blind as age could make her; but I still felt flattered at the compliment, and fancied myself more of a match for the rivals that might be advancing in the distance, to snatch away all hope of Celia Silvernot.

Having deposited the missive intended for Miss Osborne's hands in the Wharnby post-office, I turned my horse's head, and trotted homewards.

About half way in my return route, when a clatter of horses' hoofs sounded in the distance, and a minute more saw two ladies and a gentleman, well mounted, galloping towards me.

My quick eye detected the graceful figure of Celia Silvernot, the object of my thoughts, her sister Arabella, and the rector.

I had not seen her on horseback, and there was fresh subject for secret admiration as I reined in my mare to greet them.

"Not knocked up from last night's dissipation, Mr. Luke?" inquired the rector; "I feared for you—I did indeed."

"I might have felt a little dizzy when I awoke, but I have ridden off all effects."

"Been to Wharnby village, Mr. Elmore?" inquired Miss Silvernot, who looked somewhat gaunt on horseback, and terribly sharp about the nose and lips.

"Yes, Miss Arabella," I replied; "a special call at the post-office."

"I suppose we return," suggested Mr. Silvernot, junior. "Shall we keep this young scapegrace company, eh, Cely?"

"I am agreeable," with a bright glance at me.

"Right about—wheel!

They turned their horses' heads in my direction, and we all cantered off together.

By a lucky incident, perhaps by design of the warm-hearted rector, who was a shrewd man at times, I rode on a little in advance of him and Arabella, and by Celia's side.

"How your sister Agnes has improved," she observed, after three minutes' silence, during which I had been nearly bursting every vein in my head in search of a subject to converse upon.

"She has altered, I think."

"Wonderfully."

Another horrid pause, and we cantered on at a rapid pace.

"When shall we see you at 'The Rest,' Miss Celia?"

"In a day or two papa will call; I heard him say this morning that he intended shortly paying you a visit."

"And not you?"

I said it much too earnestly, for she coloured as red as the scarlet tie round her pretty white neck, and seemed embarrassed.

"I shall come and see Agnes soon," she said at last.

What a terrible bore it was that I could not dash into talk—although it were common-place talk—with Celia Silvernot!

The third silence between us. How annoying, to be sure!

"Do you remember Master Redwin?" she suddenly asked.

"To be sure I do," I replied; "is he coming home?"

"Mrs. Redwin came over in her chaise yesterday morning to say he was shortly expected at Wharnby. She was very proud of her grandson, if you remember."

"Has he altered, I wonder?"

"Really, 'tis so long a time since he came to Wharnby House, that I remember him but as a pretty boy, with a great taste, or vanity, in dress."

I felt relieved by the fact that she had not seen him lately.

We talked of Paul Redwin, and of Agnes, and of "The Rest," and even the great Cliverton ball, to which, with diplomatic skill, I managed to bring the subject round.

How that ball perplexed me!

"Are you fond of dancing, Celia?"

"Oh, yes! I am very fond of dancing, are you?"

"No—that is, yes—if I knew how to dance."

"Not dance!"

Her dark eyes opened to their fullest extent, and she suppressed a comical little smile from extending over her face, by pursing her red lips closely together.

"But I may know all your elaborate figures before the ball comes on. If so, may I engage you for the first dance?"

"I am very much obliged," with a bow.

"And you consent?"

"Can I do less, to so gallant a proposal?" And you intend to emerge from 'The Rest,' and go to the Cliverton ball?"

"Oh, yes!"

I could not help being surprised at my own cool determination; but I had settled it all in my mind, and had no doubt of satisfactorily arranging everything. What could I not arrange, with the prospect of Celia for my first partner? With my companion it seemed more of a jest, and there were one or two merry laughs over it, before I reached the road that bore round to my home on the cliff.

"I shall say no more about it, Miss Celia," I said, as we stood in a group, enchanging salutations; "but it is a promise of which I will remind you."

"Very well."

"What—what is it?" cried the rector, in his bustling manner; "a concerted scheme of elopement, or what?"

I was red, horribly red again. Why had I not Celia's self-command?—and why was I not capable of so quiet a smile?

But I was in love, and Celia——? I hoped—I believed; but I was ignorant, and all was dark and all impenetrable.

Yes, I hoped and believed; and I rode to "The Rest" happy in my hopes!

CHAPTER X.

PROGRESS.

THE change that had dawned upon our home during those years which I have but cursorily glanced at, was not without its prototype, in the fisherman village of Wharnby itself—a village destined for a greater transformation than ever came upon "The Rest."

Some royal personage, a great duke or a grand prince, thoroughly wearied with hard travelling, had stopped at Wharnby for the night instead of posting onwards at full speed to Cliverton, and had risen early in the day and sniffed the sea breeze from the cliffs with his royal nostrils, and being in good humour with himself and the world on that particular morning, had declared his excessive astonishment that Wharnby was not a fashionable watering-place, and his regret that no pier or harbour marked the spot and made it picturesque, or convenient for shipping, or even handy for the fishermen and dredgers. Royal words never fall unheeded; they alight on good ground, and take root and flourish vigorously, and these formed no exception to the rule. Wharnby began to look about itself from that time; Wharnby was remembered by many fashionable families, and immortalised in the records of fashionable news, as the resting-place of this peer of royal blood. A Wharnby genius built a large hotel, and advertised in London papers—a gas company started business in Wharnby—visitors began to arrive—two bathing machines made their appearance on the sands in the summer and the autumn months—buildings were rising right and left—and a subscription for a harbour was set on foot, and a fair amount speedily raised, owing to the five hundred pounds heading the list, the donation of the royal personage before alluded to, who from that moment bitterly regretted making any allusion whatsoever concerning Wharnby, and was particularly careful of passing remarks commendatory of anything from that time forth.

Wharnby steadily kept on the change, encouraged by the public patronage received; the harbour described a greater curve seaward every month, and was not far from completion at the time my story treats of. "The Rest" stood still in solitary grandeur on the cliffs, and my father, fearful of encroaching neighbours, had bought up many an acre of meadow land that formed the boundary of our park and garden, and refused to treat, or hold an interview, with any speculator or enterprising builder who sent his card up to the house, in vain hope of arriving at some profitable conclusion.

Still there was not much apparent change to the Elmores; the only signs of "the season" from "The Rest" were a straggling dandy with a telescope, or a party of ladies promenading in a melancholy manner on the sands, or a carriage or two on fine days tearing along the chalky roads.

But everybody talked of the rising fame of Wharnby, and the future glories destined for it when the harbour was finished, and the railway had completed its thirty mile branch from the great line (the world talked of nothing but the daring innovations of steam at that time), and formed a station about a mile from the old church—a link between the little village and the roaring, ever busy city of great London, more than a hundred miles away.

I had something better to reflect upon than the prospect of the rising greatness of Wharnby village; Wharnby might sink to utter desolation, the harbour might never be completed, and High Street, and Cliff Terraces remain "carcases" for evermore, so Celia Silvernot were well in health, and flourishing, the rarest of all flowers, at Wharnby House, and not entirely unmindful of the love increasing in my heart with every day, and never swerving from its idol, and never straying from its beaten track.

A second love may be more strong, and capable of longer duration, than a first—the wild, unprofitable first-love of the boy; but there is nothing so absorbing, so never wearying in reflection, so half grotesque in its extravagance, and yet so painful in its very minuteness, as the bright dream-world which most of us pass through, and date from thence many of our purest recollections.

My love was the more romantic for the trifles that it had to feed upon—the lightest words and smiles—the sitting by her side—the accidental contact with her hand against my own—the casual, unthinking glance—all kept me thoughtful and reserved, and very, very happy.

I made no progress—I was not contented, perhaps, with standing still—a watchful sentinel by the fire burning in my heart; but the outposts were secured, and there were no enemies advancing from the mists of the distant valleys, that my vigilant eye could detect or challenge. I preferred to wait. I had no moral courage to act otherwise; I had built my castle in the air, and peopled it with fairy faces; and in my belief, it had so long been fostered, that I could think it nothing but the strongest fabric, whose foundation was dug deep, and proof against all storm and tempest.

I had no occupation to wean me from my thoughts of her. It was part of my father's pride to keep us aloof from men, and from mingling with the world. He was rich enough to leave to each of his children a fair independence, and he loved us round him, and had a deep love for us beneath the cold, invariable manner with which he iced over his better self. Each hour was Celia's—I was ever studying love-speeches that I never had the courage to make manifest—I dreamed of her at night—I started from my sleep with her name upon my lips.

Mrs. Silvernot, with a maternal eye upon me, received me with the sweetest and crispest of welcomes, and was skilful in arranging my place at Celia's side, and was full of praises in my hearing of the budding graces of her younger daughter, and evidently intended to be down upon me presently, when symptoms set in more violently, and we gave surer sign of an affection in the bloom of youth.

Mrs. Silvernot was an estimable lady, but she had an interest in seeing her daughters off her hands, and had tried in other days to transfer the care of Arabella to some worthy man capable of appreciating the merits of so rare a prize, but had signally failed in the attempt, and at one eventful period had precipitated a promising flirtation between her elder daughter and a weak-minded young man, studying for the Church, and who had come to Wharnby to go through a course of reading with her son, preliminary to setting out for Cambridge; and had so startled him by a sudden onslaught of "intentions," that with an embarrassed air, and stuttering speech, he had backed out of the room, packed up his portmanteau, and flown away for life, leaving Arabella a monument of blank despair.

But there was a slight difference between Celia and Arabella; one was very beautiful, and the other——. Well, peace to the past, Miss Silvernot—the days have long since gone, the night has long since deepened on me, and shut thee from my sight!

There was one scheme to be set about directly, and made haste with—I must learn to dance. Unless I hovered and glided mechanically about, veering gracefully right and left on the tips of my patent boots, to the seraphic harmony of a full band, at the Great Cliverton ball, I shall be undone for ever.

How to make the first step? There were no dancing academies at Wharnby; and Cliverton, supposing it to possess that valuable desideratum to promising young men, was twelve miles from "The Rest." Then, there was a stern father to consult. I had been brought up under such careful surveillance, and taught to lay all my puny schemes and childish propositions before my father for consideration and final judgment, that the thought of keeping secret from him any plan I might form struck me with a sharp pang as of remorse. Yet that thought crept into my brain, and grew stronger and stronger with every day, and became fixed at last into resolve.

I could not bear the chance of a refusal, and I knew my stubborn nature too well to believe that it would give way to my father's wish—backed, as my inclinations were, by the love for Celia Silvernot. Consequently, I reasoned, that keeping secret my intentious would be better for all parties; that it would spare my father much pain and mental distress, and Agnes much jealous envy. So I would learn dancing, and no one should know of my acquired accomplishment; and I would go alone, and in secret, to the Great Cliverton ball.

And afterwards?

Let the future take care for itself; the ball was where all thoughts halted. I could not look beyond that event; it was the great era in my life.

It was my first secret, and I felt a keen sense of humiliation in my father's presence. I felt I had betrayed the trust reposed in me; that I had begun to think and act for myself, uncaring for the feelings of the one to whom I owed my birth, my education, my station in the world. I was a moral coward, and feared to face dispute, and, perhaps, entreaty. I preferred the tortuous path. I made the first step from right when I rode away to Cliverton, one sunny morning, full of my new project.

Cliverton was a large town, with three churches, a dissenting chapel, a small theatre, an assembly-room, a large market-place, a town-hall, and an ornamental pump, by way of public edifices. The railway was stretching out, Briareus-like, another arm in this direction—railways were giving promise of what they have since become, and shares therein were high and flourishing—and the bricklayers were busy erecting a station in the grandest Gothic; and the horses that started from the "Black Bull," with the "Pegasus" coach, every morning, weather permitting, looked as depressed in spirits, with the shadow of coming events cast on them, as did their masters, guards, and coachmen.

After putting my horse up at the "Black Bull" aforesaid, I strolled through the town in search of a dancing academy. I looked in vain at every glazed card in the shop-windows, at every brass plate on street-doors, and, at last, felt inclined to give up the wild intention, having a dread idea that there were no professors of the saltatory art in Cliverton, and that I was a doomed young man for life.

I walked to the railway station, and gazed with an apathetic manner at its large proportions. I went further into the country, and hung over half-finished cuttings, watching the navigators at work below. I looked at the pump and the market-place, and took a vast interest in a dirty old woman opening oysters, in a left-handed manner, for a knock-kneed plasterer; and finally strayed into my tailor's, and gave an immediate order for a white satin waistcoat to Mr. Stippins, who smiled significantly as he took my measure, evidently labouring under the impression that it was a wedding garment.

Whilst Mr. Stippins was encircling me with his yard measure, a bright idea suggested itself to me.

"So you are going to have a ball here, Stippins?"

"Yes, sir," he replied; "always once a year. Grand ball, sir. Given by the officers, sir."

"How do you obtain tickets?"

"Why, sir, they can be got, but it's difficult, sir."

"Oh! could you manage it for me, Stippins?"

"For you, Mr. Elmore?"

"Yes, for me."

"Why, I'll try, sir. You see, sir, the officers send tickets to all the gentry round about Cliverton, and—oh! I have it, sir—it's plain enough—very plain."

"Then I may rely upon you, Stippins?"

"Why, sir, it has just struck me that if you wrote a letter to Colonel Stalker or Captain Clifford, they would be most happy to forward you a ticket. Very courteous gentlemen, the military, sir!"

"Are they?"

"To the heads of the county, sir," remarked Stippins, very drily.

"Thank you for the hint, Stippins, and"—coming round to

the principal object I had in view—"the rising generation of Cliverton, the *beaux* and *belles* of future balls, I suppose they have some celebrated artist to prepare them for their *debût ?*"

"Oh, yes, sir; there is Bentboys."

"Bentboys is——"

"Professor of dancing, sir."

My heart felt quite light again.

"Does he reside at Cliverton ?"

"Opposite the Assembly-room, sir. Large music shop—glass chandelier—little man with red nose."

Five minutes more, and I was looking intently into the music shop, and admiring the chandelier suspended from its roof, and on the watch for a small man with a rubicund landmark, by which I might steer the way to an introduction.

After half an hour's stupendous efforts to overcome my natural timidity, I shut my eyes, and plunged into the shop, as if it were a cold water bath, and I a nervous patient.

I was soon at my ease. Bentboys was just the man for me. Bentboys would undertake to initiate me into all terpsichorean mysteries in less than two months, by a series of private lessons. Bentboys, eager to secure a new pupil, undertook to commence immediately, and several steps were analysed and gone into, in a spacious room over the shop, before I quitted the house.

It was all arranged. I had begun to learn dancing, and "The Rest" seemed frowning upon me a reproach, when I rode home that afternoon.

I let no one into the secret; I kept it as closely within my breast as that greater one which linked me to Wharnby House and those within it. I rode over to Cliverton three or four times a week, and practised dancing with Miss Bentboys—a very small lady, in a constant state of lisp—and got on amazingly.

I wrote to Colonel Stalker, and received an immediate reply, and an enclosed ticket for the ball. Colonel Stalker would be most happy and highly honoured, and the pleasure of my society would—upon his own showing—entirely overwhelm him with delight, &c. &c.

I learnt afterwards that Colonel Stalker was an ardent lover of field sports, and a crack sportsman into the bargain, and had often cast longing eyes at the dark shrubberies of our estate, as he rode by on September mornings.

My correspondents were very few and far between, and this

epistle might have been detected as an extraordinary and important one, had not the Cliverton post-mark boldly stood out in relief. I had trusted to it, and it did not fail me.

"Another tailor's bill!" said my father, tossing it to me. "Are you going to open shop?"

His quick eye had for once deceived him, and the griffin and stars, with the Latin motto on the seal, he had mistaken for a lion and unicorn, and "Stippin and Co., Tailors."

They were pleasant rides to Cliverton, and there was something worth looking at, and worth sauntering an hour away in an inspection of Cliverton shop-windows.

I had not cared for shop-gazing before I was in love; indeed, I had had a decided distaste for that particular; but how the boy-god had changed all my inclinations! Every shop suggested thoughts of Celia—that is, every shop that appealed to the imagination.

I stood admiring the jewellers' windows, and picturing the ruby brooch on Celia's neck, and the emerald bracelet on Celia's arms, and the diamond hoops on Celia's fingers. I bought more than one trinket for her, which I set aside in a little drawer, biding my own time.

Then there was the bookseller's; and I used to wonder which book she would select—which of the last fashionable works she would like to read: and I bought two or three sets of them also, and took them home to Wharnby House, and lent them to—Mrs. Silvernot!

And every bonnet in the large milliner's shop with the plate-glass windows, I fancied Celia's pretty face within, and have stood realising it, till the apprentices' heads in the back parlour have kept up an incessant bobbing over the blind, evidently impressed with the idea of my being desperately in love with one of them, or of having some felonious intention in my mind, only requiring time to be carried out with satisfaction to myself.

And the linen-drapers at the corner of the street, and all the music-shops, and the piano-forte makers from London, and that immense furniture warehouse, so suggestive of keeping house and home with Celia, all had their attractions, and weaved an ideal life around me.

I had my portrait taken on ivory, too, for seven guineas, by a German artist, with a stormy head of hair, and gave six sittings for it, and bought a gold locket of *that* jeweller's, and had my likeness set therein, and then laid it along with the trinkets in the drawer, that were biding their own time.

What a picture I drew of the day when I could give her my likeness, and she could take the miniature and prize it as something above all worth, and we should be engaged, and such a happy couple !—ah ! such a happy couple !

So, waiting for that day, I lived in hope and built my plans ; and tower after tower, turret after turret, rose on my castle in the air, as fair a fabric as ever dream-land raised, or poets mused o'er in their haunted brains.

CHAPTER XI.

THE NEW GOVERNESS.

MEANWHILE Miss Osborne had replied to my father's letter, and my father had written again, and a second reply had determined the matter, for all preliminaries had been arranged, and the day had been settled on which Miss Osborne was to come.

"Miss Osborne informs me in her last note," said my father one morning, "that she will be at Cliverton to-morrow, and will take the coach to Wharnby on the following day. I have not answered her letter, but shall send the carriage."

"Your courtesy to the fair sex reminds me of old times, Elmore," said Vaudon ; "it is almost an unnecessary attention to a governess or housekeeper."

"I do not like the idea of my daughter's preceptress arriving by a public conveyance," remarked my father, with a proud air.

"Humph !" mused Vaudon ; then, after a pause, he asked abruptly, "what does Miss Osborne want at Cliverton ? Why not come straight to Wharnby ?"

"Ever suspicious, Jacques," said my father, with a half smile ; "may not Miss Osborne have a relation or an old friend to meet ?"

"Or a lover, Elmore ?" then, in a lower tone, "and that would be a bad beginning for a quiet life at 'The Rest.'"

"Miss Osborne's lover must keep ever in the background, then," said my father ; then, turning to me, he asked—"Luke, do you mind going to Cliverton the day after to-morrow ?"

Having an engagement already at Bentboys', I did not mind at all.

"And Agnes?"

"I should like to be the first to welcome Miss Osborne," replied my sister.

"Then, Agnes can take the carriage, and bring back the lady. She will probably be at the coach-office about three or four in the afternoon. Luke, you will go on horseback, I suppose?"

"Yes, I think I will."

"But how am I to know Miss Osborne?" inquired Agnes.

"I very much doubt the probability of a second lady travelling to Wharnby by coach from Cliverton, at this season of the year."

"You forget Wharnby is becoming a trifle more fashionable, Elmore," said Vaudon.

"Fashionable!" sneered my father; "none but fools will ever set the fashion at Wharnby."

The day arrived, and early in the afternoon Agnes took her seat in the carriage, and I rode by the side in my usual dreamy state of half-consciousness — half-conscious that this was Wharnby, and I was riding from it to meet Miss Osborne—but with an entire knowledge of my desperate condition in matters of love, and of the bright face that lit up Wharnby House with radiance, and dazzled and blinded all the poor mental faculties I fancied I might possess. There was half an hour to spare at Cliverton, and Agnes wanted to make some purchases at the aspiring linendraper's near the market; so, whilst she was being bowed into the shop by the master of the establishment, all smiles and white neckcloth, I rode round to Bentboys', and was soon deep in the mysteries of waltzing.

I was getting on in waltzing rapidly—I had passed the unwieldy kind of spin which characterises beginners in the art —I no longer crippled Miss Bentboys for the remainder of the day by coming with elephantine precision on her dirty satin-clad toes; I really could waltz; and Bentboys himself, who played his kit like a Paganini, would launch forth into rapturous expressions at my proficiency, as I whirled round the room with my lisping partner.

Being a youth of strong imagination, I tried to picture the room over the shop as the ball-room opposite, Mr. Bentboys as the full band, and his accomplished daughter as Celia Silvernot, but signally failed in the latter impersonation; for Celia had not red hair and a pink nose, and did not lisp, neither was she afflicted with convulsive sniffs at uncertain intervals, as most undoubtedly was Miss Bentboys the Small of Cliverton. So, giving up these abortive attempts to forestall the happy night, I took everything in a literal sense, and progressed on at a rapid pace, and looked triumphantly through the windows at the dark room opposite, with its chandeliers in holland bags, and its windows very dirty, and its whole appearance unaccountably oppressive, like the ghost of a ball-room that was never more to see life—that had been eternally laid to sleep in its great yawning grave.

But it only looked so, I knew better. I knew that the time was coming when charwomen would be flitting in and out at side doors (not the state entrance with the enormous lamp over the wide stone portals), and men would be cleaning the window-panes, and there would be noises of moving forms and music stands within, and carpenters with paper hats and mouths full of nails would be appearing and disappearing fifty times within the hour, and packages would be arriving, and chandeliers would be unswathed, and taught to glitter in the daylight, and signs of that eventful night would be seen within, without, at Bentboys' music rooms, at the Barracks on the high road, where those kind officers were quartered, at every shop in Cliverton, on the faces of the dirty boys who lived in the choked-up streets, at the back of the market, and which faces would be packed together round the doors, to see the company go in that night, not many weeks away.

Agnes had not completed her purchases, when I emerged stealthily from Bentboys' and mounted my horse. The coachman was asleep on his box; the horses were baking in the sun, and much concerned about the flies; and through the glass doors of Messrs. Trimmer and Co., I could see Agnes very busy amongst lace and satin.

I rode round the town, and met the carriage on the move as I returned.

"Luke," said Agnes, from the window, as I rode close beside it, "do you see anything of Miss Osborne?"

We were at the coach-office, which formed part of the Black Bull; the coach had not arrived, but there were ostlers and porters hanging about the place, in expectation of it.

I looked up and down the street. No one bearing the

slightest resemblance to Miss Osborne was to be seen, and I made known the result of my observation to my sister.

"Where can she be?" cried Agnes, impatiently; "how I abhor waiting about, and everybody staring so!" and she drew down the blind of the carriage window nearest the office with a sharp jerk.

There was a large private house a few doors distant, with a brass plate on the door, and another on the gate, and a page leaning over the latter was evidently looking for something also, in an earnest manner, for he kept attracting my sudden attention by stretching his body so far across the spikes, in his eagerness for a long range, as to threaten a fall into the street, or a frightful impalement on the spot.

Whilst fearfully interested in the gymnastic performances of that remarkable boy, I caught a glimpse of the coach in the distance, advancing at a brisk pace towards us. The page, who had evidently been on the watch for the same object, darted into the house.

At a sign from me, our coachman drew the carriage to the opposite side, and the London stage came rattling up to the office at the same time as the door of the private house before alluded to opened, and a young lady emerged therefrom and descended the steps. An old white-headed gentleman, without a hat, stood at the door, smiling his adieux.

"That must be Miss Osborne; look, Aggy," I exclaimed, pointing in the direction of the house.

Agnes looked out.

"I do not know; I can hardly think it; and yet she is in slight mourning—see."

"It is she, I feel assured," said I, riding towards her.

I reached the house, and leaped off my horse.

"Miss Osborne, I presume?"

The lady stopped, and looked full at me.

She was pale and delicate-looking, with large brown eyes, of a thoughtful cast, which gave a gentle and winning expression to a countenance not otherwise particularly beautiful, although placid and intelligent. She was not tall, hardly reaching, perhaps, to the middle height of woman, but of graceful figure, and very slightly made.

"Yes, sir, I am Miss Osborne."

She waited quietly for my explanation.

"My name is Elmore, miss," I said; "my sister and your new pupil have come from 'The Rest' to meet you."

"I am indebted to your sister for so kind an attention, Mr. Elmore," she replied, with a smile; "pray let me offer her my acknowledgments forthwith."

The carriage drew up beside the pavement, and the footman having been dispensed with for so long a journey, I officiated in his place for the nonce, and turned the handle of the door.

"I intended to go by coach," she said, half reluctantly; "Miss Elmore is very kind."

Miss Elmore herself responded to the compliment as Miss Osborne entered the carriage, and, dispensing with an introduction which I was formally about to make, with lady-like grace she welcomed her governess and set her at her ease.

Agnes was chatting very busily as we rode off to Wharnby, and Miss Osborne was listening attentively, and smiling occasionally, and evidently studying the new pupil by her side.

They were both mistaken in each other. Miss Osborne had looked forward to a girl some years Agnes' junior, and had found a young woman, gracious, perhaps a little condescending, and yet with very winning manners, and apparently requiring no tuition that she was capable of bestowing; and Agnes had expected to see a staid lady of some thirty years or so, and had been agreeably surprised to find Miss Osborne evidently not more than twenty years of age, who made no pretension of her learning, and no assumption of her delegated authority, but was more of a friend and a companion, and one whom she was sure she could love and be very happy with.

I had my doubts on that point, but I kept them to myself, as I rode on a few yards in advance, and pictured my father's astonishment at the appearance of the new aide-de-camp to the household of "The Rest." I fancied I could detect on the gentle features of Miss Osborne a calm firmness, that would resist any attempt to undermine her sense of duty or of her position, which would not agree with Agnes Elmore. Agnes would strive for the mastery—would strive to be pupil and yet mistress—and I doubted the result. Whether my doubts were ever confirmed, future chapters will bear evidence. Vaudon, my father, and his two sons were awaiting us, and their glances were all directed to Miss Osborne, as she entered the room with Agnes.

My father started somewhat at the appearance of Miss Osborne. Vaudon, possessed of more self-command, bowed, and almost unconsciously rose from his seat. Gilbert and Edward slightly acknowledged the presence of the lady.

"I have pleasure in welcoming you to 'The Rest,'" said my father, advancing; "but——you are very young."

"You anticipated——" she began.

"Your pardon, Miss Osborne, but suffer me to interrupt," cried my father, quickly. "Age matters very little in the case of my daughter; it is the qualification for the task you have undertaken that is alone necessary, or that I have to care for. I believe I shall not be disappointed."

Miss Osborne bowed.

"You are aware that my letters entered into full particulars, and spoke of your assuming the duties of housekeeper, upon the completion of my daughter's education. I must say again, you are very young for a housekeeper."

"Mr. Elmore is a lover of the antique, Miss Osborne," broke in Vaudon, half satirically; "and yet, 'it is not the age, but the qualification, &c.,' as my friend has ably observed."

"I hardly venture to assert that the duties of housekeeper are suitable for me, Mr. Elmore," remarked Miss Osborne; "but I aim not at position; and, though a governess be a more ambitious title, I have not found such happiness with it as to cling tenaciously to the name. I am young, sir; and more, I am alone and friendless."

"I grieve to hear it, Miss Osborne," replied my father; "it is a sad as well as a frank confession. Alone and friendless! Well, well—there are more alone and friendless in the world than yourself, although they may be stately persons, and fare sumptuously every day, like Dives of the parable. One can believe in friends, and yet be friendless—live in the crowd, and yet be a great solitary."

"Besides," said Agnes, full of her new governess, "shall I not soon be a young woman? and then, although Miss Osborne be housekeeper, I can arrange many little things for her, and superintend everything, like a true lady of the house."

"And head of 'The Rest,'" said Gilbert, quietly; "but your ladyship forgets Miss Osborne is a traveller, and has not dined."

"Let me correct your last assertion, sir," said Miss Osborne; "I dined at Cliverton."

"I have prepared Miss Osborne's room," said Agnes; "it adjoins my own. If she will favour me by accompanying me thither, I am quite ready."

"Thank you, I will do so willingly, Miss Elmore."

The two young women glided out of the room, and my father and Vaudon looked significantly in each other's face.

"Well?" said Vaudon.

"Well?" echoed my father.

"She will do, I think. There are no airs of the *parvenu* about her. For the daughter of a naval officer, she has a surprisingly aristocratic air with her."

"I wish she had been ten years older," murmured my father.

"Why?"

"She would have had more influence over Agnes; her superiority of years would have enabled her to assert more command."

"Pooh!" cried Vaudon; "she will be more of a friend, and Agnes will imperceptibly catch her tone and manner. What think you, lads?"

Gilbert and I expressed it as our opinion that Miss Osborne would be a valuable addition to "The Rest;" and Edward, who had not the slightest interest in the subject, said nothing, and continued the book he was perusing.

Agnes returned to the room alone.

"Miss Osborne begs to be excused returning to the room this evening. Her travelling from London, during the last two days, has greatly fatigued her."

"She appears of a delicate constitution," said Gilbert.

"Poor girl!" mused my father; "friendless and alone—friendless and alone!"

We dined without Miss Osborne (our dinner-hour had changed from the old-fashioned hour, "one," again, and "six" was the appointed time), and during the evening, the boxes of Miss Osborne, which had gone on by the coach to Wharnby, were brought up to the house.

Agnes retired immediately after dinner, and went to spend the evening with her new governess. There never was such a nice girl as Miss Osborne, in her opinion, and she was so well educated; she had found out that—and mixed in such society: oh, she was sure of loving her like a sister! What a contrast to Miss Berncastle!

I was not particularly hasty in forming my opinion, yet that of mine for Miss Osborne was a favourable one at first sight.

Friendless and alone! Who were they in whom she was

interested at Cliverton, then?—that perplexed me. What mattered it? the circle at "The Rest" was closed—the last face pre-destined to have its influence on the fortunes of that gloomy house on the cliffs hanging over the bellowing sea, had come at last, and the life of home and pictures by its red fireside was fading into the life of action—the battle with the world.

CHAPTER XII.

THE DREAM ENDS.

"I SAY, Luke, what do you keep in that drawer—your money?" asked Edward, on the evening of the following day.

I was fully equipped for a journey to Wharnby House, and had just locked my drawer containing the trinkets and the miniature, to be transferred some day to their rightful owner.

"Yes," I replied.

It was not a falsehood, for there were a few shillings and a solitary sovereign locked within. My purchases had made terrible havoc in my funds, and I was looking forward somewhat anxiously to the next quarterly remittance.

"How much have you saved, Luke?" anxiously inquired my younger brother.

"Saved!" said I, "saved! Not much."

"Fifty pounds?" interrogatively.

"Fifty pounds!" I cried; "pooh Why should I save fifty pounds?"

"*I* have saved fifty," said Ned, coolly; "I shall save more next year. Father places us all on one footing then, Luke."

"You are worth fifty pounds, then, Ned," said I. "I wish you joy. What are you going to buy with it—a new pony?"

"I am going to bank it, and get interest for it, and put more to it, and keep saving up, and becoming richer every day," he answered.

"What a strange taste in an Elmore!" I observed.

"There ought to be one prudent member of a family," said Edward, very gravely; "now, you fling your money about anywhere. Last week there were two sovereigns on this carpet—flung about like rubbish."

"There were no thieves in the house."

"How do you know? How can you answer for all the servants? I can tell you, I mistrust half of them."

"Prudent Ned!"

"There's Agnes spends every shilling on finery, and borrows of Gilbert, who is not much better himself—look at the new books he's always buying!—so, *I* shall save."

"To provide for a rainy day, Ned," I said; "to help your poor brothers and sister, when they are in grievons distress, eh?"

"That's very likely!" replied he, with a laugh. "No, no, I'm for myself."

"A good motto, and you are not the first wise man that has set up his banner with it," said I; "ay, and has won many a fight, although the victory in the end may have proved a barren one. To change the subject, are you for Wharnby House?"

"Not I," said he; "I see the Silvernots often enough. I say, Luke," with a sly expression, "it's a nice ride over there of an evening, is it not?"

"Very."

"Some of these days you'll ride to Wharnby House, and never come back again; stop there for good, and marry Cely Silvernot, eh, Luke?"

What a transparent individual I was! Here, in less than a minute, had my own brother seen through me—my younger brother—and was twitting me with my secret.

"I think you have talked enough nonsense for this evening," said I, indignantly. "There, my young miser, you go and make money, and be happy!"

"And you go and make love, and be jilted!"

He did not wait for my reply, but left me, with a merry laugh at his own rejoinder.

"Be jilted!" that was an ugly conclusion to our conversation, and I rather disliked it. I thought of it going down the broad stairs, and tried to laugh it off. Why should I be jilted? It was not known I was in love yet. Edward Elmore was most decidedly an unsympathising brother. He was always selfish, and now he was a money worshipper, and but sixteen—a few months over sixteen years of age. He would never be a hero!

"Out again?" said my father, as I entered.

"Merely to Wharnby House," said I, carelessly.

"You will never be a home-lover, Luke," said he; "you are fond of life."

He sighed audibly.

"Where is Agnes?"

"Practising the piano with Miss Osborne. Do you want her?"

"I thought I would ask her to accompany me."

"Let her stay where she is," said my father; "she goes out often enough."

Gilbert was in the room, and suddenly broke in with—"I promised to spend an hour with old Mr. Silvernot one evening this week. Shall I be your companion, Luke?"

"Do; I will order the carriage."

The carriage was ordered, and Gilbert was prepared to start.

"You will not come, father?"

"No, Gilbert," shaking his head; "it never pleases me, and invariably fatigues. You will present my compliments."

"We will not fail."

Gilbert, leaning on my arm—not for support, but in friendship—limped along the hall.

"I did not ask you, Gilbert, because you so seldom go out; care so little for it."

"I have not come for my own sake, to-night," he said.

"For mine?"

"Yes, for yours," he replied. "You do not like to call at Wharnby House always unaccompanied; it looks particular."

Another decipherer of my hidden motives; what a shallow deceiver I must be!

We were in the carriage, and moving on to our friends.

"Half-past seven," said Gilbert, referring to his watch. "It is not late. I hope the rector is there."

"You are attached to him?"

"I esteem him highly," said Gilbert; "I believe there is the warmest little heart that ever beat beneath his quaint exterior. He is a learned man, too, and I like his conversation. Now, old Mr. Silvernot is the slightest degree prosy."

"Granted."

"Still I am a staid fellow myself; I hardly feel a young man, Luke; I am out of place with the young."

There was a grim look on his pale face that passed away as quickly as it came—a mere shadow of the twilight.

"Here we are, Luke," said he; "holloa!"

"What is it?"

"What is it!" repeated Gilbert; "nothing—but—but my dear Luke, keep your place—don't move."

"Why?" I almost shouted, as I sprang to the window, with the intention of looking out.

"Did I not tell you 'Nothing?'" said Gilbert. "I think I must have been dozing in the carriage, and talking nonsense. What did I say?"

"'Keep your place, and don't move,'" I reiterated, looking anxiously towards the house.

"I was decidedly talking nonsense," said Gilbert; "I imagined the carriage was lurching too much to the left to be safe. Will you get out first and assist me?"

Perfectly bewildered by my brother's incomprehensible explanation, I did so, and we entered the house.

"How d'ye do, my lads—how d'ye do?" cried out Mr. Silvernot, senior, tumbling off the sofa on which he had been dozing, and forcibly shaking hands with us. "Sit ye down. Mrs. Silvernot and Miss Wigginton are up-stairs; Arabella's practising a new song somewhere—but they'll be here presently. And how's your father? I half expected to see him and Mr. Vaudon—and how do *you* both do?"

A few common-place remarks, and then Gilbert said—

"And Miss Celia—she is well, I hope?"

"Well!" cried the old gentleman, polishing his bald head with his handkerchief; "to be sure she is; she went into the garden after dinner with young—what's his name?"

Mr. Silvernot had been so suddenly aroused from his customary nap, that he was a trifle confused at present.

"There is a heavy dew to-night," said Gilbert; "I trust Miss Celia will not suffer from its effects."

"God bless me, I hope not!" said the father, alarmed; "they merely strolled up and down the terrace outside, and—Lord deliver us! if I haven't been sleeping with that French window open!"

He ran towards it, and, looking out, cried—

"Come, it's getting late there, and we've visitors, Cely. How very imprudent not to shut the window after you; I might have been as blind as a bat by this time."

"Celia certainly closed it, Mr. Silvernot," said a clear, deep voice, that made me start from my seat and listen more attentively; "I can take my oath she closed it carefully as we went out."

I held my breath, and glared at the window, through which two figures were passing into the room—one the lovely figure I knew so well; the other, that of a tall young man—so tall, that he had to stoop considerably, in order to enter and follow Celia.

"What, Mr. Gilbert!—Mr. Luke!" cried Celia, as she shook hands with us. "Here is a very old friend of yours, Mr. Luke; you remember Master Paul Redwin?"

"I remember Master Redwin well," I answered, hoarsely. I felt that I was trembling as I held her hand; that my cheeks had lost their colour, and my voice its natural tone—like one who had seen a phantom.

Yet it was not the appearance of Redwin that alarmed or unmanned me in itself—it was something that seemed to have snapped at my heart, as they came in together from the terrace looking on the garden.

I turned to greet him. There was a slight flush on his face, for a moment, as he extended his hand.

"We have not met for many years, Mr. Elmore," he said; "and we meet now for the third time. The last interview was a well-remembered one for me, I think."

"Somewhat harsh," said I, shaking hands with him. "You came at a bad time for your disinterested errand. For my share in that day I ask your pardon."

"Your share! Do you think I bear *you* malice, then?"

"I should have said 'No,' when you spoke of coming to 'The Rest,'" said I. "As for malice, I hope you bear none in your heart, Mr. Redwin. My father was severe, but he is a severe man, and has strange ways with him. I have always resolved to ask your pardon, too, when we should chance to meet."

"Say no more about it, Elmore," said Redwin; "we are talking as if it were but yesterday; and Celia looks on, all wonder, as well she may. And," turning to my brother, "I believe I have the honour of addressing Mr. Gilbert Elmore?"

"Such is my name, sir," replied Gilbert, bowing very stiffly.

"You do not remember the occurrence of which your brother speaks?"

"Yes, I do," replied Gilbert; "and have to express my regret for the same, Mr. Redwin."

Gilbert turned immediately to Mr. Silvernot, upon completing his answer, as if to preclude further conversation with my old companion. Redwin crossed to the couch on which

Celia had taken a seat, and leant over her, talking earnestly; and I stood in the dark recess of the window, watching them.

It was almost too dark to distinguish the changes that time had made upon Paul Redwin; but I could see that he was a handsome young man, with a proud, aristocratical look on his face, which was partly softened by two bright, dark eyes, sparkling with intelligence and humour; and there was a saucy curl of the lip, too, that I remembered in the boy.

There were lights brought in a few minutes after the entrance of Celia and Redwin, and the latter came more prominently into view. It was the same boy on a larger scale. The same air of foppery pervaded him. There was the dress in the height of the prevailing fashion, the same parade of wealth more extensively displayed in an immense emerald on his little finger, and in diamond studs glittering on his breast.

Would he assume the old air of superiority over me when he knew me better? I doubted its effect a second time.

Still, I might like Paul Redwin. Put aside his artificial manner, and he would be good company—perhaps a good friend; but, then—— he certainly talked a good deal to Celia Silvernot, and Celia listened and smiled, and looked happy.

Mrs. Silvernot and her daughter made their appearance; and Miss Wigginton entering half an hour afterwards, completed the family group. The rector was expected, but he was late. No, I should not like Paul Redwin. He had kept Celia from me all the evening, and I was growing feverish, and my hoarseness had returned, and I could not listen to anything, or respond to anything, but in an abstracted manner; and ah! the heart-ache that was growing worse each instant, and making agony of every word they said unto each other.

How my temples throbbed; how I wanted to be home in my own room, at "The Rest;" and yet, how I wished I could live at Wharnby House, and watch for ever as I sat watching at that moment!

I had a dreamy consciousness of Mrs. Silvernot making tea, and my dropping my cup and saucer with a crash on a pet spaniel, and apologising to Gilbert, as if he were master of the house, and had a material interest in the carpet; and then the rector was amongst us as if by magic, and shaking hands; and there they still sat on that couch, and he was still looking into her eyes so confidently, so boldly, as I had never dared, in all the long, long time measured by my love, to look.

I knew, too, that I was watched in my turn; that Miss Silvernot had expressed an opinion that "I was dull," and I had answered, "Not at all, if you please, ma'am," in an incoherent manner; and that the little rector looked with more than common interest at me, and fidgeted on his chair, and coughed, and came across to speak.

"Well, Luke, I half expected to see your father here, to-night."

"Did you, Mr. Silvernot?"

"You have a cold?"

"No—that is—yes—I hardly know."

"You perceive we have a very old friend here, to-night?" said the rector.

This was a home-thrust, and I winced perceptibly.

"Yes—Mr. Redwin."

"Do you think he has altered?"

"A little."

Half ashamed of my laconic reply, I said—

"Has Mr. Redwin returned many days, sir?"

"Only three or four. I expect he will be here very often."

"What's that for?"

"Dear me!" said the rector, jumping at my impetuous query. "Why, he will not return to Paris, and is a near neighbour—that's all."

"Oh! of course—of course."

I began to answer in monosyllables, and became more abstracted each instant, so the clergyman passed to Gilbert's side. I joined the party at the table, and sat beside Mrs. Silvernot, who, not caring much for a talker, and hardly observer enough to detect a bad listener, was a capital shelter for that strange manner which, try how I would, I could not shake off or conceal.

There were some scrap-books on the table, and Redwin opened one carelessly, and listlessly glanced at the plates. Celia pointed out some particular beauty, and he was immediately deeply interested. He had made great progress in those three days he had been at Wharnby, and his manner, which was fascinating enough, and his attentions (how marked—how very marked to me!) had done their work on Celia's heart, and I was lost!

I saw it in her bright eyes, in her happiness at being near

him, so ill concealed, so girlishly apparent, so devoid of that disguise which a few months would bring to her—a part of woman's nature!

I knew at once that all my hopes were shattered at my feet; that the first affections of her heart—those affections made up of the best and purest feelings—would be his, if he sought them, as surely as I felt convinced he was striving steadily to win her. I knew my castle—that gloriously-constructed edifice of vain imagination—had all vanished now, was heaped ruin on ruin, and, Marius-like, I stood a solitary mourner. I saw the one I had loved so long won from me by a few careless words, an old, flippant manner, that had not so true a light within it as the brilliants sparkling disdainfully across the table at me.

I felt very thankful when the conversation took a general turn, and we were all engaged in it, and they could not talk so much in an under tone, and have a topic entirely to themselves. I laughed with Redwin—a melodramatic kind of laugh it was though—and hazarded a few words to Celia in my old friendly manner, with indifferent success. The evening was long and tedious; all was, to me, unprofitable and pulseless. My interest in Celia was gone; she had never looked at me beyond a friend, and I had looked too far, and suffered for it.

We were in the carriage again, Gilbert and I, and rattling homewards. Shrunk back, in the thick cushions I lay, silent and miserable.

I felt Gilbert's hand upon my shoulder.

"Cheer up, Luke," said he, assuringly. "You are not downcast because a rival springs to light."

He had never sought my confidence, never shown, till this evening, that he had known my secret, and kept it to himself; but in my bitter grief and loneliness, he came with his cheering words and open heart.

I could not help it; I wrestled with it long, and bit my lips till the blood streamed from them to restrain it; but all was nugatory and unavailing. It was the action of a disappointed child; it showed how little of a man I was at heart, and what a boy in my experience and strength. I covered my face with my hot hands, and struggled with my tears, and sought to stop them streaming down my face.

"One moment, Gilbert; I will be a man in one moment. How foolish!—is it not?"

He looked out of the window, and returned no answer.

A long pause.

"I did not think it had gone so far as this, dear Luke," said he, mournfully. "I know not what to say."

"It is useless saying anything, my brother; it is past."

"Did she hold out to you any hope—any encouragement?" he asked, sternly; "or have you been led on by your own illusions?"

"By mine own," I answered in a hollow voice; "I have but been encouraged by my own foolish chimeras. I have no fault to find but with myself."

"That's well. Do you think they are engaged?"

"Not yet; they will be."

"You have given up all hope?"

"All."

"Well, you are not nineteen years of age yet, Luke," said he; "that is not the time for a broken heart."

"No, it is not, Gilbert."

"You will not let those at Wharnby House see your disappointment?"

"If they have not seen it already—no."

"It was a first love—a boy's love—that was all."

"It was my life—my ambition—my sole study!" I cried, passionately. "I had no other thought—no other care. Don't speak again. Let me think."

We were silent till we reached "The Rest."

"Gilbert!"

"Yes, Luke."

"What did you see from the carriage-window as we approached the Silvernots?"

"Why ask? The story is finished; let us not turn backward to pore over leaves long since read," said Gilbert.

"I ask it as a favour."

"I saw them on the terrace; he was talking earnestly to her, with his arm lightly thrown around her waist."

"And she—listened?"

"She listened."

"He was telling his love then!" said I, with a half groan.

"Luke," said he, as he walked by my side, supported by his crutch, along the hall, "I have not offered to condole with you—I know it would be a foolish and a vain endeavour. You have deeper feelings than most young men—you are a true Elmore; so I will not affect to make light of all that has passed this evening. I wish we had never known the Silvernots, as it has ended thus. You will try to forget?"

"I will," said I; "and, Gilbert, let me thank you for that forbearance. When condolence is of no avail, it is cruelty to use it. Ah! Gilbert, Gilbert, what should I be without you!"

"You will come in?"

I stood with my foot upon the stairs.

"Not to-night. Say I am unwell—that my head aches, as it does fearfully; say anything. Good night, Gilbert!"

"Good night!"

When alone in my old room, I lit the fire, already laid to my hand, although it was summer, and a sultry night, and sat before it, glaring with blood-shot eyes into its depths, as if my life were written in it.

When it was late, and all was silence at "The Rest," I opened the drawer consecrated to one lost to me, and drew the trinkets and my miniature forth, and dropped them silently into the fire. They shrivelled, cracked, and flew beneath the heat—then mingled in a mass, grew red, and were gone! My love dreams had faded; why should they, part of them, exist to mock me with their fallacy?

I shed no tears over them—of the happiness they might have brought me in seeing her happy at my lover's gifts. I thought of the past, and suffered from many a keen pang; but there was a new-born sternness in my breast, and it was hardening me to iron.

I looked through my window; it was very dark and starless, and occasionally the lightning played in the distance, and shed a momentary radiance over the scenery of home. The dark sky overhead was but the type of the first clouds that had thrown their shadow on me, and the lightning fit emblem of that influence which had blasted the green young plant that might have grown unto a tree, and sheltered me from evil beneath its friendly boughs, in lieu of withering with a breath, and dying in unfriendly soil.

CHAPTER XIII.

NEWS FROM PARIS.

WITH the death-blow to my hopes of ever calling Celia Silvernot my wife, there died not out the love I had for her. It was existent still—it burned the fiercer, confined in its narrow bounds, and with so small a vent. Wharnby House saw me as often as heretofore, and I sought the flame of jealousy that scorched me as I fluttered round it.

I hid my feelings more completely: I obtained that command over my inner self that I had once striven for in vain, and could smile like truth when stung by the lover's tenderness to Celia. He had not proposed; he had made no statement to the parents of the beautiful girl yet: he was probably awaiting his twenty-first birthday, when he should be, as he used to boast of in his younger days, a rich man.

Mrs. Silvernot was in no hurry: she was sure of him, and it was a good match; and, although she had had her intentions concerning a Luke Elmore, yet here was a bird that probably carried more gold on its wings, for Paul Redwin was an only son. Still, I was welcome at Wharnby House; I was a bit of a favourite, and Celia had always liked me, never loved me.

Vaudon — keen, watchful Vaudon — taking in everything with his black, rolling eyes, detected my position in less than five minutes after a chance call at Wharnby House.

The next morning he took an opportunity of being alone with me, and began—

"So you rejected my advice, and the new gallant has arrived —not the least attractive of gallants either—and Luke Elmore resigns, checkmated, with not a piece brought out upon the board."

"Did I ever own to being engaged in the battle?"

"Yes," he replied, "with your eyes; your true lover's manner—your fits of thought; your constant rides to the right of 'The Rest' at all hours of the day."

"I do not appear particularly affected, do I?" was my second question.

"The lake in the garden looks not particularly deep, does it?" he inquired; "yet it is; one could drown very comfortably therein."

"You may be mistaken for once, Vaudon."

"Not I," said Vaudon. "I am never wrong; but then I am a conceited man in my opinions, Luke. Shall I tell you now those reasons for never marrying, which I spoke of when riding home from the Silvernots, one moonlight night?"

I looked up suddenly. He was standing before me with a strange, unearthly expression, with a mocking smile, and deeply-contracted brow. His arms were crossed upon his broad chest, one hand in that old habit of toying with his beard; he looked down upon me as the tempter of all men might look down upon the tempted, and I shuddered as if the Presence of Evil were in the room, and circling over me, and threatening.

"You may tell me, if you like," said I, lowering my gaze.

"Because," in a low, suppressed tone, as if he were speaking with his teeth close set, "there is no woman worth the marrying; they are all false and black at heart—they inherit sin from Eve. It is the truest religion of all holy faiths that excludes them from the highest heaven."

I felt the blood rushing to my face at this damning doctrine of my father's friend; but I could but sit and listen, conscious that he stood glaring down upon me.

"You colour up," he said; "that shows the superiority of your nature. Women never blush but for a purpose."

"Cease—cease! I have a sister."

"Some pass for good, we know," he continued, savagely. "Some die, and have 'good Christians' written on their gravestones; but, believe me, Luke, there is no woman that cannot be tempted from her duty."

"Why do you tell all this to me?" I asked, abruptly.

"Because you are easily impressed, and one more artful than Celia may yet ensnare you, Luke," he answered; "because I would teach you that marriage is a hideous mockery, an iron chain to men, and more especially to one like you, a quick observer with a sensitive heart. Women are men's prey, not men's equals."

"I will hear no more," I cried, starting to my feet; "it is Satan's own hellish promptings!"

He caught my arm, and stopped me.

"You will acknowledge I am right some day," said he. "It may be a dangerous precept to teach, but you are aloof from the world, and have a mind tolerably well-balanced. Seek pleasure where you will, the days of man soon sink into an endless night."

"Vaudon, do you believe in God?"

"Another time—another time," said he, evasively; "my belief in many things, you see, is strange; my whole being is a mystery, and I dare not even attempt the solution to myself. I force my counsel on no man. I have, for the first time, told you a strange truth; it will be years before you have courage to believe."

"Teach no one in this house that accursed precept, Vaudon; let the moral contagion spread no further. I feel, try how I will, that I have drunk in poison."

"I will say no more," said he; "I have but told you in what I put faith myself. I am a man who has seen more of the world than most men, and have judged it as it deserved—with its false pretensions, and its hollow professions, and its varnished surfaces, turned so that society may admire and worship. The world has been my study, and I am a master of the sciences it taught me."

"You will keep them to yourself," said I. "It is not fear for myself, but for others."

"Do I ever expound my doctrines?"

"I have never heard you before."

"Trust me, then."

I left him.

What horrid reasoning had I heard—what a fearful promulgation of his evil theories! What man could this be to seek to lower and debase a youthful mind (so easy to be marked and blackened at the best), and point the way out to him—that broad path from which there is no turning back?

What reason had he in telling me that woman was a living lie; that there was no truth or candour in her; and that my study should be her degradation, asserting that I should not be equally degraded, though I lowered her, and cast the brand with my own guilty hands? What project could he conceal? Then, there was the strange look, that seemed akin to hate, which I had noticed bent upon me—what did it forebode?

And then came the torturing inquiry—had he confined his words to me alone, or was he seeking to bring us all to his own standard—to poison the minds of Gilbert, Edward, even Agnes, and my own father? My impulse was to confront him with each of them, but of what could I accuse Vaudon? What had he said to me, in fact, but that which many men, soured by disappointment, believe—that which I knew my own father gave implicit credence to—the want of faith in woman's purity—the disbelief in woman's love!

During the last few days I had also detected a marked and distant manner of Gilbert's towards Vaudon, and I had no doubt that some dialogue, like that which I have related, had passed between them, and Gilbert had resented his advice, and foiled it; but my brother made no mention of the same to me, and Vaudon was more of a friend to our father than ever.

There were many things I could not fathom at "The Rest." They seemed to have sprung into being lately, and wore all the air of mystery and confusion.

I had entered the study in an abrupt manner one morning, and found my father alone with Gilbert, who was expostulating, and whose whole manner was excited, and at variance with his habitual calmness.

"Be assured, my dear Gilbert, you are mistaken," said my father; "think no more of it: let it pass."

Gilbert was about to reply, when my entrance checked him.

"I beg pardon," I exclaimed; "I merely require a book that I have mislaid—I——"

"Don't go, Luke," said my father, evidently glad of a pretext to avoid a prolonged *tête-à-tête* with his son. "We are not talking treason. How are the Silvernots?—have you seen them lately? And the rector, is he well?"

Gilbert, perceiving the object of his father's anxious queries, lingered a few moments, and then left the room.

There was another deepening calamity that gave much concern to Gilbert and me, and of which we silently took notice, but spared ourselves the pain of commenting upon to each other.

It came upon my father like a sudden affliction—it seemed making the same insidious, but fatal track as of a ravaging disease—it showed itself at intervals of weeks, then days, and threatened to settle, and become inevitable. It told its secret in the flushed face of my father; it spoke aloud from between his parched lips; it was seen in the shaking hands and faltering, unsteady footfall—it pointed out the *drunkard* to the sneering menials of home.

Amongst all the phases of drink—and it has as many as there are phases of society—I know of none so full of horror, of so fearful a humiliation, as the man of genius or of education giving way to that strange curse; flinging away his talents, prostrating a great mind, lowering all self-respect, casting aside all thought of home, and children's love, and men's esteem, and passing straightway to something lower than the brutes.

The knowledge of this sudden calamity came upon me with a fearful blow—I could not believe the testimony of my own sight; I could not imagine that he, of all men—so proud, so stern, so rigid an anchorite in his lonely hermitage—could descend to the burning consolation of the wine-cup.

It was known throughout the house immediately. It was my own father—my own dear father—who, stern and unyielding as he seemed, loved us all so much, so very dearly—as spars from the great wreck of that past life to which he clung, and of which they were a part—who went reeling to his room, with vacant looks and glassy eyes, or was supported along the passages by that mysterious man who was ever with him, and who seemed his fate.

There was one disgrace kept from us. The Silvernots knew not of the awful change; when they called, it was invariably in the early morning, when, though pale and haggard from the solitary debauch of the preceding night, my father was sober, and as they had ever known him.

If he made one of his chance visits to Wharnby House, he still preserved his old character in their eyes; but it was at home that he was changed, and another man.

It was nigh unto the celebrated Cliverton ball; that ball which I had still a firm resolve to attend, and remind Celia of her promise, and show, if the Silvernot family had suspicions of my disappointment, and my bankruptcy at heart, what a gay young fellow I was, without a care in the wide world! Celia had forgotten our conversation concerning the ball, and the idea of Luke Elmore, from the gloomy "Rest," mingling in a scene of so much pleasure and excitement, had never suggested itself to any other imagination.

The summer was nearly gone—some dry, yellow leaves, few as yet, were flitting to and fro, along the garden paths and chalky roads, indicative of coming autumn. I was sitting under a favourite tree in the park, watching the deer in the distance, when Gilbert, who had noiselessly advanced, stood before me.

"Always in thought, Luke."

"You seem to guess my thoughtful moments, Gilbert, and kindly come to dissipate them."

"I wish I could come upon you, now and then, and see more of the old looks, and less of that brooding face."

"Time, time," said I, half smiling; "give me a little grace; you know the wound of love takes long in healing."

"Sometimes," said Gilbert; "has not Vaudon given you better counsel?"

I started.

"I thought so," said Gilbert, almost fiercely; "this man requites my father's hospitality well! This Vaudon is in everything; he has a hand hovering from one unto another, apparently each one's friend, yet giving lessons that the bitterest enemy could only wish to inculcate. He tells them not as with a purpose; but, by some devil's scheming, they appear in common conversation, and wound our ears, and stab our hearts with venomed words. What has he told you?"

"He spoke of my—my disappointment."

"Well?"

"And congratulated me in his cold, sneering way, as from an escape. He pointed out to me an old picture enough,—how easy it is to sin—how great a task to think of marriage—how the part of a fool to hold the last in reverence, or think that it commands respect."

"'Tis like him," mused Gilbert, with a heavy frown; "like my father, I believe he has at one time met with some fearful blow from woman's hands, and it has shattered every confidence. Still he could keep his busy tongue more quiet."

"What has he said to you?"

"Nothing that I could bring in evidence, or even explain," said Gilbert; "but full of dreadful doubts and evil promptings, that make one almost doubt himself. Good God! how strange it is that such a man as Vaudon should be my father's best friend!"

"He has great influence."

"Terrible," cried Gilbert; "what does he seek or want, or is there any motive in all this? With you or me, Luke, his suggestions will never have great weight; he has mistaken us. But——"

"But what?" cried I, alarmed at his pause.

"But with Edward—with Agnes—with our father."

"Have you any proof that——" I began.

He interrupted me.

"Not any," he said; "but they change, they grow more

worldly. Edward becomes cunning, almost low-minded, greedy of gain, fond of money for its own intrinsic value. Agnes seems to have ever a secret purpose; she never boldly seeks her object, though it be a small one, but undermines, and reaches her end at last, by foreign means. And father (in a faltering voice), how has he altered!"

"But why attribute all this to Vaudon's influence?"

"There is the mystery," said Gilbert. "I cannot do so, and yet I feel convinced that his power rules them. All three are more attached to him than you or I; they have more confidence, and are more with him. I do not say that he has taught Edward to grow miserly, or Agnes to be designing, openly; but I do not think him the man to discourage the growth of any evil weed in us, even if he had the power to uproot it by a word."

"You have said something like this to father," said I, remembering the conference I had interrupted in the study.

"I have, and you know the result."

"Too well," I said; "and yet we may be doing Vaudon more than common injustice. He is an eccentric man, full of wild ideas, I confess; but we know no more."

"Not at present," said Gilbert; "but we will watch."

"You spoke of that dreadful change in our father's habits," I said; "can we do nothing—we, his eldest sons—to stop the ravages drink must surely make upon his health?"

Gilbert looked full at me.

"Have you the courage?"

"Try me."

"Do you know our father is in the park?" said Gilbert, eagerly, "and Vaudon is not with him?"

"What would you do?"

"He is very dull this morning, and I think there is a shadow of remorse on his pale face," said Gilbert. "Let us go to him, and urge him to consider the grief and misery he is breeding for himself and us. We are his sons, and it is our duty."

It was so sudden a proposal—so contrary to all we had ever done—that I hesitated.

"I will go myself," said he, setting his crutch firmly; "if you fear to tell him the truth, I will go myself. I came into the park to do it, but I thought the united persuasion of his sons would have more power to make him think."

The hesitation was but momentary. I cried, springing up, "I am ready."

We struck into a less frequented part of the park, where the grass was long, and the great furze and brambles grew thicker at every tread.

"He went this way," said Gilbert.

"Hush!" I cried; "there he is."

At a few yards from us to the right, stood the tall figure of my father. He was standing with his back towards us, intently interested in something he held tightly clenched within his hands. His whole appearance was that of a man contending with some powerful emotion. As we advanced, a newspaper that he had held folded in his hands, fell from them to the ground, and he flung his arms above his head with a cry of anguish that blanched our cheeks, and made us halt.

"Father!" cried Gilbert.

He wheeled round and confronted us.

"What do you here?" he cried, in a rapid tone; "what have you been dogging my footsteps hither for? Go to the house—go to the house and leave me—I am not well, I am sick and ill. Where's Vaudon? Where's Vaudon?"

He caught sight of the newspaper at his feet, and snatched it from the grass, burying it deep in his breast pocket.

"What do you do here?" he asked again.

"We have followed you, dear father," said Gilbert, in a clear, distinct voice, "to reason with you, to beg you to strive against that all besetting sin that has come upon you like an affliction from God and poisoned every hope."

"A curse of God, you mean," he muttered.

"We are your children, your loved children," urged Gilbert; "and we can see, none more sure or quick, the awful doom it will bring on you, the early grave it will prepare. If any great affliction, if any irreparable misfortune have fallen on you, bear it with the old heroic courage that has sustained many other sorrows, and share the evil with your sons, who have a right to lighten it and aid you. We pray it on our knees, for the sake of home and love, and Him whose will it was that it should fall upon you."

Gilbert bowed his form before his father in earnest supplication, and involuntarily I knelt beside him.

My father covered his eyes, and his whole frame shook violently.

"Rise, rise," he cried; "do not kneel to me like that. Oh! this is more than I can bear!"

"You will promise?" we urged.

"If you remain like accusing spirits, kneeling there," he cried, "I will leave you—I will go hence—I will fly from home, from all."

His manner was so wild and agitated, and withal so imploring, that we rose. Gilbert laid his hand gently on his arm, and drawing away his hand, said—

"But you will promise, father?"

"Promise what?"

Gilbert was about to reply, when he said—

"No matter, I can guess. Gilbert, there are but two things to choose between—drunkenness, or madness. If I abstain from the former, my shame will drive me to the latter."

"You have borne that shame without so grievous a calamity happening to you," I ventured to assert.

"No, Luke, not this new shame, this accursed blot that makes us known to all the world."

He tore the newspaper from his pocket. It was a French one, and published in Paris.

"Look here," striking the paper with his hand violently; "here is her name again, that accursed name which I gave her, your own unworthy mother, at the altar. That mother who should have loved you and died for you if needful, but who flung away all maternal ties that bound her to her children, and fled from us and brought disgrace upon us. There is that name again, the cause of a duel between a French noble and an English banker, both fighting for the false smiles of the vile courtesan. The duel and its origin are the talk of Paris, the topic at the London clubs, the revival of that old truth in London newspapers which drove me mad, when you were children. 'The wife of Mr. Elmore, that unfortunate gentleman whose deep attachment to her was so remarkable,' and a thousand repetitions of mock sympathy. They will all know it—even Wharnby will associate the name with me; I am branded, degraded, dishonoured even here!"

"You take too prejudicial a view of what your friends will say; you do not do them justice, father," said my brother.

"I know them well enough—too well," he muttered.

"And supposing that we were the common talk and jest of people in the streets," said Gilbert, "have we not the courage to look back their unworthy scorn, and value it at its just worth?"

"And should we lose a father as well as a mother? and will the sire have no more love and consideration for his children than she who left them motherless?" I added.

He looked at us long and steadily; then, suddenly advancing, extended a hand to each of us.

"I will not promise, boys," he said, "but I will try; I cannot do more than try, can I?"

My father returned to his old self for several days, and he was more affectionate and less irritable towards his children than he had been since Vaudon darkened the threshold of "The Rest."

Then disgrace—the disgrace to his name, which he had dreaded reaching him in that lonely spot upon the English coast, came even to Wharnby, and the county paper heralded the news, and published its translation from the French in large type, and added fresh intelligence of the death of Count de L——, and heaped more coals of fire upon my father's head. Then rumour grew round Wharnby, and the name was associated with the owner of "The Rest," and dates were examined, and found to tally with each other—the date of Mrs. Elmore's flight, and that of the purchase of "The Rest"—and we were known and pitied!

Oh! that mock pity!—that lying affectation of interest in our misery which is so hard to bear! That born of vulgar curiosity is so difficult to struggle against, so vain to satisfy!

The Silvernots, with more care for our feelings, refrained from any recurrence to the subject, and my father was grateful for it in his heart, and inwardly thanked the considerate rector, whom he knew to be the cause, for his kind silence and charitable reserve. But the effort at trial had passed, and he had given way. The same unsteady step, the bloodshot eyes, the wild flushed looks came again, night after night, and with it grew (strangely enough) that indomitable pride, that arrogance of wealth and learning, which had always been his characteristic, and which now became fiercer every day, as if, by his haughty bearing, he sought to keep down, with a giant's strength, the knowledge to others of that moral abasement into which he had degenerated.

CHAPTER XIV.

THE GREAT CLIVERTON BALL.

THE day registered in the chronicles of Cliverton as the brightest of Red-Letters, came at length—the day of the great ball. I felt very nervous and excitable all the morning with the knowledge of my secret; I felt assured the eyes of each respective inmate of "The Rest" were upon me, and read my plans upon a self-accusing front.

Twenty times within the hour had I arrived at the conclusion that I would resign the opportunity of seeing life in the gayest of gay colours, and let the ball pass without the presence of an Elmore. I had no strong wish to go for the sake of the pleasure it might bring me, and in which I might take my share—that had all vanished with my disappointment. I thought that I should experience no gratification in the crowd, save the melancholy one of dancing with Celia Silvernot, and foiling Redwin for once with his own weapons. And yet there *was*, despite the jealous envy which gnawed at my heart still, a pleasurable thrilling of blood in my veins, when I thought of dancing with Celia—dancing with her at the great Cliverton ball! They had spoken of the ball, too, the preceding evening, at Silvernot's, and Redwin had been there, and full of information concerning the preparations that were being made for the company's reception; and Celia's and Arabella's ball-dresses had arrived from London, and they had flown to their rooms with them, and spent half the evening gossiping over them, much to the suppressed chagrin of Paul Redwin, Esquire.

I was very glad of Celia's absence, when Mrs. Silvernot hazarded the following—

"I wonder you do not learn dancing, Mr. Luke?"

"It hardly seems necessary—I see so little society."

"But, then, you could have gone to the ball with us."

"Ah, yes!"

"I suppose you have a moral objection?" said Redwin, laughingly.

"Not at all, Redwin. On the contrary, I dare say I should like it."

"Oh! then, we shall see you start forth some day, perhaps?"

"I have no doubt of it."

The subject was changed. And now the morning had

dawned, and I, with my secret locked so close and kept so dark, was ready and prepared.

My father was very pale and thoughtful all the morning, and whenever his eyes met mine, they seemed to my accusing conscience symbolical of a reproach. I felt that I was about to deceive him, to betray his confidence, and I could not meet his glance without a scarlet cheek. It was ever on my lips to tell him of my resolution, and then the turning of a leaf of his book (he was reading by the fireside), or a movement of his arm on the favourite leathern chair in which he sat, checked me into silence.

Unable to remain longer with him, assuming a calmness that I did not feel, I strayed about the rooms of the house in a listless manner. I could not read or write, or do anything but think of the ball.

I gave no thought as to the means by which I should return to "The Rest." I knew that it would be very late at night or in the early morning, and that they would be greatly alarmed at my prolonged absence, and that all must be known in a few hours; but I did not care for that—I thought I could stand against and respond to all just words condemnatory of my deceitfulness, after the ball was over and the reaction had set in; but I could not fix my mind as to the probabilities that might arise now. I had but two ideas—the Cliverton ball and Celia Silvernot.

I met Agnes on the stairs, whilst I was ascending them for the fifth time. The reader will probably remember an old habit of mine, in wandering up and down these stairs, when perplexed or excited.

"Do you know what to-day is, Luke?" she asked.

"The day of the month?" I asked, in return.

"No, no—what will happen to-day—what this day will celebrate?"

"Why, a good many things, I have no doubt," I replied, very much confused.

"Ah! you boys have not so tenacious a memory as I have. Why, the Cliverton ball takes place to-day—the ball which we are to be kept from on account of a silly prejudice that has no meaning. I dare say, Luke, we are the only representatives of the gentry, within thirty miles, who will not be there."

"I shouldn't wonder," assented I, with the gravest of countenances.

"You're too phlegmatic and indolent to wonder at anything, Luke," said she, curtly; "and—but Miss Osborne will wonder, too, if I stay here."

She tripped gracefully away, and I resumed my meanderings from room to room, and got rid of a few heavy hours in a close scrutiny of Nature from every window of the house.

Our friend the rector called in the morning, too, and the old subject was revived, to my prolonged embarrassment.

"I have no doubt, Mr. Elmore," said he to my father, "that I shall be spending this evening with you—no matter that I have made up my mind to some hours' dry study over mathematics—a furbishing up of old lessons, at home; still, nevertheless, I am sure, impulse will make me shut up my books, and come and see you."

"I shall be glad of your company, Mr. Silvernot."

"What a time it is since we have had a long chat together, Elmore. Do you remember the old nights, years ago, when we argued and expounded over the fire—they seem all gone now"—with a slight sigh of regret.

"It is not my fault, my dear friend."

"No, no," said he, quickly; "I do not imply as much—I do not imply as much. How is Mr. Vaudon?"

The inquiry came so quickly after the last assertion, that it sounded like a reason for his less frequent visits. It may have been so.

"He is very well. You must come to-night, Silvernot," said my father; "I shall be quite alone. Vaudon has business to transact, he tells me, which will take him to Cliverton."

"To Cliverton!" cried the rector. "I cannot fancy our friend figuring in a ball-room, or I might suppose he was going to the assembly with the rest of the world."

"What, Vaudon!" said I, with a laugh.

"No, it don't seem likely," said the rector; "about as likely as my making my appearance there in full dress, or you, Luke—ha! ha!"

"Ha! ha!" I reiterated, in my best deceptive manner.

"But the girls are going at the house," said the rector—"and Mrs. S. goes to take care of them; and my worthy father goes because other worthy fathers are going: and there's a card-room—and, I regret to say it, Mr. S. has a sneaking attachment to whist. He never plays it at home—that is, when I am there—out of respect for my cloth; but I am very much mistaken if they don't have a quiet rubber at Wharnby House when my back's turned. But it does them little harm, I dare say—and they only play for bone fish and ivory halfpennies, and that's not extravagant gambling, is it?"

"Decidedly not."

"Besides, there's no reason why my father should be a parson, because I chance to be one, or a stern disciplinarian,"—looking fierce—"and a rigid moralist, like me. He could not do it."

"I suppose," continued our friend, warming his hands at the fire, "the Cliverton ball does not affect in any manner the denizens of 'The Rest?'"

Neither my father nor I replied.

"Hardly worthy of an answer, eh?" looking up sharply; "well, I don't think it is myself. There's one opinion of mine, that will ever be unalterable—I hate dancing. I try to reason Celia out of it, and laugh at Arabella in the most satirical manner, but I make no impression—they *will* dance."

"The ladies are all fond of dancing," I said.

"So they are, Luke," with a merry chuckle peculiar to himself; "that's why they are so giddy and full of fancies—their brains get in a whirl, poor things! I'm not fond of public balls either, and I wish the officers of the —th were quartered in Canada, with all my heart."

My father and the rector entered into another field of discussion, and I left the room, and continued my restless progress, waiting for the day to pass.

It was time to dress, at last, and I stole into my room and locked the door, fearful of intrusive eyes. It wanted three hours to sunset, and six or seven to the ball; but, to elude suspicion, it was necessary that I should leave "The Rest" in the broad daylight. I trembled as I dressed myself, not with cold, or fear, but with an indescribable and violent thrilling in every joint in my body, that almost made the teeth chatter in my head. After I was dressed, I took an admiring stare at myself in the dressing-glass, and thought that, taking moustache and white satin waistcoat seriously into consideration, I did not appear to be such a bad-looking fellow after all, and should pass muster even at Cliverton Assembly Rooms. I felt, for the first time, that I should like to join in the scene merely for the pleasure of it, and, for a few moments, even forgot my love for Celia Silvernot.

Having enshrouded my elegance in a great coat, and, with extraordinary forethought at the last minute, taken off my white tie and placed it in my pocket, substituting my customary black silk neckerchief, I boldly sallied out of my chamber, and strolled leisurely through the house and into the stable-yard, in the most hypocritical *nonchalant* manner in the world.

"Tom."

"Yes, sir."

Tom, in his shirt sleeves, emerged from one of the stables.

"My horse."

"Going alone, sir?"

"Yes; I shall not want you this time, Tom."

"Sorry for that, sir. It lowers the respectability of the house, a good deal, going without your groom so much, sir," said he, insinuatingly.

"Well, to-morrow we must assert our dignity, Tom."

"Yes, sir, if you please."

Tom, who had taken to heart my frequent journeys without his attendance in the rear, brightened up, and disappeared into the stable to fetch my horse, with wonderful alacrity.

In a few minutes I was mounted.

"You're sure I'm not to come to-day, Mr. Luke, sir?"

"Quite sure."

I was on the move when he called out—

"Stop, sir, please. There's a white something or t'other hanging out of your tail pocket, sir."

"Oh! it's nothing—it's nothing," said I, hurriedly thrusting my neckcloth to the lowest depths of that great coat, which Tom had been eyeing half wonderingly, and half suspiciously, probably thinking I was rather warmly clad for so mild an autumn month.

I looked back at the house, as I cantered along the drive. My father was standing at the window of a sitting-room seldom used, and looking in my direction, and I fancied I could detect a few paces from him the figure of Jacques Vaudon. I waved my hand in farewell greeting, and he gave a wan smile of recognition. There was nothing singular in my riding from "The Rest" without a preliminary announcement; it was my invariable custom, when setting forth alone, yet I half fancied I was detected, and that he was about to throw the window up and call me back in the old peremptory manner that he had used to me when my preceptor and admonitor. I gently touched my horse with the whip, and we started off more quickly, and were through the lodge gates that Johnson had thrown back, and on the road to Cliverton.

How thankful I was that my quick-eyed groom had caught sight of the "something white!" What an ignominious exposure of my deeply-laid plan it would have been, to have exhibited to my father's eyes, as he stood there at the window, the ball-room tie streaming from my pocket, and flaunting like a banner in the wind!

It was oppressively hot in my great coat, but it could not be helped in any way; it was a minor suffering, essential to my after amusement. Why did the officers of the —th have their ball in the beginning of October, when December would have suited my great coat so much better?

There were other mortifications in store for me. There had been no rain for above three weeks at Wharnby, and the chalky dust flew in clouds around me, and peppered my black dress trowsers (new for the occasion), and took all the lustre out of my patent boots, and settled in my hair, and round my upper lip, and on those very fringy whiskers that made so little progress, and gave me the appearance of a hard-working miller, who had been more than extra busy lately. Then I had no money in my great coat, and upon arriving at the first turnpike, I had to exhibit all my hidden glory to the toll-keeper's gaze, and display my white satin waistcoat and embroidered shirt to his undisguised admiration, whilst in search for threepence-halfpenny. But I got to Cliverton in good time, and put up at the Black Bull, and hired a private room and a couple of clothes-brushes, and passed half an hour in hard exercise, and three quarters of an hour in re-adornment, before a looking-glass over the mantelshelf, the frame stuck about with cards and bills of auction, and houses to let. Then I dined, and after that washed my chalky face in an adjoining room, and re-dressed for the occasion itself, and spun the time out till it was quite dark. I was only a few doors off Bentboys', and consequently could obtain a tolerable view of the Assembly Rooms, and watch how affairs were getting on therein from my window, which drawing a chair close unto, I constituted as post of observation.

I looked at my watch. Seven o'clock—and the ball commenced at nine—two hours to wait.

Two hours! More than that. I couldn't go dashing over the way immediately they flung open the entrance doors, as if it were essential I should be a first arrival, and have the ball-room entirely to myself!—no, I must wait till there was a goodly muster assembled, and then enter unobserved.

I began to feel excessively nervous about it altogether. The room was already lighted up very brilliantly, and, although the blinds were drawn and the curtains closed, there was a flood of radiance streaming into the street and lighting up the houses opposite, and making my room quite lively.

A tap at the door.

"Come in."

"Will you have lights, sir?" inquired a smart chambermaid, looking in.

"If you please, yes," I replied, with a start. I felt uncommonly confused. This would never do, to be embarrassed before a chambermaid, because I was in full dress. How should I ever face the terrible crowd of fashionables over the way?

The door re-opened, and the maid entered with wax candles, and placed them on the table. I could not help it; had it been for my life, I should have jumped up and looked into the street with an absorbing interest, for I knew she would glance at me curiously, and my courage was at a very low ebb, indeed.

Never mind! there were two hours good to screw that up into its "sticking place"—I should be full of Spartan fortitude by that time.

What a miserable length the hours were! I read every placard stuck about the looking-glass and mantel-shelf. I could have recited every bill of auction with perfect ease, and have painted every article in my private room on canvas, with my eyes shut.

Eight o'clock. I looked out of window again. Something pattered against the glass. Could it be possible the rain had come at last—had chosen this night of all nights to break the long dry season? Yes, there it was, smothering the window-panes with thick, heavy beads, and falling steadily into the street, and darkening the dusty road, and making the white pavement in an instant as full of spots as a leopard's skin.

Perhaps it was only a shower. I took half a dozen turns up and down my room, and looked out once more. Raining faster than ever, the drops chasing each other down the glass like mad, the street looking very misty, the road full of puddles, the pavement glossy with the wet, and giving back the rays of light from shop windows with undiminished brilliancy.

I sat down, clenched my chin in both my hands, and stared out, holding a council of war with myself.

What shall I do now? To cross over the road was to smother myself in mud, and make my *début* in dirty boots. That wouldn't do. To hire a glass-coach to be taken over the way; that was ridiculous in the extreme. To jump across the mud in three springs, the act of a lunatic. To hire a pair of boots of the ostler, or some one, and take my patent boots in my hand, and put them on either in the gentlemen's room or on the stairs—that would expose me to severe criticism. To go across on horseback—that would give rise to some broad jests from the damp mob round the doors. It must be the glass-coach, ridiculous as I thought it, if it pour like this much longer.

Half-past eight. Raining worse than ever.

Nine o'clock. The doors were opened. There was an immense oil-skin canopy attached to the portico, and erected over the pavement. I could see men in livery at the doors, and flitting about the hall, and the slightest glimpse in the world of a broad flight of stairs, carpeted with crimson cloth. All this looked inviting, but then, what a ride home to Wharnby I had in perspective. How it did rain!

There were glass-coaches going out of the Black Bull yard, possibly to fetch visitors. The dreadful idea suggested itself to me, supposing that all the glass-coaches were engaged! I rang the bell immediately.

The maid promptly made her appearance.

"Can I have a glass-coach?"

"I am afraid not, sir, at present," she answered; "but I'll ask."

Five minutes elapsed, and the landlord himself, after announcing his presence by a preliminary tap, entered the room.

"Very sorry, sir, but all the glass-coaches are engaged for the ball, sir."

"I merely wish to be taken across."

"I suppose so, sir; I'm afraid you must wait an hour, sir."

"Very well. Let me know when it is ready."

"Yes, sir."

Another hour to wait. Should I get into the ball-room at all? I resumed my post at the window; the place beneath presented an appearance of bustle at last. There were a great many people hemmed round the doors, totally indifferent to the heavy falling rain; there were two or three link-boys, tearing about the road, with spluttering lighted torches; the carriages were arriving in all directions, and getting jammed in masses down the street, and trying to form in something like a line, and failing wofully, and coachmen's voices in high altercation with each other made the night resonant with noise. I could not see the visitors for the shining wet tops of the carriages, and wondered whether it was possible for me to get across at all, even without the aid of a glass-coach.

I could see the figures of the visitors thrown in shadow against the window-blind; some were promenading up and down; others had already began to dance, and I could hear distinctly the music of the large band as I paced my room in a high state of excitement.

The whole scene, so full of life and action, had made me nervous and extremely agitated; I wanted to be gone, yet shrank from going. I heaped a thousand curses on the head of the landlord of the Black Bull for being behind the hour in his promise for a coach, and yet, when the coach really was ready, and waiting for me, I invented half a dozen unnecessary delays, in order to protract and retard the final move. The glass-coach had to emerge from a back entrance of the Black Bull into a dark country road, and then wind about for above half a mile, until it reached the leading thoroughfare at Cliverton, and joined in the rank of carriages, so slowly moving to the ball. It rained very heavily, and the constant rattling on the coach-top did not tend to calm my nervous state of being.

Twenty minutes' funereal progress, and the lights were blazing round me, and there were noises in my ears that seemed to stun me, and make me feel as if I were under water, and fast drowning; then the carriage stopped, and the door was wrenched open with a jerk, and the steps lowered with a crashing noise.

"As quick as you can, if you please, sir."

I managed to get out of the carriage in a confused heap, and brought a sally of boisterous laughter on my head from the unwashed citizens of Cliverton, by striking my hat against the top of the coach-door, and sending it in an ungraceful manner over my eyes.

I reached the hall; there was a flight of stairs before me; and what with the exertion of struggling from beneath my hat, and the passing up the stairs of gentlemen in full dress, and officers in scarlet and gold, and ladies in silks and satins, and gauzy materials of ethereal texture, peeping from opera-cloaks and mantles, I stood perfectly bewildered.

I ascended the stairs, and tendered my ticket to a gentleman who stood behind a green baize table on the first landing, as if he were about to deliver an impressive lecture to the crowd that flowed towards him; and, observing the gentlemen filing off into a retiring room, imitated their example. I laid down my hat, looked vacantly at my pale face in the great glass, at which half a dozen gentlemen were going through elaborate fantasias with ivory-handled hair-brushes, and breathed a little freer.

Feeling, in a remarkable manner, out of my element, I brushed my hair to gain time, drew on a pair of white kid gloves—in imitation of a very cool young ensign at the end of the room—and tried to summon resolution to dash into the great ball going on a few yards distant.

Observing the ensign, after a lingering look at the glass, saunter towards the door, I made a plunge after him, fraught with the sudden resolve of entering with him, and, trusting to the glory of his martial appearance, to pass unobserved into the assemblage.

There were several gentlemen hanging about the doors—as gentlemen will do at balls—and I had some difficulty in keeping the ensign in sight as I passed through.

I could not have entered at a more unlucky moment, for the last note of the finale ceased as I set foot in the ball-room; the dancers of the quadrille seemed all walking towards me, as if with the intention of shaking hands, and my first impulse was to fly. I paused. The ensign continued his way unmoved by the crowd of guests; the talking, laughing, the chandeliers, the wreaths of flowers on the wall, the crowds of faces—he disregarded them all, looking right and left, as if for his party, grouped somewhere on the crimson ottomans ranged around the room. If he discovered his friends, I felt that I should be lost. He walked to the end of the spacious ball-room without attaining the object of his search, and then turned, and, putting his hands behind him, stood calmly surveying the scene, as if it was all his property, and all under his entire management. A vacant seat attracted my notice; I left my pilot and took possession of it, and began to grow more composed and rational.

The orchestra was erected at the side of the room, near the

door by which I had effected my entrance, and was crowded with musicians, and round its sides were hanging fancy programmes, printed in gold letters, of the dances. There were already some hundreds of visitors assembled, and the constant shifting of colours presented to the eye, heightened by the officers of the ——th regiment, in their scarlet uniform, was, to one so habitually quiet as myself—one who had never seen a large party since he was a child—a bewildering scene; and the effect from which was not easily got over.

They began to dance once more; the music of the magnificent band restored me to myself, and made me long to share in the pleasures of the moment; the figures whirled by me in rapid succession, all with happy faces—lovely English faces, that are seen only to perfection in crowded scenes of gaiety like this.

I could see neither Celia nor the Silvernot family anywhere; they had evidently not yet arrived, and I was alone in the midst of the bright world.

Oh! stern father, hater of such scenes, couldst thou see thy son now!

Whilst the waltz was proceeding, a very little man—perhaps, half an inch smaller than the rector of Wharnby, but with an immense head, that would have matched Goliath's—escorted a lady down the room with great care, keeping close to the ottomans, in order to avoid contact with the ropes.

I drew my feet closer together, to allow them to pass, but they suddenly halted, looked round the room, and then took the vacant seat beside me. The lady was of somewhat diminutive stature, like her companion, but of exquisite proportion, and a bright flashing face, round which showered a myriad of the blackest ringlets, that reminded me of Celia. She wore a light satin dress, thickly decorated with lace, and the large diamond spray scintillating in her raven hair told of some high-born or well-to-do lady in the county of Cliverton. She glanced, as if unconsciously, towards me; and I felt the colour rising to my cheeks beneath the quick, momentary glance of two of the brightest eyes I had ever seen.

"I do not perceive the Colonel, James," she said to her companion, in the most dulcet of voices.

"He's always late," he replied, in a voice of the shrillest treble; "and yet he should be first man at a thing of this sort, Ernestine."

"I do not see any of our friends or acquaintances," said the lady, opening and shutting a carved ivory fan very rapidly; "we are isolated here."

"If I mistake not, Stalker's just entered the room," cried her escort, jumping to his feet, and striving to catch a glimpse of the door through the maze of waltzers; "yes, it must be he; I saw his bald head."

Slowly advancing in a similar manner to that which the last arrivals had adopted, came a burly man of four or five and forty years of age, of florid complexion, and with a broad, open face, somewhat prepossessing, which lit up with recognition as he caught sight of the lady and gentleman seated near me. He advanced at a more rapid pace, and stretching out a hand to each of them, shook theirs heartily, and disclosed a set of large, white teeth, in the jolliest manner possible.

"What, my old friends, I am delighted to welcome you," he said, in a rich, hearty voice. "Mr. Dartford, you are looking well, my dear sir; and," turning to the lady, "you are looking better than well, Mrs. Morton."

"Ever a flatterer, Colonel."

"But you do not introduce me to your friend, Dartford," with a half smile at me.

Here was confusion worse confounded for me; but I, summoning up fortitude, hastened to reply.

"Your pardon, Colonel Stalker," I said, in a rapid tone of voice; "I am quite alone here, and have not the pleasure of an acquaintance with this lady or gentleman. I trust you will allow me to express personally my thanks for the receipt of your kind letter, which has obtained me admittance to this ball."

"You are, let me see, you are ——?" he stopped short.

"My name is Elmore."

"Mr. Elmore!" extending his white gloved hand towards me; "to be sure. I am very glad to have the pleasure of introducing myself to you."

He shook hands very heartily. I never saw a man so delighted to see me in my life. It was quite embarrassing.

"Did I understand that you were quite alone?" he asked.

"At present, sir."

"That is excessively awkward at a Cliverton ball," said the Colonel; "will you allow me?"

Without waiting for my answer, he turned to his friends, and said—

"Here is a young friend of mine I have much pleasure in introducing to you, with your kind leave, Mrs. Morton."

"I shall be very happy to have the honour," with another quick glance at me, and a winning smile lighting up her face.

Colonel Stalker made the required introduction and repeated the ceremony with Mr. Dartford, without asking his permission at all, said a few more common-places with the freshest of looks, and then, the waltz having come to a conclusion, turned to greet other friends who were clustering thickly about him.

"A very affable man, the Colonel," suggested Mr. Dartford, in his piping tones.

"He appears a perfect gentleman," I replied.

"Yet that man is a complete tyrant to his subordinates," said Mr. Dartford, "a complete tyrant, sir. He'd flog a man within an inch of his life for a saucy word. An advocate for the *cat*, sir."

"Indeed!"

Not relishing the conversation of Mr. Dartford, which turned on an uncalled-for topic, and which appeared to me somewhat false and at variance with the manner in which he had received the Colonel, I ventured to address myself to Mrs. Morton.

"The ball is very well attended, is it not, madam?"

"It appears so," with a shrug of her white shoulders; "I have never been at a Cliverton ball before. I am not partial to *country* balls; there is so much pretension about them."

There was the slightest curl of her red lip as she glanced round, indicating the same comment applied to the company. She looked full at me as she spoke. How very beautiful she was, how young, and yet a Mrs. Morton!

"You Cliverton people," she said, lightly, "have such grand ideas, such exalted notions, which never come to anything. Now this ball is a very common-place affair, and yet the officers of the gallant —th consider there has never been its equal. As for the ladies, they must all be peeresses in their own right, they are so grand and imposing. I beg pardon, *self*-imposing."

The little handsome lady was evidently out of temper, or she could never have uttered such bitter remarks on the Cliverton beauties.

"You are severe, madam."

"No, Mr. Elmore, I am only just," she replied; "but you

are a gentleman, and are chivalric in the ladies' defence. I dare say," her eyes sparkled with meaning, "you know of an exception to the rule, sir?"

"I am quite a stranger, madam," I replied, evasively.

"You do not live at Cliverton?"

"No, at Wharnby."

"Wharnby," she said; "that is a charming little place, I have heard. My brother, Mr. Dartford," with a wave of her fan, "has lately purchased some ground at Wharnby. You have a sea view there, Mr. Elmore?"

"A very fine one."

"Ah, I have no view but London smoke, in my choked-up square in town."

The walk was concluded, and we were silent; I, for want of a subject, Mrs. Morton deep in observation of the passing visitors who promenaded to and fro, and not one of whom escaped the quick searching glance of the dark eyes beside me.

A quadrille was forming; I felt I ought to ask Mrs. Morton to dance with me, but she appeared so immeasurably above me, so great a lady, that it would be almost impertinent to solicit such an honour.

I hazarded it at last, and the graceful bend of the head in assent made me feel proud of my partner, and highly flattered by her compliance with my wish.

We took our places ere the music commenced, and James Dartford sat perched on the ottoman with the gravest of faces, holding his sister's fan and vinaigrette.

Certainly there was something particularly fascinating about Mrs. Morton, and I stumbled two or three times in my figures whilst absorbed in watching the gliding movements of my partner. Who could she be? Where was Mr. Morton? If she had been taller, how her figure would have resembled Celia's!

Oh, Celia, where was she? Life had its charms, and society much attractive power, for I had not dwelt on my own sorrows these last few hours, and had nearly forgotten Celia Silvernot.

I was sorry when the dance was over, and I had led her to her place, and resumed my own by her side. It was my duty to take my departure now; I was monopolising her attention, and keeping other gentlemen, who passed with envying eyes at my position, at arm's length; but it required some strength of mind to break away and mingle with the crowd. The Colonel made his re-appearance with a lady on his arm, whom he introduced to Mrs. Morton as Mrs. Colonel Stalker; and friends of the Colonel and his lady coming up fast around us, Mrs. Morton was soon the centre of an admiring circle.

She was very witty, very much at her ease, very brilliant in conversation, and I took refuge in Mr. Dartford.

"Your sister tells me she is a resident in London, sir."

"Yes, a true Londoner, or Londoness," replied he, with his shrill, whistling voice; "but it don't agree with her, poor thing. I must persuade her to live at Cliverton, I think."

"The air of Cliverton—— excuse me."

I darted up and hurried towards the door.

She had come at last—she, Celia, my first love—the last hope of my life!

I advanced towards her. She was leaning on Paul Redwin's arm, and blushing beneath the gaze of so many ardent eyes. Mr. Silvernot, senior, with Mrs. Silvernot and his eldest daughter on his arms, followed behind the young couple, exchanging bows and smiles with many of the guests.

"Is that a Silvernot?" I heard a voice exclaim.

"Yes, the youngest of the family. What do you think of her?"

"A fine girl. Who's her companion?"

"Don't know; but he's a lucky fellow—eh!"

"Lucky! I wish I were in his place!"

I heard no more—I was standing before them, and intercepting their progress.

Celia raised her dove-like eyes, and, for a moment, did not know me, I presented so changed an appearance in my full dress; then her pretty eyes and mouth rounded into perfect O's with amazement, and she cried, almost breathlessly, "Mr. Luke!"

Redwin stared, and looked in a puzzled manner at me, and the senior members of the family gasped with astonishment.

"Good God!" at last ejaculated Mr. Silvernot; "is anybody ill?"

Why I should come to the Cliverton ball, in a white satin waistcoat and a spotless tie, if any one were suddenly attacked at "The Rest" with a serious malady, was above my comprehension; but I nevertheless replied—

"I hope not, Mr. S."

"Bu—bu—but, what—what brought you?"

"My horse."

"Yes, yes; but you have not come to dance?"

"Oh, yes, I have!" very calmly.

"And you never mentioned a word to us about it," said Celia, reproachfully.

"Your pardon. Try and remember a ride from Wharnby one summer afternoon, Miss Celia."

The whole incident sprang to her recollection, and I know not why, but her face flushed scarlet, and she looked down upon the ground.

"You're an extraordinary fellow, Elmore," said Redwin, in somewhat of a drawling tone; "you are fond of mystery and surprises. Quite romantic, on my honour."

"There's nothing mysterious in coming to a ball, Redwin," I answered. "I presume I have an equal right, even with yourself."

"But why did you not tell us?" chirped Mrs. Silvernot; "it is so singular, Luke."

"Does your father know it, too?" asked Arabella.

"I am not a school-boy, Miss Silvernot," I replied, "and I certainly have not asked permission."

"Come, Celia," said Redwin to the lovely girl, whose hand rested on his arm, "we are making quite a blockade. Let us diminish the number of barriers." He moved on with her. I looked after them with an envying, jealous gaze. They were a handsome pair; they were a fair couple, and attracted more than common notice as they walked down the centre of the room; and I thought his place might have been mine; that hand might have rested on my arm so confidingly, so full of trust; and she might have loved me—ay, have loved me had he not come home from France!

"Lancers! lancers!" cried the M.C.

There was confusion and much pressing immediately. The room was getting crowded, and the stewards, of which Colonel Stalker was one, had much difficulty in obtaining the requisite space. I lost sight of the Silvernots, and, full of that purpose which had led me hither, I hastened in quest of Redwin and his charge.

They were waiting for the set to be formed, at the farther end of the room, and I was just in time.

"Celia," I said, in a hasty voice, "I claim a promise, made

that summer afternoon I spoke of. You have not forgotten it, I feel assured."

"What *does* the fellow mean?" murmured Redwin, half angrily to Celia.

"Fellow! Mr. Redwin," I cried, fiercely; "curb your tongue, sir. I am a gentleman!"

His face reddened.

"It was a harsh expression, Elmore," said he, frankly. "You will pardon me—but your sudden challenge, I must confess, irritated me. There, look over it."

He extended his hand, and I took it in all friendship. The apology was made so heartily—for none knew or was more scrupulous of good breeding than himself—that I regretted my interference, and wished that I had let the promise drop. I knew he loved her, and that her heart was wholly his: why should I stand between them and thrust myself upon their notice, seeking to mar the happiness I could not enjoy myself? I would retire.

"Well, let me return," said I, with forced cheerfulness. "I am hardly in the right myself. Miss Celia," turning to her, "I absolve you. Considering *all things*, I resign my claim. Time cancels a long debt."

There was a rosy blush on her face as I concluded; but she arrested my departure, by saying, quickly—

"Nay, a promise is a promise; it is fair that I should fulfil my share in it. Paul, you must excuse me this dance for the sake of my true word. In an idle conversation, many months ago, I said that, if he were at this ball, I would be his partner for my first dance."

Redwin looked as if he would read my soul, but I was thinking of how strangely "Paul" sounded, and how earnestly she sought extenuation in his eyes. "*Idle conversation!*" To me it was full of meaning and of interest, and every word was graven on my mind.

"You do not care?" she said, in so low a tone, that it was a marvel my quick ears caught the import of the words.

"Oh, no!—do as you like," he replied, carelessly; "Mr. Elmore and I will not cross swords about it. You must break one promise or the other; break mine, of course. *Au revoir.*"

He strode away with a very cloudy brow, and left me Celia's partner, and two big tears in Celia's eyes.

He was not worthy of her. So rough a speech—so crude and

sharp a return for her high sense of honour, was far from just or gentle. But is not love all injustice, and made up of folly? and jealousy, its twin sister, has she not the passions of the tiger?

The dance that I had looked forward to so long was not a happy one, after all; for Celia was grave, and forgetful of her part, and now and then I saw her meek eyes looking for the tall form of Paul Redwin in the distance, who, as a sort of sacrifice, was dancing with Miss Silvernot, and scowling at her with savage intensity.

Mrs. Morton and an officer were our *vis-à-vis*, and she smiled a recognition, and, when waiting for her turn, stood evidently analysing Celia.

"You were not chivalric in vain, Mr. Elmore," she whispered, with a merry smile, as, for a moment, I went through the usual complications of a figure with her.

I had not time for a reply, for she was with her partner again.

Celia had seen her speak to me, and, forgetting her sorrow for a moment, in her surprise, said—

"Do you know that lady, Mr. Luke?"

"I have been introduced to her this evening."

"Why, you are colouring!" with the prettiest smile I had seen that night.

"Colouring, Miss Celia!"

"Oh, I see! You must introduce me. Our turn."

Redwin had seen the smile of Celia, and he frowned gloomily, and looked more savage than ever. Smiling and flirting, too!—was that a part of her promise? Very well—very well!

The Lancers reached a termination. I was bowing my acknowledgments very gratefully, and Redwin, with Arabella on his arm, was coming towards us, and evidently studying how to transfer that worthy spinster to my care, when a suppressed whisper thrilled through the room—a low murmuring, that sounded like a sea, and that appeared to pervade the whole assemblage, rang in my ears, and nearly all eyes were turned towards the door.

"Who are they?"

"How superbly lovely!"

Celia's hand grasped my arm convulsively.

"Look! look! There, by the door!"

I staggered with intense astonishment, and passed my hand across my eyes, as if waking from a dream; for there, entering the room, slowly, calmly, and regally, were Jacques Vaudon and my sister Agnes.

Vaudon, full-dressed, and with his jet black beard descending almost to his chest, although a striking figure, was almost unheeded in the interest excited by the young girl who ,eant upon his arm, and who, in the costly dress of richest l -- with gems shining and sparkling about it, and a jewelled spray—resembling Mrs. Morton's—in her hair, appeared like the queen of this grand fête, as she moved towards us, perfectly at her ease.

Questions were flying around us on all sides concerning them.

"They must be foreigners!" "Who can *she* really be?" "Did you ever see so striking a face?" "Have you seen them before?" "Who is he with her?"

Celia and I were before them.

"Vaudon—Agnes!" I ejaculated; and "Agnes!" cried Celia, at the same time.

It was their turn to be astonished, for my appearance was as undreamt of as their own; and Agnes exhibited her surprise by a cry of "Luke! You here?" And Vaudon for one moment elevated his eyebrows in mild surprise. I was too much confused to notice the effect my sudden appearance had upon them in the eager questions that I poured upon her, and which she paid little heed to, being now in the centre of the Silvernots, with Celia close to her side, and Paul Redwin looking on.

I turned to Vaudon.

"Unravel this mystery, Jacques Vaudon," said I, sharply; "there is more beneath for me to hear, man."

"Let us take one turn up this room together, Luke," said he, linking his arm within mine; "it is soon told, and easily explained."

"I listen," said I, when we had commenced our promenade.

"You are surprised at the presence of Agnes, Luke?"

"Yes."

"Yet, if I mistake not, there is a more valid reason for her presence than your own."

"How so?"

"Your sister came with your father's consent, Luke," said he, smiling sardonically; "did you, my prodigal?"

"I did not," I answered; "but how did she obtain it?"

"Easily enough, I believe," he said; "your father was not in an obstinate mood; and Agnes's whole heart was set upon the ball, and it would have been a cruel harshness to dash all her girlish anticipation to the ground. Your father sacrificed all his old resolves in according her his permission; as your father's friend, I could do no more than offer the sacrifice of my time as a fitting escort."

"You are very kind."

"Spoken in a satirical vein, friend Luke, or I am in great error," said he, as we wheeled round to return; "but, in faith, it *was* a sacrifice—for there is nothing in this gaudy scene, this raree show to charm one to whom all pleasurable feelings are dead and buried. I shall take my post by one of these pillars, and watch the many springs at work, within this crowd of puppets; I may find amusement, perhaps here or in the card-room, if I look philosophically at it. There, go to your friends."

"But you have not spoken to the Silvernots yet, Vaudon."

"If they desire my company, Luke, they will know where to find me," said Vaudon; "so go to your friends. If you have a spirit in you, Paul Redwin's night at Cliverton should not be a very happy one."

"Why not?"

"He robbed you of a prize; if you cannot win her back, you can at least sting him, by a false attention to her."

"I have more charity within me," I replied.

"Good boy," he said, drily.

I left Vaudon to occupy the position he had indicated, by one of the pillars wreathed with flowers and laurel, against which he fixed himself rigid as a statue, and, perfectly unmoved by the inquiring looks and curious stares bent on him, composed himself to observe all that passed beneath his notice. I joined the group of Wharnby friends round Agnes. Agnes laughed merrily, as she said to me, half-aside, "I shall never forget your stupid look of amazement, Luke; it was worth coming from 'The Rest' to see."

"Let us talk seriously a moment. Will you walk with me?"

"They will dance in a minute," she said, evasively.

"Not for five minutes, at least, Aggy."

"How very tiresome you are!" said she, taking my arm. "Now what have you to say?"

"Firstly, how did you obtain my father's consent? It seems so strange, so incomprehensible, that he who has kept so strict a watch over your lightest actions all his life should let you come to this ball."

"I do not ask by what means you obtained admittance, Luke."

"You do not care."

"Not much," she replied, with a smile; "you are here, that is enough for me."

"But *I* care," I answered, quickly; "there has been some trick, in which Vaudon has connived, and my father has been misled, or duped by false representations, that you or he both have made. I *know* it."

"Nonsense!" said she, looking admiringly at her bouquet; "there have been no false representations made. I merely said, 'Father, Miss Osborne has taught me to dance; Miss Osborne sees no harm in dancing. I have learnt that I might go to the Cliverton ball, where all my friends are going; will you give me your consent?'"

"And he?"

"Why, he demurred at first, and then said, 'Go.' Mr. Vaudon offered to accompany me hither, and my father merely bound me to secresy with my brothers. He was so afraid they would want to see life, Luke; would you think it?" asked she, lightly.

"Rail on," said I, still doubting this *naïve* statement.

"Now take me back again!"

"One moment," I said—a frightful thought suggesting itself—a thought which stunned me: "when did you ask my father?"

Her cheek crimsoned, as she replied, "In the evening."

"Yes, in the evening, late in he evening, was it not?" cried I, almost stifling.

"It was late, certainly."

"*When he was drunk!*" I hissed; "when he was incapable of thought, and hardly had a knowledge of where he was, or whom you were. Oh! Aggy, Aggy—God forgive you!—that was not a woman's action!"

Her scheme discovered, she looked back my reproach, and drew herself up haughty and defiant.

"It was my only chance of coming hither, and I see not the evil of the means. I asked him when at least he was more rational, and took not such ungenerous views of life or life's duties. I did not steal out like a thief, and play the selfish hypocrite; at least, I asked."

"I would rather you had stolen out at night, and come alone in the darkness and the rain, than have had you walking in this room with me—you, but a child, too!—with the knowledge of the reproach you must be unto yourself."

"I bear my self-reproach very lightly, then," she said, snatching her hand from my arm; "and you will please spare me your comments, which are but those of a poor coward."

"Another question," I cried, "and then rejoin the Silvernots, and enjoy your first ball if you can. From whence came these jewels?"

"They were my mother's."

"Does *he* know you wear them, Agnes?"

"That is a second question," said she, hurrying away from me.

She had answered it by her evasive manner, and her humiliation was complete to me; and, although in her own esteem she had not abated one jot of self-respect—nay, rather had taken to herself the vanity of success—my heart bled for her want of right—for that lack of moral principle, which, seeking an object, cared not for the eyes with which others looked upon her.

And Vaudon, who leant against the pillar, watching us, and clutched his great black beard with his white gloved hand, with what look did *his* eyes take in and estimate the daughter of the Elmores? With no feeling of sorrow, with no regret for his best friend's child, could that man's nature be affected; all that he thought lay buried in that broad breast, and that high, white forehead, along with the many secrets his mysterious life could tell of.

Another dance had commenced, but Agnes and the Silvernots were too full of discussion to pay much attention to it; and, far from inclined to join in it myself, I entered into a fragmentary dialogue with Paul Redwin, in the place thereof.

Redwin was in as abstracted a mood as myself, so we were not particularly lively or witty during our discourse, and both were half-listening to a dialogue on the seat beside us.

"But, Agnes dear, what a bold stroke for a young lady!"

"Why is it bold, Celia?"

"You are not yet '*out!*'"

"Pardon, dear," replied my sister; "I do not consider

myself a school-girl; and Miss Osborne I look upon as a friend, not as a governess. I am your own age, Celia."

"Yes, yes," said Celia; "but you think I am blaming you, whereas I am so very glad to see you—I cannot tell you how glad, Agnes."

"'The Rest' is an unfashionable place, and I have not studied etiquette in coming hither; the Elmores do not bestow much consideration upon the usages of polite society," said Agnes; "besides, who is to know at this ball that I am not quite seventeen, and have still a governess?"

"Ah! who, indeed!"

"And then I am a young woman. Do not I look a young woman, Celia?"

"I hardly knew you, Agnes," answered Celia, very much perplexed, for Agnes was as argumentative, as perfectly unembarrassed, as graciously pleasing, as if she had been the *belle* of the Cliverton season, and reigning beauty of all balls and parties for the last six months.

Redwin, who wished to do something, and who felt conscious of appearing particularly "stickish," turned to the young ladies who were conversing by his side, and said—

"I presume Miss Agnes Elmore scarcely remembers the Master Redwin of old times, and yet Miss Celia hardly considers a second introduction to an old friend necessary."

"I beg your pardon, Paul," said Celia; "I was just puzzling my poor memory with endeavouring to think if Miss Elmore had not seen you at our house since your return."

"Poor memory!" said Paul, somewhat meaningly; "what a shocking affliction is a bad memory!"

Paul Redwin had not yet got over the first dance, and was chewing the bitter cud of his reflections with a grave intentness.

"A second introduction is assuredly out of place, Mr. Redwin," said Agnes, smiling; "I have a perfect recollection of our interview, and apologise for not arresting your attention towards my humble self some minutes since."

Paul Redwin took the extended hand, and bowed over it with great gallantry.

"Miss Elmore need not apologise," he said, laughingly; "for my part, I think an introduction almost necessary, for time has made a great change in her; and it is a new face I greet."

He looked a compliment, and Agnes half inclined her head, as if acknowledging it.

Poor Celia sat between them with a blank expression on her pretty features. She hardly liked Mr. Redwin to sit by her side and talk across to her dear friend, and smile and look compliments at her; but she did not know for what reason she disliked it, and thought, perhaps, it was her low spirits and concern because dear Paul was disappointed in his dance, that made her feel so dull.

Yes—so dull! She had anticipated spending the happiest of evenings, and yet she was very dull. How strange it was, to be sure!

Redwin and my sister still sat chatting gaily, with Celia between them, who joined in occasionally with a forced smile, and on whose countenance the shade of perplexity seemed more deep than ever. Mr. Silvernot had got tired of sitting still, and was yawning perceptibly, and hinting to Mrs. Silvernot that he thought he should adjourn to the card-room for half an hour or so. Mrs. Silvernot and Arabella were criticising the dancers, and Vaudon, in the distance, stood still, immovable, and deeply interested in the study he had chosen.

"Are you engaged for the *next* dance, Celia?" asked Redwin.

"No, Paul."

"No other engagements made in *idle conversation?*"

"How cruel you are this evening," she said, in a tone not intended to reach my ears. "Have I offended you?"

"No, Celia," he answered in the same low tone; "but I did not know if——"

I moved away from them lest my contiguity to them should give me the appearance of an eavesdropper, and slided four seats down, and engaged Miss Arabella for the next dance, purely out of respect to the family.

The ball grew more lively; the spirit of Terpsichore seemed hovering over its votaries below; dance followed dance, hardly without a minute's intermission; all the guests had assembled; the great Cliverton ball was in the flower of its strength, and going off with great *éclat*.

I danced with Miss Silvernot, and Redwin and Celia were partners, at last; and Agnes had been introduced to Captain Clifford, a friend of the Silvernots, a very pale-faced young man, with white hair and pink eyes, like a rabbit, and who, I have no doubt, was of an easy and impressionable nature; for he had been smitten, and, in fact, was observed to stand gazing dreamily at her from distant parts of the room for the remainder of the evening.

Agnes was in the full glory of her heart; her eyes were rivalling, with their light, the diamonds in her hair—her cheek was flushed—her red lips parted—her whole look that of one carried away by the glowing excitement of the hour; and despite the quarrel we had had together, and the deceit I was fully aware she must have practised to have gained the position she was holding, I felt proud that the beauty of the room was my own sister.

Proud, and yet fearful. While my heart thrilled with vanity, I trembled inwardly at I knew not what. So fair, and yet her little brain so full of scheming, and of craft. So young in years, so old in thought!

Her mother's jewels were blazing ostentatiously about her form—Heaven preserve her from inheriting the smallest portion of that mother's nature with the gems that have descended to her, or she has taken, as her right—a sinful legacy at best!

The smallest portion of her nature! I dared not breathe that hope to heaven, for it had shown itself to-night with her duplicity, when her guardian angels were sleeping.

Oh! angels, wake!—'tis time! The distant scene is indistinct and dim, and there are figures veiled and dark, standing as in the luridness of night, beckoning her towards them!

She was no longer a girl—she had shaken off all childish thoughts—she stood before me in all the glare of myriads of lights, with music swelling through the room, and crowds of faces round her, and dancers whirling past--a woman!

And that strange look, which no one seemed to notice but myself—that look which made her beautiful and dazzling, and triumphant, and which had no heavenly stamp of holiness upon it, how fearfully cognisant was I of it to-night!

She moved through the dance all grace, and did more than justice to her teaching; she attracted all eyes near her into a strange, earnest gaze; and her name, Miss Elmore, of "The Rest," at Wharnby, was murmured many times that night.

Redwin danced with Agnes the following quadrille, and Celia had Colonel Stalker for a partner.

Agnes and Redwin were capital partners for a quadrille; they had so much to say between the figures, and Redwin inclined his tall form very earnestly to every word, and was entirely forgetful of the beautiful great eyes of the younger Miss Silvernot, which were more than once hidden by their trembling lids.

My aristocratic friend was evidently interested in my sister; there was a fascination in her manner that bewildered him, and made his heart beat faster when she spoke to him, or looked into his face with her own steady, undecipherable gaze.

Mrs. Morton and I were companions again, and I mentally compared my position to Redwin's; for certainly there was something that attracted me to Mrs. Morton.

We were quite a friendly pair, this time; and I could hardly reconcile myself to the belief that I had not known her years ago, and this was only a re-union. I found myself getting witty and indulging in repartee, and escorting Mrs. M. to the refreshment-rooms, and listening eagerly to every brilliant, flashing sentence she could turn so well, and use so ably.

"That lovely girl is your sister, Mr. Elmore?" she said, as we promenaded—I holding my head very loftily, and proud of the lady on my arm.

"The lady in the white lace dress?"

"Of course. How I should like to know her!"

"Will you allow me to introduce her to you?"

"Oh! willingly. Nothing could give me greater pleasure."

It was done. I escorted Mrs. Morton to where my sister sat, and where Paul Redwin lingered, although Celia, white as death, sat with her mother, and plucked the flowers unconsciously from her rich bouquet, and scattered them at her feet.

I introduced Mrs. Morton to my sister—they were excellent friends in five minutes. Mrs. Morton's winning manner soon attracted sister Agnes. They joined the Silvernots, and entered into fresh introductions, and we all made a party on the crimson ottomans. Vaudon left his post, and came and joined us; and the small brother of Mrs. Morton brought his great head, which he rolled in an unpleasant way on his shoulders—over to our side, too—and was introduced by his handsome sister Ernestine, and began to flirt in an awfully heavy manner with Arabella Silvernot, who smiled graciously at his attentions, and whose visage wore a far less acidulated aspect than had been represented thereon since she had entered the ball-room doors.

The night wore on. It was two o'clock before I had thought it twelve; and one or two parties of ladies and gentlemen had taken their departure. Redwin had danced with Celia twice, and with Agnes once more, and was now pressing my sister a third time.

"I am engaged three deep."

"The fourth dance?"

"Nonsense—I shall disappoint my third by going home. Mr. Vaudon is getting tired of the fête—are you not?"

"I think I am"—stifling a yawn.

"You do not dance, Mr. Vaudon?" asked Mrs. Silvernot.

"No, my dear madam," he replied, "unless some one of my own age condescends to take pity on me. What say you, Mrs. S.?"

This was somewhat flattering to Mrs. S., who was fifteen years his senior at least, and she beamed with smiles. "No, I never dance; I am content to see the young enjoy themselves, Mr. Vaudon."

"So am I," said Vaudon; "if you reject me, I must decline entering into this giddy vortex. Suppose we look in at the card-room, and see how many half-crowns Mr. S. has lost in following Deschappelles' counsels."

He offered her his arm, and they walked towards the door.

Redwin renewed his proposition.

"I will not promise, Mr. Redwin," said Agnes, shaking her head with serious resolve at him. "Celia, can I?"

"What can you not, dear?" with a faltering voice.

"Dance any more with Mr. Redwin."

"I do not know, I am sure, Agnes," said Celia; "I should have thought the question could have been better answered by yourself."

"Are you engaged next dance, Celia?" said Agnes.

"Yes, am I not, Arabella?"

"I believe so," said Arabella, sharply turning her head for a moment from Mr. Dartford, who was talking something about pockets of hops.

"I did not know if it were the next," said Celia, wearily.

"And the next?"

"No."

"Then, Mr. Redwin," in a quick whisper to Paul, "I shall dance with you no more."

Redwin looked up, met her glance, and looked down again.

"Oh! how my head aches, Arabella," murmured Celia. "Oh! when are we going home?"

I heard the low words so faintly whispered, and my heart yearned for her again, and my old love went flowing back towards her, in an unchecked torrent, in sympathy with her gentle heart. It was beating dully or throbbing wildly, through *his* manner, his reserve and inattention, but I loved her for the suffering I read upon her face. I could have stood before Paul Redwin, and pointing to the slighted girl, have said—

"See there, man! You won her heart—you took her from me when I might, by earnest, unremitting love, have gained her for myself; bruise and rend it not, now it is wholly yours—and beats for you alone."

But it was an idle moment or two, that would soon be forgotten in the even tenor of their future life, and the doors of "The Rest" would close upon Agnes Elmore—and Paul Redwin would be wholly Celia's. Who should say he was not hers now? May not he devote one half hour to a lady he has not seen since his childhood?

Mr. Silvernot, accompanied by his spouse, and Vaudon, re-entered the ball-room about three, when the company were thinning.

Colonel Stalker joined our group, and begged the honour of Miss Elmore's hand, but it was getting late, and Vaudon was impatient.

"Then my entreaty is a hopeless one, Miss Elmore?"

"For this time I must be excused," replied Agnes.

"I shall certainly give you a call in a day or two," said the Colonel to me: "I shall bring my gun, and have an hour's sport, Mr. Elmore, with your leave."

"I shall be delighted to welcome you at 'The Rest,'" I answered, although perfectly aware I should not be delighted in the slightest degree whatever.

Mr. Dartford and his sister had risen, and the latter kissed Agnes affectionately, like a dear relative and old friend.

"Our carriage is waiting," said she; "I must hurry off. You will come and see me at Cliverton, before London engulfs me again, my dear Miss Agnes, will you not?"

Agnes readily assented.

"And Mr. Elmore," piped her brother, "I should be happy to have an hour's chat with you. Thornville Villa—the first house on the high road—mind, I expect you."

"I certainly shall avail myself of your kind invite," said I, bowing low.

"Oh! yes, Mr. Elmore *must* come," cried Mrs. Morton, as she extended her hand to me.

I felt confused, and my heart fluttered as she placed her hand in mine and smiled her adieux, and looked so very beautiful that I could but see her face and dancing ringlets in the room. I slightly pressed her hand, in my excitement, and then felt I had taken an unwarrantable liberty; but she did not observe it, for she smiled and said—"Remember."

She was gone, and still the bright black eyes were part of a vision before me, and the dulcet tones of her voice, "Remember," were ringing in my ears.

We were waiting under the great stone portico for the carriage to come up, and the Silvernots had been carried off to Wharnby House, with Celia still very dull, and Redwin, gloomily thoughtful, by her side.

"What do you mean to do about your horse, Luke?" asked Vaudon.

"I shall send Tom for it in the morning, or—fetch it myself."

"Ah, fetch it," mused Vaudon.

"And call on the pretty widow, Luke. Thornville Villa will not be far out of the way," said Agnes.

"The pretty widow! Is Mrs. Morton a widow?"

"Were you ignorant of that fact?"

"Yes."

"What a young widow! She must have seen great misfortune," I thought, "in her few short years of life. Poor Mrs. Morton!"

It was still raining heavily, and in the few moments after we had quitted Cliverton, we had relapsed into a rigid silence, which remained unbroken hour after hour as we glided towards our home. Vaudon fell asleep with his great cloak wrapped tightly round him. Agnes sat looking at her bouquet, and thinking for herself deeply, and the diamond spray kept flashing in the meagre light of the carriage lamp, like some fiery life hovering above her head: whilst I half dozed, and, though still conscious of the presence of Vaudon and my sister opposite, was dancing at the ball with Mrs. Morton, who faded into Celia and back again to some one I had never seen before, clothed in widow's weeds and wailing for the dead.

"The Rest." Servants were awaiting us, and we entered the house. Standing in the hall was a dim figure, which, upon advancing nearer, proved to be my father. Agnes covered the diamonds with her hood.

"You have returned," he said to me, and me alone; "it is

what I expected. I have not been deceived in you, for are not you all the children of deceit? What have I to look forward to? Poor Luke! Poor Luke!"

Why did he pity me, and shake his head so sorrowfully, as he went slowly up the stairs towards his room? Why had he this night, when he had been alone so long after the rector had gone home, abstained from the evil draughts which lowered and degraded him?

All mystery—no sun—no light of day around "The Rest."

* * * * *

I pause at the close of this era in my life.

The figure born of fever that has marched side by side with me so long, pauses likewise, but points towards the distance, and covers with one shrouded arm his face of stone. It moves again, surely, slowly, and I drag my aching feet along the rugged path we tread—that path from which the snow of youth has vanished for ever!

CHAPTER XV.

POLITE ATTENTIONS.

My head ached the morning after the ball. I felt listless and apathetic—a youth without an object in the world—now the great event at Cliverton had passed, and the stately room wherein I had danced so lightly and found so much of the pleasures that my home denied, was already passing into mourning, and the chandeliers and crimson ottomans were being shrouded in their canvas coverings, and looking repentant for last night's dissipation, and wan and meagre in the accusing daylight.

Ah! that daylight, that accuses so many of us, that stings so many consciences, that covers so many cheeks with shame, that sheds its broad effulgence, and brings us into the glaring noon, and presents to our bleared eyes the gaunt spectre of the joyous yesterday, and mocks us with the brightness in which we stand a mark!

There were no comments made upon the incidents of the preceding night; had it been a great crime, the lips could not have been closer sealed.

Gilbert and Edward were kept in ignorance of Agnes and

myself having been at the Cliverton ball, and my father and Vaudon were more than usually silent the entire morning.

Miss Osborne was a trifle more grave than ordinary, and looked wonderingly at my father, and was, on the whole, evidently perplexed with the Elmore family, each member of which was a little mystery to her. Miss Osborne and my sister had gone on amicably together to the present time, and the former had, by her gentle manners and calm authority, at least won the respect of her pupil, and probably as much of her affections as it was in Agnes's power to bestow.

Miss Osborne was a graceful ornament to "The Rest." More of a companion to Agnes than a governess, and more of a housekeeper (the most lady-like of housekeepers!) than either, she seemed to fill a vacuum that had ever been apparent in the Elmore household, and to relieve the dulness that had centred round it with the cheering influence of her presence.

She was like a daughter to my father, and a sister to us, and a general favourite with all.

Gifted as she was with intellectual powers, of which we never knew the full extent, she hid them all beneath a natural reserve and a quietness of demeanour that had been habitual to her from a child. She had ever a soft, winning smile for her friends, ever a cheerful word for the servants; but, nevertheless, it would have struck an observer that her natural expression of feature was one of grave and deep thought. Had he seen her sitting alone, looking at the fire, or from the window at the sea, as I have seen her scores of times, with her deep, thinking eyes, looking far beyond the hour, and a saddening look upon those features, so delicately pale, he would have found conjecture ripening into certainty.

Miss Osborne was a very early riser, and would be out of the house and straying along the sands, or on the cliffs, hours before the shutters of "The Rest" had opened to the morning; or we should find her in the park, careless of the heavy dew that bent the grass earthwards with its weight, absorbed in some choice book, some prized author, that "lent enchantment" to the passing hour.

Vaudon, so ready with his sneers—so quick with a sarcastic allusion to anything that was singular, or out of the common way—refrained from his acrid commentaries on the housekeeper of "The Rest;" he seemed to subside into the general respect that was entertained towards her, and listened with more attention—often with marked interest—to that conversation in which she took a part. Then there was Gilbert—poor, methodical, great-hearted Gilbert—always consulting Miss Osborne on some subject connected with his studies, or holding some argument with her upon a topic to which it might give rise, and listening—he hardly knew it himself—with suspended breath to every word she uttered.

I felt a sinking in my breast when I noticed his rapt attention one morning, about three days before the ball. What a fresh misfortune it would be if he ever conceived an affection for Miss Osborne! What a dooming of my crippled brother to the same throes and agonies which I had felt myself! The pain without an alloy for him; for Miss Osborne had an inward pride, that would allow of no injurious motives being attributed to her, and no linking of the name of Mr. Elmore's son with hers. I felt assured of that. And if such misfortune should ever be for Gilbert, there was another pride to thwart him—the strange, evil pride that was the grand attribute of my father's character. But all this was surmise. My brother Gilbert in love! Tush! it was one of my dreamy follies, that vanish into air—that fade and die ere many minutes born.

But the day after the ball, the day which put an end to my father's visionary idea of keeping his eldest and youngest son in ignorance of our having been (how had he ever calculated in stopping the hundred currents by which the news might come to them?), is the subject of the present chapter.

The Elmore family were scattered about the house in divers occupations. About one o'clock in the day, Vaudon and my father were in the garden, sauntering up and down before the lake; Gilbert and Edward were in the parlour; Miss Osborne was busy over the account-book; Agnes was practising the music of several dances played the last evening; and I was trying to read Shakspeare's "Henry VIII.," and thinking of Celia, and Mrs. Morton, and sister Agnes, and Jacques Vaudon, between every line. A loud ringing at the bell, horses' feet clattering along the path, a pause, and then one of the servants entered the room in which I sat with my brothers.

"Well, what is it?"

"A card, sir, for Miss Agnes."

"For whom?" cried Gilbert.

"Miss Agnes—a gentleman, sir."

"Take it to her, then," I observed.

This expedient seemed never to have suggested itself to the domestic; he had been so habituated to submitting everything to my father, that it was not till after some reflection he retired, murmuring something about "he thought that Mr. Elmore," &c.

Agnes, with a flushed cheek, came hurriedly into the room with the card in her hand.

"Oh! Luke, here's Mr. Redwin."

"Redwin!" cried her brothers, simultaneously.

"Yes, don't shout so," said Agnes, involuntarily smoothing her glossy hair. "He will be here directly. He has come to inquire after me."

"What a considerate fellow, to be sure!" bawled Edward. "To inquire after *you*, Aggy! Are you certain it is not my unworthy self?"

"Mr. Redwin," cried the servant.

For the second time Paul Redwin entered "The Rest;" and his first coming, and abrupt departure, recurred to him as it did to us, and flushed his cheek somewhat. He glanced round the room, as if seeking some particular object, and then advanced with extended hand to Agnes.

"I could not pass 'The Rest,' Miss Elmore, without calling to inquire if you were well, and free from any ill effects that late hours and fatigue will sometimes bring, by way of counterbalance to our pleasures."

"You are very kind, Mr. Redwin, to think of me."

"Think!"

"My brothers," said Agnes, quickly, with a wave of the hand; "you have seen them?"

"To be sure"—wheeling round, and shaking hands with us—"Mr. Edward Elmore, I should not have known you. Mr. Gilbert, we have met but lately. Mr. Luke, you appear to be suffering from no ill effects of yesterday—or this early morning, more correctly speaking."

"What is——?" began Edward, when Gilbert gently touched him on the arm, and commanded silence by a look.

"Be seated, Mr. Redwin," said Agnes.

"I thank you," said Redwin, taking the seat indicated; "may I venture to hope you spent a pleasant evening?"

He was speaking to Agnes; and I, in conjunction with my brothers, observed Paul Redwin, as, leaning forward in his chair, he addressed my sister.

He was scrupulously exact in his dress, of course, and was

very fashionable and dandified, without a thread awry in his clothes, or a curl out of proportion in his dark chestnut hair; but still he hardly reminded me of the Paul Redwin I had seen before. There was not that cool and easy way that sat upon him so naturally and complacently—not that perfectly contented, ever-at-home demeanour which he exhibited at Wharnby House, with the Silvernots. He seemed forcing his old way and style with a great effort; he tried to appear as he had ever appeared at Wharnby House; and yet he stammered a little, coloured a great deal, and once or twice (a very rare event for Paul Redwin) made a dead pause, as if at a loss how to proceed with a common-place conversation.

It was time for Mr. Redwin to put an end to a visit of courtesy; but he lingered, and looked in his hat, and then shily askance at Agnes, sitting before him, and looking so pretty in her morning dress; and then, meeting my glance, became as red as fire, for no cause that was perceptible to me.

"Well, I am prolonging my visit," said he, jumping to his feet suddenly; "my grandmother will be puzzling her poor head as to my whereabouts."

"Are you going to Wharnby House, Mr. Redwin?" asked Agnes.

"I—I—oh, yes; I am going to cut across the country to the house directly," he said, confusedly.

"Will you be the bearer of a little note to Celia from me?" asked Agnes. "I am ashamed to trouble you, but I——"

"Do not mention trouble, Miss Elmore," said Redwin; "I shall feel highly honoured by the post of messenger."

"Ever flattering, Mr. Redwin," cried Agnes, opening a small rosewood desk by the window, and seating herself thereat.

"I *shall* feel honoured, *indeed*," said Redwin; and then, as if he thought he had reiterated his assertion too earnestly, added lightly, "Are not all gentlemen honoured by commands given by a lady? You will bear me out in that, Luke?" turning to me.

"Oh, certainly."

There was a pause, broken by the hurried scratching of Agnes's pen. Redwin, who had not re-seated himself, stood, hat in hand, looking at her in an abstracted manner; Gilbert, as if unaware of his presence, conversed with Edward, in a low tone; and I, with the consciousness of appearing particularly stupid, sat, with Shakespeare in my hand, staring at all in turn.

At this juncture the door opened, and my father and Vaudon entered.

"Good morning, Mr. Redwin," said Vaudon, as he shook hands.

"Mr. Redwin!" murmured my father, half vacantly; "Redwin—Redwin! who is Redwin, Vaudon?"

Before Vaudon could reply, the object of his inquiry interposed.

"Permit me to call to your remembrance, Mr. Elmore, the Master Paul Redwin of some years ago, who had the temerity to propose a change of education for your sons, which proposal was not received in such good faith as I, poor boy, had looked for. We parted with an ill grace, if you recollect."

"I recollect," said my father, stiffly; "have you called for an apology? If I remember rightly, you were going to remind me of the time when you became a man. I presume you consider that time has arrived, by your second appearance at 'The Rest.'"

Paul Redwin jerked up his head proudly, and looked back my father's supercilious glance. There was a sharp reply on his lips, and the second appearance would probably have brought about the same result as the first, had he not remembered Agnes, *his* daughter, was sitting before the desk at the window, and looking at him and her father half-entreatingly.

The words to which he might have given utterance were checked, and Agnes, rising with her note, said—

"Papa, this is a friend of mine; for he is a friend of the Silvernots, and we respect them, all of us. This gentleman was at the ball last night, and has called this morning to pay a common courtesy;" then, in a lower tone, inaudible to all but me, close unto their side, "You forget yourself, papa—*we* are Elmores."

"True, and the Elmores were all courtesy themselves once," he muttered; then, turning to the visitor, he said, "Mr. Redwin, I ask your pardon. I am an irritable man, and have more than a common share of man's infirmities. I pray you to excuse my harshness."

Redwin bowed.

"We will not detain you, Mr. Redwin," said Agnes, delivering her missive into his hands; "time may be precious to you. You will not forget my note?"

"You may rely upon me, Miss Elmore."

Mr. Redwin was bowing his adieux, when I cried—

"I am going to Cliverton, Redwin. I will accompany you a little way on the road, with your permission."

"That will be capital."

"To Cliverton, Luke?" inquired my father.

"Yes; I left my horse at the Bull Inn last night. Tom started this morning on foot to Cliverton, and will await my coming."

"Why do you go, then?"

"I have a small bill to settle."

"Ah! true."

He said it with a half groan, for the change that had come upon me. But a little boy a few years back, all confidence in and obedience to him, and now talking of settling my bills at the Black Bull Inn!

Gilbert restrained his exhibition of surprise before Redwin, and sat with a contracted brow, brooding over the mysterious incidents of the morning.

I took my departure with Redwin, and we were soon some distance from "The Rest," with Redwin's groom clattering behind our horses' heels.

"What a surprising father you have, Elmore," said he, as we rode on; "I don't know whether I like or hate him. You see I'm frank with you."

"Very."

"If it were not for my doubts as to the reception I might receive, I should often give you a look in at 'The Rest,'" he said.

"Never fear, Redwin."

"You see I've no male companion of my own age about Wharnby," said Redwin; "and when I am not at Wharnby House you cannot imagine how dull my evenings are at home with my grandmother, Elmore," said he. "I have a bright thought. Come and see me!"

"Thank you!" I replied. "But excepting a chance visit to Wharnby House, like yourself, I seldom leave my home."

"But we are young men, each wanting to kill time, Luke Elmore."

"Kill time!" said I. "Surely Paul Redwin's time is wholly pre-occupied! There's a young lady who would chide you, methinks, if you spent *many* evenings from Wharnby House." He turned his head away from me with a start, and for a moment we rode on in silence.

Presently he looked at me, with a laugh.

"You're a shrewd fellow, Elmore; but I hardly understand you. Surely you are not like the fair sex in general, and detect a proposal in every slight attention?"

"But you are engaged, Redwin," said I, smiling faintly. "Why seek to hide what all Wharnby is well aware of, friend?"

"Engaged!" he cried; then moderating his tone, said, "So they say I am engaged? Do *you* think so, Elmore?"

"I have not much doubt."

He looked very sternly before him, and once his upper lip quivered as with pain, and over his strikingly handsome face flitted a softening expression that usurped the old look of haughtiness so peculiar to his countenance.

He did not speak again till we were near the home of the Silvernots.

"Are you going to join me?" asked he, pointing to the house with his whip.

"I have not time; I may look in as I return."

"Good day."

He extended his hand, and shook mine warmly.

"Is it a compact?" he said.

"What?"

"Our future merry meeting."

"As you will. We shall see each other shortly at Wharnby House, and then I shall find you have changed your mind, Redwin."

"Perhaps so."

His look returned to its old haughtiness as he spurred his horse and rode on, leaving me to continue my way alone.

I reached Cliverton about the middle of the afternoon, and found Tom awaiting my arrival at the bar of the Black Bull Inn.

Having settled all demands that my host of the preceding evening had upon me, I re-mounted, and my groom imitated my example.

"This way, sir?" inquired Tom.

"Yes, this way."

I had turned in the direction towards London, much to the astonishment of my groom, who, whistling softly to himself, shook his head and followed.

A quarter of an hour's trot took us out of Cliverton and on

the high road. It was not long before a tasteful villa, of small dimensions, caught my eye, and arrested further progress. There was a winding gravel path leading to the house, bordered on each side with beds of scarlet geraniums, which, late as the season, were in full blossom, and looked bright and fresh. On the stone pillar to which the gate was attached was written "Thornville Villa," and on the brass plate of the gate itself shone forth the name of "Dartford."

"Wait a few moments, Tom," said I, leaping from my horse, and pushing back the gate.

"All right, sir."

But Tom's looks, as I hastily caught a glimpse of them, evidently said, "All wrong." There was a queer twist of his lips, and a knotty appearance about his whole face, that suggested an idea of great mental exertion used to solve some exceedingly tough problem, which indicated no signs of giving up.

Was my manner a problem to myself? I thought not. May not a gentleman inquire after a lady's health, after having met her at a ball, without incurring suspicion and bringing grave doubts to himself? Pooh! ridiculous! Had I not received Paul Redwin at "The Rest" this very morning as a visitor to my sister? To be sure. Rat-a-tat-a-tat-a-tat, tat, tat, TAT! What an extraordinary little brass knocker!—it seemed charged with electricity; the contact with it sent such a peculiar thrill through my veins.

A small footman (everything seemed on a small scale here, as in a doll's house) answered my imperative summons.

"Is Mrs. Morton within?"

"Yes, sir."

I slipped my card into his hand, and followed him to a sitting-room in miniature, the walls of which were ornamented with several portraits in gilt frames, all of Mr. Dartford, in simpering attitudes, with books and blue sky in the background.

The room was chilly and disconsolate, and there was a large inkstand on the table, as big as Mr. Dartford's head, and was the only article that suggested magnitude in the establishment.

A few books, a desk, and a green-baized table by the window, led me to imagine that the room into which I had been shown was Mr. Dartford's study, and I was not mistaken.

"Will you please to follow me, sir?"

With my eyes bent upon a twinkling pair of calves, of unexceptionable proportions, I kept in the track of the small footman.

He stopped, and flung back a door.

"Mr. Elmore."

I was in the room, and Mrs. Morton was advancing towards me.

"This is an unexpected honour, Mr. Elmore."

She was as pretty as ever in the daylight, and I fancied (was it fancy?) that there was the slightest of slight rosy blushes for an instant on her face.

"I hope you will forgive the liberty I have taken, Mrs. Morton," said I, with her tiny hand in mine; "but I could not resist the opportunity of looking in at Thornville Villa."

"You have not come with that sole purpose all the way from Wharnby, Mr. Elmore?" said she, laughingly. "I surely have not received so great an honour."

"I certainly had business at Cliverton; but had I not——"

"There, there—be seated, Mr. Elmore. You are very kind to think of me at all; but spare me protestations."

I took the seat indicated by a wave of her white hand, and she resumed her place before the fairy work-table, from which my arrival had disturbed her.

"Your sister—she is well?"

"Quite well, I thank you. May I hope the same for Mr. Dartford?"

"Oh, Mr. Dartford is never ill!" said she, lightly. "He has an iron constitution, and late hours never affect him. He will be here directly; I have expected him home this last half-hour."

We fell into a hasty chat about the ball, the company, the Silvernots, and my sister.

Of the latter she said—

"I have a promise from that charming girl, Mr. Elmore—I look to you for its fulfilment. I return to London in a few weeks, and Miss Agnes and I must be great friends by that time."

"My want of persuasion shall not detain her at Wharnby, Mrs. Morton," said I, rising to depart.

"Going so soon?" said Mrs. Morton, rising also; "this is a hasty call. Will you not stay till Mr. Dartford returns, and dine with us? It is a long ride to Wharnby."

"My best thanks, but you must excuse me, madam," said I.

"Mr. Dartford would be delighted to have the pleasure."

"Pray present my best respects to him."

"Ah! Mr. Elmore, there are other calls to make," said she, looking at me with all the power of her dark eyes; "that young lady to whom you hastened, on her entrance last night, and whom you danced with immediately. Am I right, Mr. Elmore?"

I coloured. I could not hear any allusion to Celia Silvernot unmoved; and it was with a stammering tongue I hastened to reply, when Mr. Dartford relieved me from my embarrassment by his sudden appearance at the door.

"No, no, Mr. Elmore!" screamed he, pumping my right arm in a vigorous manner; "not off, sir—we shall never allow that. You must dine with us, sir—must he not, Ernestine, eh—eh?"

"Mr. Elmore has, probably, other engagements," answered his sister, moving away from us somewhat indifferently. "What attraction can we offer, to prolong his stay—we two prosy little people?"

"Why not stay, Luke Elmore?" was the whisper at my heart; "what inducement have you to hurry homewards and fly the new friends who offer hospitality so warmly?" I glanced almost unconsciously at Mrs. Morton; she had seated herself at the work-table once more, and was bending over some lace upon it till her ringlets showered before her face, and hid it from my view.

"I have no other engagement, Mr. Dartford," said I, hesitatingly; "but really I am such a stranger, and my riding coat is so out of place, and have merely called to——"

"No ceremony, Mr. Elmore—a fig for ceremony," whistled Mr. Dartford; "it is decided; stay you shall."

He skipped to the bell-rope with an ape-like agility, and rang.

The small footman appeared at the door.

"Tell the page to call in Mr. Elmore's groom, and show him to your room and make him welcome, and let John look to the horses."

"Yes, sir."

"There, sir, it is done; be seated."

"My brother has more influence than I have, it appears, Mr. Elmore," said the young widow, without looking up; "yet I am the oldest friend by half a minute, at least."

"He! he!" laughed Mr. Dartford; "half a minute! that's precise, anyhow; he! he!"

Such a horrid laugh, or attempt to laugh, I had never heard in the course of my life, as Mr. Dartford's. I fairly shuddered, and set my teeth hard to keep them from experiencing that peculiar sensation called "on edge."

It is not my intention to dwell at great length upon this scene, which familiarised me to the inmates of Thornville Villa, and increased the strange interest I took in one of them. It is almost sufficient for the future development of records that have to pass beneath this hand, to say that I dined with them and sat next to Mrs. Morton, who was at one time brilliantly conversational, flashing sentence after sentence of witty allusion to present life at home, or of interest in the world, with a rapidity of utterance and fluency of speech that was perfectly bewildering, and at another, in an abstracted mood, which, no doubt, carried her thoughts far away from present company.

She left us after dessert, and Mr. Dartford tendered me a cigar across the table.

"Thank you," said I, putting it down.

"You do not smoke?" he asked, lighting his cuba at the same time, and puffing behind it till he seemed swelling towards me like a figure in a phantasmagoria.

"Never."

"Well, it is a bad habit, but it's one not easily got over," said Dartford; "I smoked myself into a jaundice with bits of cane at school, and that gave me a taste for it, I suppose. My poor sister's husband, too—ah! he *was* a smoker! It is my belief"—lowering his voice—"he smoked himself as dry as a stick, broke up, and died. They said it was a consumption, I think it was exhaustion."

"You speak of Mr. Morton?"

"Yes; he died at twenty-five; that was three years ago."

"He was Mrs. Morton's senior by many years, I should imagine."

"Two years; that's all; my sister is only five-and-twenty now, and looks younger, I take it."

I ventured to agree with him.

"Between ourselves, sir, if he hadn't died, she would have looked five-and-eighty by this time. He was a bad man, sir; a thorough—— but he's gone, he's gone now. You don't drink!"

This was the second person I had heard Mr. Dartford comment upon during my short acquaintance with him, and neither had received a flattering eulogium from his lips. It was an unpleasant way with him, and made me fidgety. Before we went up-stairs into a tastefully-furnished drawing-room in miniature, where Mrs. Morton awaited us, he had in all confidence picked to pieces, for my especial delectation, three more characters appertaining to the gentry of Cliverton, and bestowed no word of praise on any single being existent in the neighbourhood, with the exception of the slight allusion to his sister that I have already mentioned.

Mrs. Morton had no more dull fits during the evening. She played the piano at my wish, with the skill of a great master. She replied, "She did not sing—she had no voice," to my solicitation, and then, after some pressing, broke into a flood of such entrancing melody as is seldom heard out of the precincts of the Royal Opera—a melody of voice, so clear, so full of tone, that, with my senses ravished from me, I sprang to my feet, and leant across in wonderment and ecstacy.

"You do not sing!" I exclaimed, upon her rising from the music-stool; "you do not sing, Mrs. Morton! What could you mean by telling me you had no voice?"

"Oh! but you may be a bad judge, Mr. Elmore."

We sat before the fire, a curious trio, perhaps, and Mr. Dartford brought up the Silvernots as a topic for conversation, and made such deep inquiries concerning them, and waited so patiently for answers from me, with his large head on one side in fixed attention, that beginning to imagine he must have some hidden reason in the back-ground, I answered more evasively.

Mrs. Morton detected my rising doubts, for she changed the subject to Wharnby, and Wharnby's coming greatness, and interested Mr. Dartford in it immediately, and drew him out into a lengthy, but a very dry, discourse on property and land-tax, till my head fairly ached again with the shower of statistics he kept flinging against it for my mind to grapple with.

Mrs. Morton sang again a plaintive ballad—a song of mourning for one lost—so sweetly, so pathetically, that I could hardly see her graceful figure at the piano for the swimming in my eyes. I thought of her husband, who had died so young, and how she sat there, recalling him to her memory at that moment, and venting her sorrow in such heart-piercing strains of heavenly music—music that I could scarcely think akin to earth.

It was a shock to me to see her look up from the pages of

music before her with the old bright smile, the eye sparkling and tearless, the tone of voice melodious but unfaltering, and say—

"It is rather a pitiful strain, is it not? But the composer is a German, and the Germans are a melancholy-mad sort of a race, and dull in the extreme."

She rattled over the first few notes of the waltz we had had together last night, and added—

"That is better music."

"One will be remembered equally as well as the other," I said, gallantly.

"Ah, Mr. Elmore—take care. I mistrust a flatterer."

She looked full at me, and shook her curls, and held up one finger encircled by many a gem, and laughed a low, musical, heart-stirring laugh.

Oh! that look: it stirred my blood, and made my chest heave, and my eyes betray the admiration I felt at the dazzling beauty seated at the piano, before which I stood; that beautiful woman whom, for the wild moment, I loved. That look has never left me. It is beside me as I write, distinct and palpable as ever; but where are the visions, fleet and maddening, of that moment, when she hid her deep-liquid orbs with her long Circassian lashes, as if fearful of my glance?

I went away reluctantly—the hours had sped with winged celerity—and "The Rest" was twelve miles from Cliverton.

I left her standing in the drawing-room, bidding me "good night," with a sunny smile of farewell greeting, and her brother followed to the hall, and stood talking several minutes with me.

Out in the road at last, with Mr. Dartford, shrieking "Good night!" in a wild falsetto, from the door.

I looked up instinctively at the lighted windows of the drawing-room, as I leaped astride my horse.

The slight figure of Mrs. Morton crossed and re-crossed the light within: to and fro, to and fro—backwards and forwards, backwards and forwards rapidly flitted her shadow by the blind, as if she were pacing the room, actuated by some strong feeling, convulsive with grief or maddened by rage.

I could not forget it, even when I was miles away.

Tom's dry cough—a very hard, grinding cough—evidently intended to attract notice, finally aroused me.

"Well, Tom, have you spent a pleasant evening?" I called out.

"Thankee, sir, I hope you have," he said. "No offence to the gentleman and lady of the house, Mr. Luke; but, axing pardon, the evening might have been pleasanter in the servants'-room—take it all together, sir."

"How was that, Tom?"

"Why, sir, I'm an Englishman, and hates being pumped—that's all, Mr. Luke."

"Pumped!"

"Yes, sir. I hate your inquiring, inquisitive set of fellows, that want to know all about your master and master's family. But that's like lawyer's sarvants."

"Lawyer's?"

"Yes, sir. Why, of course, you knowed Mr. Dartford was a lawyer; he's got a great office near the Bull."

"Has he?"

"Yes, sir. But they didn't get much out of me that'd stand for positive fact, sir, *I'm* inclined to think."

Tom relapsed into a silence, which was occasionally broken by a deep chuckle, significant of his own diplomacy, as we rode towards home and Wharnby.

CHAPTER XVI.

CHANGE!

WINTER has fallen again upon "The Rest;" the north winds blow furiously across the cliffs, and freezingly sweep onwards from the dull restless sea, whose heavy waves break with a rolling crash against the rocks of Wharnby, and vanish into spray. I have attained to nineteen years, and bear them with a proud consciousness of the importance they bestow upon me, and the manly look they, in my vain belief, have brought unto my personal appearance.

The gradual march of events, from my call at Thornville Villa unto the present time (the snow-flakes are falling heavily and noiselessly from the murky heavens overhead, and making of hill, and dale, and woodland one icy blank around), is worth noting, by those who may have found a passing interest in the characters which this story brings back to life long gone before.

With Mrs. Morton—gay, fascinating, accomplished Mrs. Morton!—I have had many interviews previous to her departure for that "choked-up square," her residence in which she had so regretted on the night of the great ball. My sister Agnes and I have paid Mrs. Morton a visit at her brother's house, and been warmly welcomed, and made much of; and Agnes thinks her preferable to Celia Silvernot. My father, who has sunk into an apathetic indifference concerning the progress of his children, makes no comment upon our going or return, but looks at us with his bloodshot eyes, and passes a wasted hand across his forehead, as if endeavouring to call us to remembrance, and to find out what business we had at "The Rest" in which he chanced to be concerned.

My feelings for Mrs. Morton are beyond analysis: I cannot fathom them, or dissect the real influences that bind me towards her as with a mighty spell. I do not try to do so. I am content with the present, and seek no clearer insight through the dim fluttering veil that hangs across the threshold over which I am destined to pass foot. I know that in her society I am as one infatuated by her beauty, whose eyes are dizzy with drinking in her charms, and whose head appears to whirl and throb beneath the strange power which she wields over me, and which increases each time I see or sit beside her. In the first few hours of absence, I can think of little else but the songs she has sung so melodiously before the piano in the little drawing-room, and the glances we have interchanged. Sometimes I think that I am not indifferent to her; and she, who has mingled with the world—the bright glittering side of the world—so much, has found in me something not of her sphere—something unlike those with whom many months of each year are passed, and is attracted by it for the very adverseness of its nature. But this may be a youth's vanity, or she may be testing the strength of her powers of caption on my inexperience to while away dull hours at Cliverton. I do not love her—I feel assured of that. There are none of those swayings of the whole soul—those sensations of reverence, and almost holy adoration, that I had had once, and that had been blasted by the lightning; but there is, in place thereof, a fevered, burning recollection, which I cannot grapple with, and which leaves but empty air in my clenched hands whenever I vainly seek to grasp the reality which shackles my thoughts to Mrs. Morton.

We part, with many promises.

"You will come to London, Mr. Elmore?" she says. "I shall be able to receive you at my house in Cavendish Square with more satisfaction than I have done at Cliverton."

"Rely upon it, my dear madam," I reply, "if I ever visit London, I shall eagerly avail myself of the opportunity of renewing our acquaintance; but I fear it must be your return to Cliverton that will give me the pleasure of seeing you again."

"Oh, I hate Cliverton!" cries the little lady; "and my brother is so tiresome and prolix over his papers and red tape. You *must* have some business to bring you to London, now and then, I feel assured."

"I can scarce remember being in the mighty Babylon, madam," I answer.

"Well, there is my card," she says, tendering it to me; "if you ever deign to pay me a visit, you are welcome. Good-bye—I shall write to Agnes."

She passes from my sight, and I am very dull and out of spirits for the next few days.

Miss Osborne has assumed all the duties of housekeeper to "The Rest," and has resigned the office of governante over my sister Agnes, to whom teaching would be now out of place, indeed. There is an existent affection between Miss Osborne and her late pupil, which is exhibited by the latter, despite all her angry fits of impatience and sharp rejoinders to questions quietly asked of her by Miss Osborne.

Miss Osborne is attached to Agnes more than she herself imagines, and takes great interest in all concerning her late pupil, and often hazards friendly advice and counsels, when she considers it necessary on her part to offer them. Agnes is sometimes reprimanded, too, in a sweet manner, full of sisterly reproof, which, though not always a counteracting agent, subdues at times the variable nature of my sister, from its very power over her better self.

Still, not a hundred Miss Osbornes could move her one jot from her own determinations when they are fixed and bent upon, and not a hundred more could decipher all the thoughts that throng busily, ever busily, in the recesses of that heart, of which no one has the key.

Friendly meetings pass between Wharnby House and "The Rest," week after week, and in addition, Paul Redwin often comes riding up the avenues to see his old friend, Luke! He has become so attached to me, that my heart bounds to him like a Pythias to a Damon; and in my new-formed friendship I forget that deep attention to my brother Gilbert, which should ever be his due—forget that Redwin has stepped between me and my first love—forget everything but that he is very often at "The Rest," and that the great red-brick house in which his grandmother resides occasionally holds Luke Elmore within its walls.

Mrs. Redwin improves upon further acquaintance, and setting aside a weakness on her part, in conversing on no other subject than her dear grandson Paul, is an amiable old lady of an aristocratic order.

Paul Redwin's visits to "The Rest," at first frowned menacingly at by my haughty sire, are tolerated for my sake, and his dashing manner and frank ways often cause my father to smile behind his hand, and have even worn off the first unfavourable impressions which Gilbert entertained for him—impressions which had birth in their susceptibility for me.

And Paul Redwin, with all his dashing frank manner, his volubility of discourse, his loud ringing laughs,—is peculiarly alive to every movement of my sister Agnes, and has an attentive ear for every word she utters, and falters in his voice if he speak a dozen syllables to her in succession.

Yes, it is all over with Paul Redwin! He has forgotten his first vows, although he dare not say so to himself; he has left the first image he set up in his idolatry alone on the dry sands of a desert, standing grimly in the light of that burning sun which seems to mock its desolation; he has sought another shrine, and, with blazing eyes and panting breath, kneels down and worships with a tenfold passion—a passion he had never dreamed himself capable of being so great a slave unto.

The crisis of so many first loves is fast advancing. Celia's cheek grows more ashen, and her look more wan, and her red lips are tightly compressed as with pain, when she hears of Paul, *her* Paul, paying such frequent visits to "The Rest." Agnes, on the contrary, wears a brighter look upon her face and a more sparkling light within her eyes, and her cheeks are flushed with the glow of conquest—the first conquest of the girl of seventeen! She thinks not of her dear friend Celia, sitting at home with her great heart that held so much of love broken at its outset, misplaced at the beginning, shattered in its youth. She flirts with Redwin, and bends her head to hear his whispered compliments, when we are altogether at Wharnby House, and the flush of scorn, and of awakened pride, gleams across Celia's face, and shows the woman—she who has been to Redwin but little more than a poor jest—rousing herself to a sense of her position. The night is well remembered, with the fire burning and crackling in the grate, and the Silvernots and Elmores circled round it—Vaudon taking down some books from a case in the recess, and reading them as he stands—and Mr. Dartford (yes, Mr. Dartford) next to Arabella, and quite a large-headed gallant in his attentions. My father and Gilbert are absent, and the rector is at home in his villa near the church.

Agnes and Celia are side by side, and Redwin next to Agnes. The old by-play, as at the Cliverton ball, but more divulged on Redwin's part, whose very look is intense love; and which Agnes meets so oddly unconscious, and flinches not away at, in her simplicity and innocence! Mrs. Silvernot looks restlessly from the corner seat, and fidgets with her nervous hands at the gold watch-chain round her neck.

The night is well remembered, with its partings, with the cold kiss which Celia gives back to Agnes—she is not false enough to lavish the old warm caresses on the pretty robber—with the earnest, searching gaze Celia gives Paul Redwin, as he extends his hand.

In the confusion of adieux, Celia forgets that I am standing at the back, and says to him, in a voice that is hardly articulate, from its suppressed agony—

"Paul, you will not come here again? Please don't, for my sake—for I cannot bear it."

"Celia!" he stammers forth.

"Do not say a word; it would be a folly or a falsehood, and either would be unworthy of you. I am so glad you have never said a word to mamma about it—it is so much the best."

"Celia!" he says again.

"I do not reproach you—*she* is so beautiful, how could you help it, Paul? She is so much above me, and is so different in her manner from my old way of pleasing you in everything. I only wish—I—I only wish you had not come so often here."

"You say, come here no more?"

"Oh! no more—no more!" she pleads. "I shall soon get happy, if I do not see you, and know that you are really engaged to her, and have forgotten the silly talk we had one day together."

"But, Celia——"

"It is useless," she interrupts, in a firmer tone; "if you gave me your oath this night that all should be altered, I could not love you truly any more. You never loved me—your heart strays away too soon."

I hear all this unseen; it is spoken so quickly, that hardly a moment of time has intervened; and it is ended—that short dialogue of despair—and Celia has stolen unnoticed to her room, ere all "good-nights" have been interchanged.

The night is cold, and the snow falls thickly on us in our passage from the street-door to the carriage-steps. Redwin's face is dark and frowning, as he escorts Agnes quickly across the strip of snow.

"Why, what is the matter, Mr. Redwin?" I hear her ask. "A fresh quarrel with poor Celia? How black and angry you are looking, to be sure!"

"*Miss Silvernot* and I never quarrel, Miss Agnes. We are hardly interested enough in each other to quarrel."

"Jesting again, Mr. Redwin."

"Nay,"—he whispers something, and she darts away from his arm, and is in the carriage.

Vaudon, Edward, and I follow. Agnes sits silent, and I fancy her hand trembles.

"Good-night, gentlemen," cries Redwin.

We echo his good-night.

"Good-night, Agnes."

She is close to the window, and yet does not answer.

"Good-night, Agnes," he says a second time.

My ears are very quick to-night, for, though low is the response, I hear her whisper back at last—

"Good-night——Paul!"

CHAPTER XVII.

PAUL REDWIN KEEPS HIS PROMISE.

THE evening of the following day I rode over to Mrs. Redwin's, to keep an appointment with her grandson.

I found the old lady and Redwin seated together by the fire, the former listening to some energetic speech of Paul's with great attention, and wiping her eyes from time to time with her lace handkerchief.

"You are but a boy; indeed, my dear Paul, you are but a simple boy."

"Oh! nonsense, grandmother; I was of age last week, you know."

"Your poor father was thirty——"

"Mr. Elmore!" announced the servant.

"Ah! Luke, old fellow, you are late," and "Good evening, Mr. Elmore," were my salutations.

Mrs. Redwin lingered a few moments, asking some unimportant questions, and then, at a sign which my quick glance detected the grandson bestowing upon her, departed with an audible sigh.

Redwin was not in his usual spirits; there was a forced air of hilarity in his manner which was not natural; and more than once, for the want of something to say, he snatched up the poker and battered ferociously at the coals.

With an inward guess at the coming disclosure, I was content to wait patiently for the *dénouement*.

"Shall we play that gambit once more?" he asked, pointing to the chess-table and ivory men thereon.

"With pleasure."

He drew the table between us, and silently we arranged the men. Paul knocked the king off the table in his attempt to make the first move, picked it up, and then swept the pieces *en masse* to the centre.

"It's no use, Elmore," he said; "I have some advice to ask you, some disclosure to make known."

"What is it?" I asked.

"Some months ago, friend Luke," commenced he, plunging into the subject, "you twitted me with a partiality for the society of the Silvernots, and hinted that I was not entirely free from an affection for the younger daughter. In confidence,

Elmore, I own I was touched—slightly impressed, that was all. I never proposed to the parents of Celia, understand."

"But to Celia herself," I remarked.

"No, no," he quickly replied; "a few gallant words—a flirtation, if you will—no more, upon my honour."

"Then, you have to tell me that with the first love you are tired; and that to have won her heart, and not to wear it, was your object. Do I comprehend you?"

I said it sternly, with the pale face and trembling figure of last night's Celia before me.

"Not my object, as God's my witness, Elmore!" he cried, passionately; "I was in a dream, and all was unreal and full of visions. I have remorse burning at my heart for the few words of love I ever said to her. But she is young, and we have seen but little of each other; and so the delusion will soon wear out, and die of its own weakness. But, Elmore, I have found out my first fancy was delusive through the real love, the fierce passions which men know, and which wrings the heart-strings with its intensity. I have seen the one without whom my whole life will be a curse, my existence a dead blank. I love your sister Agnes with my whole soul."

"Oh, Redwin, I expected this avowal. I know not what to say."

"Listen," said he, placing his hand upon my arm, and speaking in a tremulous voice that told of the depth of his excitement; "from the night of the Cliverton ball, I have loved your sister. She is so beautiful, so good."

"Spare me her praises, I am her brother."

"But you must know her virtues, her loveliness; you, happy fellow, see her every day," he ran on rhapsodically; "she is perfection, is she not?"

"To your tale. Is there not more to tell?"

"When I first saw Agnes, and first loved her, Luke, I thought of Celia, and felt like a traitor in her sight. Candidly, my friend, I tried to wrestle with this new-born passion for Celia's sake—for my own word, my own half-uttered expressions, made though they were in a light hour, and jesting mood. I started the following day for Wharnby House, and yet, impelled as it were by destiny, I found myself at the lodge gates of 'The Rest.' We met more frequently. I saw Agnes every time I called on you. I loved her, I felt my whole happiness was bound up in her consent."

"And she so young!"

"Young!" he cried; "she will be eighteen soon, Luke."

"True."

"Now, Luke, I believe that Agnes is aware of my attachment, and that—that she would not reject me."

"You are lucky in your loves, Redwin."

"Oh, I have great hope," he said, without heeding my remark. "It is that which lightens my heart and makes me happy. But I spoke of advice; it is necessary, you will own. How shall I proceed, Luke?"

"Proceed?"

"Yes, with your father."

He looked blankly at me for a reply.

My father! I had not thought of him. What would he say or do, and how would he receive so startling a revelation?

Redwin saw my dubious look.

"Your father is an enigma, Elmore, and I dread an interview with him more than all. He may crush me with his bitter tirades, he may forbid me the house—he—Agnes's father!"

"You must watch your opportunity, Paul."

"I wish to be engaged to Agnes; to know that no one can step between me and her; to call her my betrothed, my promised bride."

What a difference had love made in Paul Redwin! Where were the foppish airs; the pretentious style so characteristic of him; the self-conceit in which he wrapped himself; the mannerism which had grown with his growth? To me, all gone.

"And what has your grandmother to say concerning this engagement?" I asked. "There are two sides worthy consideration, Redwin."

"Oh, my grandmother thinks I have just come from school, and am hardly fit to be trusted alone yet," he said with a laugh.

"She has objections?"

"Hardly objections, Elmore," said he; "but she is alarmed at my strength of purpose. She has so long considered me a little boy, who requires careful watching, and who must not go out in the night air without a woollen comforter and a respirator, that I am not a man in her opinion, and never shall be, were I to live to threescore years and ten. But I have her consent for all that. She has but one name on her heart, and that is 'Paul.'"

Mrs. Redwin rejoined us by the fireside, and Redwin brought up the topic of his second love, and the old lady smoothed her silk dress with her white, jewelled hands, and crossed them in her lap, and listened attentively to her grandson, gazing at him with a mingled look of love and anxiety. Whenever he spoke of Agnes's beauty, and his own unworthiness, which he did fifty times within the hour, she grew fidgety, and tossed her head indignantly from side to side. Paul unworthy of her! There was not a crowned head in all Christendom that would not have been honoured by the alliance —her own dear Paul!

"Paul is so young a man, Mr. Elmore," said she, turning to me with an odd, commingling look of friendship and dignity, "that he may not know his own mind—youth is so changeable, so full of caprice. He may be in love with your sister; perhaps he is, poor boy, perhaps he is."

"Perhaps, grandmother!" indignantly reiterated Paul.

"My dear Paul," she answered, quickly, "how *can* you know? Have you not been as variable as the wind, like your poor father, from a child of three years old? Did you ever make up your mind resolutely to anything? You know you never have."

"I have made up my mind at last."

"He thinks so," said she, turning to me pityingly, "so let him have his way. He has nothing to do but to make known his intentions and his wishes to your father, Mr. Elmore, and to become engaged, and to forget his old grandmother as quickly as if she had never been."

"Never to forget her, or to change in his deep love for her," he said, laying his hand affectionately on hers.

The old lady brightened up directly.

"Ah, youth, youth! would that you could all be furnished with perspective glasses," she said, holding his hand in hers, "or that your wisdom teeth came earlier. Well, you will be a happy couple, I hope; I'm sure I don't see what is to hinder you, myself. But don't be rash, Paul; you don't think of marrying directly. Let it be a long engagement, my own boy. Don't throw me off too soon; let me prepare, and get reconciled to our separation."

"A long engagement! How many months do you——?"

"Months, child!" cried the old lady, "years—years."

Paul gave a blank smile at me, and passed his hands through his hair, but said no more.

"Paul will never desert Wharnby, and will never mingle in the dissipations of London seasons and London frivolities. Your sister must not expect that," she said.

"I am not aware what expectations my sister may build on or look forward to, my dear Mrs. Redwin. I have but heard of my friend Paul's attachment to Agnes this evening, from his own lips."

"It will be better not," continued she, not heeding my remark; "she will, doubtless, think so herself. That unfortunate occurrence which has——"

She stopped. Redwin looked embarrassed, and I felt the blood mounting to my face. It was the first sting I had received from strangers; the first sign of the inheritance of disgrace left me by my erring mother.

"But we need not continue the subject," she said, quickly; "from all that I can hear, Miss Elmore is a quiet, amiable young woman, and will make Paul a good wife. Dear me, how very strange it sounds! *Paul's wife!* Lord bless us!"

Agnes was the principal subject of conversation during the evening, and I returned home with my ears ringing with her praises. Paul came, day after day, and left, morning after morning, or evening after evening, with his undivulged confession to my father. He sat by Agnes's side; he talked alone to her—he had no voice or ears for any one save her alone—he sat as one entranced; and even Edward, who took little heed of events passing around in which he was unconcerned, knew all about it, and teazed Agnes into a frenzy, after Paul's departure, or in my father's absence.

But my father sat moodily eyeing them, without dreaming of the secret of their love, or went to another room with Vaudon, and spent the evening thither, returning late at night, after Paul had ridden home, with bloodshot eyes, and the drunkard's stamp on every movement. Paul summoned up his courage for a final effort; and, after begging me not to leave the room, took advantage of being with my father, one winter's morning.

My father was sitting in his leathern chair by the fireside, holding a book in his shaking hands, when Paul, with an unsteady voice, dashed into the subject.

"My dear Mr. Elmore," he began, "you—you will excuse my abruptness, I hope; but the matter upon which I desire to arrest your attention is so very important, that——"

He came to a dead stop upon my father closing his book, and looking him steadily in the face.

"I am your servant, Mr. Redwin," he said, languidly.

"Mr. Elmore," Paul began again, after a re-assuring look from me, "you will pardon my embarrassment, but I would speak upon a subject all-important to myself, and in which my whole life is bound. You cannot have been blind to my affection for your daughter Agnes, and——"

"Affection!—Agnes!" he murmured. "Agnes! affection? Go on, if you please; I surely comprehend you not."

Paul, fearful of a second interruption, dashed into the heart of his discourse, and, having once broken through the ice, gave vent to a flood of eloquence and passionate exhortation which carried my father out of his dreamy state into a man eagerly attentive, and tremblingly alive to every word. Paul concluded at last, and, white as death, awaited the reply. My father glanced from him to me, gave a groan, as if of pain, and was several minutes silent. We waited patiently till he broke silence, which he did in an almost inaudible tone of voice—

"It matters little what I say or assert; my children think and act for themselves. You speak as if Agnes's love were already won—the love of a child of seventeen!"

"I speak—I hope——"

"Give me an attentive hearing, Mr. Redwin," he said, calmly. "I have listened to your discourse; nay, I have been moved by it. I was not aware of the changes time has made upon me and my children—children that were little boys and girl when I first made my rest upon this coast; and now, as with a turn of a hand, the scene changes, and a suitor for my daughter comes to tell me I must rest no more—I must awake to the old bustle of the world and action, and live no longer for my own peace. You love her?"

"Beyond all the expression that my speech can give," cried Paul.

"You are a rich man; the son of a gentleman?"

"I am."

"Then what have I to urge against my daughter's choice? My brain has echoed with thoughts about her future life so long—has schemed for her—has trembled for her after destiny—ay, trembled, sir—that I can resign my charge with a light heart, and thank God she is in good hands. Mr. Redwin, you have my consent. You have fulfilled your promise, and reminded me you have become a man."

He extended his hand towards my friend, who grasped it warmly and poured forth his thanks.

"I have one wish to express concerning this engagement, Mr. Redwin."

"And that is——?"

"That it be a long one."

"I trust——"

"It is better in some cases; it is the death-blow in others. I think it will be better for you both that three years, or thereabouts, intervene (she will be twenty then) before you think of a home of your own and a wife at your hearth."

"But my dear Mr. Elmore, for what reason?" urged Paul.

"Supposing that you have formed too high an estimate of my daughter's character—or, rather, my daughter's love for you—would it not be wiser policy to find out you have been deceived, ere the wedding-ring binds her to you for a life-time? Agnes is but a girl, hardly released from the tasks of a governess, and the routine of a child's education; and her mind is not yet formed, and she may take her fancies for love till the bloom of romance is brushed away, and the fruit is sour and unripe, or turns to ashes on the lip."

"I have every confidence, Mr. Elmore."

"Ay, now!" bitterly replied my father; "we enter life all confidence, but how many quit it with those feelings at the breast, with which they start in the race, all energy? I do not say I will bind you to three years, Paul Redwin; I will watch the progress of your engagement; yes, I, so apathetic, will watch closely, and will rescind my decree, if all I hope prove true."

"There is no cause to doubt."

"No cause," said he, hollowly; "you have not found the gauge to detect the real from the ideal—you are a lover."

My father grew moody and depressed, and Redwin, taking his absent manner as indicative of a wish to conclude the conversation, took his departure light of heart, happy and expectant.

"Luke," said he to me, after the door had closed upon my friend, "this Redwin, what does he intend doing after his marriage, do you know?"

"Doing?"

"Yes; will he stay at Wharnby—will he go to London and become a politician, and an ambitious man, and mix with the world, and grasp at shadows on the wall?"

"He looks for happiness in Wharnby."

"That is well," he said. "Oh! Luke, I cannot believe in Agnes's life passing on so smooth a sea; I dare not think so, looking on her face. That face gives the lie to peace and contentment. I dream of it mingling with the crowd, I see it with other faces bent down and observing—faces of men and women, and grinning devils."

"Father!" cried I, alarmed at his increasing passion.

"It is her mother's face—the self-same face that I stood before God's altar with when sixteen summers had but shed a beauty on it bright as heaven, but false as hell. She has the old ways—the superficial airs of society, as if she had mixed with throngs of fashionable people all her life, and knew them thoroughly. Luke, Agnes has been my mental curse from a pretty child with golden ringlets, dancing about the house—from a grave, thoughtful little girl, wandering about the chambers of 'The Rest'—to now, a young woman, distinct again, and full of schemes that have herself in view. God grant all this to be but hallucination, but I hear a voice thundering in my ears like doom—'No rest for Agnes Elmore; no life of home, or angels 'neath the roof-tree. Her destiny is otherwise—the seal is set upon her fate.'"

"A morbid fear, dear father."

"It is not alone in Agnes, but more or less in all of you; the taint of the guilty blood inherited from one lost to every sense of right," he cried, vehemently. "I have no faith in my children. They put no trust in me: I put no trust in them."

"Have you learned to disbelieve in all our affection and respect, then?" I asked, reproachfully.

"What have you done indicative of a son's honour to his father?" he retorted. "What confidence is there between us? All self—self."

I could not reply: I felt the accusation was not altogether groundless. That I had a son's love for him, I knew; but that I had ever shown it by word or action, ever let it step between me and my inclinations, I could not prove, and so remained silent with bowed head.

"And Gilbert, is there confidence there? Do I know the secrets of his heart, or hold the love that is my right. Do I——"

"Stay, stay," I cried. "Doubt Agnes, doubt me, doubt us all, but that true heart—that faithful and unselfish son."

"Would that I could," he cried, wringing his hands; "would that it were possible! and Edward, crafty and miserly, a young usurer, with no Elmore blood or honour in him. All false!"

Was this part of the secret of the solitary debauches? had he sought relief in the wine-cup from such delusive ideas as these, which seemed engraven on his brain indelibly, and burning? What a terrible misconception of us all—what a fatal disease preying upon his once generous mind, so full of noble motive.

"My ambition, Luke," continued he, gloomily, "was to pass my life with my children, to die in their arms, with their saddening faces bent weepingly over my death-bed—to have rest from my great misfortune and disgrace here upon the cliff. Now, when Agnes is married, when you have all gone from me, and have homes of your own, and wives of your own, and cares of your own, this will be 'The Rest.' Not till then."

I exerted my endeavours to dissuade him from the crude opinion he had formed upon his children without avail; the more argument I strived to enforce as the truth upon his stubborn mind, the less did he seem open to conviction.

I must see Gilbert, and disclose all particulars of the interview, and we must take counsel together against this growing darkness of my father's mind, and wrestle against his unnatural prejudice, and find the weapons that we have to combat against, and the enemies we have to meet.

But the day expired without a conference with Gilbert, and the next morning there were more urgent thoughts, and too much distress in a new shape to give my old suspicions utterance.

In the morning my father was found in his bed with a livid face and half-deadened form, marked by the silent leaden hand of paralysis that had drawn the heavy folds of his curtains away in the still night, and with its noiseless strength struck at him in the dark and left him a poor helpless clod of earth upon his bed.

CHAPTER XVIII.

THE WANING LIGHT OF HOME.

It was many weeks before my father could pass from his room, leaning heavily on Vaudon's arm, and griping at the hand-rail for support at every tread.

Weeks and weeks before he sat in his leathern chair, shrunken, emaciated, and livid as the dead with the changes of years and years upon him.

The black hair had become an iron grey—the eyes were sunken, bloodshot, and glaring, his left hand was palsy-stricken, and his right was dead and withered like the side on which the leaden hand had fallen.

The tall form was no longer erect, and unbending, and he appeared one over whom the Psalmist's allotted period of years had passed and bowed him to the earth. With the changes on his outward form came another change in his seething brain that was never still and never calm, and that had been diseased since she who should have been a mother to us dishonoured him in the proud days of his strength. All the evil nature, the sinful pride, the wild irritability, the gloomy mistrust increased a hundredfold in his affliction ; and all the good, the high sense of honour, the father's love, vanished and became a void.

From the day he came down stairs, a tottering old man, side by side with the dark majestic figure of his mysterious friend—so great a contrast, with his broad chest and sturdy giant frame, to the one who leant upon his arm—he seemed to have no more thought for his sons—to have no more consideration for them—hardly to be aware that they were even present with him.

To Gilbert's affectionate concern he replied by a cold apathy that was not feigned, or by a mocking irony as if he were returning sarcasm for sarcasm—to Edward and me he never addressed a word, and hardly deigned a reply, although I have seen his wandering eyes glancing suspiciously at us if we spoke together in an undertone, as though we were plotting against his life. To Redwin, who came every evening, he was equally indifferent, and never commented on the engagement between him and Agnes, and indeed seemed to have forgotten all particulars of the interview, although future events will prove that his recent affliction had not cancelled the recollections of the day when Paul Redwin kept his promise and proved his manhood. To Miss Osborne he was coldly polite; but to Agnes he was a doting father, lavishing upon her the most extravagant marks of affection, and exhibiting a father's pride in praises of her beauty, intellect, and grace, which, so contrary to his old manner, he would repeat in rapid succession with his arm round her or his hand in hers. He never stirred from "The Rest" now; he could not listen patiently to the remonstrances of his old friend the little rector, and seemed never at ease in his presence, and but released when he was gone.

And that accursed pride had assumed such wild authority over him, that even Vaudon had to succumb to it, and give way to his new arrogance. He would speak of his riches and his position for hours at a time; and in one interview between Mrs. Redwin and him, he had assumed such lofty airs, that the old lady had abruptly taken her departure, without a word concerning the "engagement," and had registered a vow never to cross the Elmore threshold again on any pretence whatever; and he would draw his dressing-gown closer round him when he passed the servants in the passages, lest their touch should bring contamination. Added to all this the besotting influence of drink (fatal habit, that knows no change till its victim lies within the grave!)—the ravings, or childish weepings, whilst beneath its influence—and one may conjecture the little happiness contained within the walls of "The Rest."

And though my father knew it not—and though I never whispered the secret to my brothers, to Agnes, to Miss Osborne, or Jacques Vaudon—and I never read upon their faces the terrible conviction that seared my own mind, and made me tremble with a mighty fear—I knew all these signs were of a second madness, and that his reason was unsound and shaking since his illness, if even before that time he had been wholly sane; or that his misanthropy of old days, or his sudden love of drink, were not but different phases of an intellect that had never recovered from its fall.

Redwin, with consummate tact, steered clear of my father in his sullen moods, and forgot any restraint he might have felt, in his close attention to Agnes, and in his unconsciousness of events drifting before his eyes.

To Redwin and Agnes the time seemed passing magically; and the influence of that new born-passion appeared to have a salutary effect upon the character of my sister, whose dark shadings seemed receding in the light.

But time went on—the north winds went back beyond the sea—the drifting spars and floating remnants of old wrecks were no longer washed ashore—the green, young buds expanded into leaves, beneath the glowing sun that set later every night behind the distant sea-line far away—the earth grew bright with flowers, and spring was young and golden.

The loves of Redwin and Agnes made steady progress; and, if Agnes were a trifle more capricious and more exacting towards her lover, there was nothing antagonistic to female nature in that; and Redwin bore all most complacently, and kept his loftiness in the background, and his old off-hand way completely out of sight.

Mrs. Morton having left Wharnby, and Redwin coming to "The Rest" night after night, my old ways were returned to perforce, and I seldom quitted home for two hours together, excepting when I paid occasional visits to Wharnby House, where I saw nothing of Celia Silvernot. She had gone to London, to spend the winter at a distant relative's, Mrs. Silvernot informed me. She had not been very well, and change, Mrs. Silvernot thought, would do her good.

But there was a frequent guest in the place of the smart Paul, in my new-found acquaintance, Mr. Dartford, who had resigned his bachelor tactics after five-and-thirty years of single blessedness, and had come, lance in rest and helmet fixed, into the lists, with the Arabella colours in his plume.

Yes, hope had again sprung into being, and the elder daughter of the Wharnby House was soft and amiable, and had accepted the proposals from Mr. Dartford, and had become engaged to his large head, and the day was fixed for some early date in summer.

I had another subject for my marked observance in the person of Miss Osborne, who began to attract an uncommon interest towards her. I noticed that Miss Osborne had paid a visit every week to Cliverton for some months past, and had not considered it worthy of comment or observation, till the regularity of the time and day struck me as peculiar. Connecting this incident with the day on which Agnes and I escorted her from Cliverton, I, although not naturally inquisitive, puzzled my brains in the endeavour to attribute some feasible motive for her somewhat eccentric conduct; but, none presenting itself, I was contented to remain in ignorance, perfectly assured of her honour and integrity.

I have said but little of Miss Osborne, but what pages could I not fill of her gentleness—her sisterly attachment to us all—the love and esteem in which we all held her—the hold she had upon our hearts? Her life had been of such an even tenor, so little disturbed by our petty troubles or household trifles, that, until the time of my father's sudden illness, she had almost dreamed away her life.

Since his recovery, she appeared to me to have become suddenly depressed in spirits, or to be suffering from ill health; her face was paler than ordinary, and her lips almost bloodless; and more than once I had entered the room appropriated to her, on some slight errand, and found her with her thin, white hands spread before her face.

"You are not well, Miss Osborne," I ventured to observe, upon discovering her position in the manner indicated.

"Yes, I am, Mr. Luke," said she, snatching her pen from the desk, and writing, hurriedly, a few lines on some paper before her. "Oh! I am very well. What reason have you for thinking otherwise?"

"You are looking pale, Miss Osborne."

"Oh! it is only my contrast with your rosy cheeks," she said, with a forced laugh; "I am naturally pale."

I shook my head in doubt.

"You will pardon me, Miss Osborne," I said; "but I must not place credence in your statement. You are harassed, and have some weight upon your mind; I can see it in your face. Surely you have known us long enough to put trust in us, and to believe that we can assist you."

"No, no!" she said, shading her eyes, "you mistake me—I am not ill—I am very well. I thank you for your cheering words—I have every faith; but I am well, Mr. Luke, indeed, I am."

It would have been useless, as well as cruel, to attempt to press her further, or to convince her against her will; so I let the matter drop; and Miss Osborne seemed growing paler and more wan with every day.

I had seen but little of my brother Gilbert for several days; he had been closeted in his room, writing very earnestly, and we had but met at the dinner-table in the evening; so, more and more interested in Miss Osborne, and concerned for her failing health, I resolved to enter my brother's study, and confer with him upon the subject, trusting to his keen perceptions to throw some light upon the mystery.

To my surprise, no answer was returned to my knock, and I softly entered the room, and stood amazed.

The white blinds had not been drawn up since the preceding night, and threw a sombre shadow over everything—on the books upon the table, and the despairing figure of my brother Gilbert, who was leaning over his unopened desk, with outstretched arms and weary head.

The thought immediately suggested itself to me that there was a sympathy in the grief or inward sorrow of Miss Osborne and Gilbert, and that my power might go far to alleviate it.

I closed the door, and locked it on the inner side, as a preventive against intruders, and advanced towards Gilbert. I had never seen him overcome by distress and doubt before, and I knew that it was no common power could have bowed his strong nature to submission.

"Gilbert!"

I laid my hand upon his shoulder, and he started to his feet, and, holding by the table for support, looked at me wildly, almost defiantly.

"Gilbert!"

His features softened, and he replied.

"Oh! Luke—what is it?"

"I have come to seek you, but I have not come to see my elder brother prostrated by affliction without offering him a brother's help."

"There is a true heart yet," he murmured; "I had imagined the new life of society—the new friends at your side—had weaned you from the cripple."

"There is no power in society, or friend that could do that," I answered.

"Thank God for it."

"But, Gilbert, what has happened? What fearful mystery could lower you to that sad figure of despair?"

He hesitated.

"Do you fear to confide in me? Do you fear I shall abuse your trust, or offer you no comfort?"

"'When condolence is of no avail, it is cruelty to use it.'"

They were my own words, uttered on that summer evening when we stood in the hall of "The Rest," after that visit to Wharnby House, in which my love died before its time, and my hopes were trampled to the ground.

"Do not mock me with my own words, Gilbert! Remember those more true, spoken on the sick-bed of my youth, when you came, changed in all but a brother's heart, to sit beside me and say, 'I shall have you to help me—your kind heart to guide me. A brother's love unites us in a bond, which no misfortune will now ever separate.'"

"I will tell you."

He said it in a low tone of voice, motioning me at the same time to his side.

We stood by each other, his hand upon my arm, his large, black eyes fixed steadily on my face.

"Luke, I have loved."

That was all his secret—all his powerful grief—told in the few words just uttered, proved by the haggard features turned towards me.

"My dear Gilbert!"

Where is the alleviating balm for that burning pain which seems as if it would never die, but grips at the heart-strings, and tears away all self-control?

"But——"

"But whom have I loved? ask you. Can I love but one? Have I seen but one face worth the loving?"

"Miss Osborne?" I replied, half interrogatively.

"Yes, Miss Osborne—beautiful, intellectual, gifted by God with rare powers, of which you know nothing, but which I worship. Thrown into constant companionship with me, I loved her above all earthly bliss, all earthly ties. I told my love a few weeks back; I poured out the burning secrets of my breast, but (bitterly) I was a cripple, a poor, deformed outcast."

"It was not for that."

"How know you?" he asked, sharply; "for what else could she so coldly, so silently reject my love, and turn from me with her haughty step and her cold expressions of respect, esteem—all, all but love?"

"Did she say there were no obstacles on your side—no father's pride even?—a barrier as insurmountable as destiny?"

"She would not express one word for good or evil in the case. At first she struggled to be gone, and then, overpowered by my excited speech, she stood and listened, white as death, and trembling like a leaf. She heard me out, and then replied, 'That it was madness to hope on my part, for it was an impossibility, and beyond all hope.' She said more."

He stopped and drew a long breath. I waited patiently for him to continue.

"She concluded in icy words, and to the effect," he resumed, after a long pause, "that she trusted there would be no recapitulation of the subject to her—that it should pass, and be forgotten: but for a word, a look, to betray my feelings, and wound hers again, would be the signal for her to leave 'The Rest' for ever."

"Did she offer no kind word to mitigate the harshness of her refusal?"

"She was deeply pained with the knowledge that I had ever looked so beneath my position, and regretted she had ever come to Wharnby. No more."

"This is a terrible revelation," I said, "but there is nothing to advise but forgetfulness. I believe it is better that Miss Osborne should have annihilated all hope and love, than that she should have responded to your passion, and brought misery on both of you."

"Why do you think that, Luke?"

"Our father's pride, I have already said; a pride that would not give way to save you from disgrace or ruin."

"I do not know," he answered, dubiously; "I have never asked it, and I cannot think he would step between me and the ambition of my life."

"You know him not. Your ambition, in his eyes, would have been a degradation."

"And he despises the world," said Gilbert; "strange inconsistency!"

"And Vaudon——"

"Oh, Vaudon!" he interrupted; "that man knows my secret, I feel assured. He meets me in my walks, besets my path, and hints what folly it were to degrade oneself by a low marriage; and tells me stories of elopements and disgrace, as if the story of my own mother were not graven deep enough."

"What think you Vaudon counsels?"

"He never speaks enough to give me ground to meet him, or refute him," said Gilbert; "but my blood boils with his cold sneers. He would applaud my lowering Miss Osborne to a grave of ignominy, if it was in the power of man, and curse my folly by an honourable marriage. But we are pitted against each other, and there will be a battle ere long—ay, a battle to the death."

"What do you mean?"

"No matter, Luke. Time, time. We shall see the mask drop ere long, and then—Heaven for the Elmores!"

"To return to your distress—which I do, Gilbert, most unwillingly—suffer me to ask one question. Supposing Miss Osborne had refused your offer, not for want of appreciation of the generous and unselfish affection which prompted it—not for want of love for you in return, but for her own true estimation of our father's character, her knowledge of the grief and the division she would call up in the household, and the certainty of a dark futurity for both—do you not think, if she had acted for such reasons, she has acted well?"

"I do not know. I think that would be a greater torture to me—a more cruel fate. God forbid *that*, for her sake, as well as mine."

Seeing the agony my supposition caused him—a supposition which I believed nigh unto the truth, I forbore to increase his anguish by particulars of Miss Osborne's sorrow—a reason for which was now apparent to me—and let the darkness rest over both their lives, knowing how unavailing any efforts of my own would be to draw aside the curtain, held down by stronger hands than mine.

CHAPTER XIX.

THE CHOICE.

Oh, that contest where the battle-field is home! Where sons take part against the sire; where sire hurls his maledictions on his offspring, who stand defiant and accusing; where wife and husband, sworn one at God's altar, have every thought and wish distinct; where the fire goes out upon the hearth, and the wailing notes of the heavy-laden sound like spirit-voices through those echoing rooms and passages, deserted by the Presence!

Gilbert was right. A battle to the death was threatening, and my brother was buckling for the contest, and arming with a sense of right that should have been invincible.

Roused to a deeper observance of passing events, by my last conference with Gilbert, I saw the mask he spoke of slowly but steadily dropping to the ground.

Vaudon was not the Jacques Vaudon of that time when he sat before the fire, and told the children stories that held them spell-bound till the evening was passed—not even the Vaudon of years back; he had taken higher ground, and, emboldened by my father's infatuated attachment to him, become the dictator and tyrant.

The servants feared him more than their rightful master; and though he seldom spoke above his usual tone of voice, and hardly deigned to bestow upon them a single glance, there was a perceptible dread amongst the domestics of "The Rest," and his lightest word was a command too fearful to be disobeyed.

What did he seek? That was ever the mystery that wrapped round him an impenetrable cloak. If he sought riches, why mingle with the children of his patron, and seek to win their confidence, and teach them nothing that was good? Why plot and scheme against them, and lay trepans to ensnare them with the lurking malice of the great father of evil? For what purpose did he, day after day, full of a new project, suddenly veer round and talk of nothing but Miss Osborne to my father, and spare no withering comment upon her actions, and adjudge no worthy motive to them?

He had had scarcely an angry word with any dwellers beneath "The Rest," and yet how truly Gilbert and I judged his false smiles, and the glittering deceitfulness lurking in his flashing eyes. As for my father and his twin-children, they were blind, and the light seemed never coming.

It was in the spring. So bright a morning, so full of sunshine, that I took no evil augury from the day that was ever marked in deepest characters—written with an iron stylus on my heart, for ever ineffaceable.

Entering from the garden through the French window, as the clock was striking twelve, I came upon my father in his chair before the fire, listening intently with his white, upturned face to Vaudon, who leant, with folded arms, across the back, and recited some engrossing tale. Vaudon started upon perceiving my entrance, and ceased speaking.

"Go on, Vaudon; go on!"

"It is Luke," he whispered.

"Is the subject one so full of conspiracy, that I may not listen thereunto?" I said; "if so, I will retire."

"Tell him," said my father.

"Tush! for what object?" said Vaudon, turning on his heel.

My father seemed very agitated; his eyes were burning luridly, his breathing hard and fierce.

"Stay, Vaudon!" I cried, actuated by a motive that was undefinable; "it is my father's wish. Save not all your evil news and torturing anxieties for one poor mind so ill able to bear them; let a son share the distress which unmans the sire thus."

Vaudon turned, and faced me with a deep-browed, lowering look, and his hand upon his beard.

"Tell him, Vaudon; it will strike home."

"Strike home!"

"Let him know all," continued my father—"see the fresh disgrace plotting against me—my eldest son—my Gilbert!"

"Who couples his name with reproach, or breathes a word unallied to purity and honour concerning him, lies!" I vociferated.

The indignation of my manner fired all the passion in my father, who leaped from his seat, fell back again, and raved madly and incoherently, with his left arm brandished above his head.

I turned away, heart-sick.

"Calm him, Vaudon, if you have the power," I cried, appealingly.

"He will recover speedily," replied Vaudon, with composure, as he crossed his arms on his broad chest.

My father ceased abruptly, passed his hand across his face, looked at me fiercely, then broke forth again.

"He would disgrace the Elmores! He would marry her! He has kept it all from me, caring not if its shock brought me to the grave. It was all arranged by this unworthy son—this serpent I have nourished till it stings me—this son I once had faith in—I once loved!"

"Who says this?"

"Who, but my only friend—the true rock, that has never flinched from me in my distress—the only landmark in this dreary waste?"

"This man?" I said, pointing to Vaudon, and turning on him a stern gaze.

"I spoke of it as one who had your father's interest at heart, and who, being your father's friend, could not see him betrayed by a son so unworthy of his confidence," replied Vaudon, meeting my look with one equally as stern.

"And you believe him, father? believe all the guilty colouring he has thrown around some fragment of a truth, caught eavesdropping, or learnt from some prying servant, who retails his news, with exaggerated statements, to this spy and coward?"

Vaudon recoiled with amazement as I gave vent to the long pent-up passions in my breast: he had never dreamed of me as champion of my brother's cause.

"Spy and coward!" he yelled, recovering from his amazement, and advancing menacingly towards me. "Recall your words, or your father's presence shall not save you from the chastisement you merit."

"Chastisement!" I echoed; "not at your guilty hands! Keep back, for I cannot trust myself."

"*I* am the defender of my own honour, brother Luke," cried Gilbert, as he entered the room, and advanced towards my father.

We stood transfixed: my father turned away his head as Gilbert came beside his chair, and touched his hand. It was the one spared to him from the shock, and he drew it hastily away.

"Father."

No answer.

"You have not a word to say—not one question to ask; but, believing in all the accusations that that evil man has chosen in his blackened soul to fix upon your son, are content to let them rest there, without listening to the defence he has to urge."

His voice was very firm: his whole look and manner betokened some decisive project which he had come to carry out.

He waited long for a reply. None came.

"You are content?"

"I am."

"Would nothing have its weight?"

"I believe all."

"That I have loved Miss Osborne, I have no compunction in asserting."

"False—false in all but that disgrace."

"And that, if I had won her love in return, I should——"

"Cease!" thundered my father, looking up at last. "Why come to this room to taunt me with all you would have done, or the ignominy that you had in store for me? Go!"

Gilbert coloured, but flinched not.

"This is the first time in our lives we have interchanged an angry word; has your confidence in me faded all at once?"

"I have no confidence in your protestations. I know everything."

"I am your eldest son."

"You are one of the many curses God has heaped upon me."

Gilbert turned to Vaudon.

"To you, and you alone, can be attributed the evil that has grown and grown with many a long day, until the fruit has dropped at my feet at last, full of corruption and of poison. There will be a day of recompense between us."

He turned to his father.

"Mr. Elmore, you have a choice to make."

"Well?"

"Between that man, whose shadow lies a heavy and impenetrable darkness on your heart, as on those he has studied many years to injure, and your son, whose love has never lessened, and will never droop or fall away, no matter what result this day may bring about. Choose!"

"What mean you?" with a deepening frown.

"One roof shelters us not. It is not in my power, had I the will, to cringe beneath the iron rule of that false-styled friend, who asserts my place and ousts me from a love that is my right. This man you bid begone, or I, an injured son, go forth to seek my fortune in a world that cannot be more unjust, and look for protection in that mighty Father who knows the secrets of us all. I go with hope—I go without an angry or revengeful feeling, ere another hour has passed, or I stay without the man who pays his patron's bounty by a slander that drags him to the grave."

"Go, unnatural child of a false wife! it is better for us all. I have no choice to make."

"So strong a hold as this!" murmured he. "Well, then, it is better for us all, indeed."

"The day that parts us shall never have an end," cried my father; "I shall have no son named Gilbert from that hour."

"You have no son named Gilbert, *now*, sir," replied my brother; "he died when he was young. Remember!"

"I will not forget," was the bitter answer.

"I go, sir."

"Go."

There was no relenting in the fierce, red eyes, no quivering of the lash. Vaudon, with a smile of triumph, stood, like a trophy of his craft, by my father's side.

"I will not ask your blessing now, sir; but in a future time, when the curse of blindness is removed, and you are suffered by Him above to judge, think of me then: a son, for ever lost to you."

"But, Gilbert," I cried, finding speech at last, "you will not go? This is sheer madness."

He shook his head.

"Then you go not alone."

"Folly!" he cried: "a rash assertion that cannot be maintained. You, Luke, must remain here, a foil to *him*," pointing to Vaudon. "It is your duty."

"And yours."

"Not mine—not mine! Judge by what has passed to-day."

He stood at the door, hesitated, went back, and, stooping over my father, lightly pressed his lips upon the furrowed brow, that neither moved nor shrunk back as he advanced.

"It is the last in life! Forgive me, sir. The last!"

He moved quickly from the room, hardly leaning for support upon his crutch, or conscious that he used it.

I lingered a moment to watch the effect of Gilbert's departure on my father; but he moved not in his chair, and I left him with his evil genius standing motionless and erect by his side.

I followed Gilbert to his room, and found the trunks already packed and corded.

He noted my astonished looks.

"I had expected the sequel, Luke," said he, "and prepared for it."

"And you will go and leave us all?"

"Ah, what have I to stop for? A father's love exchanged for hate—no faith put in my word—my name commingled with a curse! And I his son!"

"But it is his madness."

"No, no; it is an uprooting of all trust—no more."

"You will not stay? you leave me here your heritage of sorrow? you will not let me share the world with you?"

"For my father's sake, and not for mine, dear Luke," he answered; "he can spare me—my absence will be a relief to him. But you—you *must* remain."

"What do you intend? What ideas of the life before you can you have?"

"Plenty."

"And if you fail?"

"If I fail entirely, I will write to you for help."

"You will?" I cried.

"On my honour."

"And if you succeed?"

"Then, some day we shall meet again, God willing! We have not parted for life, dear Luke; it is a 'good-bye' for a few years, at the most."

"I cannot but think it all a dream!" I cried; "it is beyond my comprehension. It is so wild and strange—a leaf out of romance, not reality, existent and before me."

"Luke," said he, sadly, "it is hard to part, to go forth alone with no father's blessing on my head, and leave that villain beneath this roof. I trust in you to fight my battles, to step between him and his evil purposes, when they start into the glaring light."

"And yet you have not the courage."

"You do not know me," he replied. "I have not a father's love; my will is set aside, my word unheeded, my name blasted and dishonoured. Can I remain here so great a mark of scorn?"

"No, no!" I said. "But if my turn come, can I do less than act the same; or must I cringe and fawn at Vaudon's knees, and intercede with him for my father's mercy?"

"Your turn will never come, my brother," said Gilbert; "one sacrifice will be enough, and mine be it. If there be good to follow, I go willingly."

No protestations, no prayers and entreaties of mine, could for a moment shake his resolution. He heard them with quivering lips, and big, heavy tears, and straining chest; but there was not a moment's wavering in him.

He was going! "The Rest" was no more for him; he, a child unto the world, fraught with no experience, strengthened by no advice, was departing from his home without a settled view before him, in the midst of dangers and temptations, of which he was as ignorant and helpless as an infant.

He was going! The bright sun that streamed into his room and poured a flood of gold upon him, appeared to shine but for his misery. His room! that old room, wherein he had lain a cripple, and beside which bed that father, so stern and unyielding, had once prayed and wept for his first-born, and watched night after night in feverish anxiety over him he now discarded like a hireling.

He was going! I should see his pale, noble countenance no more, hear no more welcome from his lips, sit no longer by his side, profit never again by his counsel, nor be heartened under affliction with his cheering speech, and guided by his hand.

He was going! There would be a great void in "The Rest" that no time could fill, no fresh face cover. It would remain for ever a black gap, speaking of the one gone; it would tell of Gilbert's absence in a thousand little things; even his birds, singing in their golden cages by his study windows, would miss him morning after morning; and the dull faces of servants would be ominous of loss and significant of mystery.

He would take no leave of his sister, or his brother Edward—he did not feel he had the strength to support more trials. He bade me watch over them, and give to them his best love and his most sincere wishes for their happiness, with a prayer to meet again at some future time, and find affection still burning for him in their hearts.

He said nothing of Miss Osborne, but went out for a few moments, and gazed at her through the window of the room, where she, unconscious of the watcher, sat and thought.

He came back more pale and wan, and rested for some time on the chair by the bed-side, the same chair in which his father had watched him some years ago.

He rose at last with a heavy sigh.

"You will forward my boxes to Cliverton, Luke," he said, "and let them proceed to London by the morning coach, and remain at the office till I send for them."

I could not speak, but bowed my head in acquiescence.

"Is there anything more to say but good-bye?"

"I will go with you to Cliverton."

"I am going to Wharnby, to procure some conveyance."

"I will accompany you."

"No, no, Luke, I go alone. Let me depart a solitary traveller, and have my thoughts free, and my step unwatched. I could not bear even my brother's presence in the first mile from home."

I did not press him further, I saw it was his wish—his last wish!

A servant tapped at the door. I went to it, and opening it slightly, asked his errand.

"A note from Mr. Elmore for Mr. Gilbert." I took it, and the servant departed.

"He has relented, Gilbert," I cried; "I knew his heart was not iron, and that he loved you."

"Dreamer, dreamer," said Gilbert, tearing open the letter—"look here. The old panacea for human wrong—the smoother of rough paths, rock-hewn and stony."

He let several bank-notes, for a large sum, drop from his hands to the floor.

"Let them remain," said Gilbert. "It is not his gold I covet, or his wealth I envy. I will not so humble myself, and give way to his pride, as to start in life with all its necessaries bought me. There is no lesson to be learned from that. Even a son he hates—a son he believes guilty of machinations against his rank or his position, he showers his money on—not for old love, old memory, or kindred ties—but for the name of Elmore! Return them, Luke, when I am gone. I work my way alone."

He put both his hands in mine, and looked at me long and earnestly—his favourite brother!

"This is the hardest parting, Luke—there is none so poignant, or that wounds so deep. I pray God to bless you."

We both had much to say, but yet our lips were white and motionless, and our tongues refused to move. If we, two young men, wept like children, ere the bitter parting came, there was no selfish grief mingling with the disruption of ties, that we, in our narrow conceptions of fraternity, had pictured knit for ever, and proof against all shock. If we were less than men, we had thoughts more pure, and feelings deeper, in those few fleeting moments, before he—my elder brother, loved above them all, and endeared to me beyond all word-expression—left "The Rest," never to come back.

Oh! never to come back! The wind might moan around "The Rest" in sympathy with the lost; the waves might dash against the white cliff, sea-beaten and rugged, 'neath the storm, whereon in happier days, freer of limb and bolder in his strength, he had carved "Gilbert" three feet above his brothers' names—aspiring record left for Time! But he was of the Past, and wind and wave told me in my loneliness of what had been once, and what would never be again!

* * * * *

The figure stands, and waits once more, and gives me time to reach it ere it slowly glides on, leading me and beckoning. The way is steeper, and more wild, and childhood far beneath—a green valley in the mist—breathes of Peace departed.

High above my head, the tortuous path proceeds; and there are briars and weeds, and tangled brushwood in my course, and night seems deepening over head. There are no stars to light my way, and the shadowy figure grows more indistinct, and I can see but the drapery of crape fluttering in the wind, and the extended arm pointing to the distance. Across my path, a few stumbling footsteps in advance, I see a darkness impalpable and strange, over which the figure, bound to me for life, passes, and then halts. It makes a threatening sign to the lowering heaven, unlit by heaven's light, and then awaits my coming by an open grave!

I reach it, and a sudden knowledge comes unto me, and I shrink back and call aloud a name. The figure motions to me, and once more I advance; and, kneeling at the open pit, round which flit shapes indistinct and visionary, that seem weeping, I pray for an erring soul, called back to render its account, and tell of all its stewardship.

The spectre stands and gazes on me with its mysterious face of death, waiting for the traveller at that landmark where life ends, and maketh a last sign!

CHAPTER XX.

WHARNBY'S GREATNESS.

WHARNBY has risen into greatness, and into fashion—without which, what is greatness in itself?—and has become a living spot in a green waste, to which come streaming, in its season, the myriad pleasure-seekers of great London, who, needing health, wives, heart, or excitement, come to the sea-shore and sit beneath the white cliffs, and make a world of Wharnby.

The sands—those lonely, deep-strewn sands, where three brothers wandered, in time past, as on the sands of a wild desert—are thickly sown with human creatures, who have brought their passions, plots, and worldliness to face the restless sea, and their loud jests and noisy laughter to rouse the echoes of the dear old rocks, that frown a hundred feet above them in their rugged grandeur.

Did my father conjecture, even in a madness full of wild improbabilities, such a change as this? Did he look forward to faces he had shunned and fled from after his disgrace, following him to that solitary "Rest," and holding festival beneath, mocking him with the old frivolity, the old heartlessness, the old love of show, the old giddy turmoil for an object that was never good, or held a worthy season?

Two years and a half have stolen away since Gilbert left us for a new and unknown life, and there has been no sign made, and we know nought of him. He has gone for ever from "The Rest." We feel it in his unyielding silence; and my father has a son, and I a brother the less. My father has forbidden all mention of his name, and holds him dead in his remembrance, though bearing enmity against the power of his will, that could throw off all allegiance, and disown an ability to be a slave.

It is early in the autumn. Every morning the sands of Wharnby are densely thronged; music floats upward to "The Rest;" amusements of various kinds go on unceasingly; romantic young ladies, with faces screened from the sun's rays, sit on the sands and read the last new love story, or stand contemplatively at the water's edge, and think of Robert and James at their ledgers, in dusky London counting-houses. Bathing machines, clumsy and innumerable, are dragging about their human burthens; horses and donkeys are racing to and fro; fathers of families gravely dig holes in the deep sand for the edification of their offspring, or go to sleep with coloured silk handkerchiefs over their faces, and telescopes and umbrellas clutched tightly in their sun-burnt fists; men about town—moustached, high cheek-boned men—well known in billiard-rooms and hells at night, or in Regent Street and broad West-end thoroughfares by day, promenade to and fro, with their bold, libertine gaze in every female face; sprigs of nobility, fast running to seed beneath the influence of late hours and endless dissipation, strut listlessly about, and kill time by slow degrees. Life varied, and of all colours, is in full flower at Wharnby.

And Wharnby in itself—streets on streets full of bazaars, assembly-rooms, fifty-windowed hotels, libraries, jewellers—all that a fashionable can desire, or hold dear in his capacious mind.

And the cliffs, for half a mile on either side, are lined with rows of houses termed Terraces and Crescents, private hotels, and boarding-houses, all white, with green balconies and jalousies, fronting the murmuring sea, with promenades of great length before them, and seats for weary visitors, and circles marked for military bands.

Such is Wharnby; and Cliverton, jealous and full of envy, hides its diminished head, and sinks to insignificance. Wharnby has its harbour all complete, with light-house and landing-place, and dry docks, and inner basins, and forests of masts point upwards from their refuge; and the stone monument at the entrance records the laying of the first stone by the Royal Highness mentioned in a preceding chapter, whose idle words made Wharnby famous, and of worthy note.

Upon "The Rest" there hangs a deeper gloom; there is no confidence between its members, each buries its secrets and says nothing. We move about like phantoms with closed lips and thoughtful gaze, and have no knowledge of each other. My father sits huddled in his chair all day, more chary of speech than ever, more irritable, and with look more vacant. One thing remains; the sudden demonstration of affection for his daughter Agnes has not subsided, and her power over him seems greater than Jacques Vaudon's. He can refuse her nothing, and she is not backward in requests.

Agnes has become still more the woman. There is a self-consciousness of her surprising beauty in every movement that she makes, there is self-study in every action that sets a grace upon her.

Paul Redwin is more infatuated with my sister than ever; a long engagement has but riveted upon him stronger chains. How proud he is of her, too; how h struts behind her into Wharnby Church, and flings back his head, conscious of the value of his prize, and of the many admiring glances—side-long, askance, or full, as the crowded congregation chance to differ in mode of church observance—bestowed upon her. He sees not Celia, of less commanding beauty, but of that gentle loveliness that wins unto the heart, in the pew by the side, with her parents; he has forgotten her, and she, perhaps—for her bright look has returned, and there is no sign of inward pain or gnawing care upon her face—has learned to smile at the first fantasy of her young life.

Agnes, fully conscious of her power over Paul, and of the boundless extent of his affection, asserts her supremacy at times, and acts little comedies for her own amusement. She is variable in her manner towards him, astounding him by a freezing reception at "The Rest" on some occasions, or feigning indifference to all he acts and says on others, or teazing him to a frenzy with a simulation of intense interest in some stranger, coined expressly for the occasion, from her own imagination.

But a smile subdues the angry storm she has raised, and Paul emerges from his sulks at a sunny glance, and forgets unpleasant reminiscences in the hour before him, and is the beau-ideal of an attentive lover. He is anxious for his marriage, and only waits his opportunity to have a long conversation with my father, that will put an end to suspense. Agnes vexes him sometimes by expressions of a desire to extend the engagement another year, and laughs at his reproaches, and pleads her youth and unsettled mind with such mock earnestness, that Paul tears his curly hair in his delirium. To me, she appears even in no hurry to leave "The Rest," and become Mrs. Redwin; and when I plead for Paul, whom I esteem and have a brother's love for, she answers with a curl of her red lip—

"Why should I be so eager to resign my freedom and shut myself out from the world before I have caught a glimpse of it? Paul is of a very jealous disposition, and will lock me up in his convent, and make a lady abbess of me, and give me a bunch of keys, and think me perfect."

"With such a father confessor your convent will be gay enough."

"But, nevertheless, a convent," continued Agnes, still harping on the world, or that artificial life which she considers it.

"Do you know, Agnes, I almost doubt if you have a true attachment to Paul Redwin?"

"Why so, my special pleader?"

"Oh! for many reasons, Aggy," I reply.

"I cannot say," she remarks, lightly; "I have had no choice, Luke. He is very handsome and loves me, and I—I don't dislike him very much."

I say no more. She is in a humour of her own, and would take an opposite side to any point of argument, whether right or wrong, I might think it worth while to stand upon or endeavour to enforce. Redwin arrives at "The Rest," and his reception, owing to our late converse, is far from warm or complimentary.

My brother Edward has not improved with years, and has an affinity in selfishness to his twin sister, although a selfishness distinct from hers, having no ambition intermingled with it to elevate its grossness. He has become stout, thick-set, and heavy-looking. A keen searching look, characteristic of the Elmore family, and said to be seen more or less on every face pertaining to it, he is entirely free from. He is stolid, dull, and inexpressive. He has a large sum hoarded in the Cliverton Bank, which he intends to transfer to the New Wharnby firm when he thinks it safe enough to invest his capital therein. He has no pleasure in society, and is, on the whole, an uncompanionable young man. If he has one friend in the world without, it is Mr. Dartford of Cliverton, with whom he sometimes spends an evening, and finds possibly some congeniality of sentiment. Mr. Dartford has married Miss Silvernot, and a great maternal care is set at rest in her respected mother's breast. She is provided for! Holiest of mottoes in a calculating mother's book of precepts is this "provided for." It matters not whether disparity of age, or mind, or taste stand in the way, so that Benedict be rich, and have a heavy bank-book, and a respectable name in society—though the latter qualification can be waived upon emergency—it is enough to say, "She is provided for." If Benedict, aforesaid, after the honeymoon, keep late hours, and score his dissipations on his wife's heart as well as on his own face, if he make a slave of her, and rule a despot and grind her down beneath his iron heel, teaching her *his* way to obey and love, and honour, "she is provided for, thank God!"

Not that I would impugn the sobriety or morality of Mr. Dartford; he is like ice, so chaste and cold. He is a hard-headed as well as a large-headed man, and lives in his deeds and parchments, and japanned boxes full of family secrets and family decadence, and has entered upon marriage as he would upon a mortgage.

Mrs. Dartford, late Arabella Silvernot, is not an imaginative person; neither is she imbued with any of youth's romance or folly, any more than with youth itself; so she is content with her liege lord at Thornville Villa, who is a rising man, and has the reputation of having the sharpest eye for flaws in the county. I believe it.

Miss Osborne is still at "The Rest," and still makes many journeys to Cliverton. She has a face of care, but her voice is still as gentle and as kind. She is still unconscious of the reason for Gilbert's departure, and in ignorance of the many aspersions Vaudon had once affixed upon her name. My father has forgotten all about them, and though never expressing a word to the effect, has evidently a respect for Miss Osborne as a housekeeper and a lady of education, and is still proud of her as presiding genius at "The Rest." Agnes, in odd moments of affection, sometimes seeks Miss Osborne, and sits at her feet, and rests her head in her lap, and talks and listens to good counsel, and appears to me to be some one else—not Agnes Elmore; she is so patient, and attentive, and affectionate.

And in those times Miss Osborne seems to set aside her grave earnestness, and to bend over her as if she were a younger sister, dearly loved, and to rest her hands upon her glossy braids or ringlets of fair hair, as if she blessed her as she sat. But when weeks pass, and Agnes seeks her not, the light upon her face fades gradually and perceptibly, and she retires within herself, and holds communion with thoughts congenial to herself alone.

Vaudon, dark and mysterious as ever, is still my father's friend and counsellor. To spare my father more pain and dangerous excitement, I am courteous to Vaudon in his presence; and there is a false peace between us, which we both are cognisant of, and both feel, as we face each other at our father's table. There stands between us the Disowned—we both feel that he has left a legacy of hate, and we think of it and him each time we intersect each other's path, and love each other none the better for the recollection.

When Gilbert first left Wharnby, there were many embarrassing circumstances that naturally followed. The rector of Wharnby, always greatly attached to Gilbert, harassed my father to madness by his inquiries, and finally received an imperious summons to be silent, which offended the rector for six months; and the servants went about the house looking amazement; and Agnes and Edward held a consultation with me, and could not understand my explanations. What had good, quiet Mr. Vaudon to do with it? It was a silly whim of Gilbert's; they were sorry, and missed him for a time, and then they grew accustomed to his absence, and forgot him.

The Silvernot family—decreased by one provided for—are happy enough at Wharnby House, and I have become more frequent in my visits lately, and am led thither by an old attraction, or a new one that has sprung from out its ashes. I see Celia very often. I note the roses once more blooming on her cheeks—I hear her voice—I see her smile—I feel again old passions claiming an ascendance. Month after month has passed unto this time, and I have rode with her and her brother, and seen her meet Paul and Agnes on the road and betray no signs of distress, or blush at her old lover, or seem envious of Agnes's sway over him, but always calm and self-possessed, and lovely.

I begin to look forward once more in my dreams—my old love seems coming back to me; but I build no more daring fabrics in the future. I hold my heart in check, and wait and watch, and give no indication that the old wound is still unhealed; but take once more to my load of doubt and anguish, concealing this time from them all my secret, with tact bought by experience and my riper manhood.

CHAPTER XXI.

OLD FRIENDS AND NEW FACES.

"LUKE, I want an escort."

"Paul will be here in about half an hour, Agnes," I replied.

"Paul will not come till the evening, brother," was the answer.

"Indeed!"

"Paul Redwin, Esquire, went away seriously offended, last night, about some trifle or other; so I give him till the evening to smooth the ruffled plumes of his dignity; he will not descend from his stilts before then."

"Miss Osborne will have much pleasure in accompanying you," I remarked.

"But I shall not have much pleasure in accompanying Miss Osborne."

"Really, you flatter me by so decided a preference, Aggy. Might I recommend Mr. Edward Elmore?"

"You may recommend no one but yourself, scapegrace!" said she; "so, put on your hat and your best looks, and take me a walk along the cliffs."

"You insist?"

"I insist!" she repeated.

"May I venture to inquire wherefore my society is so indispensable, Agnes?"

"Why, Mr. Vaudon is engaged, and Miss Osborne is so serious a companion, and requires more energy to rouse than I can afford this morning; and as for Edward, I would as soon walk with that great mastiff in the coach-yard."

"Then I will sacrifice an hour to please you, for once."

"For once, you may well say," she remarked; "but 'sacrifice' is a misplaced word. Sacrifice—with such a handsome sister! Fie, Luke!"

"There, there, Miss Vanity, I consent. Let me know when you are ready."

Luke Elmore and his sister Agnes were quite good friends that morning; and considering the latter had parted with her betrothed rather distantly the preceding night, she was in excellent spirits, and far from depressed.

In half an hour we were strolling in the direction of Wharnby Harbour, which looked picturesque in the distance as it swept boldly into the blue sea. There was a fresh breeze on the cliffs, which caught Agnes's veil, and blew it far from her bright face, and deepened the roses on her cheek. Beneath us lay the sands, dotted with innumerable figures; and the murmuring of many voices, the creaking of wheels appertaining to bathing-machines, the noise of vendors of toys and shell ornaments (made in London, and forwarded to Wharnby!), the roll of the tide as it came in rapidly, the strains of music from wandering minstrels—some lame, some blind, some extravagantly dressed in old theatrical costume, the refuse of the wardrobe of some country theatre—formed a medley of sound which came welling to us from the giddy mass below.

Agnes kept her looks fixed on the busy scene, enacting more than a hundred feet below, as if fascinated by the murmur of the world—the stream beneath her vision ever passing and repassing.

"Shall we descend?" she asked, suddenly.

"Descend!" I exclaimed; "the saints forbid. What, mix with that vulgar mob—that *olla podrida!* You are jesting."

"I see no harm," calmly replied my sister; "there are many amongst 'the vulgar mob' who hold a higher position, and have a greater name than we have."

"And have a more vulgar taste," concluded I.

"Have your own way," said she. "I thought it might be a change from our eternal dreariness; but I am all obedience."

We continued our walk, and as we neared Wharnby, two or three straggling visitors passed, and honoured us by lengthy stares.

"With your permission, Agnes, we will return."

"Oh! this is the promenade," cried Agnes, "and the new terrace. There are very few people here. Let us stroll to the end, and then return. Have you an objection?"

It was a level grass-plat, stretching a considerable length, flanked on the right by a row of white houses of pretentious size, profusely ornamented with stone-work, and gaudily painted balconies and blinds. There were a few persons about—one or two fine ladies seated in the balconies of the houses mentioned, busy over fancy-work, or water-colour sketching, and some used-up dandies lolling on the seats, with the knobs of their riding-canes between their teeth.

"Well, we will take the promenade, Agnes."

I repented of my acquiescence before we had proceeded many yards; there appeared such a cool survey taken of us by the visitors, which, to me, was not so peculiarly embarrassing as annoying. Agnes, as collected as at her home, walked by my side, her hand on my arm, unmoved at the fixed looks of passers-by, or the simpering, lackadaisical ogling of more than one dandy and prim fop, perfectly self-convinced of the great impression he was making by a glance.

One of these gentlemen attracted my particular attention, and caused me once or twice to instinctively clench my right hand, as if I had him by his lemon-coloured stock. He was a tall man, of about thirty years of age, with sandy whiskers, thin nose, and large, grey, meaningless-looking eyes, one of which was adorned with a gold-mounted eye-glass attached to a broad silk ribbon round his neck. His head was surmounted by a small white cap, with a capacious brim, which had been carelessly thrown on his head in a jaunty, look-at-me sort of a way, which, I have no doubt, he considered particularly attractive. A loose coat of a light colour, and waistcoat and trousers of an enormous check pattern, together with a pair of patent-leather slippers, completed the attractive portions of his morning costume. This man, after a careful survey of Agnes through his eye-glass, and a half-smile of admiration, wheeled round as we passed, and proceeded in our wake, cutting at the grass with a small riding-cane as he followed us.

I glanced over my shoulder at him, and he honoured me with a steady, undiscomfited gaze, which made my blood stir a trifle quicker in my veins.

"We have an attendant cavalier, Agnes," I said. "I am afraid I must bring my gentleman to reason, if he dog us like this."

"Nonsense," said Agnes, "let him be, poor fellow; he is happy now."

Agnes made the remark so ludicrously compassionate, that I could hardly refrain from exhibiting signs of my appreciation of her humour to the Wharnby visitors, who were coming thickly on parade.

The gentleman in the rear being accosted by a party, consisting of two ladies and two gentlemen, and forced to halt, we were for a few minutes rid of our intruder.

We reached the end of the promenade, and turned to retrace our steps.

The individual with the lemon stock and eye-glass was still talking to his friends as we passed.

I have said there were four. They consisted of an old gentleman, very much bent—a stout and imposing lady of about fifty—a youth of seventeen or eighteen, in a midshipman's dress, with a curly head of hair, of a reddish hue—and a young woman, a few years his senior, also of a sanguine complexion, with a flat little nose, pressed tight against her face.

The gold-mounted young man leaned forward, and made some comment concerning us, for the midshipman and the two ladies instantly bent an inquiring gaze upon us. I threw back a defiant glance, which was quickly changed to an expression of astonishment, as the stout lady cried out loudly—

"Sir John—Sir John! I never saw such a likeness!"

"Good *Gord!* madam—what do you mean by startling me like that for?" savagely retorted the old gentleman, without paying any heed to her remark.

But the lady was absorbed in her surprise, and stood clutching the arm of Sir John, and pointing to my sister Agnes.

"Do you mean to say, my dear madam," asked our first friend, "that you know any young lady resembling that charming creature?" He raised his glass, and said again, in a more drawling tone—"Charming creature!"

The remark was evidently intended for Agnes's ears, and, letting her hand drop from my arm, I advanced with an angry frown and a menacing intention.

"I do not know who you may be, sir, and I have no desire to know," I said in a voice suppressed with passion; "but let me assure you, sir, that another such offensive remark, or studied impertinence, shall be rewarded as it deserves."

"And how, my good fellow?"

"By horsewhipping you," I replied, with a significant glance at his riding-cane.

"Ri-di-cu-lous in the extreme," he drawled; but I detected a perceptible change of colour, and a backward flinching movement.

The stout lady looked at me, and again at Agnes, gasping forth—"It is very strange—all very strange."

"Chastise the puppy, my good sir! chastise the puppy!" cried the elderly gentleman; "he's an arrant coward, sir: by Jove! sir, he sold out of his regiment last week because it was ordered to Calcutta, and he was afraid of yellow fever. Thrash him, sir; it will do him good."

"Sir John Boyington!" remonstrated the individual alluded to, "I am shocked at your absur-di-ty."

"Luke!" cried Agnes, indignantly, "why do you wrangle with those people in that coarse manner? Take me away."

She flung upon the group a disdainful glance, and took my arm.

But the stout lady, unobservant of the repeated chuckling cry of Sir John, expressive of his full consent to my awarding chastisement to the young man so lavish with his compliments, of the scorn expressed in Agnes's countenance, or the fury in my own, cried to my sister—

"I ask your pardon, but can it—is it—are you—Elmore?"

"Elmore!" I reiterated.

"Your name is Elmore?" she asked of Agnes.

"Yes, madam," replied Agnes, haughtily.

"I knew it; how very like your unhappy mother and my poor sister. Oh, good gracious! Sir John, it is my niece."

"The devil!" replied Sir John, with remarkable emphasis.

"Aunt!" exclaimed Agnes; "what, my aunt that I have not seen since a little girl—Aunt Witherby?"

"Hush! my dear," she said; "Mr. Witherby has long since slept in peace. Three years since, I accepted the hand of Sir John Boyington. And it is you, really—my dear, dear, *dear* child."

She folded Agnes in her arms, and kissed her on both cheeks.

"And this is your brother?" turning to me. "My nephew Gilbert, that I remember so well."

"My brother Gilbert is in London, madam," I replied. "I am the second son."

"Oh! Luke," extending her hand; "Luke is the name, to be sure."

I answered in the affirmative, and greeted that sister of my mother, whom I had not seen since the night which celebrated my poor father's wedding-day, and brought a curse of dishonour in the train of its false festival.

"Let me introduce you to your cousins, Miss Jane Witherby and Mr. John Witherby. You remember when you used all to play together at our house? Oh, those past times!"

We bowed to the young midshipman—who was a pleasant-looking young fellow enough, with his red, curly hair, and swarthy face, and twinkling little black eyes—and his sister. It was like cousins meeting for the first time, we were so young when we saw each other last. I felt there was a tie between us, as I shook their hands.

"Lady Boyington," cried Sir John, in a tone of reprimand.

"My dear," she answered.

"I should have thought etiquette would have suggested that a baronet was not to be placed last on the list of introductions—and be hanged to you!"

This was a most uncourteous method of terminating his speech, and Agnes and I exchanged wondering glances.

"I really beg pardon, Sir John, but in the natural embarrassment of meeting, I had quite forgotten you. Sir John Boyington—Miss Elmore. Mr. Elmore—Sir John Boyington."

Sir John, with an odd smirk on his features, wrinkled and seamed into a complicated net-work, took off his hat, and bowed profoundly.

"And to complete the circle, suffer me to make known to you Mr. George Boyington, a very amiable step-son, and a great blessing to me."

Mr. George Boyington, my sister, and I exchanged salutations. Mr. Boyington bowed very politely to me, and totally unmindful of our altercation, half-extended his hand in the coolest manner imaginable, an action which I affected to overlook.

"So you are still residing at Wharnby, or have you come hither for the autumn, my dear nephew?" inquired Lady Boyington, as she took my proffered right arm, and Miss Jane Witherby, with becoming graciousness, took my left. Mr. George Boyington, with enviable pertinacity, attached himself to Agnes, and was using his best endeavours to rub off any unfavourable impression he might have made, and Sir John and his step-son, young Witherby, followed in the rear.

"We have lived at Wharnby many years."

"*Since*——?"

"Yes, madam."

"Your father is still implacable in his resentment?"

"My father is bowed down by his cares, my dear madam, and never speaks of *her*."

"It was sad, it was very sad," shaking her head; "what a disgrace to the family, to be sure! For months, my dear nephew, I assure you, I trembled to meet the eye of society."

I had nothing to reply.

"What a beautiful girl your sister has grown, Luke!" said Lady Boyington, rambling in her speech from one subject to another; "and we used to call her little dame Elmore—she was so prim and quiet, and old-fashioned."

"She has improved."

"She is a matchless girl," cried she, quite enthusiastically. "What a sensation she would make in London! What a pity she should be buried alive in Wharnby!"

"Oh! London is well stocked with loveliness, madam."

After devoting some portion of my discourse to my cousin Jane, who was a quiet, chirping little body, with a very musical voice, I ventured to remark to my aunt, that Sir John seemed a pleasant, candid old gentleman, and to congratulate her on her standing in society.

"Candid—yes," said she, "a trifle too candid; do you not think so, Luke?"

"I am hardly competent to judge."

"But, then, Sir John has served in the navy all his life; and sea-faring men are blunt and rough. I suppose it's the salt water."

"And Sir John has been in more than one great battle," added Jane Witherby, full of her step-father's praise; "and was once cut down by a cutlass, and left for dead on the deck."

"Ah! a frightful wound in the head—just a hair's breadth within being an idiot," added Lady Boyington; "and, indeed, there are some invidious persons who have ventured to declare he is somewhat more than eccentric, but there's no truth in it; sane, my dear nephew, sane as I am."

I looked at my aunt—she was stout and large-featured, and her good looks had been lost many years, and were beyond redemption. There was a small degree of eccentricity in Sir John offering her his hand, I thought; but if there were few charms about my aunt's personal appearance, there were certainly a less number of attractions in Sir John.

But, then, he was a baronet, and his title gilded seventy-five years, and glossed over a little eccentricity. Why, of what value would a title be, if it did not? a mere name!

Lady Boyington had made up her mind to see the present residence of my father, and so continued by my side, as a matter of course, and asked innumerable questions respecting members of the family of Elmore, their present pursuits and future intentions, totally excluding her daughter from any share in the conversation.

Agnes and her admirer were positively flirting together in the background, when I bestowed a glance in that direction. George Boyington had dropped his eye-glass, and was particularly attentive; and had become so interested in his fair charge, that he had let the riding-cane slide from his hands, and was wholly unconscious of it being already in the possession of two dirty fisherboys, who were strolling in the opposite direction, and exulting over their prize, much to the satisfaction of the midshipman and Sir John, who were laughing, one against the other, till the tears streamed down their cheeks.

"You have found something par-tic-u-lar-ly lively for a topic, I presume, gentlemen?" said Mr. Boyington, aroused by a more than common shout of exhilaration.

"By Jove! we have, sir!" cried Sir John. "Tell him, Jack, by all means; he will enjoy it so. There's a real amethyst in the handle; I heard him say so this morning."

But Mr. Boyington had become entranced again, and Jack Witherby was too bashful to enter into any explanation before the pretty lady his half-brother was escorting so cavalierly.

We were within a few yards of home. I hesitated how to proceed; I could not shake them off my arms, and tell them they could accompany me no farther; and I knew my father's nature too well to believe he would give them anything but a freezing welcome to "The Rest;" dreading, also, the result of an interview with the sister of my mother—this worldly woman hanging on my arm.

"And that is your father's estate?" she asked.

"Yes, madam."

"A fine place. Has it a title?"

"'The Rest.'"

"'The Rest?' How strange, to be sure! 'The Rest!' Dear me!"

"He had resolved to rest from the world, to shun his fellow-men, and so he gave it that name; a forbidding one to strangers!"

This was a good hint, but it was not taken.

"Ahem! yes; so I should think. Strangers must be particularly annoying to him, but near relations and friends, who claim affinity with him, what a relief it will be to see those old faces once again! How surprised he will be!"

Fearful of the effect of their abrupt appearance on my father, I was about to enter into an explanation of a more decided character, when the voice of Sir John hailed me from the rear.

"Mr. Elmore!" he shouted.

I felt a tingling in my ears, at the rough salutation, but stopped, and looked back.

"That horrid ship's habit of vociferating at the top of his lungs," peevishly said Lady Boyington to her daughter.

"Mr. Elmore will excuse him, I am sure," said my cousin to me.

"I beg you not to mention it."

"Mr. Elmore, I'm dead beat, sir! I'm as lame as an old cart-horse, and as dry as a ship's cow after a six months' voyage. I hope we have not a much greater distance to go before we partake of your hospitality."

This was the last turn of the screw, and I could struggle against fate no more; I resigned myself to circumstances, and re-assured the worthy baronet, by indicating "The Rest" with my hand, not feeling disposed to carry on a dialogue at so considerable a distance from my interlocutor.

"Aunt!" cried Agnes, "you must step in and partake of luncheon, and see father."

"Oh! I think we had better return—say, till the evening."

As that expedient would have been worse than the present, I added my entreaties to Agnes's, and we passed through the lodge-gates; old Johnson, aghast with consternation, tremblingly looking after us.

"Upon my honour, Mr. Elmore, a very fine estate!" expressed Mr. George Boyington, in a conciliatory tone, as he looked right and left with his eye-glass, and drawled out his encomiums as if he were reciting a lesson in words of one syllable—"a mag-ni-fi-cent estate!"

"'Tis somewhat large," I answered, coolly, and anxiously debating within myself the best mode of procedure.

We were advancing up the drive: a few more steps would bring us round the curve of laurel bushes, and face to face with "The Rest." I resolved.

"Your pardon, ladies," I said, rapidly, "but my father is in delicate health, and I think it would be better to prepare him."

I did not wait for their replies; but, letting their hands gently drop from my arm, I hurried to the house, through the front entrance, along the hall, and into the room where my father sat. He was alone.

"Father, a strange series of incidents has occurred, which has thrown us into the presence of old friends—very old friends—who were known in London. I have hastened hither to ward off any shock that their sudden arrival might create."

He looked bewildered, and I had to repeat my tidings in a slower tone, my rapidity of utterance having failed to convey to his mind a clear statement of the facts.

"Coming here!" cried my father: "old friends known in London! Why do you bring them here? Send them away: say I am ill—say I am dead—say I am in my grave!"

"But——"

"Vaudon, Vaudon, come to my help! A plot against me—*a plot against me!*" he cried, wildly: "help, Vaudon, Vaudon!"

The man sought for opened the door of the room, and, at his usual slow pace, came silently gliding into the room.

"What has happened?"

"Bar the door, and keep them out," cried my father, vehemently. "This son brings the accursed faces of the past back with him."

"Gilbert Elmore!" exclaimed Vaudon, catching at a ray of light.

"Not Gilbert Elmore," I said, sternly; "there would be cause for God's blessing on the day that brings him back—not fear."

"Explain, explain!" demanded Vaudon.

For my father's sake, I yielded to his imperious summons. "Lady Boyington, or Mrs. Witherby, my aunt, is within a few yards of 'The Rest,' with her husband and my cousins." My father shrieked out like a woman, and his colour changed to the lividness of the dead. He tried to speak, but the words seemed choking him. He pointed to the door with frantic gesticulations.

"It is too late, Elmore," said Vaudon, cool and unmoved: "we must see them. Brandy, Luke."

I rushed to the chiffonier, and filled a wine-glass.

Vaudon, snatching the glass from my hand, poured its contents down my father's throat.

The effect was instantly apparent: he sat up, and the death-like look faded from his face.

"That woman—that woman of all others. *Her* sister. Oh, Vaudon! is there no resource?"

"None," said Vaudon. "Rouse yourself, and look at the trouble fearlessly; it is a passing shadow that will soon be gone. Let her not return to London to spread a thousand reports of your condition, for the pity of her friends, and the false condolement of the clubs. You are tracked; stand at bay!"

The pride of Elmore flushed on my father's cheek, beneath the bold counsel of Vaudon. He would meet them.

"Let luncheon be prepared, Vaudon," he murmured, "and let the servants wait at table. See to it all."

"I will. Listen! they approach."

They came into the room—a crowd of unwelcome guests—and my father stood up to receive them. Lady Boyington rushed at him with sisterly affection and extended arms; but my father, shrinking back, held out his left hand.

"You will forgive my left hand, Mrs. Witherby," he said: "an attack of paralysis has deprived me of my right."

"My dear Elmore," cried my aunt, seizing it, "I can scarcely believe it to be you. How you are changed: how pale, and haggard, and afflicted! Oh, dear, dear me!"

"My health has improved of late years, and my afflictions I can bear, madam."

Introductions were gone into, and passively received by my father.

"You are acquainted with Mr. Vaudon, I believe, Mrs. Witherby," said my father, indicating that gentleman to her.

"Lady Boyington, sir," corrected Sir John. "Why do you persist in groaning out 'Mrs. Witherby?' Lady Boyington!"

My father and Sir John frowned at each other in an inauspicious manner, whilst Lady Boyington advanced to Vaudon.

"I had quite forgotten the name, and years have changed you, Mr. Vaudon, also," said she, extending her hand, "yet you were an old friend, too."

"We soon forget old friends, Lady Boyington," said Vaudon, with his hand in hers, "although I should have known you at first sight. Time has not dealt so harshly with you as it has with me."

Lady Boyington turned away with a smiling face at the compliment, and resumed her conversation with my father, who, having overcome the first effects of their unlooked-for visit, became more of the host and less of the misanthrope, although his bright, restless eyes boded no good effect from the suppressed excitement their arrival had created.

Lady Boyington had attached herself to her brother-in-law, and was showering on him her worldly narratives and incidents of her artificial life, till he sat heart-sick and stupefied. Becoming aware of his wandering attention, she changed the topic, and spoke of Agnes's beauty, and went into raptures of expatiation on the subject. Then Edward made his appearance, and she asked after Gilbert, and my father sternly forbade a second inquiry concerning him; and Lady Boyington looked puzzled, but held her peace, as desired. Mr. George Boyington had taken a seat by Agnes's side, and Agnes seemed bent on achieving a conquest over the exquisite: she smiled so winningly, and chatted with him so confidentially, and looked playfully reproachful, or dubious, at his flatteries. Sir John having attached himself by two fingers to the button-hole of Vaudon's coat, had left the young midshipman and his sister in an isolated position, so, full of charitable intention, I took a seat by their side, and made their acquaintance more fully.

They were very agreeable cousins, mine, and I felt that to know more of them would not be displeasing to me; I felt still more the link there was between us, and we were soon far from strangers. Jack Witherby (he detested the name of John) was a bold, spirited young fellow, and his sparkling little eyes were full of fun and daring. He had been in one engagement, and spoke of it as "capital" and "first-rate," as though it were some exhibition or grand novelty. He had nothing to talk of but the sea; it was his one hobby, and he made much of it.

It is needless to add, in this place, that he was an especial favourite of Sir John's.

Vaudon, watching his opportunity, had left the room, and abandoned Sir John to his own resources, and we were all talking and forming quite a friendly group, when Paul Redwin, with the familiarity of a friend of the family, darted in, unannounced.

"Well, here I am, Agnes, and——oh!"

Amazed at the unexpected assembly into which he had unceremoniously precipitated himself, he stopped short, and made a half-bow, as if of recognition.

"Oh, Paul," cried I, "here are some new friends, or rather old friends with new faces, I shall have great pleasure in introducing to you."

"I am highly honoured."

Paul, recovering from his embarrassment, was the perfect gentleman, and went through the ceremony of introduction in a graceful manner, keeping his great brown eyes on Agnes and Mr. Boyington.

There was no vacant chair near his betrothed, so he came towards me, and entered into detail concerning some carriage-horses he had lately purchased. But carriage-horses were not uppermost in Paul's mind, and he kept turning from me to look across at Agnes, and was very forgetful of his part, and extremely inattentive to my answers.

Agnes pertinaciously kept her head away from Paul, and continued her lively dialogue with greater spirit, adding a few more thorns in her lover's side.

"Upon my soul, Luke," he said, "its terribly warm to-day."

He fidgeted with his fingers at his neckerchief as if it were unpleasantly tight, and wiped his forehead with his pocket-handkerchief, and tried to look unconcerned respecting anything but the oppressive heat of the atmosphere.

"Don't you find it sultry in the extreme?" he asked.

"The autumn *is* mild," I asserted.

"Mild!" echoed Paul—"pooh! I never was in such a heat in my life!"

Poor Paul Redwin! He had come over full of repentance for yesterday's little difference, and had been full of a delightful reconciliation, and had anticipated all that he would say, and all that Agnes would reply; and he had found the house full of company, and Agnes listening, and more than listening, to a young man very particular in his attentions, and very much entranced and wrapt up in *his* Agnes. No wonder it was warm!

How plainly to my memory did his wounded feelings recall that night at Wharnby House, where I saw him after many years, and where he played the leading character and thrust me into the background, and won Celia's heart, but to set it aside for another beneath it in all variety of comparison.

But he was too much my friend for me to take any gratification in his pain; I had forgiven the past, and could feel for every sting that made him start, and writhe, and jump from his place to look out into the garden, and perform numberless absent actions illustrative of his tortured mind. I read all that he suffered, and endeavoured to relieve him.

I advanced to Agnes, and said, in a voice inaudible to her new admirer, "Think of Paul Redwin."

I left the words to have their proper effect and returned to my friend. But Agnes was not to be reprimanded, even by a brother, and my remonstrance might as well have never been expressed.

Luncheon was announced in the dining-room, and Paul started forward to offer his arm to Agnes; but he was already forestalled, and Mr. George Boyington was the favoured individual.

Paul came back very crestfallen, and hotter than ever.

"I say, Luke," he asked, in an angry whisper—"who did you say that—that *mincing fool* was?"

It was a strong expression—and Paul was generally very choice in his expressions; but I made a due allowance for his case, and had not a very flattering opinion of the heir to the Boyington estate, myself.

"Mr. George Boyington."

"Then I don't mind telling you, Luke, that Mr. George Boyington had better be less particular to Agnes, or Mr. George Boyington and I will come to a private understanding with each other."

"Never mind him, Paul—you're not jealous, surely?"

"Jealous—ha! ha!—that's a good idea, Luke," he cried; "no, no—jealous, indeed! I'm not of a jealous disposition—far from it, Elmore. Oh, no!"—and he glanced poisoned daggers at Boyington and Agnes disappearing through the doorway.

We had luncheon in the dining-room, with more than extra state, to please my father's pride, and to demonstrate the grandeur of his position; and Paul picked at his cold fowl, and fell into thought, and began to grow haughty and reserved, and declined to return an answer to Sir John, who was seated next him, by anything more conversational than a freezing monosyllable.

The luncheon was concluded, and there were rumours of departure, and Lady Boyington was pressing my father to come and see her at her marine residence—hired for two months, at a hundred pounds per month, servants included, Sir John grumbled out—and my father was replying in a decided negative.

"Well, Agnes and the boys must come—I take no denial from that quarter. I take no denial, understand?"

"Oh! we shall be too happy!"

My father looked half inclined to contravene this statement—but, meeting Agnes's glance, he turned away with a stifled sigh.

We were all standing.

"And, perhaps, Mr. Redwin will favour us?" suggested Mr. Boyington, drawing on his gloves.

"Thank you!" said Redwin, in the dryest of voices.

"We shall have very great pleasure in Mr. Redwin's company," added Lady Boyington.

"Thank you!"—with the regularity of an automaton.

They had left "The Rest" at last, and my father had returned to his old room, and sunk exhausted into his chair.

"Go with them—see them as often as you all like, if there can be any gratification in their company; but a curse on the one who brings those wolves and vultures to this house again!"

Paul was buttoning his coat up to the chin.

"Are you going?" calmly asked Agnes.

"Yes, I am, Agnes," said Paul, decisively; "yes, I *am*, Miss Elmore. I shall come to-morrow evening; but, at present, I fear my society would be an intrusion on pleasant thoughts; and"—in a voice intended for Agnes alone—"I think, Agnes, you have been more than unkind and inconsiderate, as well as unmindful of the relative positions we occupy towards each other. Think of it, if you please; and—good morning!"

Agnes replied but with a merry laugh; and Paul strutted out of the house, still suffering from the weather.

CHAPTER XXII.

CELIA!

A WEEK sufficed to put us on terms of the greatest familiarity with the Boyington and Witherby family, making of them and us dear relatives and friends—thanks to the efforts of Agnes Elmore to bring about the same. I had very little objection to urge; for, despite my antipathy to George Boyington—an antipathy that did not grow less upon closer intimacy—I felt there was a claim upon Lady Boyington existent in my breast. She was the sister of my mother—her own sister; and, despite her worldliness, and mannerism, and airs of pretension, I took no common pleasure in her society. Although several years my mother's senior, yet I fancied that, in the features marked by Time's relentless scythe, I could distinguish some faint glimmerings of my mother's patrician look, as I remembered it so long ago! And she would speak about my mother, too; and tell me stories of my father's courtship and his adoration, and wonder how such love as they both had had, when they were married, should have died away an unprofitable vision. She mingled with her stories and lamentations much selfish counsel that the head teaches and fashion gives allowance to—much of precepts telling of the earth, earthy, and little of the heaven beneath which we busy ants grope on—on to a futurity; but the charm was still visible to me through all, and afar off—like a dim figure in a wild landscape—passed the figure of my mother.

My father, firmly resolved to avoid all intercourse with our new friends, kept to his first intention, and closed "The Rest" upon their visits. He was content to be alone, and though irritated and dissatisfied at the resumption of that acquaintance began in childhood, regarded it as a lesser evil, which a few weeks would soon remedy. So we paid frequent visits to No. 54, Belle Vue Terrace, Upper Cliff, Wharnby, and saw more of life, and heard more of the din of the world.

There were plenty of visitors at the Boyington residence, and they were pleasant *réunions* in the autumn evenings, when the brilliant drawing-rooms were full of guests—real, high-bred, London-polished guests.

Agnes seemed more than ever in her element, and more fitted to adorn. She had quite won the affections of Lady Boyington, who was never happy out of her society, and whose eyes would look admiringly at her from distant corners of the room, when she sat surrounded by half-a-dozen young men, all rivals with each other for a word. George Boyington, fearfully interested in Agnes, became more of the man, and less of the fop; and once or twice I had been the witness to variable changes of colour on his brazen cheeks, when his particular friends kept too long, or danced too often, with his cousin Agnes. George Boyington persisted in calling her cousin, and reminded his acquaintances that she was his favourite cousin, too. And George, how fond he was of me!—how entirely forgetful of our first meeting, and its threatened result!—how partial to anything appertaining to an Elmore! Yes, this man about town, this boaster of his conquests at his club, this fellow who had been a lady's man all his life, and who had ever a scurrilous jest or covert insinuation to make respecting the weaker sex, was caught by a smile from a country girl!

I took a fancy to my real cousins, and we were great friends. Jack Witherby (he would be called Jack) was the best tempered, wildest, jolliest of fellows, always getting into some mischief, and scrambling with cat-like agility out of it, and as full of pranks as a monkey. He was very partial to long strolls with me across the cliffs, where he would jeopardise his life, and freeze every drop of blood in my veins, by walking on the extremest verge, in order that he might attain greater facility in his aim at parties on the sands beneath, with small cubes of chalk, or pebbles, or pieces of hard earth—he was not particular as to his selection of material. Yet for all this, he was the most sheepish, and most bashful of lads; he would colour up and stammer out an inaudible series of words, if Agnes had a question to ask of him, or an observation to make, and would sit in a corner of the drawing-room, full-dressed and uncomfortable, on reception-nights, with his carroty and curly head bobbing aside every minute to elude detection and evade mortal glance.

And prim, quaint, cousin Jane, what good friends we were, and how little of your mother's teachings had you inculcated! for you cared nothing for the world's attractions, and were more happy in a solitary evening walk than in a dazzling ball-room.

Sir John Boyington did not appear much on the scene. Lady Boyington's chief study was to keep him as much as possible out of the way on reception-nights, lest his nautical manners and his unfashionable style of address should jar upon the sensitive nerves of her guests, and Sir John preferred his pipe in the back-room, looking over the slate roofs of the new town, and took great interest in the smoke of the chimneys, and the patent cowls and waterspouts, and was seldom wearied with the study of them.

There was little doubt in my mind that Sir John Boyington had never completely recovered from the effects of the cutlass in the last naval engagement, despite Lady Boyington's incessant protestations to the contrary; he was a shade more than eccentric, or there would never have been a mysterious kind of valet, of powerful build, attached to the establishment, who kept Sir John in sight, when the family were engaged, and sat with him for a few hours whilst he smoked his great meerschaum over Wharnby house-tops.

Paul Redwin had a great objection to the whole of the Boyington family; he excepted not even Jack Witherby, and kept him at a distance, with stately bows and ceremonious deportment; he accompanied Agnes occasionally to her aunt's house, on the Upper Cliff, and was exceedingly disagreeable during his stay thither, and terrifically ill-tempered and argumentative when we walked home on fine evenings to "The Rest." As for Mr. George Boyington, if there ever was a mincing, namby-pamby, insignificant, conceited, twaddling, self-sufficient jackanapes, it was he, in the opinion of Paul Redwin, and he expressed the same to Agnes, and Agnes laughed and thought Paul severe, and that Mr. Boyington was very agreeable, and quite a gentleman. Paul sneered at *gentleman*, and thought Agnes prejudiced. Agnes considered Paul rude, and uncivil in the extreme, and begged to inform him that Mr. Boyington was her friend, and should command more respect. Paul became satirical, and fell into raptures concerning Agnes's taste, upon which Agnes appeared charmed likewise, and coincided with him in everything, which acquiescence finished Paul, and sent him home with a "Good evening, miss."

Lady Boyington had broached a topic in conversation, after some dozen meetings, which had set more than one thinking deeply, and had sown the seed of many desires in fruitful ground. This was the expression of a wish that Agnes should accompany the family to London for a few weeks or months, after the expiration of the Wharnby season.

"Not that London is in full flower of society at this period of the year, my dear niece," said Lady Boyington; "but Sir John is a strange man, and *will return*, and I should be so happy if you would form one of our party. Oh! you must contrive to obtain Mr. Elmore's consent. I shall insist upon it."

"Oh! no denial, pos—i—tive—ly no denial," cried Mr. George Boyington.

"Yes, we shall decide upon it; and you, Luke, must join us, too," ran on Lady Boyington. "Agnes has not seen London since she was a pretty little girl; it will be so great a change, and do her so much good. And there's Mr. Redwin will give his consent, I am sure."

Agnes tossed her head playfully, and cried, "Mr. Redwin, indeed!"

Mr. Redwin was not present to make a reply, but I hazarded a few words condemnatory of the proposed expedition.

The subject was changed, but Agnes was thoughtful the remainder of the evening; the idea of going to London never left her from that night.

She brooded on the feasibility of the plan; and set her brains scheming to bring about the result; she made a study of her wish.

When we were alone together, she said to me—"What do you think, Luke, of going to London?"

"I have no wish, and you——"

"And I——?" said she.

"Should have none," I concluded.

"Because I am engaged," she said, in a rapid tone. "Oh! this eternal engagement, how you din my ears with its one single monotonous note! Every word and gesture of your own and Paul's seem to imply 'you are engaged.' I see it in Paul's look, in your own manner; I read it a hundred times a night at my aunt's; it is universal, and you torture me with its unchangeableness. Am I to forego a few weeks' pleasure with my own relatives—the only relatives we have—because I am engaged? If you do not choose to accompany me I shall still go. I have already made up my mind."

"Agnes!"

"It is truth. I have made up my mind," she repeated.

"To go to London, with the Boyingtons—you?" I exclaimed.

"Yes, to go to London—and with the Boyingtons."

"But—Paul?"

"Paul will not deny me the gratification of so natural a wish; but if he assume his dictatorial airs, and assert his right of prohibition then—I shall still go."

She closed her red lips, and set her small white teeth, and I read the inflexibility of her purpose in the determined look upon her face.

"And our father, Agnes? Set aside Paul Redwin, as with a callous indifference you feign to do, there stands still a great barrier in the way."

"It can be removed."

"I do not believe even your influence can exert so great a force."

"It can; it shall!"

"But——"

"Shakespeare said 'No buts.' Good night, Luke."

"She tripped away to her room, leaving me full of doubt, and harassed by this new project, so suddenly formed, but so unshaken in its indomitable strength.

It was three weeks before I heard more of it.

Meanwhile, those three weeks contained the nucleus of all the real happiness I have ever known, and set me thinking more about myself, and less of the troubles that seemed hovering around "The Rest."

Does it matter now if they were formed of empty air, and illusive, lasting a few weeks at most, and then swiftly vanishing before me, tending, in the events they brought about, to make me what I am? They were weeks of unalloyed happiness, in which all was forgotten—father, absent brother, present relatives, and home faces, and I can look back upon them without remorse, and feel my yearning heart still throbbing at the memories they recall to me.

I have deferred to this time—save a faint allusion to a hope that I believed had been for ever cast adrift, or foundered—the new purpose of my life.

It is all mockery, and yet I live those three weeks o'er again, and read my lesson from them.

They were the old days, before Redwin came home from Paris. With every hour the spell grew stronger on me—the hope took deeper hold—my past feelings came flowing back with tenfold strength—the first love of my life!

Wharnby House again held me within its walls, day after day, and "The Rest" seemed ever deserted by my presence. There were a few hours devoted to my aunt and cousins once or twice a week, and the remainder of my time to Celia. I had forgotten everything, save that I once more loved her. I had succumbed to the gentleness and purity that encircled her, as with a halo, and made myself her worshipper. We were much together; we had been brought into contact with each other from our childhood; we recalled old scenes and old associations, that came naturally with them; we spoke of Paul, and she blushed not; of his engagement to Agnes, and the smile left not her lip, nor the brightness her full dark eyes. We were like sister and brother, and my heart was young.

Slowly, steadily, I worked onwards to her love, gaining

progress every day. I noted a change at last—a silent understanding of the attentions that I ventured to offer—a rosy cheek more than once, or twice, or thrice, when I have greeted her, and the thrilling sense of happiness I had never felt before was making heavenly visions of the future. It was so pure a love—it had so bright an object—that I trod enchanted ground, and painted life in vivid colours, that glowed before me on my way.

It was in the beginning of the three weeks when I ventured to make a confidant of the rector. I told him of my love, its death, and its revival; I laid every fibre of my heart bare before him, assured of his advice, his generous appreciation, his great unselfishness. He had expected the disclosure; he had long seen the love within me for his sister; and yet he broke down like a child, and fairly cried.

"Bless my soul, what a fool I am!" he said, wiping his eyes; "but I am so happy, my dear Luke; you do not know how happy you have made me. I have wished for Celia and you to become betrothed for years and years, and when young Redwin stepped in, I was as miserable as you were. But that's past," shaking my hand. "Paul was not fit for Celia; there was not spirit enough in her dear, lovable nature for him, and the folly expired of sheer weakness. But the last year, Luke, I have detected symptoms in both of you of something stronger than mere caprice—something like the oak of slow growth, but of sure strength, defiant of tempest and misfortune."

"And do you believe that Celia has forgotten Redwin, and that she would not reject my proposals? Do you give me hope?"

"Every hope," cried he, releasing my hand with a warm pressure. "I should be the last to offer one word of encouragement, if I had not seen the state of the weather long since, Luke. There, take your first opportunity, and wait for *Impulse;* there's nothing like it—and God bless you both. Amen."

Fearful of another break down, he dashed out of his room, and left me to get out of the vicarage in the best manner I could under the circumstances.

Ever considerate, he framed an excursion next day to Cliverton; and, early in the afternoon, I accompanied Celia and him to Mr. Dartford's. We were on horseback, and the little rector hung very kindly in the back-ground, and stopped his horse more than half-a-dozen times to admire a sea view, or a country prospect, till Celia grew alarmed at his non-appearance. But the opportunities given were not made available; each time we were cantering together along the road my courage left me, my hand trembled, my lips became parched and dry, my head swam, and I rode on in a busy whirl, with a tongue that felt like a leaden weight upon my speech. The thought kept ever before me—if I should have been mistaken; if I were doomed to the old terrible agony of the heart—that dreadful feeling of loneliness and despair which there is no shaking off, but which hangs on mind, and thought, and action? She was so beautiful, I could not give credence to a return of that love which I felt myself within my breast; I could not speak, though my life had been the forfeiture.

She was very silent, and embarrassed, too; a secret consciousness of impending disclosure kept her head turned from me, and her eagerness to discuss common-place subjects, and to remark common-place things, added to my reserve; so that we rode into Cliverton still occupying our relative positions, and the rector, blue with cold, on account of repeated stoppages, joined us a few minutes after our entry into the town.

We found an old face at the Dartford's. Coming suddenly upon me with all its beauty, its well-known fascinating smile, I started, and cried out her name.

"Mr. Elmore, it is some time since we have met."

"It is, indeed, my dear Mrs. Morton. I am happy in welcoming you to Cliverton."

Mrs. Morton and Celia exchanged greetings; they had met but for a moment at the ball in years past (for the marriage of her brother had not induced Mrs. Morton to leave London), and the rencontre was somewhat frigid on both sides. Arabella, a more agreeable hostess than a spinster, welcomed us heartily; and Mr. Dartford, coming in a few minutes after our arrival, completed the family circle at Thornville Villa.

Mrs. Morton and I talked of our past meetings, and she appeared more lovely and more winning; but the rich, soft voice, so low and musical—the brilliant eyes shadowed by their silken lashes—the small perfect figure, the undefinable charm that had been ever apparent in each look and movement, were all of no avail towards me. I was unmoved, cold, courteous, and complimentary. The strange glances that half-returned your own, and spoke volumes of encouragement, were harmless, and fell upon one clothed in armour and invincible. I could not believe it was she who had exerted so mysterious an influence over me; I felt but the admiration I should have had for a beautiful portrait, or a matchless work of sculpture—nothing more.

Throughout the afternoon there was no thought more than this, and the fevered passion of my breast was dormant, or had died.

As I stood looking upon Celia and Mrs. Morton, a wild fancy came across me—born of imagination, within the room, as I watched them talking by the fire—that they were my good and evil angels! They were both dark-haired and eyed; and yet, looking at them from a distance, I could not divest myself of this impression, and of the great difference between them, and that heaven and earth were not more distinct, or had a greater line of separation drawn between them, than their respective natures.

And yet they were both so lovely! But Celia, to me, appeared the type of love, seeking the stars, and soaring upward; and Ernestine Morton, that of the earthly passion, full of aspirations and wishes akin to our mortality.

I gazed at them, full of the startling idea that had formed itself within my brain, that they were the antithesis of each other, and that my future life was linked with both of them. So great a hold had the thought possessed itself of my common sense and reason, that when Mrs. Morton came towards me at a later portion of the day, my first impulse was to make a backward step.

The day wore away, and we were going back to Wharnby.

"Then I am never to see you in Cavendish Square, Mr. Elmore? she said to me. "You are perfectly content at Wharnby?"

"I do not know of any reason that can give me the pleasure of visiting you in London."

"Ah! you are contented, I see, Mr. Elmore," she said, gaily. "Well, I am going on to Wharnby in a few days. Perhaps I may meet you before I return to town. I will not say good-bye."

"I look forward to many meetings."

She changed colour.

"No, you do not," she cried, in a quick, stifled tone; "you

have no place for me even in your memory. We each take a different path in life, and shall soon forget each other. By your sudden start and astonished looks to-night upon our meeting, I saw you had not thought of me—not given me one poor thought—since we met last at my brother's house!"

She turned from me with a haughty step, and left me bewildered at this accusation. She was distant and repelling till the last moment of our visit, and drew her hand from mine ere it had been hardly tendered me, upon taking my farewell.

There would have been food for much perplexity in the eccentric courage of Mrs. Morton, had I not had a topic of deeper import to myself to dwell upon. I had no remembrance of Mrs. Morton, and was conscious of Celia alone, and of her riding by my side.

"We shan't be home till dark," said the rector, looking up at the sky; "that's decidedly unpleasant. I merely intended a call, and here we've made it two hours or more. It's nearly sunset."

He looked at me with an inquiring glance, and read my wishes on my grave face.

"Ahem!" coughed he; "it's so cold this evening—for it *is* evening—that I shall gallop a mile or two, and wait for you at the cross roads."

"We may all increase our pace, I think," suggested Celia.

"Not for the world!" cried the rector, with a feigned alarm I could never have supposed him capable of assuming. "Your horse might take fright, and a pretty thing that would be. No!" said he, decisively; "I've an impulse on me to get to the cross roads before"—looking at his watch—"before six o'clock; and get there I will, too."

And, without waiting for further remark or expostulation, he was off at a pace more consistent with a fox-hunter than a peaceable and praiseworthy minister of the Church of England.

The old symptoms began to return before he was out of sight, but I controlled them, and resolved to know my destiny.

A few minutes—silent, agonising minutes—then my heart gave way; the flood-gates of my passion were beaten down beneath the tide of love that poured forth from my lips. It was uttered quickly, suddenly; and she drew the veil of her riding-hat close over her face, and rode on with heaving bosom, and shaking hands—but not away from me, I thanked God—not away from me!

"Celia, I can remain no longer silent, nor must you be longer ignorant of my one secret—the all-powerful secret that has dwelt with me so long! It is my love—the great love of my life—a love with but one object, having but one ambition. It is my love for you, born ere we were man and woman, increasing month by month and year by year—though silent and despairing often—until it has come to this avowal, and seeks an answer to its long idolatry. I have loved you from my boyhood; you have been the bright figure in the foreground of all my dreams; and to cast me away without a hope, is to blast the current of a life—to annihilate all settled purpose in me! Oh! Celia, not to love in vain—not to tear aside the cold formalities of friendship in a wild belief that has no foundation but in my visions—oh! not for that, this prayer to love me in return—oh! not for that, dear Celia!"

She tried to answer me, but could not. We rode on silently together, then she essayed again, but in so low a voice, that I, greedy listener, could hardly distinguish the reply, although bending in my saddle eagerly towards her.

"Oh, Luke! I wish it had not been. I wish—no, no—I cannot say *that*, even—but——"

"Oh! frightful '*but*,' rising up black and ominous to mar my love!"

"But I have loved before," she murmured, after a long pause.

"But it is past!" I cried, anxiously.

Another pause, and she resumed—

"Luke, you have been candid with me; I will be so with you. Whether my first love be past or not, I cannot say; I do not know. Mine are affections not lightly won, and not easily turned away or drawn aside. I have tried to forget him, and I believe and hope I have succeeded. I have prayed to do so, night after night, for years. Can I, for the strong love of your nature, make so poor a return as a divided heart, or a love made old before its time?"

"But you do not love him, now?"

She reflected; then, looking me full in the face for the first time, said, "No."

"Then, you can love again; there is no death of love in the heart of a young girl. Oh! Celia, do not for vague scruples, which have no definition and can command none, throw away my every hope of future happiness. I will be all to you—I will be happy, if you will give me hope to win you!"

P

"Luke," she answered, in an agitated voice, as she bent her head towards the saddle, away from my ardent gaze, "had I not believed that I could love and prize the heart you offer, I would not have listened to you so long, or entered into so strange an explanation. If you are content to know that I esteem you more than any other living at this moment, and will give me time to learn to love you as you deserve, I—I will learn that lesson with a true devotion."

She drew aside her veil, and smiled through the swimming tears, as she extended her hand frankly—the sign of her engagement. Bewildered by love, by happiness within my grasp, real, tangible, as I had scarcely dreamed of, I felt too light for earth, my whole being seemed transformed—the world had changed—there was more light and sunshine in it, although but a faint mark—a blood-red curve, was lingering above the heap of dark clouds beyond the tinted sea.

What a happy ride to the cross roads! Sacred from this record, those few brief minutes of existence, that interchange of confidence, that halcyon era in my new-born bliss.

CHAPTER XXIII.

THE FIRST LINK BROKEN.

I SPOKE of three weeks' pure happiness, not implying that the term of my engagement but extended to that period, but that there were no other cares, no other thoughts of anxiety or trouble, to counteract the sensation of deep joy. I had informed my father of my engagement, and he had but inclined his head, in the habitual indifferent way with which he received all intelligence not immediately connected with his own thoughts or feelings.

He had scarcely sufficient interest in the matter to betray much surprise, or to offer any congratulation, in his morbid ideas—fostered by the evil friend so constantly. He believed we were all working for ourselves, all wrapped in our own selfish views, and but estimating him as a nonentity; as one to be set aside and disregarded in all we undertook.

Agnes had promised secresy with the Boyingtons respecting my engagement, but either through forgetfulness of our mutual compact, or pique at my former revelations concerning her own engagement to Paul Redwin, she whispered it in confidence to her aunt, who, worthy old lady, informed the remainder of the family.

I had to suffer a myriad of congratulations at Belle-Vue Terrace, and to bear up against some very rough jests of Sir John, who had taken it into his head to make his appearance in on old dressing-gown, as we were sitting down to supper, and on whom no persuasions of Lady Boyington to induce him to retire, could have the slightest effect. Lady Boyington murmured something about "so nautical!" gave a sickly smile at the company, and resumed her place.

After those three weeks there came the alloy. I was perplexed in the gloom that seemed increasing and gathering over "The Rest," and this was more apparent, and came with greater force, after returning with so light a heart from Wharnby House. Agnes was determined in her project—there was no shaking her from it—no argument to counteract the force with which she clung to her first resolution.

I had promised to let her be the means of making it known to the family and to Paul—to set about her plans in her own way, and work the end of her ambition for the nonce, as her own judgment might suggest. I had sought to wean her from this new fantasy by speaking of Paul and of my father, and of the opposition she must expect from them, and the evil it would bring on all of us. To no purpose. The one thought of London was a talisman which drew her on, which overlooked all obstacles, which would set aside all entreaty of her lover, all threat of her stern sire.

There were bounds to the apathy of my father. I felt assured that his love for Agnes would not give assent to her going to London with her aunt, and that the very suggestion would madden him with its overwhelming force. I set this picture before Agnes with all the power I was capable of. I drew it in its deepest shades, forming a parallel even with her and Gilbert. She heard me out attentively, looked at me with an unflinching gaze, and answered defiantly, "I shall go to London."

The circle in which the Boyingtons moved—the glittering radiations from its circumference—had dazzled one of Agnes's temperament beyond the bounds of reason, had set aside all calculations, and framed her mind to take but one impression.

"Mr. Luke," said Miss Osborne to me one morning, "may

I inquire if any event of importance be about to take place at 'The Rest?'"

"Concerning whom, Miss Osborne?"

"Concerning Agnes," she replied. "You will think me inquisitive, but I have remarked much abstraction of manner in your sister, and yet much determination towards some unknown project."

"I will believe you earnest for her welfare, and interested in Agnes Elmore, my dear Miss Osborne, but not inquisitive."

"The interest for Agnes is deeper than my own heart knows," she said; "I cannot fathom its intensity. She is something more than a younger sister to me. This is strange, and a little romantic, seeing we are not great confidants, Mr. Luke—is it not?"

Before I could reply, she went on—

"It is because she is the only girl whose age approximates to my own that I know or love, and my affections are concentrated in her. Sometimes"—with a sigh—"I wish she would put more trust in me; I would not betray it."

"My sister will not long withhold her secret from you, Miss Osborne, I feel assured," said I; "but I have promised that from her own lips shall come the disclosure."

"You look grave, Mr. Luke," she said, quickly; "is it of importance—is it likely to do her harm?"

"I see no good to spring from the result," I answered; "but I fear all injury. Your keen discernment will place all those fears before you when Agnes makes known her wishes, Miss Osborne—wishes which I trust in you and in your influence to combat against."

"I am powerless," she murmured; "my influence is no more than a name."

"I have seen it exercised with some effect."

"But oh! how seldom," she exclaimed, "and in what small matters, and of what unimportance!"

"God grant that you may succeed in this more serious one."

"Is it so urgent?" she asked, breathlessly; "can I not divine it? Does it concern Mr. Vaudon? for he and Agnes have held long conferences together the last few days, and they are even now walking in the garden."

"Ha!"

I hastened to the window, and looked out.

In the distance, crossing and recrossing a small grass plat at a slow regulated pace, were Vaudon and Agnes. Vaudon had his heavy cloak hanging carelessly from his shoulders, and one hand—the old habit—on his black beard. Agnes, intent on all he said, and listening as to sage advice, walked by his side, and looked eagerly in his face.

What a contrast! The bronzed Egyptian-looking face, dark, impenetrable, silent-looking, and betraying nothing, and the lovely face of the young girl, flushed, eager, and expectant.

"If she profit by *his* teaching, Miss Osborne," I said, bitterly, "God help your own—for it is futile and worth nothing."

"You mistrust that man?" she inquired, quickly.

"As I mistrust all that is false and double-faced—as I mistrust a liar!"

Miss Osborne was silent.

"You must pardon my vehemence, Miss Osborne," I said, less energetically; "but my blood cannot run placidly within my veins at so sad a sight as that," pointing to them in the distance. "Agnes can learn no good from him whose fatal influence deprived my father of a son."

"Of a son!" she cried, turning a deadly white; "of a son—of Gilbert—of——"

She stopped, and a burning flush suffused her face, flickered there a moment, and then vanished, leaving her whiter than before.

"I have betrayed the secret of a household," I said, "if so great a secret could have been so long kept without incurring your suspicions. There is no cause to be more explicit, Miss Osborne, there is so little to explain, and even less that I could say to you. It is enough to know that through that man I have lost the kindest, best, truest of brothers, and my father, though he knew it not, the most exemplary of sons."

She appeared greatly agitated, her slight figure shook violently, and her thin, white hands grasped the back of a chair for support.

"I do not wish—I do not ask to know the reasons that have caused so sad a disrupture in your family, Mr. Luke," she said, looking down; "but as you have broached the subject, and spoken of it of your own free will, may I ask—if—if you have heard from him since the day he left 'The Rest?'"

"No," I answered, mournfully.

"Have you reason to suppose that he is well?"

"I had his promise to me that he would write, if he were unprosperous with the world."

"You may have thought me heedless or unmindful of his welfare, Mr. Luke," she said, still looking down as if she feared to meet my glance; "but there seemed so strict a silence kept concerning him that I felt any recurrence to his name on my part would have been unfitting and unkind. But—but it was not for want of my esteem. You have not thought me unmindful of him, Mr. Luke?"

"I have not been so unjust."

We both turned towards the window again, as if with tacit consent to preclude all further conversation. They were standing on the lawn, and Agnes was taking leave of him, and by her manner evidently reminding him of some promise he had made. She looked behind and held up her finger to him as she came along the winding gravel paths towards the French window at which we were standing.

As Agnes advanced I flung it back, and she entered, looking bright and happy.

I had formed the sudden resolution, whilst she was advancing to the house, of confronting her with Miss Osborne, ere the impressions left by her conference with Vaudon had formed into any settled shape. There should be some antidote to the poison, ere the poison was many minutes old.

"The old topic, Agnes?" asked I.

She looked quickly from Miss Osborne to me—it was a rapid searching glance, and I hastened to reply to it.

"I have made no explanation to Miss Osborne," I said; "I have left it for yourself alone, and have kept strictly to my promise."

Miss Osborne hastened to reply.

"Dear Agnes, do not think I wish to force myself into your confidence, or assert a right to share it. But if you have some great intention, we are all interested; and surely you believe we all would do our best to help you or advise you?"

"Well, then," said Agnes, taking off her bonnet and passing her hands over her braided hair; "we will have a chat about it. It is a slight matter after all; but Luke's gloomy countenance suggests a gunpowder plot at least. Are you going, Luke?"

"I think the conference might have a better——"

"Not at all," interrupted Agnes; "you know all about it. Come join us by the fire, Luke. You will not go to Wharnby House before dinner," with a significant smile.

"I am your humble servant."

Agnes was evidently fearful of a *tête-à-tête* discourse with Miss Osborne, and imagined that the subject might assume a less particular appearance if I made a third party to the conference. We drew our chairs before the fire, and Agnes leant her hand affectionately on the shoulder of Miss Osborne.

"Now the great mystery is simply this—I am going to London with my aunt."

For all the light air Agnes had assumed, the announcement was so astounding that Miss Osborne caught Agnes by the hand and cried out, "To London!" in piercing tones that startled both of us."

"It is very strange," said Agnes, peevishly, "that the name of London should have so terrible an effect. Is it the abode of giants, or devouring wolves, or full of enchanted castles kept by three-headed ogres like we read of in children's story-books, that the very name should alarm you so, Miss Osborne?"

"To London!" Miss Osborne could only reply.

"Yes, to London, with my aunt and cousins—sufficient protection for even the daughter of an 'Elmore.'"

"But, Agnes," said Miss Osborne; "what inducement is there to go to London? You will pardon me for mentioning it, my dear girl, but your engagement—your father's strong dislike to fashionable life—your own pursuits—your home."

"Miss Osborne," said Agnes, withdrawing her hand from hers, and looking fixedly at her, "these superficial arguments have been used so often, and commented upon so much by Luke, that a recapitulation of them is tedious and most unnecessary. There is a misunderstanding concerning my proposed trip. You look upon it as a grave expedition; I, as a pleasant journey, and a little change. Why my engagement should keep me from a friendly visit, though that visit be to my relations in London, I cannot see; or why my father's objections should debar me from a natural wish, and my pursuits stand in the way of its accomplishment."

"It is not the going, it is the wish to go," cried Miss Osborne, warmly; "it is the vain desire of mixing in society, of courting adulation, of mingling with that false, artificial stream, from which you have been kept aloof, that will do you moral injury."

"Moral injury!" cried Agnes, starting up with flashing eyes; "what teaching have I, then, received from you, that all your inculcations are so estimated? Am I so weak of will—so prone to flattery—so fragile in my very nature—that, like a bright mirror, a mere breath must tarnish me?"

"I have judged your character truly, I believe, dear Agnes, and you are wronging me by your vehemence."

"And my character?" asked Agnes, imperiously.

"Is this," answered her preceptor. "You are good-hearted, and there is sterling gold beneath the surface; but it is so hidden, and the warm promptings of the heart so checked, that your better self only predominates at times. You study your own will too much; and yet, a flattering speech will lead you; and your love of admiration stands out a distinguishing mark that all can see! Have I not fought hard to win your respect without debasing you by studied compliments?"

"The respect is gone for ever, Miss Osborne," said Agnes, drawing her tall form to its queenly height; "the love between us is destroyed and lost. You lower me before my brother; you seek to lower me in my own esteem. I thank you for the knowledge of myself that you have given me—a degrading knowledge that I cannot profit by."

"I have said it for your good," replied Miss Osborne, with a faltering voice; "I have told a hard truth in hope of dissuading you from the purpose you have formed. Oh! Agnes, in the deep love that my heart holds for you, place credence, and believe its promptings. Give up this scheme that can but end in ill, and that will stir up so much of misconstruction. Put aside my love, regret and shun me when we meet; nay, be an utter stranger to me; but do not go to London. For your father's sake—your own!"

"For Paul's!" I cried; "for his love that claims you as a destined wife, that holds you sacred to himself alone."

"My father will grant me his consent," said Agnes, coldly. "I will ask him before you all to-morrow, and he will give it me of his free accord. I ask none other. For Paul's sake, Luke; and why for Paul's? Have I to bow to a tyrannical dominion, that *he*, of all others, is to command my actions, and to rule them?"

"Listen unto others, not always to yourself!" cried Miss Osborne, imploringly. "I am not so urgent without a cause, although to it you are blind. This family——"

"Stop!" said Agnes, "they are my friends. All these protestations and melo-dramatic scenes are not worthy of the theme. You over-act your part, Miss Osborne. I am not affected by your eloquence; and, were it to the purpose, I am not your pupil, and am free from school dominion. Give me a will of my own, and not dictate to me as if I were a helpless child. My will is formed!"

Miss Osborne let her hands drop to her side, and her head bend, with the agony of her grief. There was no resisting the look on Agnes's face—it was immovable. Death could not have changed it, but have alone impressed it more indelibly. "Her will was formed"—was graven as in marble!

As she glided from the room, Miss Osborne, in the bitterness of her grief, cried out, as though her heart would break—"Oh! how I loved her—how I loved her in my loneliness!"

CHAPTER XXIV.

THE SECOND.

AGNES went out, with her brother Edward, a few minutes after her altercation with Miss Osborne, and did not return till within a few minutes before the dinner-hour. They had been to Lady Boyington's, and Agnes was in high spirits with her visit.

Paul came in after dinner, and took his accustomed place.

"When is Paul to learn your intention, Agnes?" I inquired, aside.

"To-night, I think," she said, carelessly; "for I go next Monday."

"Next Monday!—and to-day is Friday."

"An unlucky day for disclosures, as for everything else; but it is of little consequence—and I am not superstitious."

It was a custom for the members of the family to divide into two sections after dinner—Miss Osborne, Agnes, Paul, and I, adjourning to the music-room, leaving Edward with my father and Vaudon. Edward had no love for associating with those whose ages appeared by nature to be more congenial to his own, and was content to remain with Vaudon and my father, and to listen to their grave discourse till he grew sleepy, when he stretched himself at full length on the couch, and slept peacefully until further summons.

With the exception of Miss Osborne, who pleaded a sick-headache, we strolled to the music-room. It was a favourite lounge of ours; and there, free from all the restraint which my father's presence imposed, we have passed many pleasant hours.

Paul was in capital spirits, I had seldom seen him more cheerful, or more engaging. There were no Boyingtons to acidulate his temper, no rivals in the way, no simpering fops, sidling towards Agnes with the intention of asking her to dance, no admirers, no paper-gallants and carpet knights, sighing at her feet, or making eyes of soft persuasion.

Paul was always happy when alone with her; but his jealous temperament would not allow of a third person between him and Agnes; he was a perfect lover, fond of monopoly, and exacting in the extreme.

To-night he was the true Paul Redwin. Perfectly at home, he rattled on his discourse, with a jest, and a laugh for everything.

Agnes sat at the piano, her fingers wandering carelessly over the keys, striking plaintive chords, and looking thoughtful. Perhaps, she was thinking, like myself, of the change that would be in Paul Redwin's spirits soon, and postponing her declaration out of pity for the shock.

"I say, Luke," cried Paul, a merry smile lighting up his handsome face, "are you off to Wharnby House to-night?"

"In a few minutes," I replied, "have you any commands?"

"No; my best respects, that's all," said he.

"Play my sentimental French song, dear," said he, clearing his throat, "I'm taken musical. Luke, take a seat, and 'I'll enchant thine ear.'"

"Thank you, but I really must depart."

"Very well, I'll enchant my own," said Paul, "I shan't be gone when you come back, I dare say, and if you are pressed for time now, why I must let you off, that's all."

"Are you disposed for a ride with me, Redwin?"

"Excuse me," with a mock bow of great politeness.

"You will not?"

"Why, it is so seldom that I get a quiet evening, thanks to those confounded Boyingtons and their everlasting *soirées*, that I really must decline."

Agnes laughed; it was her policy to keep Paul in the best of spirits. She trusted to her own powers of persuasion, which backed by his love, gave her hope of obtaining his consent.

"*Au revoir*, then."

"*Au revoir*. Now, Agnes, the song, and then we will rejoin the good folks in the parlour."

I left them, he standing by her side, and looking down upon her smiling upturned face, with his dark, earnest, loving eyes. He stood by her side, tall, erect and handsome, without a care to gnaw at his heart's core, without a thought of the secret of Agnes's impending and threatening over him.

I reached Wharnby House about seven in the evening, and Celia welcomed me with a bright smile.

It was a happy evening. We were all in all to each other; there were no jarring thoughts to our own—no interruptions to our felicity. The rector was absent; Mrs. Silvernot sat at the table, with her spectacles across her little peaked nose, absorbed in her novel from the new library at Wharnby. The rector was not expected, or she would have carefully set it aside until his departure, and listened to his plans about his church, or the new infants' school he was building down the lane. Miss Wigginton was at her mother's, in London, for a few weeks; and Mr. Silvernot, senior, had gone to a public dinner at the Albion Hotel, and was not expected home till late. I played chess with Celia, and looked over some new music that had come from London, and then, tired of both occupations, I won her over to talk of our future—that golden, brilliant future which was never written in my book of destiny that I should share!

It was the first time we had looked forward, and she sat blushing by my side, and turning away her head, and yet not unhappy, or unwilling to listen to my projects.

Mrs. Silvernot had fallen asleep over the heroine's rescue from the Baron of the Black Forest, by Sir Spotless de White, of course, the hero, and a perfect gentleman—and was nodding gracefully in her chair. Her troubles were over, her vigilance at rest—her Celia engaged. She was a strange woman. Since the end of Celia's first love-dream, her whole thoughts had been concentrated in finding a substitute for Redwin, and of marrying her youngest daughter. For this purpose she had taken her to town relatives, and accepted every invitation to neighbours' parties, and given entertainments of her own, and had been foiled by Celia's own calm indifference to the admirers that crowded round her. And yet, if we were married, Mrs. Silvernot would cry bitterly at the altar, and feel the parting as deeply as mothers do feel, and be miserable and lonely the remainder of her life with Miss Wigginton, three-volume novels, and sal-volatile. Unfathomable inconsistency! So Mrs. Silvernot slept, and we painted fancy pictures in our glowing minds, and love was taking deeper root within us.

That night I told her of the past first love that had been foiled by my accomplished rival. I spoke of my agony at finding Redwin the usurper of my place, and of the memorable night of my return—a night spent before the hollow burning fire, wherein I had sacrificed the treasures and love-tokens I had garnered for so long a time. And she could so well feel sympathy for all my disappointment, and return my smile, and whisper, "If I were reconciled now with my second love?" No need to tell my answer in that happy moment—no need to dwell upon a scene like this, a scene that draws the hot tears from me as I bend over this reminiscence, and sears my heart with its old memories, and makes a child of me.

It was late when I took my leave of Celia and Mrs. Silvernot. I had not ridden to Wharnby House, having purposed to enjoy a moonlight walk on my return, with the cool winds blowing from the sea.

I had set foot on the country road, when a hoarse, suffocating voice greeted me.

"Elmore!"

I turned, and from the shade of an adjacent clump of trees came forth Paul Redwin.

"Paul! What is the matter?—what has happened?"

I could divine the cause, but the very suddenness of his appearance extorted the unnecessary queries.

"I have been waiting for you by those trees some hours."

"You have quarrelled with Agnes?"

"A quarrel not of my own seeking, God knows," he said. "Luke, I have waited for you to ask if you, *her* brother, have no power to stop this project? I ask for her own sake, not for mine, now—not for mine!"

I looked into his face. The moonlight revealed features sternly set, over which the old air of haughtiness was fluttering.

"If you have failed, how can I succeed?"

"You are her brother," he answered; "there is some tie

between you—some natural love; but I am an idler, one fitted to amuse her dull hours—nothing more."

"You misjudge yourself."

"Not I," he said; "if a woman love the man destined for her husband, she will give consideration to his wishes, and sacrifice her dearest hopes to please him. I have had right on my side; I have had all that makes right; I have sought to demonstrate all to her; I have knelt at her feet—grovelled before her in the dust to turn her from her fallacies."

"And she gives no ear?"

"She set me at defiance; she spoke of her right to command *my* actions," cried Paul, excitedly. "She boasted of these new-found friends, the pleasures she had enjoyed with them, the anticipations she had in her intended London visit; she spoke and thought of everything but the feelings of that heart she has cast aside for ever."

"Oh! not that, Redwin; it has not ended like that?"

"It has ended—it is for ever broken off," he said. "The long years of love, where I have worshipped her, and would have died for her. If she had asked me, this accursed night, to sacrifice my life for hers, I would have done it, Luke, without a murmur. But it was not in my nature—I loved her too well, her name, her future place as my own wife—to say, 'Go with your friends; go as if you were unfettered by the tie of an engagement; go with that heartless crew of fashionables; mix with their world, follow their pursuits, and forget me till you return!' I *could not* say that, Luke. I have been at your aunt's house, and seen her son-in-law and his male friends hovering about her, with their wanton glances, in my own presence, seeking to gain her smiles, to win her from me before my own eyes; and yet I was to let her go to London with them all! No, no; she loved me not, or she would have said, like a true woman, 'Paul you are the best judge of my actions, and of what wounds *you*—I will stay!'"

"Was there no relenting?"

"None," he said. "She flung me off as though I were a dog. She severed the bonds by which we were united; she brought the books and trinkets I had given her, and showered them before me in her passion; she cast me from her mind, her heart, glorying in the deed!"

"What is to be done?"

"Nothing," he said; "my pride is humbled, my hope of life

is gone. If Agnes gave up her wish to-morrow, and become as I first knew her, I could not say, 'I love you!' There is a burning within me at my heart, but it is not love, nor hate, nor anything that has a name. I feel that I am wholly changed—that I am a man seeking some object which no hand from heaven points out, and yet which urges me and goads me on. I must have excitement; I should go mad if I took to my old life. Oh, Luke, old friend! the poorest beggar in the streets may pity me this moment!"

"Courage, dear Redwin," I said; "there are many fairer and with minds more disciplined than Agnes, that will make you a good wife, and as happy a home as you deserve. This is the first overwhelming feeling, and it bears you down. To-morrow will bring its true counsel and make a man of you."

He shook his head.

"I shall not come to 'The Rest' again, of course. I shall be glad to see you at my house in a few weeks; but you must give me time to think and act. I could not bear to meet your face yet awhile. I have not the nerve. I may go abroad to-morrow, or I may live and die in Wharnby. I know not what a day may decide for me. But whatever comes about, whatever Fate deals out for me, remember this—Paul Redwin has no dearer friend, nor one he holds in greater honour and esteem, than Luke Elmore, of 'The Rest.'"

He grasped my hand, and wrung it long and silently, looking at me with a softened expression on his haggard face, and then struck into a by-path leading to his home, and was gone.

The gay notes of the piano saluted me on my return to "The Rest."

I walked to the music-room. Agnes was seated at the instrument; she was alone. The heap of presents Redwin had brought her in happier times lay in a rude heap upon the floor.

She looked round upon my entrance. Her eyes were very bright, her cheek somewhat flushed and red, but she was calm and passionless, and struck the keys firmly and with unshaking fingers.

"Well, Luke; you are late."

"Have you been here since I left?"

"No; I presided at the tea-table, and played backgammon with Vaudon; but it was tedious, so I have returned."

"I have seen Paul."

She shrugged her white shoulders and played on.

"He has told me the result."

"He is confiding."

She played the music softly whilst we were speaking, like an accompaniment.

"Is it possible, Agnes, that you can sit and play there, knowing the ruin you have made of his affections—the severance of an engagement that has extended over years?"

"Why not?" she said, looking round in mild surprise; "the engagement was a weak one—made in haste, and long since, on my part, repented. I am no fitting wife for Paul Redwin, Esquire; and we both believe it. It has all happened for the best. This is a new set of quadrilles I am playing; do you like them?"

"You celebrate your new existence?"

"New! Luke?"

The music softly playing.

"You have entered upon a new life with the heartlessness that has characterised this night. You will look back upon it some day with regret. You stand upon a threshold gazing in at a bright scene, where the guests are many, and the colours are enchanting, and where the flowers are strewn thickly for your tread. But the guests who welcome you wear masks; the colours will grow faint, and fade; the flowers but hide the snares and pitfalls into which many as undaunted as Agnes Elmore have fallen and been lost!"

"Strange, brother mine, you deal in metaphors, and I cannot understand them. This 'La Poule' is charming!"

Long after I had gone to my own room the music came softly stealing to my ears, and ringing in low melody throughout "The Rest."

CHAPTER XXV.

THE THIRD!

TRUE to her promise, and sanguine as to the result, Agnes made her appearance at the breakfast-table the next morning full of the bold determination of asking her father's consent to her intended visit.

There was a smile of anticipated triumph on her red lips,

and her full blue eyes looked meaningly at me. There was a cold "Good morning" for Miss Osborne, and then a total disregard of the presence of her best friend. Agnes was not one easily to forget.

Edward and Vaudon came in a few minutes after we were seated.

"Where is papa?" eagerly asked Agnes.

"He will be here directly," answered Vaudon, evading her inquiring glance.

For the first time a suspicion of the nature of Vaudon's good offices crossed the thoughts of my sister, and her little hand closed convulsively.

That Vaudon was in my sister's confidence I had been long aware, and there was no doubt that he knew of Agnes's intention, and encouraged it. Had Agnes relied upon this man to use his influence for her sake, and, knowing her own power likewise over her father, placed implicit trust in the combined influence working for one end? Had he played her traitor at the last moment, and struck another blow for the great scheme he was planning?

My father entered. I felt my heart beating very fast, and glanced at Agnes. She was unmoved, and rose to greet him with her morning kiss.

He turned away as she advanced, and moved on as if unconscious of her being near, and sank heavily into his seat.

I had seen many changes in my father; but from his first coming to "The Rest" in his sick bed a paralytic man, and but a step between life and death, or glaring from his leathern chair and denouncing his own son, I had never seen him look like this.

His face was of an ashen grey, a dull leaden colour that was fearfully unnatural; his long hair was tangled and disordered, and his dress had evidently not been taken off since the preceding night. The red, fiery eyes were sunken in his head, and gleamed like a wild beast's.

"You are not well, sir," cried Miss Osborne.

"Luke, go for a doctor!" cried Edward, really alarmed at his appearance.

"I am well, I am very well," muttered my father; "what makes you think that I am ill?"

He stretched a shaking hand out for his breakfast-cup, and sought to look down our fears.

It was a silent meal; we felt a heavy weight upon our tongues which kept us mute; we were conscious of some event about to take place more or less connected with my sister, and the very uncertainty of its nature kept us, all but one, and she the principal and most concerned, feverish and fearfully expectant.

My father spoke not during the meal; he sat looking before him into vacancy, and the clattering noise of the cup shaking in his hand but told of the inward agitation from which he sat there, a poor sufferer.

Suddenly the clear, musical voice of Agnes broke the silence.

"Papa!"

I sought to catch her eye, but she, conscious of my object, looked at her father, and at him alone.

"Another time," I cried; "not now, Agnes! See you not his state? Have you no reason or compassion, girl?"

"I am very well," murmured my father again.

"Agnes!" pleaded Miss Osborne.

But Agnes had commenced.

"Papa, Lady Boyington has kindly invited me to her town mansion, and offered me the shelter of her roof for a few weeks. I have become attached to her, I love her very dearly, and I have consented to accompany her. There is but your consent to ratify my own, and make your daughter happy. You will not deny it? You are not afraid to trust me to her care, or to trust me with myself?"

She placed both her hands upon his arm, and looked into his face with an old winning expression that had never failed her yet.

He neither turned nor moved, nor seemed to be aware that she was hanging over him in her false fondness; he looked still forward at the vacant space, and said—

"It is your wish to go?"

"It is."

"To leave 'The Rest' and go to London?"

"Yes."

"To part for ever from me?"

"For ever, dear papa!"

"Ay."

"I do not understand. It is my wish to see London. I have been brought up too strictly, and too well to suffer from any temptations that it may present. A virtuous girl is as safe in cities as in a wilderness."

"I came to 'The Rest' for peace. I came that I might keep my children from the curse of society and aloof from the evil that it brings. In Agnes Elmore I saw but the same face that had deceived me, and I prayed that it might never leave my side until my death or her own marriage. I feared for that face ere it grew a woman's—I find the confirmation of my fears this day."

"You have no trust in your own daughter?"

"None."

A gloomy look settled on Agnes' brow.

"You will give me your consent?"

"You are engaged to a young man of honourable principles, a true gentleman. Has he given you *his* permission?"

Agnes did not answer.

"Has he—but no matter, he has not!"

"May I go, papa?" persisted Agnes, her form dilating, and her chest heaving with excitement.

Still looking before him, he continued—

"The woman you would go with is a woman of the world one whose precepts are all worldly, and whose soul is all calculation and self-interest. I have known her in her youth; I have seen her but a few months back unchanged. This woman was the sister of your mother, Agnes, the elder sister, and from whom your mother received the greater portion of her education. You still wish to go?"

"Yes."

"I have known all this some weeks; I have heard my only friend—my only good adviser—patiently and sorrowfully. You have rejected all his counsel; all his admonitions."

"What!" cried Agnes.

"Headstrong and resolved, you pass all friendly warning by."

"May I go?" again asked Agnes, sharply.

"I have never sought to force the inclination of my children; since they have passed the boundary of childhood, I have allowed each to think and act, believing the remembrance of my teaching was strong enough to keep them from all ill. I have been deceived. Still, I put no force upon their actions each is his or her own master—I have but to express my wish, and then let them act by it or not—I have done my part."

He took a long breath, and went on again.

"My wish is, that you should stay! By going with that woman and her family, you inflict the heaviest blow upon me. You bring back all the horror and disgrace I have come hither to avoid. You dishonour me, and pile coals of fire upon my head. If you will remain, I will love you as no daughter has been loved, and every whim of your own shall have its gratification; but if you go, I never wish to see you more—I cast you from my heart—I lose all common respect—I hate and loathe you from that hour!"

His forced calmness was abandoning him, and the wild passion, more natural to him, was possessing him. "I will not deprive you of your inheritance—it is a daughter's right, and I have an Elmore's pride. Had you been a man, I would have closed the doors of this house for ever against your return, as I have done against your wilful brother's. But it is enough that your inheritance of love will be for ever lost; and if you go, may God forgive your wilfulness!"

"You put no force upon my actions, and yet you madly pile threat on threat to thwart me," cried Agnes, indignantly; "but I am not easily deterred by the imaginations you have brooded on, until you think every step I take requires a guiding hand. Father, I shall go."

He gave a low, smothered cry, and hid his face. I sprang towards him, crying—

"She will not go; it is but a rash assertion in her anger."

He shook me off, and looked up again, stern and wild."

"And Vaudon," said Agnes, "I have to thank you for your double-dealing. I see the study you have made, and congratulate you on its fair success. I should have doubted all your specious phrases, and your lying tongue, as others have doubted you years since."

"You rave, Agnes. I have done my best to——"

"No more. I am not blind."

Agnes rose, and, with the old, old look, went slowly towards the door. Miss Osborne sprang forward, but Agnes waved her hand, imperiously crying—"Back, I would be alone!"

All that day Agnes kept to her own room, and my father sat where she had left him, vacant and almost unconscious. The servants glided in and out; Vaudon sat by him; I tried to gain his ear; but, like some one stricken into stone, he sat crushed by his disregarded love.

He went to his room at his usual hour, and came down on

the Sunday and took his old place, and sat there rigid and immovable as on the preceding day. I laid a book upon his knees, and there it lay, open at the same page, until it fell to the ground. I tried one last appeal to Agnes. I begged and implored her, for her father's sake, as I had never begged or implored throughout my life; but the fatal perversity of her mind was not shaken by the urgency of my appeals, and she was adamant.

The Monday came. Her boxes had been taken from the house by the servants, and she was ready to depart. She came into the room, equipped for her journey, to bid us "good-bye." Taking no heed of Vaudon, or of Miss Osborne, as if they were her deadliest enemies—and one may have been, at least—she stooped and kissed her father on the forehead.

He murmured something like "Good-bye," but the words were indistinct and vague; and the look he gave her might have turned her even then, it was so mournful in its very sternness.

"Will you come and see my aunt, Luke, before we go?"

I escorted her to the cliff on which the house of my aunt was placed, bade my relatives good-bye, and turned to Agnes.

"For the last time, stay."

"Impossible!"

"Think what you have done. Good God! Agnes, can you really be so young, and yet so impenetrable to human sorrow? Your own father, Agnes—your own father!"

"I am going on a visit," she said, calmly.

It was a cold farewell I took of her, and we parted.

I returned home to find my father still seated in the chair as I had left him. I spoke to him, and told him that I had seen her safe with her aunt; but he paid no attention to my words, and kept the same dull, apathetic stare.

A fearful presentiment of evil came across me as I looked at him. The face seemed changed since I had seen it last; the leaden colour more intense; the lips and nose more prominent, and the breath more short.

"Vaudon," I cried, "I cannot leave him in this listless state! He is ill! I will go for Dr. Whittaker."

"I am better."

They were the first words he had distinctly spoken for days, and my heart felt relieved, and beat freer and more light.

"Will you walk with me round the garden? The air is mild, and will revive you, sir."

He shook his head.

"I think some medical advice is necessary, still."

"No, no," he cried, hastily.

But I was not content, and on my own responsibility dispatched a servant for the old physician that had attended my brother Gilbert in his illness.

I spent the time till his arrival anxiously watching my father in his chair. When he had seen him, he looked grave and walked aside with Vaudon, and held a whispered conference.

Presently, Dr. Whittaker came across to me.

"Your father must be taken to his room directly. I shall not leave to-night."

"Is there danger?"

"I regret to say the greatest!"

He was carried more than led to his room. I dispatched a second servant to Wharnby, with orders, if Agnes had already started, to follow her to London with a hasty note which I had written. The telegraph had not at that time annihilated space.

When he was in bed, he turned upon his withered side, and reached out his thin, white hand to me.

"God bless you!"

"Oh! father, father, not those words; oh! not spoken with that look—oh! father!"

There was a faint smile, and he let go my hand and pointed to an iron chest beside the window.

"What is it, Elmore?" asked Vaudon.

My father, with a prolonged ringing cry, sprang up in his bed. The doctor crossed hastily towards him.

"Keep him back! keep him back! My will, my will! Gilbert—son—'The Rest!'"

He fell back in his bed, and rose once more and struggled for his life, and raved of Gilbert, Vaudon, and "The Rest." I flung my arms round him in my agony, and called upon his name, and prayed to God to spare him to his children. But the great seal was set, the final word was written, and through my blinding tears I watched his life die out as he lay pillowed 'gainst my breast.

CHAPTER XXVI.

REST.

He rests at last! Free from his overbearing load of grief, he sleeps in peace, poor, weary, suffering pilgrim! and all the sorrows of his life are forgotten in "The Rest."

How many years—slow, dragging, cruel years—have gone by in the flight of time, since he looked so calm, so peaceful, and so untired with brooding thought, as now, sleeping in his coffin!

Through the darkened rooms and gloomy passages I wander, borne down by my loss—oppressed by an iron weight—lowered to the dust.

How many self-accusations come crowding on me now, from years back, a wilful child, to this sad time, embracing within that long, long space such myriads of reproaches! What might I not have been to him in his loneliness—what comfort to his saddened years, had I studied him the more and myself the less? Had I ever sought to alleviate the burden of his dishonour by showing to him a son's love, and giving proof of it in action? Had not his thoughts and mine been ever separate? Had not our paths diverged more and more from each other's since I became a man and acted for myself? Would it have ended thus—would his life have passed away like a fleeting vision, leaving so dark a reality to accuse me—had I made his wishes, strange as they were, my first consideration?

But it is too late—the time will never come again—the hour is passed for ever—the gulf that stands between time and eternity divides us—the grave shuts out all hope!

Day and night I move about the house without an object; I come upon my brother Edward, listlessly walking up and down the room, or sleeping in that sacred leathern chair before the fire, exhibiting his grief in a dull stupor and a heavy silence. I meet Vaudon gliding like a ghost about the house, his hand upon his beard, his dark eyes bent upon the ground. Is there any memory of love for the old friend he has parted with on earth? Is there a self-accusation in *his* breast—one sorrowful recollection at his heart? I read an appreciation of my inward grief, and a kind sympathy in all I feel, in the pale face of Miss Osborne, and I hear words of consolation breathed from her lips to me; and they fall like summer rain, and bring me comfort for the time.

And friends come to The "Rest," and pay their last duty to the dead. And the rector kneels with me in that silent room, inhabited by death, and we pray together long and earnestly; and Celia places both her hands in mine at parting, and looks her consolation through her tears; and Paul Redwin comes one night, and grasps my hand—sits beside me, silent in his companionship, and disappears, I scarce know how or in what manner, and leaves me in my loneliness.

There comes a letter, bordered deep with black, stamped with the London post-mark, and written by a hand to which I am a stranger. I break the seal and read:—

"No. —, Park Lane.

"MY DEAR, DEAR NEPHEW,

"The sudden shock which the arrival of the servant has caused poor Agnes—followed as it was by your fatal letter bringing the cruel tidings of your father's death—will totally prevent her immediate return. The dear child is very ill indeed, and I think, with your permission, it will be better for her to remain with me in London—such associations as 'The Rest' will bring to her sensitive mind being sorrowful and unnecessary. You will perceive the force of this yourself, my afflicted boy. Our own physician is attending Agnes, but she is very much depressed. Poor Sir John is also 'cut up' in a remarkable degree, and my feelings you can well imagine. Agnes desires from her sick couch the expression of her deep regret for her irreparable loss, and sends her best love to yourself and Edward, in which I heartily unite with her.

"Believe me, my dear Luke,
"Your affectionate aunt,
"LYDIA BOYINGTON."

I place the letter aside; it is of little consequence whether the daughter weep over the father's grave or not; he would have wished it, perhaps, but my sister's indisposition—I can see her, in her elegance of grief, pillowed on the couch before the fire—prevents the last token of respect. So let it be. It cannot sting the silent sleeper for whom I am mourning here.

I seal the iron chest in which is deposited my father's will, keeping home-secrets safe until a fitting time. I take his pocket-book from the desk, undo the same, and, amongst old papers, I detect a letter, the superscription of which is "To my son, Luke Elmore." Time enough—time enough for the contents of that epistle, written as from the grave to me—sad, holy record, which I treasure in my breast.

The darkness of the night steals on: we lay him in the old churchyard of Wharnby, and my tears fall thickly o'er his resting-place. There are many followers to his final home; and the long train of servants in deep mourning add to the number. It had been his wish in old time, and the last sign of pride was not denied his memory.

Returning home, leaving that dear one behind, I feel that he is really gone, and that one tie the more has broken with that new mound of earth beneath which my father sleeps!

* * * * * * *

The figure reaches the apex of the mountain, and points to the path by which we have struggled to its lofty eminence. Looking back, how dark a road, with, ah! how little light upon it, is revealed beneath my gaze! Above, one star—a star in which my vain love has built its faith—shines dimly; and, as I look, the figure shakes its head, and makes its gesture of command.

But the dull vista of my past is sunshine to the ebon gloom of that dark future, down the steep mountain side of which the figure leads the way. More rugged and more fierce, I start back from my guide, and look for help towards the star. It darts through space—that one light—and is gone!

Still onwards—ever onwards—with this genius of my life: slowly, painfully, along the downward path! There are figures in this gathering darkness known to me, and I seek to touch them, and they recede as I advance.

Still onwards, following the shadows!

CHAPTER XXVII.

THE WILL.

THE Elmore seal upon the iron chest in that room where my father died, is broken, and my own hands have unlocked the weighty mass of metal, and drawn from its receptacle my father's will.

His will; and I abide by it! I murmur not, nor speak a bitter word, nor heap one cruel accusation: it is enough for me that he has written it.

No matter in what mood, or stung by what false promptings—he has thought it best; and I fold my arms across my chest, as if to stay the wild beating of my heart, and am content.

My soul is heavy, and my mind is clouded. I am stern, silent, and yet uncomplaining. I am suffering within—not for loss of my inheritance—not for the bar he has laid upon my progress; but for the wrong estimation he has ever had of me—the ignorance of my filial love—the inability to test the truth of my own mind—the misconception of everything concerning me.

The tenor of the will is this:—

To Vaudon, Jacques Vaudon, his dear friend, his old companion—so run the phrases of affection—he leaves nearly a third of his whole fortune, adding thereunto—as if he could not pile sufficient riches upon the man to testify to him his last token of regard—"The Rest," and all estates belonging to it.

To Edward Elmore is left a sum of money equalling that apportioned to Jacques Vaudon; there is no word of comment made—he dismisses him with so many thousand pounds: a legacy and birthright. To his loved daughter, Agnes Elmore, the same portion is allotted; and then follows the name of Luke, and there is left to him—three hundred pounds a year! From all his wealth, from the riches which have accumulated by long interest until they have swollen into a fortune that kings might envy on their thrones, he leaves me this poor pittance!

Brought up as I have been, knowing no money's value, and putting no value on it, taught from my cradle to be considered the child of a rich man; the sum seems poorer by comparison, and I feel that it would have been less degrading to have been wholly cast aside and struck off from his slightest notice like his first-born son, than to have inherited this mammon's stigma which seems crushing me with its reproach.

"Within my desk is a letter for the eyes of my son Luke alone," he writes; "and therein he will find and give justice to the reasons that have actuated me in bequeathing the above sum to him."

Vaudon and the rector of Wharnby are executors to this strange will, dated a year back, and signed by witnesses and drawn up, at my father's dictation, by a legal hand. Vaudon is left the trustee over the property of Edward and Agnes, and their sole guardian until twenty-one years of age. I am, by law, a man and my own master, and there is no ruler over the legacy which my father has bestowed upon me.

I take the letter from my breast when I am alone, and open it, and reverentially gaze upon the lines written tremblingly by his left hand, and crossed, stained, and almost indistinct. It must have been a great task for him in his affliction, and the paper is blistered in many places as with tears.

I read :—

"'The Rest,'
"November 18th, 18—.

"MY DEAR SON,

"These lines, written with an aching heart and tortured mind, are intended for your eyes alone, when I am dead to the world and at peace in the grave. Yesterday I made my will. To you, as my *eldest son* it is my duty to explain some portion of it that is mysterious, and which appears to you unjust. You will blame me in your anger, but in the end you will judge me fairly, and believe that I have acted well. I have left to Jacques Vaudon, Edward, and Agnes, the same sums of money, adding to Jacques Vaudon's, the house in which I live, for he is attached to it—far more than my children are—and I would not have him cast away from its memories. He has been my only staff, my helping hand. He is poor ; I out of gratitude have enriched him. I have left you three hundred pounds a year—it is sufficient for a country gentleman. You will have shelter at 'The Rest,' and have horses, servants, all at your command while within the circle of that home you have so long despised, and instructed by that friend's advice which you have always shunned—I have left you no more for this reason. You are a lover of the world, and its temptations are great to a man of wealth. You would have despised 'The Rest,' rejected all good counsel, mixed with the lying faces of false friends, made my name as it was of old, cursed your own existence, forgotten brother, sister, home, your father's memory, and your own honour.

"I have kept you from these dangers by my will. London will offer no temptations now, for your income will not suffice to keep you in your ancient splendour. You will remain at Wharnby ; your pride will not allow of anything else. You will become a good man, and, if you marry—I hardly wish it—a kind husband and father, neglecting neither wife nor children for society ; and the wife, not having wealth before her in her choice, will be to you that which God ever denied to me !

"If I keep you from evil, from temptation, I have not done

wrong. I feel less weight upon my mind since this will has been completed, and I hope that I have fulfilled my duty by you all. To your brother Edward, cold and unimaginative, an exalted station is necessary, and will *command* respect. To Agnes, she will be the wife of a good young man, and I have given her a marriage portion, and the fears which I once had for her are subdued or wholly gone. She will never see London —that world of vanity and sin; and her whole life is changed, and bright and radiant. I feel it as I write.

"My concern is now alone for you. I have long lost your love and confidence; it is an affliction I foresaw years ago. Strong in your intentions, wilful and heedless, and not to be turned aside from any rash endeavour, I have done my best to restrain your wild impetuosity. The fierce passions that led you along the rocky paths by the sea-side when a boy; the eager desire for fashionable life when a young man, have ripened, and yet must fall to the ground by the means I have adopted. That it pains me to adopt them, believe me, my dear Luke; but there is no second course, or I would take it.

"The ways of life are varied and unknown, and evil may follow from this intended good, and jealousy, envy, and uncharitableness choke up the well-springs of your best affections; but judge me rightly, Luke, and if I have wounded you deeply and irreparably, forgive me; I mean all for the best! Looking forward to the grave, and standing, perhaps, upon its brink, I write these words to you. "Ever your affectionate father,

"GILBERT ELMORE."

Strange wandering epistle—speaking of the goodness of his heart in its very sternness! I read it, and re-read it, and ponder more upon it.

"If I have long lost your love and confidence!" Recrimination speaking from the grave, accusing me of my old apathy, my life silence, and stinging more than all! And yet he loved me, I know it now, I read it in these lines, I find it in the motive for my poor inheritance, and I am comforted.

Misjudging ever—in his eldest son denying his affection, and never mentioning his name; in Agnes, elevating her above her right or merits; in Vaudon, placing him above us all, and blind to every fault of his, and trustful only in the most unworthy; in myself, doubting, fearful, and full of apprehension; never taking a right view of the figures passing beneath his eyes.

Was there a waking light that fearful morning, when he sprang up in his bed, and pointing to his chest, cried out—

"Keep him back!—keep him back! My will!—my will!—Gilbert—son—'The Rest!'"

I believe so, and I am happier in my belief. Confirmed by his wild terror and his shrieking cries for Gilbert that succeeded, is that conviction fixed upon me.

Amongst his papers, I find another letter addressed to no son in particular, but applying unto each. There is no date, no mark to tell how long a time it is since it was written. It runs thus—

"It is the duty of a son to avenge a family's dishonour; the stain that rests upon the name of Elmore is still branding it, and a whole life's curse is covering it with shame. Seek not the quarrel, but abide the time. It will come one day to the father or the son, and then act. For the seducer and adulterer there is but one atonement!"

I raise the letter to my lips, and murmur a vow; I steal forth to the churchyard, and over the new grave renew my pledge to the dead.

I meet Vaudon on the road, and we walk home together. He is friendly in his actions towards me, and links his arm within my own, as if he would draw me to his heart. I am too moody and depressed to pay much heed to his discourse, so we walk on, two grave figures homewards. I hear words that fall meaningless upon my ears of his offer of service, and his desire that I should make "The Rest" my home—his "Rest!" He would have us still one family, still united. I try to say some words, expressive of my thanks in return, but my proud spirit chokes me, and I merely incline my head. He leaves me not till within the hall, and then he presses my hand and glides away. He seems content with the result of his long study, and would propitiate the children of his patron. Even Gilbert might receive a welcome home, if he came back to "The Rest." Edward has been won—he has great faith in Vaudon—he looks upon him as his second father, and is almost forgetful of the first, and certainly quite reconciled to the home-loss that we have suffered.

He is curious about me, and wonders what I shall do with three hundred a year. "You have such lofty notions, that I don't know how you'll get on. Certainly, there's a home now. But when you marry, Luke?"

When I marry! My heart beats fast—the blood quickens in my veins—and yet I feel that I could weep for one heart-cheering word, or one sentence of true love.

Time passes. Miss Osborne bids farewell to "The Rest."

"Your sister is constantly absent; and I accepted not the office of housekeeper from Mr. Vaudon's hands," she says to me; "and, above all, I wish to go. It was only my affection for Agnes that has kept me at 'The Rest' so long; and she has thrown me off, and we may never meet again. Nay, do not urge me to stay; a hundred nameless reasons now command my resignation."

"All welcome faces are vanishing before me!" I exclaim, mournfully.

"Not *all*, Luke."

"I cannot say one will remain long, Miss Osborne," I reply to her meaning look; "I am learning to despair."

Vaudon, more energetic, begs Miss Osborne to retain the post she has long filled so gracefully; but, to all entreaties, she gives a calm denial, and is resolved to go. The night before her going, Vaudon is very thoughtful, and the book he holds he keeps open at one place. He rises from his seat after two hours' reverie, and walks slowly to the music-room, where Miss Osborne is looking over old papers of her own, and remains there twenty minutes talking to her, and then returns and takes up his book once more at the same unread place.

The morning sees her last farewell—her last wishes for our happiness, and she goes away not tearless or unmoved. She places her hand in mine, and offers me her cheek to kiss, as confidingly as though I were her brother. Edward and Vaudon have given their adieux, and have left us alone together.

"When you meet your brother Gilbert, you will not fail to remember me to his notice, and say, in my last parting from 'The Rest,' I bore him kind remembrance."

"When I meet him, dear Miss Osborne!"

One swimming look round the well-known room, and she is gone—and one more guardian spirit of "The Rest" belongeth to the past!

I am dull and dispirited by a sense of weariness that has been upon me since my father's death. I have no power to shake it off—there is no alleviation from it. I feel no change yet, from my change of fortune; it is the old life with the old scenes passing before me, and its false calmness is deceptive.

There is little to wean my mind from the present. Celia is staying at an aunt's, fifty miles away, and does not return to gladden me, or give me brighter thoughts. I feel her absence keenly; it seems unnatural, and shrouded in some mystery. I write, and she replies; and her loving letter re-assures me, and an interchange of notes becomes some compensation for her long, long sojourn in the West of England.

"She has been so shocked by your poor father's death," says Mrs. Silvernot, "that, for her health's sake, I was forced to send her from her native place."

Her health! I am content to wait until her return, for then will she not be well again? And happiness and love, will they not come back with her?

There is a something, to which I cannot give a name, that steals upon me when I visit Wharnby House. It is not lack of kindly greeting, and yet the welcome jars. Mr. Silvernot calls me "his dear Luke," and shakes my hand for a considerable length of time; and Mrs. Silvernot is so charmed to see me, and so pressing for me to prolong my stay, and yet I am not at my ease, until the warm-hearted and impulsive rector makes his appearance, and rouses me from my depression. I set it down to Celia's absence; but am not satisfied. I attribute it to my own saddened feelings; but discontent and doubt still keep busy at my brain.

I call at Mrs. Redwin's one evening in the beginning of the February month, and find, to my astonishment, that her grandson, Paul, has been absent three weeks. Mrs. Redwin receives me coldly at first, then her thin lips quiver, and she takes off her gold spectacles, and drops them on the table, and begins to cry.

She wipes her eyes, and makes an apology for her weakness.

"He has never left me, since he came home from school, for more than a whole day," she says, "and now he has gone to France again, and for pleasure, too. Oh, your wicked sister! Oh, your wicked sister!"

I look at the fire, and make no reply. The old lady wrings her hands, and continues—

"What a terrible change is in my dear, dear grandson! Before—before this unhappy engagement terminated, he was like a bird, so gay and free, and thoughtless. It was 'Agnes did this,' and 'Agnes said that;' and that name was on his lips sixty times within the hour at least. Then he changed so suddenly; his handsome brave face became full of lines, and his darling eyes lost their merry sparkle; and he would sit staring at this fire for hours; and sit brood, brood, brood, until I thought I should come in some morning and find him dead before me."

Another flood of tears, and she proceeds—

"Six months ago, it would have been my death blow, if he had said to me, 'Grandmother, I shall leave you for a few months, and go to Paris;' but when he did say so I felt quite relieved. I knew the change would do him so much good. If he had only taken me with him, I should have been happy again. Heigho!"

"I trust the change may do my old friend good."

"Oh, I hope so, I am sure. I shall die if he comes back full of care. He is so young, too!"

She cries once more, and reproaches my sister in her grief, and I have nothing to reply. She steals a glance at me, and becomes more composed.

"But I am very selfish in my sorrow," she says; "and you have lost a father, and yet come here to cheer up a poor woman. Paul is gone, but you take your seat in the old place; and how kind and good it is of you, to be sure! When some of my dear grandson's friends called last week, and I told them he was gone to Paris, they said something about my health, and went away. But you are a very considerate young man, indeed. And Paul was fonder of you than all the rest, too. Dear Paul!"

Her grandson never leaves her thoughts; he mingles with every subject, and his name is the last word I hear, as after an hour's conversation, I take my departure homewards.

Agnes writes home to "The Rest." She has become resigned to her loss, and her aunt has persuaded her to accompany the family to Brighton.

Time passes onward—spring—summer. They talk of Celia's return. What a long stay it has been!

Agnes has written to her guardian a strange letter, and he tosses it to me, and asks for my advice.

It is expressive of her wish to remain with her Aunt Boyington. Her ladyship has become so much attached to her, and she to her ladyship, and "The Rest" would conjure up so many unpleasant reminiscences, and be a source of so much unhappiness.

"I have no advice to give," I say, in answer to his look.

"Nor I," he replies; "we know the strength of Agnes Elmore's *wishes* by this time. Let her have her way."

He writes the same night to that effect, and I sit and watch his rapid pen, and his unmoved marbled face, from behind my book, and love him not for all his new friendliness towards me.

Edward is looking over some plans and reading letters from his banker, and there is not one ennobling thought upon his face.

I feel alone with them. They have no call upon my sympathy. At home, or far away, we are all divided—scattered threads that seem impossible ever to be gathered by mortal hand again in harmony of mind and place; in mind, from my brother Edward, who has no common aim with me; in place, from Gilbert, in his loneliness, and Agnes, in the splendour of her life.

CHAPTER XXVIII.

BITTERNESS.

In the early summer, Celia Silvernot came home.

It was with a conscious feeling of that happiness, born to me when I told my love, riding home from Cliverton, that I went to welcome back my betrothed to Wharnby House.

She was changed since I had seen her last; there was less bloom upon her cheeks, and the lustre in her eyes was somewhat dimmed.

"Home at last, dear Celia," I cried, warmly.

"At last," she echoed, with a faint smile.

"You are unwell; you have been very ill and kept it from me, Celia! Oh, why did you do that?"

"I have not been well, Luke," she said, faintly; "but I am better now. You, too, are pale and looking haggard."

She seemed speaking under a restraint; she seemed mentally wrestling with some intention, and the tears were in her eyes once, when I chanced to look steadily and fixedly at her.

"Celia, you have something to tell me?"

"No, no, I have not!"

"Yes—I read a secret in your looks. Do you fear to place your trust in me?"

"I have—oh! another time—another time!"

She assumed more of her true manner, and I gave way to her intercession; and her parents and the rector joining us, the day went by without a solution to the mystery.

Not alone that day, but many others intervened, before the clue to this new riddle was given me to unravel. I thought of everything that might have its influence to work upon her health; I read something inexplicable on the face of Mrs. Silvernot, and an embarrassed stammering manner of the old gentleman towards me; and there was a sinking in my own breast each time I stood before them, as if I were fearful of some terrible disclosure.

The secret was betrayed, at last.

One morning I was shown into their state sitting-room—a room seldom used for ordinary occasions—and left alone after the servant had muttered—

"Mrs. Silvernot will be with you immediately, Mr. Elmore."

I inclined my head to the domestic, and then pondered on the meaning of this stately reception, and wherefore it was used towards me. Had I offended them unintentionally? What did it all portend?

The room, notwithstanding its Indian vases, its girandoles and mirrors, its costly lace-work and inlaid furniture, was cold and cheerless-looking; and I sat surrounded by its manifestations of luxury, a dark figure in my mourning.

The door opened, and Mrs. Silvernot came in.

She was a little agitated, and her hands were far from steady, and her slim figure shook slightly, as I rose to greet her.

"Be seated, Mr. Elmore—pray do not rise."

Mechanically I complied, keeping my eyes fixed searchingly upon her; and she drew a chair within a few paces of me, and dropped into it, and lay fluttering some minutes.

I made no effort to break the silence. I sat regarding her, my hat still in hand, in a posture of grave attention. The whole truth had come upon me. I read it on her face the moment she came with her swimming gait into the room. I was burning as with fever, and yet I kept my place, and waited for her explanation.

After two choking efforts, she commenced in a husky voice, that did but partially clear off during the whole period of our interview—

"You may have detected—that is—have seen, Mr. Elmore,

a distant manner—that is, again, not hardly distant; but a manner, on *our* side, different from that which we have generally adopted towards so old a friend as yourself."

"Well, madam?"

My cold reply added to her embarrassment, and she made more than one effort to continue.

"It is but fair that you should require an explanation, and, as you have appeared to be perplexed at our demeanour, and not aware of—of—of—I beg pardon, I am sure."

"Let us pass to the main subject, Mrs. Silvernot; this I presume to be but preliminary."

"Ahem!" she re-commenced, making an ineffectual attempt to clear her throat; "it is a painful topic, and I have to speak of it with deep regret, Mr Elmore—with very deep regret indeed—ahem!"

Another pause.

"Mr. Elmore," she cried, sud [illegible] a mother. In a mother's hands is placed the car[illegible]ters by a merciful Providence, and on the mother r[illegible]nsibility. I should not be acting a maternal part i[illegible]make them my first care. By Arabella I have don[illegible]my du[illegible], and, when it pleases the Ruler of the Universe, Mr. Elmore—when, I say again, it pleases the Ruler of the Universe—to call me to His account, no blame can attach to me for want of love concerning her."

"You mention care for Arabella, and a mother's love for her, as if that care and love were wanting for your younger daughter, or as if you had not exercised those attributes so strictly or so justly in Celia's case. I am following your meaning, Mrs. Silvernot?"

"Partly, sir—partly," she said, the flowers in her cap shaking with mild indignation at my interruption; "I should not be acting like a mother were I to be less watchful and considerate. Now a mother's first care, when the daughter is a woman, is to see her affections properly engaged—to see that they are not misplaced, and that the object of her attachment can support her in that station of life to which she has been habituated from her childhood. When you honoured her by proposals for her hand there were natural expectations of it being a suitable match, and I freely accorded my consent. Your father's will has, in a most extraordinary manner, dashed those expectations to the ground. Three hundred a year is but a poor income, if you consider it well, Mr. Elmore. You must give up horses, carriages, servants, and your own good sense will tell you what establishment so small an annuity can maintain. I am sorry—I am grieved—I am very grieved! It is painful to make such a statement, and I had hoped that you would, of your own free will, have resigned your claim upon her, without subjecting yourself to this cruel explanation—cruel both to your feelings and to mine."

"For this reason, Celia was kept away so long, madam?"

"It was best."

"Madam," said I, rising, "I cannot give you an answer till I have seen your daughter. If she wish it—if she ask it of me—I will throw aside all my hopes, and let them wither in my sight. But she is pledged to me of her own word, and I will have her ask *me* to cancel this engagement, with the lips that granted a consent to it."

"Things were so different when she accepted you."

"Mrs. Silvernot," said I, looking upon her in her chair with blazing eyes, "this difference between the present and the past is not considered by that Ruler of the Universe you study, or has one atom's weight in the scale which turns against me. 'Horses, carriages, servants,' were not my consideration when I sought your daughter's hand. It was my love for her, madam—the strength of ardour that years had matured within my breast—that made me seek her, and that has but ripened to bear fruit like this! Three hundred pounds will not keep those appurtenances of rank, but they would have supported a quiet, happy home, and left us nothing to regret; her affection would have looked beyond the trappings of the rich, and set no store by them. Our valuation would have been of the heart, and, if we had been content, God would have blessed us, and a loving mother could have wished no more. Nay, if such wish came, I am not helpless or bedridden; I have a brain to work, have great friends, who might have pointed out the way and aided me; and England has many offices that a gentleman can fill."

"Things were so different," she feebly murmured. She sat trembling violently beneath the torrent of indignant words poured forth, and had but that old worldly reply to summon in extenuation."

"Mr. Silvernot is aware of your desire, of course?"

"Most certainly."

"And the rector?"

"Yes."

"They both think and agree with you, madam?"

"My son has no voice in the matter, Mr. Elmore; he cannot enter into the delicate points of so sensitive a question."

"He preaches humility," I answered, between my set teeth.

"I have talked to Celia. She is a good dutiful girl, and has been brought up to honour and obey me, and I have no fear for her; she will give her consent to annul this unfortunate engagement for her mother's sake—her family's."

"For all but mine!"

"Dear Mr. Elmore," said she, in a more conciliatory tone; "I should have been proud of a son-in-law in you. I looked forward to it—indeed I did."

She rose and extended her hand towards me as if to conclude all further argument, and there was a self-satisfaction in her smile which gave way to a blank expression on her face, when I said, firmly—

"I will see Miss Silvernot."

"Mr. Elmore—I hope and trust——"

"I will see Miss Silvernot, in your presence if it please you, or without it, if you have compassion for me; but in either case I quit not Wharnby House without a word of parting."

"It is impossible. Her health—her——"

"Spare me your excuses; their evasiveness will avail you nothing," I said; "see her I must, and will."

I flung myself heavily into the chair again, crossed my arms upon my heaving chest, and looked defiance at her.

She made one more appeal, to which I turned a deaf ear; she laid her hand beseechingly upon my arm, but I shook it off with an indignant cry, and pointed to the door.

She went out slowly, and closed it after her.

When I was alone all the stifled emotion that had been so long pent up burst forth, and I sprang from my seat and paced the room, and dashed my clenched hand in my face, and struck the table till the vases and glass-shades clattered on the mantel-shelf and brackets. I had lost all command over reason—I was beyond self-control—I was maddened by the humiliations I had suffered. No indignity could have so abased me, and lowered me in my own eyes. I felt my pride—that Elmore pride, which was so stubborn and unyielding—stung and aroused, and overpowering my mind. Half an hour, and still alone. I grasped the silken bell-rope dangling from the wall, and rang a summons through the house.

A servant made his appearance.

"Will you inform Miss Silvernot that I am waiting?"

"Yes, sir."

Alone, and silence deeper than before. I walked to the window, and looked out at the quiet landscape, so bright and fresh that summer morning, and at the rippling blue sea, stretching far beyond and glittering in the sun's rays; its air of peace and beauty so great a contrast to my angry soul. There were two men walking on the distant road, and their faces were towards me; two homely labourers, who looked happy, and yet who were trudging along barefooted, and in search of work—and from the corn-fields, deep among the golden grain, that swayed in the gentle breeze, came the merry laughter of young maidens—sweet music borne to my ears, a melody of joy.

I turned away. I could not gaze longer into the light and sunshine, its radiance was blinding me.

She came not. The gilded time-piece struck the hour, and I was still desolate. She would not come, though I was parting from her for ever—although I might never see her more!

I rang again, and the servant re-appeared.

"Did you deliver my message to Miss Silvernot?"

"Yes, sir."

"And she——?"

"Miss Silvernot is with her mother, Mr. Elmore," he said, looking dubiously at me.

"What answer were you requested to deliver?" I asked, sharply.

"Not—not any, sir; Miss Sil——"

"Not any! You can go."

The door was closed, and I was shut in once more with my loneliness. I felt that all was lost, and that the flowers of my heart were broken, torn, and trailing at my feet, and that no bud or blossom would ever come again! I felt it in her fear of meeting me, and her avoidance of my entreaties and my prayers; there was a tacit acknowledgment in this keeping from my sight. My rage, and the hot turmoil of my passion, subsided, and in their place came such a perception of utter misery, and over which was drawn the thick, heavy folds of my despair, concealing the murder of my love, stabbed to its death, before the altar of its worship.

I looked round the room with a dark, troubled gaze.

"Not worth a word—not worth a word!"

The time-piece arrested my eye, supported by its carved wreath and group of Loves.

"I will give her half an hour more."

Slowly, painfully it passed away, and the silver bell struck once to note the progress of the hand upon the dial.

"Never to enter this house again, or of my will to meet its inmates, or seek a friendship began in an old time and ended here; I swear to God!"

With the dark, troubled look more settled on my face, I raised my hand to heaven to bear witness to my oath, and then passed out.

Through the passages to the hall door, my feet echoing on the marble pavement; into the the light of heaven, and beneath its blazing sun, I went upon my way.

CHAPTER XXIX.

FEVER VISIONS.

Well could I understand that maddening disquietude inimical to old habits and associations, that had drawn Paul Redwin from his home and hurried him to Paris, seeking forgetfulness in the vortex, whirling far away! When we lose a great faith we have had, or find deception in that which we have trusted without dreaming of suspicion, what a deep wound it makes, and what a scar is ever left upon our retrospection! Hast thou not, reader, felt a strange yearning for universal change after some great affliction that has crushed thee with its fall? or art thou some fortune's favourite, who hast known nothing of life's sorrows, and whose petty troubles have been written upon rose-leaves, and whose minor cares have not added one wrinkle to the brow? Amongst the many suffering, there may be, here and there, scattered like jewels in the mine, some much envied beings, whose guardian angel's wings have been ever spread before them, keeping aloof the vultures of the mind. I am not understood by those—it must be experience, not imagination that can follow out the train of horrors that hold all things familiar to the eye in an abhorrence, and as something desirable to be shunned and shut out from the light.

Wharnby, for the time, became hateful to my memory. It was a desert strewn with dead aspirations, and I panted to be gone and quit of it. I had ridden along this road with Celia. I had strayed in happier times down that green footpath, where the trees met over head, and interlaced their branches, and made beneath a lovers' walk, and where amongst the rustling leaves the birds were ever singing. There was not a spot but which had its story for me, and which was cruel satire now.

I must leave Wharnby. There was but that resource. "The Rest" was loathsome to my sight; the rolling sea beyond its boundaries, seemed, in its restless turmoil, to mimic the agitation at my brain; and strangers whom I met upon the high-road, or passed upon the cliffs, gazed anxiously at my face, and stopped and looked back after me.

I was harassed by the desire to leave Wharnby, and deterred by that letter written from one dead. It was his dying wish—it spoke from the grave—it accused me each hour of my life, and I dared not go.

That I was bound to "The Rest" for an entire existence, was a too frightful thought; that Vaudon and my brother Edward were doomed to be ever my companions—the sceptic and the miser—both cold, and grave, and solemn, and each an antithesis to my burning youth.

Three days after the blow, the rector came to "The Rest." The servant brought up his card to me, in my own room.

The very name of Silvernot made the glow of shame and wounded pride mantle over my face.

"I am not well. I am engaged."

"Sir?" cried the servant, half-doubting my reply.

"I decline to see Mr. Silvernot; give what answer pleases you best, and leave the room."

A few minutes had elapsed, when Jacques Vaudon stood before me.

"What has happened, Luke? You decline to see the rector—your friend and earthly counsellor, and heavenly teacher—strange!"

I saw by his curling lip and mocking eyes he knew my secret, or that the rector had informed him of some portion of it.

"I wish to be alone."

"Brood not on irreparable misfortune—'tis the wisdom of the slave. Come with me."

"No, leave me."

He was gone, and I could breathe freer in his absence. Presently he came again.

"The rector makes a last entreaty. He begs that you will see him. I can hardly restrain his *impulse*," with a sneer, "from prompting him to force his way into your presence."

"I have done with the Silvernots," I cried, "I know them not—each one is a stranger to me from this time. Tell him that he has mistaken his object in this visit; that I am a *poor* man, that my *carriage*, *horses*, *servants* are all confiscated, and I stand lower in the world's opinion. There is nothing to be gained by my friendship now."

"Timon of Athens, I will do your bidding."

When he had once more left me, a pang of sharp remorse smote me for my conduct to the rector—he had been so old and true a friend; *he* had not embittered my existence, or stood between me and my only love—had not his selfish mother even acknowledged that?

I paused—strode forward—hesitated—advanced again—*the door closed!*

I returned to my old position, and he rode away from "The Rest."

"It matters not," I murmured, "if I have offended him—we shall not meet again; and oblivion will soon erase the traces of the wound. Better to lose sight of every face that reminds me of my utter misery; better to die and be buried in my father's grave!"

Oh! fatal hour in which I refused to see that valued friend! Oh, hour, when the last red spark went out, and the gates of hope were barred against me evermore!

"Again here?"

For the third time, Jacques Vaudon obtruded on my reveries.

"An unwelcome greeting, Luke!" he said, in his deep, hollow voice; "but we are acquainted with each other too well to stand upon much ceremony, or take umbrage at a slight offence. So the engagement is broken off?"

"I require no comment upon it," I said, quickly.

"I will make none," replied Vaudon.

"Then leave me to myself; I am sick and ill."

"Luke Elmore!" said Vaudon, in an impressive tone, "there have been differences between us, and you have shunned me often, and looked upon me with an eye of hate. I will not speak of your injustice, or of my wish to be your friend. I will offer you my advice—my help."

"I ask for neither."

"I will give——"

"Stay!" I interrupted. "Offer me not the patronage of your support, Jacques Vaudon! I have inherited my father's pride."

"You are an enigma, Luke," said Vaudon, unmoved by my vehemence; "but I am your friend, for all that credulous curl of the lip. You are ill—wearied. Go to London."

"Ha! London!"—I looked up more eagerly.

He noted my roused attention, and continued—

"If you do not have change, you will sink into an idiot; there are all the symptoms in full force," pointing to me. "Let not the Silvernots pity as well as despise you. Go, and look after Agnes—and return when it pleases you."

"I will think of it, Vaudon."

"Has your faith in woman's love—love pure and disinterested—been shaken since your disappointment? or is your imaginary idol still fixed and strong, and waiting for your self-abasement?"

"Ask me not!" I cried. "I am not myself in thought or heart. For the love of heaven, leave me! I cannot think or reason."

The same night I was helpless on my couch. The fever I had had when a boy was once more my fearful visitant; and night and day I writhed upon my bed of fire, and raved of old times and incidents and hopes. The music clashed around me as of yore, or died in waves of melody, and mingled with the waves of the sea without; and the Figure—that dark Figure, spectral, and grim, and deathly!—sat ever by my bed-side, wrapped in its sable garments, and its face turned from me. It was there when Vaudon, or my brother, or the doctor came into the room, and I pointed to it, and prayed them all to drag it from my sight; but still it cowered near me, and they but looked at each other, and then at me, and shook their heads.

There came another vision in my delirium. Waking from a sleep of horror, methought the face of Celia was bending over me, and tears were falling on me as I lay. I tried to rise up in my bed, but could not—I essayed to call her by her name, and she held up her hand as if commanding silence—I heard, plain as reality, a well-known voice bidding her come away, and then she vanished, slowly, slowly, from my yearning gaze, and the Figure came once more, and took its place of watch.

That face of beauty, pale and changed, as though with some heavy sorrow, was so impressed upon me, that when I recovered consciousness, I cried to Vaudon—

"She has been here!"

"She! Who?"

"Celia—Miss Silvernot."

"You are wandering still, Luke."

"I saw her—she stood here, and looked at me. Oh! Vaudon, say she came!"

"I hoped to find you better to-day—Dr. Whittaker spoke confidently," he said, half aloud; "is it possible she would have come to 'The Rest,' or thought of coming, Luke? There, sleep."

"Possible!—oh! no."

I buried my hot head in the pillows with a stifled groan. What should she care for me?

It was a girl's fancy, not a woman's love—she was led on and urged, and I alone was the victim!

I grew better. The fever seemed to have been more intense, although of less duration, than the illness of my boyhood, and within a fortnight I could leave my couch, and sit pillowed in my chair by the open window, and feel the fresh and scented air upon my temples.

Dr. Whittaker proposed change.

"There is nothing like change of air, Mr. Elmore. Your mind requires diversion. Try London."

London again! It was every one's advice, and my own desire led in that direction.

London! I might see Gilbert there—might meet him, and share his home—his hearth—and be his brother. What had I to induce me ever to come back to Wharnby?—Paul Redwin and my brother Edward.

The first was away, and might never return; and the second would not miss me.

"London will offer no temptations now, for your income will not suffice to keep you in your ancient splendour."

He had never said "stay," and it was not pleasure that could tempt me; and my income would not suffice to mingle with those of my own station in life, and in Wharnby was a living burial.

So, I would go. It was determined. Alone, unattended, even by my groom, I had resolved to depart.

The night before my departure, I took my farewell of Edward and Jacques Vaudon.

"Do you intend to start early in the morning, Luke?" asked Vaudon.

"Soon after sunrise."

"You are eager to be gone," said Edward; "there must be something very attractive in the great city. I have no doubt we shall meet within it."

"Meet within it!" cried I; "you do not intend a visit to London, Edward?"

"Perhaps," replied Edward; "if my guardian will permit me?"

Vaudon inclined his head in acquiescence, and then said to me—

"When shall we welcome back the prodigal to 'The Rest?'"

"I do not know," I answered; "I have no scheme upon which I am resolved. I am eager for a busy life—for some honourable occupation that will keep my mind engaged."

"Can I offer you my help?" said Vaudon; "I have many friends whose influence may be of service to you."

"I thank you, but——"

"But you would be independent," said Vaudon, marking my hesitation; "well, it is best."

His thick eyebrows lowered for a moment, then the austere look passed off.

Before I left them in the sitting-room, he extended his hand towards me, saying—

"Good-bye. We have not been great friends since I came to 'The Rest,' but let all enmity cease with our parting."

I took the hand passively in mine; I felt the protestations of his service and the frankness of his concluding words were false and hollow, and I never saw him standing before me, or heard the deep reverberating tones of his voice, without Gilbert, pale and careworn as I had seen him last, rising up beside him, and keeping back all communion with my father's friend.

After shaking hands with Edward more cordially and frankly, I went to my room, and throwing up the window, sat before it, my elbow on the sill, my chin clenched between my hands, and mused upon my journey till the clock of Wharnby Church struck one in the distance.

In the morning, ere Vaudon and Edward had descended from their rooms, I was standing at the lodge gates, looking back upon "The Rest," with old Johnson whimpering by my side.

"It's hard to see the young masters go away like this," he said, wiping his left eye with the back of his horny hand; "but you will soon be back, I hope, Mr. Luke."

"It may be many years, Johnson," I answered—"many long years."

"Then I shan't see you any more, sir," said he; "for I'm nigh upon ninety now, and every winter makes me more ailing like. Ah! me!"

Still further on my way. A thought struck me as I wandered by the cliffs. It was a duty to give Edward my best counsel before I left my home, and to have warned him against too great a trust in Vaudon. Then came the conviction of his stubborn mind, and how vain would have been my endeavours to make impression on it—this twin brother of my sister Agnes.

How each offspring of the Elmores, though distinct in temperament and inclination and pursuit, was firm of purpose and of obdurate will! Would it have been better had they been less led by their own wishes and promptings? Who can tell?

Into the churchyard, and standing bareheaded by my father's grave.

"Not in wilful disobedience to thy last requests, or for a love of that world of which thou falsely dreamed thy son a devotee, leave I my home behind."

One prayer over the grave—one look at the sculptured tablet with his name and age, and then I pass out of the churchyard, and close the wicket-gate upon his "Rest."

* * * * *

In the starless night I still can see the Figure leading onwards with its extended arm.

I hear the roar of a great world—the hum of a giant hive of human souls, and near me rise spires and pinnacles, cathedral tops and house roofs, crowded in one mass, and part of the darkness in which I am enshrouded, and yet looming from it in appalling density.

I listen. From church spires and domes there ring peal on peal of marriage bells, clanging their metal tongues discordantly, and sounding dismally—not joyfully—from out the darkness.

Ring on! My heart is heavy—my spirit crushed beneath an iron heel—there is no harmony in marriage bells for me!

Ring on!—ring on! The mountain side gives echo to the jarring, clashing, peals; and to the thrilling voices of the bells I follow my silent guide, and the gates of the great city are thrown back, and noiselessly we enter.

CHAPTER XXX.

MY SISTER.

THE great city is in its height of season, and fashion holds pre-eminence; London is wreathed with garlands, and sown with sparkling diamonds. The opera is open, and carriages rank thick before its colonnade; lords and ladies, waiting for the last notes of the prima-donna, or lingering for the ballet, lounge in their draperied boxes and voluptuously-cushioned stalls.

London is in its season, and holding its rare holiday! Labour plods on as ever, early in the morning, ere the sun has gilded London streets—and creeping back at night, jaded, and worn out with toil; men of business—men bent upon making thousands in a day—jostle one another in their hurry for the gold, in the close, stifling streets, where the houses are narrow, and heaped together, and dark as cavern mouths—where the cool breeze never comes, and where the banks and merchants' firms are; prisons are full, as well as palaces, and Want, with shrivelled bony arms, stlll batters at the workhouse-gates!

I have been three days in London, and the change has already worked upon me a salutary effect. I am less depressed. My one cankering grief is so small, so lost in the stream of sorrows passing by me, and in which I have no share. Thoughts, grave as my own, hearts as heavy, faces as full of listless apathy, I meet at every step. I am but one in a despairing myriad.

For the first time since my arrival in town, I am being ushered into a grandly-furnished apartment in the mansion of Sir John Boyington, Park Lane, and Sir John himself rises from his chair to greet me.

"What, Mr. Elmore!" he cries, shaking hands violently with me; "this is an unexpected pleasure. Caught me quite alone—an ocean bird."

The mysterious valet of the powerful build, who has been seated close to Sir John's side, rises at my entrance, and walks towards the door.

"Going, Twidger?"

"Yes, Sir John," he answers, very respectfully; "if I am required, will it please you to ring."

He looks at me somewhat significantly, and takes his departure, not heeding Sir John's cries of—

"But you've not finished the story, Twidger. Did the Queen of Morocco catch him?"

We are together, and Sir John says to me, apologetically—

"Capital fellow that for stories—spin a yarn with any old salt in the king's pay, I'll wager my head. Take a seat, Mr. Elmore. How's your father?"

This is a question that sets every fibre in my body vibrating, as though I were struck by sudden illness. I do not answer my eccentric interlocutor, but take the seat indicated by his nod.

"Will it be long before my aunt and sister return, Sir John?" I ask, after a long interval of silence, during which my companion sits looking me intently in the face.

"They're at the Opera, but I understand from B——"

"B!"

"Lady B. Bouncing B. Comprehend?"

Sir John is decidedly more characteristic than ever, and his cogitations are of a more wandering tendency, for it is some minutes before I bring him round to the point from which he started.

"Opera—opera! Let me see. Yes—they've gone to the opera—be back before the last act. Like music, Mr. Elmore?"

"Yes, Sir John, although——"

He waits not for the conclusion of my reply to his question, but breaks in sharply with—

"Did you have any trouble to *see me*, now?"

"To see you, Sir John?"

"To get within hail?" he asks. "Did the servants *object* or demur?"

This is a delicate question; for had not I mentioned to the watchful porter my own name, and the object of my visit, I had not been seated before him now. But an inflammable appearance about his red, ferretty eyes inclines me to conciliate him, and subdue his rising suspicions, and I answer evasively—

"I should hope I am too old a friend of Sir John Boyington's for an interdict to be put upon my admittance."

"Oh! yes, of course. You need not mention to B. I asked, Mr. Elmore."

"Rely upon me."

I wish heartily for my sister's return. Sir John is far from a pleasant companion. Looking at him more intently, I note a great change in his form and countenance since I bade him adieu at Wharnby, and a more perceptible sign in every word and gesture of his mental malady.

He is full of inquiries.

"Your father's dead, isn't he?" forgetting his former question.

"I regret to say so."

"Was he ever cut over the skull with a sabre, now?" he inquires, very earnestly.

"No, Sir John."

"He was a civilian—eh! He went mad once, didn't he? Ah! poor fellow—terrible thing the brain! I shall never go mad—I haven't got any."

He rambles in his speech, and ends with a low muttering to himself.

"I say, Elmore," he cries, suddenly, "your sister is the girl—everybody's dying for her, and fretting for her, and getting cuts over their soft heads with sabres for her—she's the girl, Mr. Elmore!"

I am about to reply to the old man's spirited encomium, when the door opens, and Cousin Jack makes his appearance.

"What, my dear Mr. Elmore," he cries, running towards me, "I am glad to see you. Upon my honour, I am very glad to see you, Cousin Luke."

He is in evening dress, and his red curly hair is in admirable contrast to his white neckcloth. His face is such a true speaking face (masked though it is with innumerable freckles), that there is no doubt of the real heartiness of my reception. "I've been to that squalling, bawling place again, but I've given them good-bye a little unceremoniously. Oh! Luke, how I do hate screech, screech, screech, all the blessed night. But"—looking suddenly downcast, "you've just come as I'm off—that's *my* luck. I join my ship on Tuesday morning. Yesterday I was praying to be on board—now, I wouldn't mind another week ashore. Never mind. Holloa!" to Sir John, "why, old dad, have *you* been entertaining my cousin? why, you ought to be in bed—here, Twidger," ringing the bell, and causing the immediate appearance of that gentleman, "you won't mind attending on Sir John will you?"

"I shall be delighted to be of service to Sir John," he replies.

"Sir John is tired—there, there, good night, God bless you —good-night."

The baronet, confused by the entrance of Twidger, and the volubility of his son-in-law, rises with a vacant stare from his seat, shakes hands with both of us, and is led out by the valet of six feet one.

"Poor Sir John," sighs Jack Witherby, "he gets worse and worse. I wish I could cure him, or take him to sea with me. My dear Luke, you are very pale—you have been ill?"

"I have just recovered from a fever."

"We never knew that!" he ejaculates.

"I believe my brother Edward wrote to Agnes."

"Did he—then, Agnes never told me, or by Jove! you would have seen me at 'The Rest.' I'm such a capital nurse, cousin."

I inquire after his mother and sister.

"Oh! they're very well—jolly, I may say," he answers, "so's George. Poor George!"

"'Poor George!'" I echo.

He looks artfully at me, and says—

"Ah! poor George."

He makes no attempt to enlighten me further, and we change the subject of discourse.

"Will Lady Boyington stay for the ballet to-night, cousin—for if such be her intention, I will look in to-morrow evening?"

"I don't think she will," he says; "but don't talk about going, man alive—going, indeed! Why, how long is it since you have seen—Agnes?"

He pauses before mentioning my sister's name, and swallows an imaginary and indigestible substance, that impedes its proper utterance.

"Nine months—perhaps a week or two more. Sir John tells me she is a favourite."

"A favourite! I believe you, Luke. She's taken the world by storm; my mother always said she would. Of course you are aware of her engagement?"

"Engagement!" I repeat.

"Hardly an engagement, though," he says, colouring; "for

nothing has been spoken about it, and George has not formally proposed, you must understand. Still, we all look upon it as settled; and George is very desirous to conclude all preliminaries, and mother has spoken to Agnes, I think, and they go out together a great deal, and——so on."

"Not an engagement, I should think," I reply, moodily, "or Agnes would have written and informed me. At least, most sisters would have done so."

"That is why I called my brother-in-law 'poor George,'" he says; "for he's frightfully nervous about her, and jealous as an old cat, and—Agnes, she makes him look right and left, and keep lively, I can tell you—she's so merry, and has such a flow of spirits—so gay and artless."

"She is to be envied."

"Between ourselves, cousin, George is not good enough for —Agnes, and, in fact, who is? What a dear girl she is!—how you must have missed her at 'The Rest!'"

"Her spirits were somewhat variable at Wharnby."

"Were they, though?" he remarks, with a surprised air. "Here she is as gay as a lark. Do you know, Luke, I used to fancy my cousin was engaged to that stiffish, handsome maypole sort of a young chap, who used to be with you a great deal; but Lady Boyington asked Agnes, and—Lord, how she laughed at the idea! It was a standard jest for two days."

"It was certainly a strange idea, Cousin Witherby."

"There's the carriage," he cries, holding up a finger of attention.

The roll of wheels, the grating against kerbstones, the ringing clatter of the horses' heels, announce an arrival.

A few minutes afterwards, Mr. George Boyington strays into the room, with his crush hat still in his hand.

"What—wha-at, Elmore! To be sure, my old friend, Elmore! How do!—how do?"

His white kids are in my hands, and the tears are almost in his eyes—he is so glad to see me. "We were so attached, such bosom friends, from the first hour of our meeting. There was congeniality of sentiment between us, wasn't there, Elmore?" I smile and bow, and think of the horse-whipping this popinjay was nigh unto receiving, on the Grand Parade at Wharnby.

"You're looking dey-vilish queer, Elmore," he said; "but tha-at's almost natural, considering. I should be dey-vilish queer myself."

"Considering what, Mr. Boyington?"

He looks inquiringly at me, fearful of having given offence, and answers—

"Why, the will of your respected pa-rent was a horrid affair altogether. Horrid!"

"I did not suffer in health from that, sir," I assert; "I have been suffering from a severe fever, and am still pale from its effects."

"You will excuse me, Elmore, I know," he says, apologetically; "but I spoke with the freedom of a friend and a relation. *Je demande votre pardon.*"

"Granted."

After a careful re-arrangement of his stock, and a re-adjustment of his shirt-collar, he takes off his white kids and flings them on the table.

"The ladies will be here directly. We have been to the opera. A poor affair to-night. Wretched! A new tenor damned un-mer-ci-fully. Could have sung better myself. As for his figure—fat, and crooked legs, sir. To personate the leader of the Templars—a man short as a drummer-boy, and knock-kneed as a fla-mingo. Be-ast-ly!"

"You, too, have your sufferings, Mr. Boyington."

"Now, that's an ex*cee*ding-ly un-kind sneer, Mr. Elmore," he replies; "why, you are quite sati-rical."

"You mistake me."

"Ja-ack," to his half-brother, "will you make inquiry about the ladies? They are not aware of Mr. Elmore's pre-sence, perhaps. Oblige me."

Jack Witherby, ready to oblige anybody, leaves the room. A change immediately takes place in the manner of Mr. Boyington; he advances to the door, tries the lock, and comes towards me on tiptoe, with a mysterious air.

"My dear Mr. Elmore."

"Sir."

"My very dear friend, Mr. Elmore," he continues, forgetting his drawl, in the importance of his subject, "as the brother of Agnes, you are entitled to my most particular consideration, and to receive from me a full statement of my position as regards her."

I bow my head.

"Now, Mr. Elmore, I—I most decidedly love Agnes. She has bewitched me—taken away all my heart, all my mind, all my strength—just like the Catechism."

"You honour her."

"Do you think so? Thank you"—he shook hands violently. "Now, Mr. Elmore, I am rather nervous upon this point, and for the life of me—you'll scarcely believe it—for the life of me I cannot speak to Agnes about it. I have tried it twice, and she's like a butterfly, first this way, then that way, turning the topic in a most remarkable manner, that, if we keep on much longer in this style, it will stretch me out a corpse!"

He pats his forehead with his white handkerchief, rolls his ugly eyes about, and dashes into the subject once more.

"Mother—Lady B. that is," corrects he, "is interested in Agnes, and approves of the proposed match. *She* has spoken to Agnes, and——"

"And her reply?" I ask, as he pauses, with a blank look.

"Butterfly!" He still further illustrates his answer by twitching his fingers rapidly in the air. I repress a smile. "There's no obtaining a decided 'yes' or 'no.' Now, Mr. Elmore, will you use *your* influence, and let me know if a proposal would be—be—be understood?"

"Mr. Boyington," I say in reply, "each man ought to read the secret for himself; a look, a sign, an attentive ear to a single word, will tell him that, and give him a valid reason to act upon, and a light to show the way. It is not my place to interfere."

"You are her brother," he remarks with a downcast look, "and could do much for me. The look, the sign, the attentive ear are for me, but then——"

He pauses again.

"But then?" I reiterate.

"But then they are for others likewise, Mr. Elmore, and that's—that's damned unpleasant!"

"Very."

"You will ask her, my dear friend—you *will* ask her? I am getting thin with worry; I have taken to padding; I am falling away visibly—visibly, sir. Observe my condition, Mr. Elmore."

He looks piteously at me, beseeching my intercession.

"It is strange that you, of all men, Mr. Boyington, should need my assistance in so delicate a matter," I say; "I had given you credit for great powers of self-command, for an iron nerve, and an unblushing front. Remember the parade at Wharnby—there was no lack of boldness then, man."

"Mr. Elmore, before I fell a victim to the tender passion, I could have done anything; now, sir, I am on the rack."

"I will ask Agnes," I say, anxious to conclude the dialogue between us.

"God bless you! Mr. Elmore; I am indebted—deep-ley indebted."

The drawl comes back to him, and Boyington is himself again.

In a few minutes the door re-opens, and Agnes and my aunt, followed by young Witherby and his sister, make their appearance. Agnes flies towards me, and puts her hands upon my shoulders, and proffers me her lips to kiss.

"Dear Luke, this is a welcome meeting."

In sober truth she is wondrously beautiful. As she stands before me in her evening dress, and with her mother's diamonds—the old legacy—blazing upon her neck and in her hair, and the rich satin dress of violet hue, displaying her queenly form, her faultless carriage, I confess unto myself that I have never seen beauty so striking and so dazzling.

It is with a pang I notice all signs of the dead father vanished from her dress—all look of sorrow absent from her sparkling eyes—no memory of what changes Wharnby has seen, and my wrecked hopes experienced, since she left "The Rest" that fatal morning.

"Well, Agnes."

I fold her to my breast a moment, and feel a brother's love, despite her faults, her stubborn will, or the evil she has caused.

"My dear nephew, I am rejoiced to welcome you! my dear nephew, I am rejoiced beyond all expression!" cries Lady Boyington, her tall and large-proportioned form looming before me in green silk, and her ladyship's fat white shoulders a conspicuous attraction. I salute her and my Cousin Jane, who blushes, and looks pleased to see me, and then we group together, and enter into general conversation.

Lady Boyington asks after Edward and Mr. Vaudon, "lucky man," and becomes sentimental after a short time, and with a curved mouth murmurs some expressions of condolence, and talks of my "poor father," and my "dear father," and my "respected father."

Mr. George Boyington is strategic, and contrives to separate the family from Agnes and me, and to leave us for a quarter of an hour or so, together.

Lady Boyington and children are equally willing that brother and sister should exchange inquiries, and talk of home and Wharnby; and so I sit by Agnes' side on the couch, and she commences.

"How ill you are looking, Luke!"

"I have had another attack of my old fever, Agnes."

"I was sorry to hear it from Edward."

"How do you like this 'life in London,' Aggy?"

"I would not exchange five years of the life I am leading now, for immortality in Wharnby."

"So happy, then?"

She reflects.

"Yes, I am happy, Luke. There are some temperaments made for the busy world, as there are others for the quiet country hamlets and green shady nooks that hermits love. Mine is of the former."

"I regret it."

"Still regret it, brother!" she replies; "why should you regret that I love society and am fitted to adorn it? It is a vain question; but I do *adorn* it, or am lavishly flattered and made much of in derision. Oh, Luke, I thought at the Cliverton Ball I could never feel more happy, or glow with greater delight or feel prouder in my own estimation, but"—her eyes sparkle and the diamonds on her neck heave wildly—"I have seen true life, I have been in *real* society; I have found that paltry ball a mere dance in a barn."

"You compliment the directors of that *fête*."

"Oh! I have much to tell you of the pleasures I have participated in."

"And much to thank my worthy aunt for the initiation thereunto."

"Thank aunt!" repeats Agnes; "my dear Luke, I have been the making of my aunt."

"I do not comprehend."

"When I came to town with my aunt, the Boyingtons were not very high in the aristocratic scale," says Agnes, lowering her voice; "they were just tolerated; but, as for invitations, nobility balls, titled friends, they were almost entirely excluded from. Well, I 'came out,' and what is the result?"

"I am at a loss to guess."

"That day after day the carriages before this house eclipse all Park Lane, in number or in their owners' rank.

That our invitations are too numerous to accept, and that my portrait appears in 'Books of Beauty,' and shines from fashionable print shops; that I have attended the principal balls given by the nobility this season, and that I have been presented at Court."

"Is it possible!"

"You may well look astonished, Luke, but it is no romance. What a leap from 'The Rest' to the glittering palace of a King!"

"It is no wonder that poor Redwin is forgotten, or that the daughter sets aside the mourning indicative of a father's loss in such gay scenes of life, gilded with royal smiles, and coloured by her own ambitions."

She looks down at her dress, and then full at me.

"It is not fashionable, long mourning. My loss is felt as deeply as your own, despite the contrast we present."

"You think so, Agnes," I reply; "but you cannot gauge the depths of my affliction, though I can measure every drop of yours."

"No, Luke."

"Yes, Agnes. The cup did not overflow, and there were jewelled hands to keep it steadily in its place, or to take it from your sight, and mask the story that it told with flowers."

"More metaphorical than ever, Luke; you should have been a poet."

"Well, we will not quarrel, Aggy, at our first meeting after nine months' separation. The outward mourning matters little. If it were a true test of the depth of man's emotion, the sterling value of his sorrow, how many crape garments would fade to nothingness even on the grave's brink!"

"Gloomier than ever, Luke, as well as metaphorical. How is Celia?"

"Celia is well."

"Have you quarrelled?" she asks, quickly.

"We have parted. My change of worldly position did not warrant Miss Silvernot in the continuance of her engagement. It is broken off, and I wish to hear no more concerning it."

"No wonder you are metaphorical and gloomy, brother," she says, lightly; "a disappointed cavalier is a rueful knight, indeed! So you have come to London to get heart-whole? It is easily accomplished. You must join in our festivities."

"I thank you; but——"

"No excuses. Why, there is Mrs. Morton, whom I see very often, to the good, yet! She often speaks of you; and do you know, Luke, I sometimes fancy, that at Wharnby it would have needed but little persuasion to have made her Mrs. Elmore?"

"You flatter me, Agnes, and value your friend's heart too cheaply."

"What a chance it would be!" she says, musingly, "now affairs have altered with you. A marriage would reinstate you, and more than reinstate you; and Mrs. Morton is immensely rich."

"I do not covet riches."

"Neither did the fox covet the grapes, you know; but then they would not drop into his mouth, Luke. Besides, there are too many already in the lists, and the pretty widow is probably engaged."

"Are you engaged, Aggy?" I inquire, the presence of Mr. Boyington being brought to my remembrance by a violent sneeze from that gentleman.

"Engaged, Luke!" she cries. "Oh, no more of your engagements."

"But you have not set your heart upon a single life?"

"I am very ambitious, Luke."

"I suppose I shall see you a titled lady, then. My aunt's cognomen is rather grand—'Lady Boyington!'"

She glances at me with her searching brilliant eyes.

"Ah, ho! my cunning brother, are you enlisted in the service of Mr. George, too?"

"I do not desire the match; he is not fitted to occupy Paul Redwin's place, or to supersede him. Let my friend be at least cut out by one that will do credit to Miss Elmore's judgment."

"You do not like George?"

"Candidly, I do not. Things that have passed give me no high opinion of his talents, or his virtues. I promised him to——"

"There, there, Luke," she cries, "I'll hear no more. Suffice it to say, I can guess all, and my brother can bear suspense if I like him, and I cannot remain here with great propriety, if I reject him. Let the matter rest. There will come moments of opportunity when *I* wish it."

"Strange girl! to me, as unto all, a riddle."

"Strange in declining a quarrel, or a long engagement, Luke?"

"Perhaps it is best, Aggy, for you are not always of one mind. At all events, I doubt if you love your aunt's step-son, and there is no happy marriage without it, even to a woman who aims alone at station, and a title. But, Agnes Elmore may be surveying from an eminence, and be biding the arrival of some gallant with higher honours—perhaps some Giant from the clouds of Court, with gartered knee and star upon the breast."

Her hand grasps my arm with a suddenness that startles me, the red blood covers face, and neck, and bosom, and she glares wildly at me.

"What do you mean? What do you mean?"

My look of astonishment reassures her, for she breaks into a merry, ringing laugh, and turns to her aunt and cousins.

"Here is Luke drawing such a fancy sketch, aunt, picturing my future husband with the Order of the Garter, and decorated on the breast with stars. Is he not the kindest of brothers?"

"I am sure he is," says Cousin Jane, very earnestly. Agnes rises from the couch, and crosses to her aunt. I follow, and our dialogue is ended. Agnes is calm and queenly, but to my observation, there appears still a throbbing at the breast, which I cannot account for.

The night is late, and I shortly take my leave, resisting my aunt's urgent entreaties to make her house my home, and promising to dine with the family on the morrow. George Boyington follows me down the broad staircase.

"My dear friend, you have told her?"

"Yes, Boyington."

"And she—she—God bless me, I feel like a jelly! What did she say?"

"I cannot get any decided answer; but it appears to me that you have a fair chance; you are living in the same house, and should watch your opportunity."

"A fair chance!" he cries; "thank you—thank you."

He looks triumphant, and fondles his large sandy whiskers with his left hand as we stand talking in the hall.

"Still, remember the——"

"Remember the *what*, Elmore?"

"Butterfly," I answer, laconically.

He gives a feeble groan, and sinks into a half despair again, and bids me "Good night," with a heavy sigh.

Leaving Park Lane behind me, I set forth in the direction of my hotel, thinking of my sister Agnes.

CHAPTER XXXI.

MEETINGS.

It was not with any pleasurable or congratulatory feeling that I found the popularity (if I may use the term) of Agnes Elmore to be something more than a mere name. Looking over "Court Circulars" and fashionable newspapers, I found my sister's progress noted day by day; my sister ever on the list at ball, and entertainment, and grand *réunion*. Not alone in such chronicles as these met I the name of Miss Elmore, but novels and poems were dedicated to her by unknown admirers; and, as she had told me on the night when we sat side by side on the couch, in Sir John Boyington's drawing-room, there was her portrait in the West-end print shops, and the last edition of "Keepsakes" and "Annuals" had striven to immortalise her.

I felt no pride in this constant repetition of her name and face—I knew how much it brought to the recollection of that bright world, in which Agnes lived, the mother who had dishonoured us. There were many around Agnes who had known Agnes' mother, and comments were not unspared, nor contrasts refrained from being drawn.

True, that Agnes attained to a more lofty eminence, and commanded homage from men of higher rank, it was not to be denied; but it was a fearful height to which she had arisen; and from the plain I gazed upwards at her brilliant form, and grew dizzy in the gazing. It was like magic, like destiny and fate, that this should have come about. It appeared so unlike reality, that the girl I saw last at Wharnby should be the reigning *belle* of the great London season. Well might she despise home, after that—it was her nature to cast aside all recollections that told of her first estate.

How beautiful she was! In the gay life in which I thought to drown my one care, her equal never met me. She knew her power, and it was a terrible knowledge for one so ambitious—one who had ever self in view, and self alone to study.

Mr. George Boyington was not the only worshipper of my sister's fatal loveliness. Agnes had a command over many hearts—some young and true, some old and shrunken before their time, like that of the heir to the Boyington estate itself.

George Boyington had striven hard to maintain his old man-of-the-world demeanour in the new sensations of love and expectancy: he had not sunk into the maudlin lover and the nervous admirer without a desperate struggle with himself for the mastery; but he had finally succumbed, and had become the greater slave for being at one time a man without a conscience; an aristocratic hawk hungering for prey. He kept up his character, too, before his old associates, and strutted arm-in-arm with them in Regent Street and Pall Mall, or in the parks, with that bold, brazen look on his face that I had first seen on the cliffs near "The Rest." But when he came home he set aside his old style, and went sneaking and cringing into the room and towards Agnes, and was as sheepishly attentive as if he had been an amorous youth of seventeen summers.

About a week after I had made my first call at No. —, Park Lane, little Jack Witherby, in a strange bewilderment of pleasure at his second cruise, and sorrow at leaving his mother, Sir John, and all of us, took his departure in His Majesty's Ship, "The Thunderbolt."

The night before he left was spent quietly by the Boyingtons, and Jack Witherby had nearly all the talk to himself. He rattled on in fine style, and was in the highest spirits, till he walked home with me, late in the evening.

"It's the last time, for a precious while, Luke, that I shall be walking with you," he said, half whimpering, as we strolled down Piccadilly, in the clear moonlight; "and it may be the very last. I may find my quietus in a cannon-ball, or a sunken rock, or a sudden lurch overboard, or in a hundred ways that sailors manage to get off the hooks at sea. There'll be plenty of changes by the time I do return, if I am spared, won't there, cousin?"

"Every hour brings some change to man, Jack; and we shall not stand exempt. How long will you be away?"

"Three years—perhaps four or five."

"Why, you'll return a strapping fellow, Witherby! A bold, handsome young lieutenant—who knows?"

He laughed at this, and slapped his hand upon his knee in his delight.

"I hope to see you come back covered with blushing honours, Jack; and, perhaps, marry my sister, and cut out 'poor George.'"

I said it as a jest; but he looked grave, and walked on by my side without answering.

"What say you?" I inquired.

"Say!—say what, cousin?" he asked—"oh!—about—Agnes. Why, Luke, you are getting in better spirits, or you wouldn't crack your jokes at me. Agnes," he said, reflectively, "is born for rank and a high station, and she will adorn them both. We've had many a bit of fun together. I hope she won't forget me directly, Luke—do you think she will?"

"Forget you, Witherby? No."

"Don't let her, there's a good chap," he said, earnestly, as he pulled his gold-banded cap over his face; "now and then bring my name up and say, 'Jack used to do that,' and 'Do you remember, Agnes, how Jack did so and so, and said this and that?' because I am very fond of my pretty cousin—fond as *you* are."

He kept talking with the simplicity of a child about her, and I thought within myself that it was better Jack was going to sea. When he bade me "good-bye" before the steps of my hotel, he rammed his cap closer than ever over his eyes, shook me violently by both hands, made a gurgling noise in the throat, and then took to his heels and tore across the road, and, under plunging horses' heads, to the opposite pavement, from whence he waved his hand in last farewell, and ran towards Park Lane, as if it were for his life.

I have spoken of the gay existence I led in London—an existence almost forced upon me by my relatives and sister, and in which I sought to keep down the cruel memory of what I had fled from Wharnby for. I have to enter somewhat more fully into the details of this glowing life of fashion, and to recall scenes which form part of the task I have set myself, and to chronicle those incidents which are, with me, so indelibly fixed.

Amongst the powerful rivals of Mr. Boyington, I fancied I detected a Lord Chilvers, a nobleman who had lost everything but his name at the gaming-table, and would have risked that, had it been marketable, upon one throw of the dice.

He was a young man of five or six-and-twenty, with a handsome set of features, wasted by dissolute living, and marked by late hours and excitement. How he contrived to support his vast establishment was as much a mystery to his friends as to the world; debts were hanging round and hemming him in on all sides, yet he kept his head upreared, and defied the creditors whose name was Legion. His was a name always on people's lips; the press made much of it, and had ever a new story to tell concerning it. Satirical newspapers caricatured it, and held it up for a nation's scorn. I became acquainted with his lordship one morning, as I rode with Agnes, Mr. Boyington, and my cousin Jane along Rotten Row. The Row was thronged with equestrians, and Agnes, her cousin, and her admirer, were exchanging salutations every instant. Lord Chilvers, on a superb grey mare, met us, wheeled round, and rather unceremoniously joined our cortège. Agnes very gracefully made me known to his lordship, who raised his hat in acknowledgment, and said—

"I am delighted to make the acquaintance of Mr. Elmore. Well, Boyington, and how are you? Miss Boyington and Miss Elmore, you are both as charming as ever!"

Agnes smiled bewitchingly, and Mr. Boyington grunted like a pig. There was an agreeable dashing way with Lord Chilvers that interested me; he put on no patrician airs with his more plebeian companions, and he was *bon camarade* with me on the instant.

What a deal of attention a young man gets paid by his own sex when he has a handsome sister!

We proceeded in our canter. Lord Chilvers rode between Agnes and me, and Mr. Boyington between his sister and Agnes. What his lordship said to Agnes was expressed in so low a tone, that I could not catch the full meaning, but he was, doubtless, a lively and witty companion, for Agnes' silvery laugh rang out now and then, and her eyes sparkled at him as he looked into them. Mr. Boyington whipped his horse, and set him plunging against his sister's, scowled once or twice when the dialogue was animated, and kept glancing from Agnes in her riding-dress to the young nobleman in his height of fashion, and broke in with abrupt inquiries, and "spoiled sport," as Lord Chilvers thought, in all probability.

"Miss Elmore, you have not forgotten Thursday next?"

"Forgotten it, my lord!" she replied. "It is a red-letter day in my calendar of engagements!"

"Now, that's complimentary," he said, laughing; "and I thank you for it, heartily. It's my last party this season—I'm off to Paris."

How many times had I heard the word "Paris," in my life?

"That is early in the season, Lord Chilvers," remarked Agnes.

"Rather early, but I cannot flatter myself I shall be missed," said Chilvers, entirely forgetting the tenacious memory of creditors for the moment.

"Oh! we shall miss you."

"Really, now!" cried he, insinuatingly, "my dear Miss Elmore, you make me a happy man! You will positively miss me!"

As he bent forward in his saddle, with his most killing look, Agnes, ever wayward, filliped her horse with her riding-cane, and started forward, leaving the full effect of his glance to be bestowed on Mr. George Boyington.

Mr. Boyington grinned; and Lord Chilvers, recovering himself, darted forward also.

Presently, Lord Chilvers and I were side by side.

"Mr. Elmore, might I take the liberty of expressing a wish to see you at Alton House, on Thursday next? I was not aware of your presence in London, or should have more specially invited you."

"I am obliged, my lord," I answered; "but——"

"No excuses—I pray you, no excuses," he said, hastily; "you must accompany your sister and my good friends, the Boyingtons. Come, Elmore, you consent?"

I had no particular desire to go or stay; I had no curiosity to satisfy, and no ambition to mingle with those above my rank; but I had no wish to shun society—for I had not come to London to lead a hermit's life—so I inclined my head in acquiescence.

"Going!" exclaimed Lord Chilvers, as Agnes gaily bade him farewell.

"Yes; I have some calls to make with Lady Boyington," replied my sister. "For the present, adieu."

"But you've no calls to make, Mr. Elmore," he said, addressing me. "Suppose you and I have another turn—we have but a little while to get up a friendship in. What say you?"

It would have been a churlish act to refuse, so I joined Lord Chilvers, whilst the Boyingtons and Agnes cantered towards Park Lane.

"You have a matchless sister, Mr. Elmore," he said.

"You compliment me."

"Truly, you have," he asserted; "such a sister as any man ought to be proud of. Do you know, Mr. Elmore, she has made a greater sensation in our circles than any beauty that has shone upon the West-end world for years! We are to have the 'Agnes Waltz,' and the 'Agnes Quadrille,' for the last testimonials as to her myriad of admirers. She is——ah! Sir George —ah! my dear Mrs. Morton!"

A curvetting of horses, a little prancing and plunging, and we were facing Mrs. Morton and an aristocratical gentleman of about thirty years of age. Seated on horseback with her black ringlets from beneath her hat, and her cheek flushed by exercise, she was more beautiful than ever.

Lord Chilvers had not concluded his ceremony of greeting, ere Mrs. Morton, raising her dark eyes, beheld me by the nobleman's side. A slight embarrassment, a more heightened colour, then she extended her fairy hand, exclaiming—

"Mr. Elmore, this is indeed a surprise."

"You are acquainted with my friend?" said Chilvers, with a wondering stare.

"I have known Mr. Elmore some years, my lord," replied Mrs. Morton.

"Sir George Harvey," said Lord Chilvers; "my friend, Mr. Elmore."

The gentleman made a stiff obeisance towards me, and then sat bolt upright in his saddle, neither well pleased with my appearance, nor with my unceremonious introduction to him.

"Have you been long in London?" asked Mrs. Morton of me, as Sir George and Lord Chilvers entered into an iced colloquy concerning the weather, and the Parliament, and the last budget.

"But a few weeks, madam."

"Weeks! and yet there was once a promise made at Cliverton, that my poor mansion should not be neglected, if chance should ever bring you to our busy Babel," she said, half-reproachfully, as she shook her curls and laughed.

"I have not forgotten that promise, I assure you."

"So you are a friend of Lord Chilvers, Mr. Elmore?"

"I was introduced to him this morning—so he is a friend of an early date, my dear madam."

"I am glad of that," she said; then in a lower tone, added, "If you will take my advice, be cautious of him; Lord Chilvers makes his friends serviceable, if possible."

Before I could reply, Sir George said, coldly—

"Had we not better proceed, Mrs. Morton?"

"I am ready, Sir George."

"There is a letter unanswered, Mrs. Morton," said Chilvers, "respecting a ball at Alton House. 'It is positively my last appearance.'"

"I do not know if I shall witness it," replied the lady, as we all commenced curveting and prancing again; "I do not know if we are friends."

"Oh! friends upon my honour."

"Well, I will decide to-morrow. Mr. Elmore, I hope shortly to have the pleasure of seeing you again."

They were gone, and Chilvers looked over his shoulder after them.

"A stiffish buck, Sir George—eh, Elmore?"

"He appears reserved," I replied, as we resumed our ride.

"Reserved, by the holy Moses!" cried his lordship; "there isn't a prouder peacock in the Row this moment. I wish, with all my heart, pretty Mrs. Morton would send him to the right about."

"Are they engaged, my lord?" I asked, with some interest.

"Heaven knows!" replied Chilvers; "Mrs. Morton has been reported 'engaged' so many times, that I shall never believe she has forgotten her first vows, until I see her at St. George's with my own eyes."

"She has been a widow some years."

"Yes; it's rather strange."

"She sets a value on a single life."

"A wise little woman," assented his lordship: "quite an example to the softer sex in general. She did not live happily with her first husband, you see, and she fears to risk a second. With her wealth, I do not blame her—although, with her personal attractions to boot, I may envy Harvey's place in her good graces. My dear Elmore, I assure you I was in love with her, once upon a time—but then," lightly added he, "I have been in love with every woman in England."

"You estimate a single life at its true value, also, my lord!"

"Um," he said, musingly—"perhaps so."

A party of young men having met him, I took the opportunity of bidding him "Good morning."

"Good morning, if it must be so," he said, a trifle reluctantly. "Are you engaged to-night?"

"To-night I fear I am, my lord."

"Oh, it's no matter," he said, carelessly—"we meet on Thursday."

He raised his hat, and, after imitating his example, I rode away, but not before I had heard the following:—

"Who is that, Chilvers?"

"A particular friend of mine—a brother of Miss Elmore's."

CHAPTER XXXII.

ALTON HOUSE.

On the appointed Thursday I arrived at a late hour at Alton House. I had declined to accompany my sister and the Boyingtons, who were, for a wonder, going early to the ball. I had wavered till the last minute, and then had finally resolved to join in the aristocratic festivities to which I was invited. There were no feelings of bashful youth—no shame-faced reserve—as I stepped into the great, marble-paved hall, thronged with servants in rich liveries and ushers with wands, and filled with rare exotics of intoxicating perfume. I thought of the great Cliverton Ball, and of my inexperience, and of my reason for going thither, and the contrast that this night afforded. At any other time the scene might have bewildered me—had I thought more of it, or had wished to participate in its enjoyments, I might have shrunk back alarmed; but, cool and self-possessed, I followed the usher up the carpeted stairs, and my name passed from lip to lip in pompous announcement; and the reporters of the fashionable papers, still lingering for news, affixed it in their note-books, and chronicled my arrival.

At the ball-room door, and for the first time, a slight nervous feeling passed across me.

"Mr. Elmore."

The doors swung wide, and into the glaring light and glowing life I entered with my pale face and grave step.

"My dear Elmore, how late you are!"

Lord Chilvers was shaking me by the hand.

"I have been bothering your sister for the last hour about you," he continued; "and I was beginning to cogitate how I should sue you for a 'breach of promise,' and what demand I could make upon you by way of damages."

He linked his arm in mine, and we walked down the room together. The scene was dazzling and magnificent, and my sluggish blood moved quicker in my veins—some portion of the excitement of the scene communicated its contagion to me. There was not a very great number of guests, but in all there was the sterling print of the high-born and the wealthy; and I felt it was not my sphere, and that I was beneath it. A celebrated quadrille band, led by a great master, occupied one end of the room, in a gilded orchestra of skilful workmanship. I gave one glance at the walls with their rich hangings and appointments, at the painted ceiling, and the myriads of lights, and then turned my attention to my host.

"I do not perceive my sister, Lord Chilvers."

"She is promenading: I saw her a few moments since. Ah! there she is."

I looked towards the direction indicated. Agnes was in white satin, and the snowy lustre of the dress, subdued beneath the rich white lace, and scattered thick with pearls, set off her bright complexion and commanding height to their fullest advantage.

The mother's legacy was absent this particular evening, and there were other pearls glowing from her hair and clasping her white arms at the wrist. She was reclining on the arm of a tall, stoutly-built gentleman of about forty, who looked into her face very often, and evidently spoke in a suppressed tone of voice. Agnes' hands were linked on his arm, and she was listening earnestly to every word he uttered, although more than once her eyes suddenly shifted aside to look another way.

As they advanced I made a movement as if to speak to her, when Lord Chilvers swerved round, and drew me quickly in another direction.

"Wait a moment, Elmore—your sister is engaged."

"I merely wished to address a good evening to her, and to inquire after Lady Boyington and daughter."

"Lady Boyington and daughter are here to reply to that inquiry themselves, and it is a rule never to spoil a flirtation, *mon ami.*"

"Oh, I would not have disturbed them, my lord."

"There is Lady B. fanning herself on the couch by the window, and the fair Jane by her side," said Chilvers. "Haste and secure a partner in one of them; our next dance will be a waltz, and Lady Boyington waltzes like a sylph."

He withdrew his arm, and, giving me a comical, half-saucy look, left me to my relations.

The music had not struck up the waltz, although many of the guests were waiting—some of the music had been mislaid, and there was a little confusion in the orchestra. I made my respects to my aunt and cousin, and solicited Jane's hand for the next dance. It is needless to say, Lord Chilvers was wrong in his assertion concerning my aunt's waltzing qualifications, Lady Boyington not having danced, much less waltzed, the last twenty or thirty years.

Jane was engaged to her half-brother, who now came towards us biting the thumb of his white kid glove.

"How do, Elmore?" he said to me. "How pre-e-cious late you have made your appearance. Fash-ionable in the cxtreme! Now, Jane."

Two ladies, escorted by a gentleman, passed, and one was Mrs. Morton. She was more beautiful than ever to-night, and her clear, yet almost Spanish olive complexion was set off by her rich dress of amber satin and black lace. There was a dreamy, indifferent manner exhibited towards her companions that struck me even as she passed.

Almost involuntarily I uttered her name.

She looked round quickly, and her face lightened up with a sunny smile.

"Ah, Mr. Elmore!" she cried, stopping and extending her hand; "I expected to——that is, I hardly expected to see you here to-night."

"I am engaged to Percy this dance," whispered her lady companion to Mrs. Morton.

Percy, their escort, a young man of vacant expression, carried off the lady, leaving Mrs. Morton with me. I introduced my fair companion to my aunt—George and my cousin Jane were already in the crowd.

"What has delayed the waltz so long, I wonder?" remarked Lady Boyington. "Have they lost any of the music?"

"They managed better at Cliverton," said Mrs. Morton, with a bright glance at me.

"Oh, Cliverton! Do you remember our first waltz, Mrs. Morton?"

"Remember it!—ah, well."

"We cannot do better than celebrate our second meeting at a ball by engaging in this dance, if your consent be not already granted, and you will favour me?"

"It would be a well-merited punishment if I were engaged," said Mrs. Morton, gaily; "for then I should deprive you of a dance—and you hardly deserve one, coming at so late an hour. Why, some of the company have gone!"

"I did not know my fair friend was one of the guests, or should have made greater haste to Alton House," said I, gallantly, as I offered her my arm.

"Empty words!" replied she, smiling, as we moved towards the centre of the room.

The crash of the music sounded at last, and I passed my arm round her slender waist, and she rested her hand in mine. I looked down at her: she was blushing, and I fancied slightly trembling.

For a moment we whirled round, and then I stopped as if I had been shot.

"What is the matter, Mr. Elmore?" cried Mrs. Morton, anxiously; "are you unwell?"

"No, no—pray excuse me—let us proceed. The waltz struck me. It is an old one, and I have heard it under strange circumstances. I ask your pardon."

We resumed the dance. It was the old "Honeymoon Waltz!" that waltz played so many years ago, at the time when my mother glided down the back stone stairs of the house, looking on the park, and fled away from home. The waltz which my father interrupted, with his fearful look of madness, as he stood in the doorway, crushed by the first blow of his dishonour. The waltz which he tore from the leaves of the music-book, one evening in the twilight, when we were living at "The Rest."

I thought of all this as I held the light form of the beautiful woman pressed to me, her waist encircled by my arm. I glanced towards Agnes; she was not dancing, but seated by the side of the tall man with whom I had seen her at my entrance. Their conversation was animated; and, unaware of my watching eyes, my sister's admirer for a moment caught her hand and held it in his own. It was but for a moment—and then Agnes, without a gesture of indignation, or a look of surprise, withdrew it slowly from his clasp. The face of the man was flushed and red, and in our evolutions I could not forbear keeping him and Agnes in sight at every opportunity. Once he leant forward, and looked towards the door, and my quick vision discerned a diamond star glittering on his breast!

The star upon the breast, and Agnes' cry that night!

"Who is the gentleman with my sister, Mrs. Morton?" I asked, quickly.

"You do not know?" she answered, pantingly.

We were rapidly waltzing at the time.

"I have not seen him before."

"It is His Royal Highness the Duke of ——."

"The Duke of ——!" I exclaimed, "and here!"

"He has been here once before, and only once," she said. "Perhaps Agnes is destined to be a duchess, Mr. Elmore, for he follows her like a constant swain."

I said no more, and we were silent till the waltz was ended, and I led her to a cushioned recess by the window, and took my seat beside her.

"I am not used to fashionable life, my dear Mrs. Morton; so I would ask you one question," said I.

"Concerning Agnes?"

"Yes."

"Let me hear it."

"Is it etiquette for a Royal Duke to pay such marked attention to one lady in the company?—attention which, in my opinion, seems likely to give rise to much injurious comment?"

"Ah! you are so punctilious, Mr. Elmore," said she, in reply, "and are so full of scruples."

"You have not answered my question, Mrs. Morton."

"Is it etiquette? Well, no," she replied; "but, then, a duke is almost above set rules—and more especially the Duke of ——. Agnes, Mr. Elmore, is the reigning beauty, and His Royal Highness pays due homage, like a true cavalier. As for comments," she said, quietly, "dukes are above them."

"But not Agnes Elmore," I answered; "and, candidly, I dislike it."

"You must not imagine he has been entirely devoted to Miss Elmore since his arrival. She had but just accepted his escort as you entered the ball-room."

I felt relieved at this statement, although there was a weight upon my mind that was very heavy still.

His Royal Highness rose, and having exchanged a few words with some of the principal guests, took his departure, leaving the field clear for Mr. Boyington, who plunged wildly across, and superseded an extensive dandy who was mincingly advancing. But Agnes had had enough of *tête-à-têtes*, and so brought Mr. George back again, and joined us on the couch.

"So, Luke, you have arrived," she said. "If you had come half-an-hour earlier, I would have introduced you to the Duke of ——."

"I have no ambition for so honoured an introduction," I replied.

"Well, Mrs. Morton, you have danced at last, I see."

"Danced!" with a heightened colour; "could I refuse a waltz with so old a friend?"

"Have you not danced before this evening?" I asked.

Agnes forestalled Mrs. Morton in her reply.

"Oh! she has been in the worst of tempers, Luke; I am sure she has found fault with every person in the room, and has been quite satirical and severe. She has refused Lord Chilvers and Sir ——"

"Mr. Elmore does not require a list," interrupted Mrs. Morton, with a merry laugh.

"Mr. Elmore is more than contented with the preference shown him," I remarked.

There was a fascinating look about the eyes for a reply, that reminded me of old times, and thrilled me.

"I—I ha-ve not ha-ad the ple-a-sure of being intro-du-ced to Mrs. Morton," drawled Boyington.

"And I am sure I cannot spare the time, Mr. Boyington," cried Agnes, saucily; "here comes Lord Chilvers to solicit my hand for the cotillon. He has just returned from accompanying His Royal Highness to the carriage."

This was quite enough for Mr. Boyington, who, forgetting Mrs. Morton and all introductions, led Agnes off to her place in the dance.

"You see Agnes has not much respect for etiquette," said Mrs. Morton, smiling; "she is a merry girl, and a dear one."

"You like her?"

"Very much."

The cotillon commenced, and I sat in the recess of the window with Mrs. Morton. She seemed contented with being my companion, and I felt old sorrows but lightly in her presence. How ridiculous it appeared to me on that night, when she and Celia met at Mr. Dartford's house, I should have thought her my evil angel! Was not the daughter of the Silvernots my evil angel?—for had she not thrust aside the affection fostered with her false love? And Mrs. Morton—why, she was beautiful and young, and weaved a stronger spell around me each instant that I sat by her side and listened to her voice, and the music rang softly in our ears, and the giddy maze of dancers flitted by.

She spoke of Celia, and asked me if she were well, with a meaning smile.

"I have not seen Miss Silvernot for many weeks," I answered.

"But you may have heard?"

"Nor heard."

"That is strange!"

"Why strange, dear madam?"

"Nothing."

She sat gazing at the dancers several minutes, and toyed with the bracelet of rubies on her arm. Presently, in a lower voice, she asked, still looking at the dancers, and twisting the bracelet round and round her wrist—

"Are you an unfaithful correspondent, then?"

"I do not correspond with Miss Silvernot."

"But you are engaged, Mr. Elmore," with a surprised air, but still with look averted; "I heard that at Cliverton."

"Mrs. Morton cannot be unaware of a change in my position with the world. It is too well known, and the news too generally diffused."

"I have heard something to the effect," she murmured; "but still, I do not find in that remark an answer to my question."

"There is an answer contained therein, nevertheless."

She looked up, at last, with her large lustrous black eyes, and said, as if she were taking a long breath—

"Indeed!"

"I am talking as to an old friend ——"

"Am I not one?" she asked, quickly.

"Yes, dear madam; but, perhaps, hardly a fitting *confidante* for a young man like myself," I replied. "But I would not wish any friend of mine to suppose Miss Silvernot is engaged to me."

We sat together long after the cotillon had come to an end, and talked of the evenings spent at Mr. Dartford's. She had not changed; she sat before me as though a few years were but yesterday, and new thoughts arose within me and quickened the pulsation at my heart. She spoke no longer with averted look, but discoursed on those past events with that fascinating eloquence of language so characteristic of her—that brilliant, flashing wit which I had observed so many times before. I forgot all in her presence—I thought of nothing but her beauty and her talents.

"A quadrille," I said; "dare I ask you to favour me a second time, knowing your antipathy to dancing?"

"Antipathy!"

"Does not my sister assert as much?"

"Your sister is a wilful child," said she, rising, and accepting my arm; "and her brother considers the etiquette of Royal Dukes worth imitating, for he neglects everybody in the room, except my honoured self."

A reply rose to my lips—I forbore—I met her glance—I spoke it.

"I have as good a reason as His Royal Highness, and one more irresistible."

It was not so much the words as the look, that made the red blood mantle to her face and neck. She turned her head away, and the hand upon my arm trembled again.

"Have I not?"

"You are pleased to be complimentary," said she, in a half-tremulous voice. "I am sorry you have grown so gallant."

"I have not grown gallant, Mrs. Morton," I replied; "far from it. You will believe it true?"

"I will believe nothing, Mr. Elmore."

We commenced the quadrille. She was like a fairy partner for me; and, as I gazed on her, my heart felt fresh and young once more, and I felt how little it would take to make me love her.

Ay, love her! Not as I loved Celia Silvernot, but with a fierce passion that was not all soul—with an ungovernable fire that might last long, or soon burn out, as circumstances fanned it to a flame or blew it from the altar.

One dance with my Cousin Jane, who was in bad spirits and depressed, and then I felt drawn to the young widow again. It was by an influence I could not resist; it was stronger than I had known it at Cliverton—it was a new passion which usurped all control over me, and led me to her side. She was listening to Lord Chilvers, but made room for me on the ottoman as I advanced, and received me with a gracious smile.

Lord Chilvers was attentive in the extreme to the rich widow; but she was absent in her replies, and, after a long searching glance at both of us, he rose and strayed to other friends.

It was with no common satisfaction that I found Mrs. Morton quick to respond to my discourse, and that, for the third time, she was willing to become my partner.

"Once more, monopoliser?" she said, with beaming glance.

"Once more!"

I pressed the hand placed confidently in mine, and though her face flushed scarlet, she made no effort to withdraw it. Fascination more powerful, and showing signs of long endurance, and filling up the empty void left by a first love's death! I was her slave that night, and old memories helped to shackle me with chains.

Lady Boyington and daughter—the guests, who were becoming thin—the giver of the ball so perfectly at home, and hand-and-glove with every one—the throng of admirers round my queenly sister, who had a word for all, and who concentrated within herself the chief attraction to the gentlemen—were all forgotten in the bright eyes that shone full on me, in the soft melodious voice that seemed tuned to answer love.

Love! Could she ever love me?—a few years her junior, inexperienced in the world, and dead to fashion, and shut out—save on this night—from fashion's circle, standing alone and isolated, and devoid even of rank and name, without even the power of riches to bring her to my arms.

And yet those eyes—those dark, kindling eyes—the smile that gave back my own—the blush that came unbidden to her cheek—(she who had ever such command of inmost feeling)—the voice that seemed to falter with suppressed emotion. Were they not signs of love, or a consciousness of my attention?

I did not leave her side again that night; I cared not for the meaning interchange of looks between friends of Mrs. Morton, or between my aunt and Agnes. I was spell-bound; I could not force myself away, although I felt certain my particular attachment to the widow had generated more than common notice.

Mrs. Morton was equally as indifferent, if she gave it a thought a single moment. In the dance or promenade, we were constant companions, heedless of any one but ourselves; and when friends joined us, now and then, there appeared to be a restraint upon us, until we were left alone together. The lady, with whom I had first beheld Mrs. Morton, approached us, leaning on the arm of the gentleman named Percy.

"Here is my escort," Mrs. Morton said to me; "I must bid you, for the present, adieu. For a long time, 'adieu,' rather. Your memory is far from tenacious in its impressions."

"We shall see."

"Spoken meaningly," said she. "Well, adieu."

"Are you ready, Ernestine, dear?" asked the lady, with a significant smile.

Lord Chilvers, Mr. Boyington, Agnes, and my aunt and cousin, came up at the same moment, and added to the group, and made conversation general.

We were all ready to depart; and it was my arm on which she leaned, going down the broad staircase, and my hands that shawled her ere we descended.

The carriages were rattling fast away, and but a few remained.

"Mrs. Morton's carriage."

"Good-bye," I whispered.

She extended her hand, and I retained it longer in my own than I had a right or title to.

"I shall see you soon."

"I do not believe it," she answered, smiling incredulously.

"Come, Ernestine," cried the lady.

"It will be very soon," I said, pressing her hand as I released it.

"It is a promise, Mr. Elmore," she said, with a vivid blush.

"Good-bye."

I left her at the carriage steps, and joined my friends.

"Lady Boyington's carriage."

I parted with them also, promising to look in at Park Lane on the morrow, and then rode home to my hotel, forgetting everything in thoughts of Mrs. Morton—even the star upon the breast!

CHAPTER XXXIII.

ERNESTINE!

THE reader will agree with Mrs. Morton in her affirmation made on the evening of the ball at Alton House, that my memory was far from tenacious in its impressions, when I inform him that I spent the next day alone, in my own private room at the hotel, and did not call at Cavendish Square and see the enchantress of the preceding night.

But it was not for the fading away of the strong impression made on me the night before, not for an unwillingness to seek her out as I had done at Cliverton, not for a want of courtesy in my attention—but for a thousand thoughts that held me back, and kept my strong will in check.

Why should I use every endeavour to see her again, and take advantage of every opportunity to bring her to my presence? Was I not forging for myself new fetters with which to load myself, a captive, and for as little purpose? I could love her mayhap, and in the new love drown the afflictions of the past; but, was she not already engaged to the stern-looking man I had met her riding with in the Park? had not rumour named him for her future husband, and would not the lying tongues of scandal hiss forth—I but sought her for her wealth, did I seek to rival him in her affections?

Yet I could not forget her, although I formed a resolution to remain alone that day, and to restrain the temptation that with every thought of yester-night lured me to go forth; I could not frame my mind to read or write, or even to gaze out of the window into the street; I burned as with the fever from which I had but lately recovered at "The Rest."

I tried to crush my vanity—if it were vanity that glowed within me—by picturing myself a dupe, and Mrs. Morton a flirt, who laughed at my susceptibility in my absence, and added my name to her long list of conquests.

If this were true, what a natural actress was she! and why did she blush and tremble?

The day passed, and the morrow came. I had spent a sleepless night, and had thought of every incident of the ball at Alton House—each single word she had uttered, each glance, and look, and smile; and my inflexible resolves gave way.

There could be no harm in calling at Cavendish Square; besides, had I not promised to do so soon?

I sallied forth in the direction of Oxford Street, turned into Cavendish Square, and stood before a large mansion, the number of which agreed with the address she had given me at Cliverton.

I knocked, and a servant in dark green livery responded to my summons. Mrs. Morton was from home. I left my card, and, irritable and disappointed, for all my Platonic affection and self-imposed asceticism, set off for Park Lane, and spent the morning with my relatives and sister, and half-an-hour with Sir John, who was cutting fine points to all his finger-nails, with the valet of the powerful build close to his side, keeping a watchful eye upon the knife.

There was so little rationality in the baronet's discourse that morning, that I was sincerely glad when Twidger slid his arm through Sir John's, and took him up-stairs to see a bran-new sun that Sir John had been expecting these three weeks or more. Agnes and Lady Boyington were full of pleasant satire upon my marked attention to Mrs. Morton at the ball, and Cousin Jane sat and worked at an embroidery-frame, and said very little, one way or the other.

Lady Boyington commingled much sober advice with her sallies at me.

"What a good match it would be for you, my dear nephew!" she said; "for I hear Mrs. Morton is immensely rich. She is a haughty lady, certainly; and would you believe it, though I have met her more than a score of times, the night before last was the first time she ever condescended to address me? But still, what a good match it would be, Luke, considering your circumstances."

"'Considering my circumstances!' sage reason for a 'marriage made in heaven,' worthy aunt," I replied.

"Marriages have been made for reasons similar, I have heard," said Agnes.

"Now and then," remarked Jane, quietly.

Later in the day, Lord Chilvers drove by me in Pall Mall, saw me, drew up, and, leaning forward from his cabriolet, stretched out his hand.

"Ah! Elmore, lucky I saw you!" he cried; "I have been to your hotel, and could glean no tidings of your whereabouts. I start for the Continent to-morrow or the next day."

"So soon!"

"I am a true wanderer. Will you spend a last evening with me?"

I stood framing my excuse, when he said, quickly—

"Are you engaged?"

"No, my lord."

"Then you will not refuse me; it is a farewell supper—all male friends—you will come?"

"For half-an-hour I shall be most happy," replied I, giving up all hope of an excuse.

"Bravely spoken," he said. "Nine or ten in the evening is the proposed time, Elmore. I regret it is not a dance, and Mrs. Morton is not invited."

He showed his white teeth and laughed merrily. I coloured.

"You struck a fair blow for the pretty widow," said he; "and, between ourselves, made more than a common impression. I have never seen Mrs. Morton in better spirits; and yet, before your arrival—and a plaguy late arrival it was—she was as glum as a cod-fish, and as ill-tempered as a spiteful kitten. As for dancing, she did not 'feel inclined' to dance. I say, Elmore."

"My lord."

"There's something I don't exactly fathom in all this!"

"I am sorry I cannot assist you."

"Very, I dare say," said he, drily. "Will you ride?"

"I am within a dozen yards of my hotel, and will not trouble you, my lord."

"Well, to-night, remember. *Au revoir.*"

"*Au revoir.*"

At ten o'clock in the evening of the same day I fulfilled my promise, and made a second call at Alton House. I was ushered into a small but luxuriously furnished room, in which were assembled about a dozen young men, only one of whom I remembered to have seen on the Thursday. Lord Chilvers introduced me to the guests. They were all pale-faced, high-cheek-boned men—a few young, and one or two grey-haired.

"There is good news for you, Elmore," said Chilvers, in a whisper, to me.

"For me, my lord?"

"To be sure," he said. "Blankley"—to a young man of short stature, and highly-glazed eyes—"continue the story. I have no doubt Mr. Elmore will be interested."

He nudged me familiarly with his elbow, as he made mention of my name.

"I think you must have jumped rather hastily to a conclusion, Blankley," said another guest.

"Not at all," said Blankley. "I tell you Sir George Harvey came into the club, raving like a madman. I was reading the *Times*, by the window, and was unperceived, or he would not have given voice to his complaints, you may be assured."

"Not *very* likely," drily remarked one of the elder gentlemen.

"He called her 'ungrateful' and 'cruel Ernestine!'—that's Mrs. Morton's Christian name, you know—and then he espied me and must needs pick a quarrel—as if I could help it!—and so we've arranged a friendly meeting at Chalk Farm. You may depend upon it, the match is broken off."

"Not a doubt of it."

"Do you hear that?" said Chilvers. "Now, Elmore, I'll back the Favourite against the Field!"

The conversation dwelt for some time upon Mrs. Morton, and there was not one disparaging remark made reflecting on her character; and, had there been a stain to show, or a light scandal to make much of, such men as these would have been ready enough to declare it. They spoke of her wealth, dwelt a little on her capriciousness, enumerated the many matches which had been town-talk since her widowhood, but said nothing prejudicial concerning her; and I felt a secret satisfaction that her name was uncommingled with calumnious report.

Lord Chilvers proposed cards after supper, and I found myself seated at a table, engaged in Lansquenet, with wine flowing before me, and liveried servants attending at the back.

Too much absorbed in vainly endeavouring to conjecture reasons for the abrupt termination to Mrs. Morton's engagement—terminated that very afternoon—inexperienced in the game itself, and confused by the loud sallies and coarse jests of the friends of Chilvers, I rose from the table at a late hour, a considerable loser.

"You will not leave us at so early an hour, Elmore," entreated Lord Chilvers, as he received my acknowledgment for sixty pounds.

"You must excuse me."

"To-morrow you will claim your revenge, of course?"

"I am content, Lord Chilvers," I remarked; "and am of firm will enough to say, I shall never touch a card again."

"Pooh! absurd. Your loss——?"

"I am not concerned about it," I replied, hastily, "although my purse could ill afford such a continuance of ill-fortune."

"You do not like cards?"

"I can scarcely remember gambling, my lord."

"Gambling! Do you call a game at Lansquenet gambling?" he asked, in some surprise.

"To me."

"Ah! I forgot about the will."

He turned carelessly away, with a "Good evening," and after a cool farewell of the guests, I took my departure. As I went down the wide stone steps, into the street, a private carriage drew up, and the Duke of ——— leaped forth.

As he passed, he stared haughtily in my face. I made a half salutation, which he heeded not, but entered the house.

"Sister Agnes, sister Agnes," I muttered, "is it this red-faced, coarse-featured Royal Highness that flatters you by his attention?"

It was plain the night had scarce begun, and I felt an inward wish that I had delayed my departure by one half-hour, so that I might have seen more of the character of the exalted personage who passed me on the steps.

But I had soon forgotten sister Agnes, His Royal Highness, and my first debt at cards, in Mrs. Morton. She seemed shining before me, like a vision, and smiling hope and love. I read upon the radiancy of her face the one balm for my grief, the antidote against the broken vows of Celia Silvernot. I felt too —unworthy reason!—how it would sting them all at Wharnby House to learn that I was about to be married to Mrs. Morton, so soon after my first engagement was abruptly put an end to.

To marry her! As if I had more than an illusion upon which to base so bold an aspiration.

Another sleepless night, and listless, apathetic morning, scorched up with inward fever.

Resolved at one moment, and unresolved at the next, the morning passed by, marked by no decisive action. The bells rang out for church, but my thoughts were not of Sabbath calmness, and I let their metal tongues ring on their summons to the crowd of worshippers, and paid no heed. The day seemed but as other days to me. I could but find one theme to brood upon, and that was pre-eminent and powerful. At one instant it appeared as if Mrs. Morton were but a stranger to me, and at another, as if I could risk life itself to gain her smiles and bask in the sunshine of her favour. The day passed. On the evening of the Monday, her power over me asserted itself with greater force, and I seemed led as by the hand of genii onwards. I would go and see her! She might not be from home on this particular evening, and I had promised to call upon her for old friendship's sake; there could be no harm in that, even if tho laws of fashionable society were slightly outraged by my going.

It was night when I issued from my hotel. It was a hot, sultry summer's night, and the sky was heavy overhead. I resolved to walk, and so strolled leisurely towards Cavendish Square, along the crowded, lighted streets.

Why did my heart beat so violently as I stood before the door? Could it be possible that Celia Silvernot was forgotten? that that fierce passion of my wild youth and my first manhood was fading out, and a new love coming in its place?

Mrs. Morton was within. I was ushered into a brilliantly-lighted sitting-room, and left alone. Presently the rustle of a silk dress set my heart beating, and Mrs. Morton entered.

"At last!" she said, extending her hand as I rose to greet her.

"I have made good the promise at Lord Chilvers' ball, Mrs. Morton," I replied.

"I am flattered by your keeping me so long in kind remembrance," said she, looking down.

"Ever an accusation against my memory, dear madam?"

"Not a very stern accuser, Mr. Elmore," she answered; "but you will join us? Two ladies and a gentleman form my little party, and you must not flit away from Cavendish Square before you have hardly crossed the threshold of my home."

"I thank you, but ——"

"Oh, that 'but!'" she cried. "You are in evening dress, and have no excuse."

"I have walked hither."

"The streets are dry and my friends are few, and will not put you through the ordeal of their criticism."

I had ever an objection to sudden invitations, and still hesitated.

"Mr. Dartford is not here to assist me in my solicitation," said Mrs. Morton, somewhat piqued.

"It was not Mr. Dartford who persuaded me to stay that evening at Cliverton," I said, earnestly; "that happy evening at Thornville Villa!"

"You will stay, then?" she asked, in a low voice.

"If it please you," I replied, offering her my arm.

We passed into an adjoining room, occupied by two ladies and a young man of about my own age.

One of the ladies I remembered to have seen with Mrs. Morton at the ball, and the young man was the Percy, of vacant expression, alluded to in the last chapter. The second lady was of the middle age, and mother of Mr. Percy Wilton.

Mrs. Morton introduced me to her visitors, by whom I was graciously received.

"Mrs. Morton will now favour us with her promised song," said Mr. Wilton.

She shook her head, and laughed.

"Oh, do, Ernestine, dear!" cried the ladies.

"I never sing; I am out of practice," she replied.

"But you will sing?" pleaded I.

"But I will not, Mr. Elmore!" said she, gaily.

"There is no excuse for Mrs. Morton," said I to her; "despite my fickle memory, I have not forgotten some charming songs at Thornville Villa."

"Charming, Mr. Elmore!" with a smile.

"Yes, charming!"

"Surely, I cannot refuse, after so great a compliment."

She sang; and I stood by her side, and turned over the leaves of the music, and looked down upon her bright face, and my ears drank in every note of her ringing, melodious voice. It was the past night at Cliverton I was living over again, and the silvery tones brought all before me as I listened.

Presently another lady and gentleman arrived; and then two young ladies, with their brother; and then an old gentleman, with three daughters.

"This is an evening party, Mrs. Morton," I said, reproachfully.

"Not so, Mr. Elmore," she replied; "they are members of my own quiet circle. I seldom accept invitations out, and it is generally known that I do not; and so my friends take pity on my loneliness."

I could more especially converse with Mrs. Morton as the number of guests increased.

She was so beautiful, of such glowing loveliness, that every thought was attracted to her. I could but gaze upon her beauty, and grow more entranced with every instant.

There was a card-table formed, and the greater part of the guests had circled round it; so we were left comparatively alone.

"Will you join?" she asked.

"I am not partial to card-playing; but I am detaining you."

"No; I do not like cards."

So we sat together on the couch, and I felt as in a dream, with the visitors and gliding servants, and all but the young widow by my side, parts of the vision in which I was enwrapped.

"When do you return to Wharnby, Mr. Elmore?"

"Return!" I exclaimed; "I have not thought of returning."

"No fair enslaver at Cliverton or Wharnby?" she asked, with her large eyes so full and brilliant, seeking to penetrate my secret.

"I am not worth the enslaving, dear madam."

"An evasive reply, Mr. Elmore," she said, quickly.

"It is the true one," I answered; "in the new sphere into which I have descended, I am set apart from all *enslavers*."

"Mr. Elmore," said Mrs. Morton, "you affix a cruel stigma on our sex. Women do not seek to enslave; as a general rule, they are sought. You speak of your new sphere, too, as if your old title—that of the son of a rich man—would but have helped to gain a young girl's love."

"My brilliant qualities would have aided me but little," I answered bitterly.

"You are unpretending. I have known many brainless fops who have thought themselves born to conquer and command, and yet you——"

She stopped.

"Pray continue!"

"No, I will not flatter you," she said, laughingly.

"It may but assure me."

"Oh, when the right lady crosses your path, assurance will be born again."

"I do not know that."

"Doubter!"

"Supposing the lady were above me in rank, in station, in the opinion of the world," I said, hurriedly; "supposing that she were rich, how could I assure her it was not her money I was seeking—it was alone the rich treasure of her love?"

"Each woman has power to detect the real from the false in the lover at her feet; it is her own fault if she accept the false," said she, colouring and looking down.

"Then I am assured," said I, "and the dawning of my love may be already in the east."

I said it with an unsteady voice, conscious that the slight, fairy-like figure of Mrs. Morton was near me, and that she sat with roseate cheeks, almost fearful of my burning glances. There was a silence between us, broken by the murmurs of the card-players in the distance. Had I had the will, there was a lack of self-command, which, at the moment, no influence could have controlled. Looking upon her, my whole soul seemed transfused, and to have but one impression, and my heart beat loudly and painfully.

Silence still! Neither a word to say. The heightened colour still upon her cheek; her face averted; the eyes bent upon the ground; the bosom heaving; the white hand tremulous.

I found my voice at last; it was so deep and strange a voice, that it was hardly mine.

"You give me hope that all will not deny me when my time for love arrives," I said.

"When the time comes, there is ever hope."

"The time may be at hand."

"So soon!"

"The time has come, Ernestine!"

She bowed her head more and more, to hide her crimsoned face; but the white hand I had clasped in mine lay a willing prisoner within it.

"Ernestine!" I whispered, in an agitated voice.

"Not now—not now," she cried, gently disengaging her hand, and rising.

"You do not cast away——?" I began.

"We are observed."

She moved towards the card-table, and stood looking on the play, and I was left alone.

One cold, icy feeling, and then my love more powerful, and my brain more heated.

Throughout the evening she studiously avoided me. She passed from the card-table, and engaged in an animated conversation with some ladies, clustered near the piano. I watched her keenly, with the jealous eyes of one who had a claim upon her. I saw that the light manner was forced—that her flow of spirits was far from real; and that, as if fearful of disclosing it to me, she scrupulously evaded meeting my fixed glance.

She sang again, but her voice was not of its accustomed firmness; and more than one note was struck incorrectly, and jarred harshly.

The guests began to separate at an early hour, but I lingered. As they thinned, Mrs. Morton's agitation grew more apparent. Did she dread the disclosure of my love?

The last guests—Mr. Percy Wilton and his mother—took their departure, and yet we were not alone—the young lady named Helen still sat at the table, and carelessly turned over the pages of a book.

She was evidently staying with Mrs. Morton; and one inquiring gaze at her friend appeared to me indicative of some surprise at my prolonged intrusion. Mrs. Morton, with a strong effort of her old self-command, resumed her place before the piano, and played the waltz we had had at the Cliverton ball.

"Do you remember that, Mr. Elmore?"

"Well," said I, advancing to her side, and leaning over her; "it was the first step, I hope, to future happiness."

She bent over the keys till her raven curls almost touched them.

"So silent! denying me even a single word?"

She looked up, and in her blushing face I read the reflex of my love, the confirmation of my deepest hopes.

"What can I say? You would not—would not——"

The opening of the door startled us.

"Where are you going, Helen?"

"I have a letter to write; I shall not be long," said she, smiling.

There was a deeper scarlet flush on Mrs. Morton's face, as the door closed, leaving us alone together. I sank at her feet, and clasped her hand in mine.

"You will believe that it is but love that bends to you thus, and seeks your hand! You will not thrust back the true affection of my heart, dear Ernestine, and deny me the happiness I have hoped for in coming here to-night."

She let her hand rest in mine, and, with averted head, listened to my tale of love, poured forth at her feet. They were moments of deep bliss to me; for there was the consciousness that this beautiful woman loved me for myself alone; and that it was for this heart-love she suffered me to confess my passion for her—to press my hot lips to the hand I still retained.

"You will let me call you Ernestine?"

"Yes," she whispered.

"You will love me in return? you do now? you love me now?"

She turned her face towards me, and looked down upon me, kneeling before her, and said, with faltering lips and swimming eyes—"I have ever loved you, Luke."

I sprang towards her, and wound my arm round her waist, and drew her, blushing, to my side.

"Have ever loved me, Ernestine?" I cried, as I pressed her to my heart. "Good God! had I ever deemed such happiness for me?"

"It was your noble nature—your unworldliness—your free and generous heart, that spoke forth in your words," she said, in the same murmuring, bell-like tones, "that won my woman's love, ere I believed I had a love to offer. Oh! Luke, I can forget—I can forget," she said again, hiding her face upon my arm, "the terrors, doubts, and agonies at Cliverton, fearful that there was no hope of my poor heart's affection being prized by you; I have ever doubted till this night."

"And now?"

"And now—I am thine for ever!"

I stooped my head and pressed my lips to hers, and folded her to my heart, as my betrothed—my destined wife; and the world rose before me once again—gay, glittering, and radiant.

As she stood looking into my face with all her new-born love within her eyes, and I gazed down upon her, scarce daring to draw breath, lest she should fade and vanish into air—so unreal seemed all my bliss—Helen re-entered the room, and paused, irresolute whether to advance or again retire.

There was a merry smile kept back on her pursed red lips, as she surveyed us.

"Do not go, Helen," said Mrs. Morton; "I—I—have to present Mr. Elmore in a new character to you, dear."

"I can guess it—I can guess it!" she cried; "I have seen it on both your faces all the evening."

"Guess all but the deep sensations of pure happiness our hearts are throbbing with, dear Ernestine," I said.

"Ah! all but that!" she cried, returning my loving glance—"all but that, dear Luke."

CHAPTER XXXIV.

THE FIRST LOVE.

STILL like a dream seemed it to me, that I should be engaged, and that my marriage-day was fixed. Like a dream, and yet the reality was powerful; and, throughout the whirl of sense and brain, the lovely figure of my destined wife charmed me and entranced me.

At times—coming suddenly upon me in her absence, in the cold grey mornings when sleep was not for me, or in the silent darkness of the night—a morbid depression fell upon my nerves, a cold shuddering crept through every limb, which not all the looking forward to the glowing future which my life promised could throw off or set aside. There was a gloomy self-depreciation, as if I were a traitor, or had sworn falsely, or had won a woman's heart, without a heart to give back in return. But these sinkings back into my old self wore off as day after day saw me faithful attendant on Mrs. Morton, and devoted to her every wish.

And Ernestine? He would have been an anchorite indeed, who could have known her long, who could have sat by her side often, conscious that she loved him, and not have sought to prove how deep was his appreciation of the priceless gift of her affection. I could but love her with my whole soul, in return for the passionate attachment which she demonstrated for me. I could but have done so in very gratitude, had I never had one feeling warmer than a brother's. To me she was no longer Mrs. Morton, the beautiful young widow—fascinating, eloquent, and talented—she was my Ernestine, the new idol of my worship, my betrothed.

The very evidence of her affection appeared to be bestowed unworthily; I did not feel her equal, or to have a just right to all the love she lavished on me. I could believe now that she had loved me from the first night at Cliverton, attracted, perhaps, by my very contrast to other young men, who at the time were fighting for her hand. How reverently she listened to my plans for our new life, which we spent hours laying out, her hands upon my arm, her glowing face fondly raised towards me!

Entering the square, I found she was ever a watcher for my coming, behind the curtains of the window, and flew to meet me as though I had been a wanderer for years.

A month flew by, and I was within a fortnight of my marriage day. Every time I made chance morning calls at Lady Boyington's, I found signs of preparation for the great event going on within. I had informed them, a few days after my proposal, of my intended change in life, and had received all congratulations on the same. Mrs. Morton had accepted several invitations from Lady Boyington, and Agnes and she were like sisters in their long conferences together.

One morning, with the appointed day not far distant from me, I sat with my sister on that couch whereon I had heard her describe her fashionable life, late in the evening of one Saturday.

"Luke," said Agnes, "have you written to Edward concerning this engagement?"

"I wrote a week since," I replied; "and have received an answer, that he, with Mr. Vaudon, may honour me upon my wedding-day."

"Vaudon!" peevishly said Agnes; "I have not forgotten Vaudon."

"I did not desire to see him, Aggy," I answered; "there is ever a cloud upon me in his presence, and he would embitter even my marriage festival. But I could but ask him."

"Has he replied?"

"Yes, thanking me, and wishing me happiness."

"He can leave 'The Rest' now; he is not the hater of the world, now the patron, so long mimicked and made his tool, lives not to mark his hypocrisy and deceit."

"Let the past die," I replied, moodily.

"Be it so. I will meet him cordially, although——" she set her small, white teeth close; "although I hate him."

After a moment's silence, she said—

"Let us change the subject. Do you not find Mrs. Morton a graceful substitute for Celia Silvernot?"

"I find she has a truer love for me."

"Oh! she is a dear creature, and what a pretty sister she will make me!" she said; "and what a lucky fellow you have proved yourself!"

"I am fortunate in having won her heart."

"No less than in rising to more than common affluence," added Agnes.

"The Elmores, that is, a brother and sister of that name, have both had Fortune to smile upon them, Aggy," remarked I.

"Both!"

"Yes; for is there not another wedding advancing to the present? and will not Agnes Elmore soon be Mrs. Boyington, eventually to change again to Lady B.?"

"We do not advance in our courtship," returned she, smiling; "besides, I have had grander offers."

"Concerning which you have not had sufficient confidence in your brother to inform him."

"I did not accept them," she said, quietly.

"May I inquire the names of the parties favouring you by their proposals?"

"The last is Lord Chilvers."

"Lord Chilvers!"

"Yes; three weeks since he laid his name, fortunes, and estate at my feet. Generous man!" she added, ironically.

"That was before he went to Paris with my sixty pounds," said I, laughing; "and you had the courage to decline?"

"Why, yes," she said; "the name was hackneyed, the fortunes were varied and bedraggled, and the estate was deeply mortgaged; so the offer was not a brilliant one."

"The name itself would have won you once, Aggy."

"No, no—I think not," she answered.

"Will it ever be Lady Boyington, Aggy?" I asked, seriously; "come, sister, have faith in me for once, and unveil a corner of that scheming, ambitious little heart."

"You will not betray me?"

"Have I ever done so?"

"Have you ever had an opportunity?" cried Agnes, merrily; "well, I will for once be confidential and sisterly. I shall never usurp the name of Boyington, brother Luke."

"But, Agnes——"

"But, Luke, there is an end to questioning," she said, holding up a jewelled finger; "I have no more replies to make."

"Nor I inquiries," I said; "yet, Agnes, will you listen? I do not say, Take a brother's advice. It will be none the less worth hearing, and considering though it come from a brother you have not truly known all your life."

"Now, dear Luke, you should set aside that solemn air for ever, being on the point of marriage," said Agnes; "no grave-digger wears so dismal a countenance as yours, when you attempt to moralise."

"Still, hear me, Aggy."

"Well!" with a forced attitude of attention.

"Be not too ambitious," I said; "soar not with your weak pinions to a dazzling height, a fall from which may crush you. You are, despite your worldliness, easily led aside when your will falls in with your ambition; I ask you but to take heed, for I can but fear for you, Agnes!"

A shade passed over her face, a shade that changed the whole expression of her countenance, and gave it a sorrowful, womanly look, that I had never seen before; it was but transitory. She raised her head, and laid her hand on mine, saying—

"You are a good brother, Luke, and perhaps I might have been less wilful, had we been more together in the far-off days of 'The Rest.' But do not fear for me; do not—do not *think of me* too much. No matter what station I shall take, or what position occupy, I shall take it as my choice, and seek to be happy in it! There, enough of sermonising."

"I believe I am glad it is not to be Mrs. George Boyington," I said, reflectively; "although his foppishness might have sobered down, and, as a married man, he might have been a passable member of society. But I shall ever regret that you were not Mrs. Redwin."

"I should have made Paul a capricious wife, and teased him out of all love for me," she said. "It is better as it is."

"Then, there was your own cousin, Jack Witherby," I remarked. "I should not have objected to an engagement in that quarter. He will be a fine young fellow when he comes home from sea."

"The Witherbys and Boyingtons are all impressionable in Park Lane," replied Agnes; "and little Cousin Jack used to fly upon special service for me, like Cupid's own messenger. I miss him very much. Yet, what a silly fellow he was!"

Poor Jack Witherby! fostering your romantic fancies in the night-watch, or at the lonely mast-head, with sea and sky for prospect, it is as well you know not Cousin Agnes's estimation of your character!

"There's Jane, too; but I shall make you vain."

"Make *me* vain!" I cried, in some surprise.

"Oh! Mr. Innocent," said Agnes, "you do not know, you cannot guess?"

"I am really in the most total darkness."

"Well, then, I fancy Jane was half inclined to fall in love with her grim-faced Cousin Luke. She was always so full of your praises, and had so many things to relate about you; and when she heard of your engagement to Mrs. Morton, she walked steadily to her room, and no one saw her for three hours or more. When I did see her, she had been crying—I am sure of it."

"I am not vain enough to believe that I was an unconscious agent to her grief," I replied; "and God forbid that it should be so. I have hardly paid her the attention due to one so closely related to me, and so cannot give my sister credit for much penetration. I am sorry you have mentioned it at all."

"Will you go to Ernestine, phlegmatic, grave young man?" said Agnes. "The carriage is ordered, and I am going with Lady Boyington and Sir John to the drive—that is, if Sir John can be persuaded to go out in rational costume."

I left Park Lane, and returned to my hotel. A servant was anxiously lingering about the hall for me.

"Beg pardon, Mr. Elmore, but a gentleman and lady have been waiting for you more than half an hour. They called early in the morning, but you had just gone out; and so they came again a little while ago, and the gentleman said that they would stop until you did come, and so I took them to your room."

"Did the gentleman leave his name?"

"No, sir."

Unable to fathom the mystery, I ascended the stairs, and turned the handle of the door of my sitting-room. Two well-known figures rose from their position by the window as I entered, both in that deep mourning indicative of some recent loss. They were those of the rector of Wharnby and his sister Celia! I stood transfixed upon discerning them, and turned as white as death.

"Mr. Sil–Silvernot, this is an unexpected visit."

I could not express my sense of Celia being there—a few paces from me; I knew not how to address one word to her, and stood looking on the carpet at my feet.

"Luke," said the rector, advancing to me, and taking my unproffered hand, "I could not leave London without making one more attempt to see you. I have brought my sister—nay, she has wished to come, for the sake of her own name and honour. Celia, pray keep your seat."

Celia, who had remained standing, with gaze directed, like my own, upon the ground, mechanically obeyed, and resumed her place by the window—calm, grave, and silent.

"Luke, there is much explanation required on both sides."

"None, none, Mr. Silvernot," I answered; "the time for that is gone for ever. Aggrieved as I have been, or as I *think* I may have been to you, there is no explanation can do more than revive old injuries and broken faiths. It is my wish that we part as we have met."

"There has been some misconstruction—some more than misconstruction," said the rector, wringing his hands piteously, "and I *demand* an explanation."

"It is for you to make it, then; for I, sir, have no accusation ready to my lip."

He became more dignified at my implacable reserve.

"Mr. Elmore, you must not mistake the object of our visit," said he; "it is with no desire to force ourselves upon you with the claim of an old friendship. It is but to vindicate our name that we have come hither this day."

"I listen, sir."

"Your own engagement, and the knowledge that we have of it, will suggest to you that no unworthy motive has actuated us in this visit," said the rector; "we seek not to renew any tie gone past—we are here but to explain."

"Mrs. Silvernot gave me all explanation worthy of the title," I said, sharply.

The rector paused, and said in a less firm voice—

"Silence, sir; Mrs. Silvernot and my dear mother is dead."

"Your pardon, Mr. Silvernot," I said in some confusion; "I did not know you had experienced so great a loss. I trust you will forgive the harshness with which I made mention of her name."

He coughed, and blew his nose, and cleared his throat, and began again.

"My dear Luke—I beg pardon, Mr. Elmore—you may have felt naturally hurt, insulted, humiliated on that day you saw my poor mother for the last time; but when I came to 'The Rest' with the assurance that her opposition could be removed, that *others* did not desire the breaking off the engagement, why —why did you refuse to see me?"

I gasped for breath, and, reeling to a chair, clutched at the back of it for support.

"What is the meaning? I—I do not understand all this."

"When in my last message I sent up all particulars by Mr. Vaudon—you remember the day?—why still deny to see or speak to me, or write back one poor word, if you were not too ready to leap at an excuse?"

"Vaudon! all particulars by Vaudon!" I murmured, staring vacantly at the rector.

"Yes; did I not even write a last message, willing to give you every proof, and every chance?"

"No, no; it is a juggling lie, or some devil has stepped between me and you, and blasted the last hope held out to me. I know not, remember not, one word of all this you are telling me."

He looked incredulous.

"It is for Celia to explain the rest," said the rector, moving to the other window, and gazing out into the street.

With shaking limbs, as though old and palsy-stricken, I almost tottered to where she sat, and gazed at that face I knew so well—that face I had at one time pictured gladdening my home, and beaming on me all my life.

"There is but little to explain," she said, in a low, firm voice; and her eyes, for a moment, met my own, and then were shadowed by their lashes; "and Mr. Elmore may hardly do me the justice to believe it."

"Every word, Miss Silvernot—every word."

"It was my mother's wish, you are aware, Mr. Elmore, that our engagement should be broken off, after that reverse of fortune which the will of your father brought about—it was not my own! Pledged to you, no change in your social position had a right to change *me*; and I had never dreamed of it."

"And yet——"

"Do not misjudge me, sir," she said, hastily; "let me say all uninterrupted. Do not agitate me by your wild manner and excited questions. Knowing we are speaking of what is gone, and that which is irrevocable, we should both be calm."

"Gone, and irrevocable!" I groaned. "Proceed, Miss Silvernot; I will interrupt no more."

"Unless you had been engaged or married, I could not, conscientiously, have sought this interview," she continued; "now, I look upon it as my duty. If you had written, sought me out, spoken with my brother, as—as I thought you would have done, it might not have been better, but it would have been more just."

Taking a long breath, she resumed—

"I was unaware of my mother's firm determination to annul the tie between us. I had thought that the statement of my own fixed purpose to adhere to my promise, would have shaken hers. The constant excitement, harass, and perplexity had, that very morning on which the interview took place, thrown me upon a sick bed."

"You were ill!" I shouted; "it was not your wish to keep back from saving me from despair—your mother never told you that I desired a meeting—that I waited—God! how many centuries did I wait, counted my agony of suspense!—for you to come, and sever with your own lips the last thread to which my love still clung!"

"You waited—you did not know that I was ill?"

"I knew alone that I was to be cast aside."

There was a long struggle with her calmness; she could appreciate the depth of my strong suffering, for she had known the fervour of my love.

"I heard the door close, and the whole truth flashed upon me," said Celia, after a long silence. "When I recovered strength, I asked for my brother—I bade him go to your home, and tell you that, even at a mother's bidding, I could not forget that I had pledged myself to be your wife, and that I bade you to look forward, relying on—on—my love."

I groaned.

"But you cast us off—you refused to see or hear us; you came to London after your illness; you were willing to abide by my dear mother's wish, that we should part. This new engagement has proved *that*."

"It has proved nothing!" I cried. "I have been made a dupe, deceived by false friends at my own home—friends who had not heart enough to drag me from my misery. I would have been contented with a single word, a look! In my conviction of your wish to set my love aside, I had sworn, on that cruel morning, never to seek the renewal of the friendship held so long with all—never to enter Wharnby House again. I knew alone that he, that old friend, was at 'The Rest,' but not that he had come to bring me comfort—to heal the wounds I bled from. I could not have listened to consolation, such as I expected he would have to give, and I would not see him at a mere request. If letter or hope were given to me through that messenger of evil, it was kept back to break my heart!"

I flung my arms above my head in my vehemence, and then threw myself wildly at her feet.

"Oh! Celia, by the memory of that old love, believe I was not altogether heartless; believe that even now I love you as I have loved you from a child. It was the great ambition of my life to call you mine. I sought no other happiness; I looked for no greater blessing this side of the grave! I love but you —there is no——"

"Hush, hush!" she cried; "not an apostate unto all! Our re-union can never come. Now I do not wish it. Remember," she said, rising, "you have sworn vows to another, and even now you are unfaithful."

I rose with the full conviction of this truth. I felt how weak were my efforts to break through this web of circumstance.

The little rector, fairly crying, came from the window, and pressed my hands in his.

"May you be happy in your marriage, dear Luke! I have no doubt that in Mrs. Morton you have chosen worthily. God bless you, my dear boy! I had wished it otherwise, but—but——"

The tears were streaming down his face so fast, that he tore his hands away, and dashed through the door, leaving me with Celia.

She extended me her hand. The interview had been too much for her, and she had drawn her thick veil completely down.

"Good-bye, Luke. How much better it would have been for you and me, if you had never spoken of your love that ride home from Cliverton. I pray every happiness may be yours. Good-bye."

"For ever!" I cried, kissing passionately the extended hand.

"It may be so," she said, gently withdrawing it; "our paths diverge from this point, and may never cross again."

"One more—one last question!"

She stopped in her passage to the door.

"When I lay ill—when fever deprived me of all sense and will, did you come in the night, with your brother, and look upon me in my great affliction?"

"Yes," she murmured.

"God bless you for that, Celia, and—good-bye. It is for ever! I feel it is for ever!"

And it was! As I know it now, writing these chronicles, so knew I by foreknowledge, that I should never see her more, when she passed out of the room, and I dropped silently, heavily into the chair she had quitted, and covered my shaking hands over my white face!

CHAPTER XXXV

PASSING CLOUDS AT HOME, AND PASSING FIGURES IN THE STREETS.

"LUKE, dear, how pale you are to-night! I fear you are unwell."

"Unwell, Ernestine!"

"You are really very pale," said she, looking at me anxiously; "something has disturbed you. You look wild, and you answer absently. Have I offended you?"

She nestled closer to my side, keeping her affectionate glance still fixed upon me.

"Offended me, dear Ernestine!" I answered, passing my arm round her sylph-like waist; "have you been anything but kind, and more than kind, since our engagement, then, that you ask so strange and inconsiderate a question?"

"Luke, you are keeping a secret from me," she cried; "you must not deceive me by false words and reasonings. You will tell me?"

"I will tell you whom I have seen this morning, dearest," I replied, "if that be the explanation you require. I have seen Mr. Silvernot, the rector, and his sister, Celia."

"Celia!"

She sprang from my encircling arm, and looked with her great black eyes searchingly and even suspiciously at me.

"What did they want with you, Luke? What did *she* say? What did she mean by visiting you with her brother?"

I was silent.

"Mr. Elmore—Sir—Luke," she cried, trembling with agitation, "why are you silent? Speak, sir; I command you!"

The peremptory mandate was uttered with a feeble voice, and her red lips had changed to an ashen whiteness, though the eyes were kindling with a lurid light.

"Ernestine, you are jealous."

"Tell me, tell me," she reiterated, petulantly; "what did that girl seek an interview with you for?"

"I will tell you, Ernestine, but you must listen with greater calmness, or you will misjudge both her and me. Knowing of my engagement, she came with her brother to convince me that I had misinterpreted her actions, and that I had taken a false estimate of many occurrences at Wharnby, and been my own enemy in accusing and condemning them. Having thrown a light on many things that heretofore had been to me but blackest night, she parted with me coldly and dispassionately."

"It was a trick!" she said, her small white jewelled hands nervously clasping and unclasping.

"You do not know her."

"You do well to take her part," she cried, vehemently, as she sat some distance from me now, with rapidly heaving bosom; "you can admire the acting in the actress."

"Ernestine!" I said, reproachfully.

"Go on, sir—go on with your story; I am calm and unaffected by it."

She panted as she spoke, and bit her lip with her white teeth.

"That is the sequel of the story. Is it so terrible?"

"No, it is not all—you know that it is a story half completed, and you seek to blind me! These explanations were concerning the reasons that had broken off your engagement to her, were they not?" she asked, turning on me with flashing eyes.

"They were; but hear me. I——"

She snatched the hand that I had sought to touch, and cried—

"Continue this affecting love tale. What did you say? what grief, and prayer, and entreaty had you to reply?"

"Madam, I could do no less than express my sorrow that I should so unworthily have judged her," I continued, more coldly; "I had loved her once too dearly not to feel some pangs of conscience and remorse. Nay, Ernestine, I will be true to you, and tell all that you have a right to know. In the emotion, the madness of the moment, I flung myself at her feet and raved."

She sprang from the couch, her form dilating with passion,

her black jetty ringlets pushed back from her face, her hands clenched, her glance fiery and wild.

"It was easy to forget—it was easy to glibly talk of love for me when she was beyond your reach! Why, jealousy and spite could but have prompted such feelings as your own! It was cowardly and cruel. And yet for him I would have sacrificed——I—no more—go sir, go! Leave me here—I never wish to see you more."

She staggered to the door—her trembling hand reached out to touch it—she paused, and then sank crouching to the floor, with bent head, and hands folded despairingly upon her lap, and gave way to a passionate outburst of bitter, scalding tears.

I flew towards her, and attempted to raise her. With an indignant cry, she pushed my hands aside.

"Ernestine! dear Ernestine!" I cried again, essaying to raise her; "you will not hear me out—you will not let me tell you of all the self-accusations I heaped upon my head, for the folly I have spoken of, when reason came back to me; when I remembered that my whole heart was yours, and that I loved you above all. You will not, you cannot think that I would have sought your hand, had I not been devoted to you, and held you as my brightest hope. Ernestine, by all that is holy and sacred in my eyes, it was but a moment's passion, and its remembrance now endears me to you more than ever, even if those showering tears did not tell me how strong is the affection I have won, and proved how sensitive a little heart is beating for me!"

She knew by the deep, tremulous accents of my voice, that there was no alloy with the truth I murmured in her ears, and though she sobbed more than ever as I spoke, she let me raise her from my feet, and press her to my breast.

"I am forgiven, Ernestine?"

"Forgiven, Luke!" she said, looking up through her swimming tears; "yes, what can I do ever but forgive? Is not love made up of forgiveness?"

She dashed some crystal drops from her silken lashes, and held up her quivering lips, to which the bright red had returned, as proof of reconciliation.

"It is our first quarrel, and our last," I said, as I sat by her side, her hand locked fast in mine; "is it not, dear Ernestine?"

"I hope so."

"Unless there is some tiny secret of your own, dearest, to make me jealous in my turn."

She sighed heavily. Such a deep, soul-drawn sigh, that I cried, alarmed, "Ernestine!"

"I have not recovered, dear Luke, from my agitation," she said, "and my head aches; how you have made my head ache, cruel Luke!"

"You do not sigh because you still doubt my love?"

"I do not doubt it, Luke," she answered, pressing my hand.

"There is no little secret, then," I said; "remember that Sir George Harvey—you were engaged to him?"

"Not strictly engaged, dear, and certainly not attached," she said; "I did not care—I had grown callous. But when I met you in the Park, and at the ball, and you called here in my absence, some kind genius whispered hope to me; and when Sir George made his proposals, which, singularly enough, happened the same day, I declined them at once, for I had no heart to give him."

"Poor Harvey! I can feel for a disappointed rival."

"I should never have married him, perhaps, Luke," she said, musingly; "I do not think I should ever have married if the truant had not returned."

The smiles were once more on her lip, and beaming from her eyes; and we were lovers, and had forgotten our true lovers' quarrel. Those were happy days that followed, looking forward to our marriage, and the altar and the priest came more prominently to view, as hand in hand we advanced along our road in life. I thought no more of Celia, or rather, if I thought of her, it was as some fair girl whom I had known and esteemed in other days; the rapid current of events allowed me no other retrospection, suffered no truer analysis, or deeper gauge.

Every day endeared me more to Ernestine. Her great unselfishness, her study of my slightest wish, her passionate devotion for my unworthiness, even that proof of her jealous disposition and irritable temperament which I have chronicled, were all some tokens of the inestimable treasure I had won unto myself.

She had written to Mr. Dartford, and had received a cold, formal reply in return, expressive of his disinclination to make one in the wedding festivities proposed. My father's will had naturally worked a considerable change in Mr. Dartford's opinion of myself, and he looked upon the match as a bad one for Ernestine, although, once upon a time, I could not have found a more faithful brother-in-law in the wide world. But Mr. Dartford's opposition did not affect me or my betrothed, and we formed our plans, and laid out our lives, as if there were no ruling hand to thwart us.

One striking proof of her faith in me was to give up all claim and title over her large property, despite my earnest persuasions to turn aside her resolution.

"Will it not appear as if I sought to marry you but for the money to be gained by the alliance?"

"Do I not know better?" she asked, affectionately.

"But, Ernestine, forgive me if I broach a painful subject."

She changed colour, but prepared herself to listen.

"This fortune was not left you by Mr. Morton, your first husband?"

"No; it was left me by an aunt of mine, ere I was twelve years old, and my guardians and executors insisted upon its being made over to me, and excluding Mr. Morton from all participation in and power over it. Perhaps for this reason our marriage was an unhappy one."

"Unhappy with you, Ernestine?"

"Ah! rash believer in my power to charm," she said; "but it was so. A few weeks after my marriage heralded in the first storm, and all confidence was shipwrecked before I had been a wife six months. He was a villain!"

An angry flush swept across her face, and her delicately-pencilled eyebrows contracted as she proceeded—

"When I discovered his gross selfishness and his eagerness to frame a hundred schemes to obtain possession of the money in my hands—for he was a gamester and a profligate—I maintained my power over my own wealth until his death."

"He died young?"

"Very young."

After an embarrassing silence, she said—

"It appears cruel to carry my enmity beyond the grave, but I cannot think of him without living the dreadful past over again, and experiencing sufferings and humiliations more than man can well imagine."

"God was merciful in removing the agent of such affliction."

"He died of consumption in Sicily."

"You were not with him?"

"We had parted by mutual consent: his love and my girlish idolatry had turned to hatred, and seas were best between us. Oh, those bitter days!"

She shaded her eyes with her hand, and a few tears sprang upwards and dimmed their lustre. I changed the subject, and, speaking of our new life and of the bliss in store for us, charmed her to believe that her sorrows had found an end for ever. On my return home, I found my brother Edward awaiting my return.

"Well, Luke, old fellow."

"Well, Edward, I am glad to see you."

We shook hands, and took somewhat of a lengthened survey of each other. He seemed to have grown stouter since we had parted at "The Rest," and the features to have become more coarse.

"When did you arrive, Ned?"

"This morning; I dined with the Boyingtons and Agnes. Vaudon will not come to town; he sends his best wishes for your prosperity."

"Vaudon will not come! He has changed his mind, then?"

"Yes."

"Has he seen the rector since his return to Wharnby?"

"Why do you ask that question? Yes, he has seen him; and a pretty row they made of it, two evenings ago. I never saw little Silvernot in such a tremendous passion before—tremendous, Luke!"

"Vaudon, Vaudon!" I muttered, dwelling on his last act of duplicity—the last sign that his hatred still endured.

"That reminds me that I am the bearer of a letter from him."

"To me, Edward?"

"To you, of course."

I took the letter from his hand, and, without opening it, tore it into a hundred strips, and strewed the pieces on the floor.

"With Jacques Vaudon I have ended all communication. To know him is but to heap misery upon all I do and act. When you see him again, tell him that thus I treated his lying words, and honoured them! And, Edward, be warned, and put no faith in the master of 'The Rest.' Judge for yourself; and rather take counsel from the first man you meet with on the highway than of Vaudon."

"Oh, you never agreed, and never will agree," said my brother, yawning; "and as for me, I judge for myself pretty well, Luke, I can tell you. I live at 'The Rest' because it saves money: but I think London may suit me better."

"Will you lodge with me?"

"No, thank you: I have accepted my aunt's invitation, and shall be very comfortable there. When is *the* day?"

"Thursday morning next."

My brother supped with me, and I walked home to Park Lane with him, and listened to his dry details of Wharnby, and his moneyed speculations of Wharnby's land and houses.

I did not enter the Boyington mansion with him; it was nearly one o'clock—the morning was too early, and the hour was too late.

I was in a musing mood. Edward's arrival from Wharnby had brought associations of that well-known place forcibly before me: and I walked slowly down Park Lane, seeing, in my imagination, "The Rest" upon the cliffs, with its dark, waving trees topping the gaunt white rocks, and hanging over the deep green sea.

A woman, in a dark dress and thick veil, came hurrying down the street, and her rapid pace arrested my attention, and brought me back once more to the present. I stepped aside to let her pass, and something indistinct about the common dress she wore, or in her gait, her height, her figure, struck me so forcibly as corresponding with my sister, that I cried out, wildly, "Agnes!"

The woman hurried by, paying no heed to my interjection; and for a moment I stood transfixed, watching the receding form. As it neared my aunt's residence, I held my breath with a frightful suspense, and kept one glaring look upon its progress. Once I fancied it gave a hurried glance over the shoulder, and then increased its pace. It reached my aunt's house; it passed, and then ran on more swiftly, and was soon lost in the darkness.

"What folly," I muttered to myself as I resumed my walk, "to cry out my sister's name! Probably, it was some poor woman on a sad mission, and I must needs startle her with my vociferations. My sister, alone, and at such an hour, and equipped like that!—I am becoming childish!"

The absurdity of the suspicion re-assured me, and I strode homewards, smiling at my own excited imagination.

CHAPTER XXXVI.

MARRIED!

It has come! The appointed day—my marriage-day, and carriages are thick within the square, and wedding-bells are pealing out; and Ernestine, surrounded by her bridesmaids, and in her beauty eclipsing all around her, is ready to set forth.

It has come! Within St. George's—most fashionable of London saints—I wait her coming with a beating heart—a heart full of love and fevered expectation. I think not of Celia Silvernot, lost by my own rashness, and cast aside by my own impetuosity—of Celia, so unhappy in her loves; I think not that that fair virtuous girl might have come on some such sunny morning into the echoing church, and, resting her hand in mine, have said, "I, Celia, take thee, Luke, to my wedded husband!"

No more such dreams for me!—no more such thoughts, so vain, and impotent, and self-accusing! Do I not wait a more accomplished bride, as beautiful, more talented, and more devoted to me? What have I lost?

My friends are round me; my brother and sister, my aunt and cousin, Sir John and Mr. George, and a host of faces that I have seen before—friends of the Boyingtons and Agnes.

The clergymen—there are two—enter the communion, and at the same time, as though by some signal preconcerted, the doors swing wide, and Ernestine advances; and I, impatient bridegroom, hasten to meet her, and take her from her surrounding friends, and move with her to the altar.

With the rich lace veil sweeping from her head, and falling over her in gauzy folds, she looks a bride well worthy of a monarch. Her step is firm, the hand upon my arm moves not tremulously; there is no hesitation, no backward lingering of soul.

I murmur forth her name, and press the hand linked to my arm; and she replies, "Dear Luke."

Her face is very pale and white when she flings back her veil, and more than one behind me note the same, and whisper concerning it.

"The excitement has been almost too much for my Ernestine," I say to her; "and the blush roses, for a time, have vanished from her cheek."

"Am I so pale?"

"You have not your usual colour," I reply; "but you are not fearful, at the last, and before this altar, dear?"

We are standing round it now, and the clergyman has opened his great book of prayer, and an officious individual is hovering at the back to prompt and give advice.

"Fearful of you!" She presses my arm gently with her fingers, and looks up and smiles.

The weak tones of the minister's voice rouse all to attention, and Lady Boyington, who is interested in the ceremony, hooks one finger into the button-hole of Sir John's coat, and cowes him with a look. Sir John is restless, and had been better in Park Lane. He keeps standing on tip-toe, and straining to peer over all heads in the direction of the church-door, and is continually asking, in husky tones, of Lady Boyington and cousin Jane—"Where's Twidger? where the devil's Twidger?" My brother Edward is alarmed at the baronet, and edges from him at all opportunities; and Agnes is more attentive to a flirtation with a Captain Evbell than to Sir John's eccentricities, or her brother's marriage.

The assistant clergyman—we are great people, and play a well-known farce—commences, after the preliminary discourse, with his impressive exhortation. His voice is deep and almost sepulchral, and, in contrast to his fellow-minister's, strikes deeper into the heart, and rouses all to listen. He is a young man to whom such ceremonies as our own are not yet hackneyed and grown flat, and, standing before Ernestine and me, he says, forcibly and impressively, with his looks fixed on us, as Becket or Wolsey might have looked upon some penitent before them—"I require and charge you both, as ye will answer at the dreadful day of judgment, when the secrets of all hearts shall be disclosed, that if either of you know any impediment why ye may not be lawfully joined together in matrimony, ye do now confess it. For be ye well assured, that so many as are coupled together otherwise than God's Word doth allow, are not joined together by God; neither is their matrimony lawful."

Ernestine's gaze is fixed upon the ground, but her colour has not yet returned, and she is, if possible, paler than before. The marriage rites proceed, and our hands are clasped together, and I place the ring upon her finger, and it is said—

"Those whom God hath joined together, let no man put asunder."

We are man and wife ; and what tie can sunder two such faithful hearts as stand before God's altar, and plight their troth unto each other ?

The ceremony is complete, the names are signed, the death-like pallor has been replaced by the scarlet blush, the friends are thronging round us, heaping congratulation on congratulation, and Sir John is shaking me violently by the hand.

It is with some difficulty that I get my hand away from Sir John, who holds on as to a raft, and turn to Ernestine, and lead her from the church.

The wedding breakfast is to be given at my aunt's, and to Park Lane carriage after carriage rattles fast away. Alone within the carriage, I draw her to my side, and ask if she is happy.

"Too happy !" she murmurs, with her head upon my breast ; "I cannot think such joy can last—such deep bliss must be ever transient !"

"No, my dear Ernestine, do not say that," I reply ; "whilst two hearts are knit together, having but one kindred feeling, one impulse, and beating with one sacred love, no storms from the outward world can separate them, or make a fleeting vision of their rapt devotion."

"Dear Luke, I am not worthy of such love as yours."

"Dear Ernestine, your love is priceless."

"Not worthy, Luke, not worthy !" she reiterates. "Oh ! dear husband, promise never to fall off in this affection you have confessed to-day—to turn aside from me, and from my love, as one hath done before. Cease to love me, and I cease to live !"

"May I cease to live myself, when I play so false and recreant a part !"

Is there no foreshadowing of the future, in these suspicions of my bride—no glimpse of an *afterwards*, over which there is no controlling, and against which there is no preparing ? Ring on, wedding-bells, ring on ; for there *is* harmony for me in these voices of the Lares, and the world is a gay world, and all the sombre repinings of my life are gone with the gentle figure of my wife, nestling to my side—my wife that has come from out the depth of my despair, like a bright angel from the shadow land, and sat beside me, and charmed away all evil !

It is a day of gladness, of feasting, and of revelry. There is the reflex of our joy on every face around us, on every lip that drinks to our prosperity in the sparkling wine. Mr. Boyington is a constant hanger-on to Agnes, and not a word in coy aside to rival swains does she attempt to utter, but what he thrusts in his drawling voice, and mars all meaning responses with his officiousness. Sir John is missing, and Twidger has been seen to flit up-stairs, and keep him company in his own private room. Ernestine has little to say; she is thoughtful, blushing, happy; and Edward has grown conversational with cousin Jane, and is telling her of his last investment.

At an early hour our post-carriage stands before the house, waiting to bear us from the guests and the dwelling of the Boyingtons, and Ernestine has retired to change her wedding-dress, followed by the ladies.

The time hastens on, and we are going away. With Agnes, Edward, Jane, and my aunt, we take a more affectionate farewell; and as I press Agnes to my heart—so young, and beautiful, and vain—a cold shudder creeps through every vein within me.

"When we meet once more, dear Aggy," I say, "a year, or even more, will have passed by: it is a long time, judging by our glances into futurity; and we can but wonder what relative position we shall occupy ere the curtain rises again upon our re-union. How shall I find my sister?"

"Do not ask."

"Not ask!"

"It is impossible to give an answer, is it not?" she said; "and does it matter much to you or me, seeing we have no power to avert it. I shall not be the reigning beauty then. There will be fairer blossoms bursting into the full flower of their charms."

"And you?"

"And I, Luke, may be like flowers that have bloomed too long in the sun—a withered leaf at best! You see," she said, returning to her light manner suddenly; "I can be metaphorical and weave similes of flowers, as well as prosing brother mine."

She pressed my hand, and glided across to Ernestine, and kissed her.

"Good-bye, dear sister," said my bride; "keep me a list of your conquests, that I may read them on my return, or send them to me in your first long letter."

"The postage would be heavy, Ernestine."

Lady Boyington folds me to her like a wrapper, and blesses me, and slips a diamond ring on my finger as a parting gift. Cousin Jane murmurs her best wishes, and offers me her gentle lips; and Edward bluffy says, "Good-bye," and clasps my hand tightly, but there is no fraternal warmth in the hard grip he gives me.

We are off. The windows of the room we have quitted are alive with smiling faces, and more than a dozen handkerchiefs wave in friendly farewell to us.

The liveried menials flock from the open door, and stare after our carriage, and a window opens from an upstairs room, and Sir John's red face and half his short figure, ornamented about the shoulders with two great hands for epaulettes—the property of Twidger—leans out. Sir John, mindful of old customs, flings a heavy shoe into the road, and seems in the excitement of the moment to be struggling with Twidger in a wild attempt to follow it—the crowd of idlers set up a cheer—the post-boys whip their horses, and we have started on our honeymoon!

* * * * *

From the dark night of the city on the mountain side, from tower and pinnacle, from spire and mass of house roof, from sound of marriage bell and hum of human voice, the figure slowly takes its way, and I, bound to its will and helpless in mine own, follow it. To me it seems as if now, in my new life, a second figure, and that a woman's, should have been with me hand in hand, participating in this mysterious journey; but still I am alone, and still the figure beckons and points to the downward path, and goes on before—a silent, death-like guide.

Past cities, that look like foreign capitals, with bold cathedrals looming from the haze in the grand, dark outline of their majesty—past flowing rivers, bright with light, as if the sun were rising, and on which falls the shadow of the purple clustering vines—and then the figure, for the first time as it were, vanishes, and day breaks on the mountain-side, and my wife comes to me with her gladsome smile, and all is fairy-land.

The night comes on again—the light was but a gleaming meteor, although it may be counted by days and weeks of mortal computation—and the figure stands as before, and waits for my approach; and I look round for my second self, and she is gone! We halt at a villa, near some glassy lake—for I can see lights from windows reflected in the dark sheet of water spreading out before—it and my conductor makes a gesture of attention. My heart leaps with strange exhilaration, and even the presence of the spectre is forgotten in a wailing infant's cry! I move—but the figure warns me back; and, as I have seen it once before, covers its grim, corpse-like face with the black folds of its garment.

I watch until he re-assumes the old, stern attitude, and once more motions me to follow.

Past the silent lake—down into the gloomy wilds—more towns, lakes, nigh unto a sea—and then once more, the city from whence our last journey dated—from whence the marriage bells pealed forth—from whence we rode away a bride and bridegroom of an hour.

"Again!"

The figure nods its head, and still precedes me. The gates of the city fly back as before; there are faces in the streets that I have longed to see for years—and faces missing that I last left full of health—and faces changed and marked by sin and care—and faces on which disgrace is masked by forced smiles that have no merriment within them—and faces coming from far and near, from life and the grave—all pressing forward and awaiting me!

CHAPTER XXXVII.

THE MOTHER'S LEGACY!

Two years have glided by in the current of my life—have passed as years of contentment do pass to the contented ones—swiftly, magically, evanescently. They were two such happy years, spent far away from the cliffs of Albion—far away from those recollections which had bitterness in them for us both.

Years spent in the south of France—by the banks of the Rhine—in the romantic Fatherland—in Switzerland, beneath its mountains, and by its glassy lakes—in Italy, "the sunny land" of Europe—in Venice, gay, brilliant Venice—in islands studding calm blue seas—oh, those halcyon years! We shunned the cities—there was too much noise—too much of the world for us within their bustling streets: we sought the shadow of the vine—the banks of the silent water—the foot of the mountain crag—the villa on the shores of the silvery lake! We followed no paths struck out for tourists—we abided by our own counsel—we sought but each other's approbation—and love made every resting-place a paradise. And in that villa by the lake—the villa we had engaged for six entire months, it was so fairy-like a palace—what a hallowed home did it become to both of us!

For therein was born unto me a son. I folded it to my heart, and invoked God's blessing on its baby head, and thanked him for this gift. I felt a better man—a greater Christian—for the boon bestowed; and when Ernestine could take my arm again, and wander by those shores lining the great silvery expanse, I was beyond all care—my bliss beyond all earthly knowledge.

So two years faded away, and in the summer-time we came back again to London, bearing our cherished boy. We had returned for no particular reason—it was not that we were surfeited with life far from our ancient world, or longed for the attractions that that world presented—not that we sought to meet other faces, or that our love had been toned down to a less romantic passion. Our love was ever a romance! Yet we came home, and took up our residence in the house in Cavendish Square.

We had heard but little of those left behind, two years ago; some letters had been received; others, in consequence of our constant change of place, had miscarried, and been lost; and we, ourselves, had been far from regular correspondents.

It was early in one evening in July that we arrived in Cavendish Square. Being desirous of seeing my sister and my relatives, and of surprising them by my sudden return, I sallied forth at about nine in the evening, leaving Ernestine watching the slumbers of little Luke.

"It is a bad omen when the husband abandons his wife at so early a date, Luke!" she said, laughingly.

"Shall I stay?"

"No; go and persuade them all to come and see me to-morrow, and bring me all the news, Luke—every scrap."

My carriage drew up at the house in Park Lane at about half-past nine. The house seemed full of guests; there were lights behind every window blind, and shadows of many visitors passed to and fro.

The porter admitted me, and stared vacantly in my face.

"Tell Lady Boyington that——"

"Lady Boyington!" he ejaculated with surprise.

"Have they gone from home?" I cried. "Where are Sir John and Lady Boyington? My name is Elmore. Have you forgotten me, Pilchers?"

"Ask your pardon, Mr. Elmore, but I really had. Glad to see you back again, sir. Thankee, sir."

As he pocketed my douceur, I made further inquiries.

"Lord, sir! Lady Boyington and daughter have left Park Lane these nine months. You see, after the death of Sir John——"

"The death of Sir John!"

"Why, didn't you know *that?*"

"I have but just returned—Sir John dead!"

"He cut his throat, sir; did it all of a sudden, when Twidger's—dare say you remember Twidger, sir?—back was turned. Twidger tried to get the razor away—too late for anything but the tops of his own fingers."

"Can you give me Lady Boyington's address?"

"Yes, sir. But will you not see Sir George?"

"Sir George!" I said. "Then, Sir George still lives here?"

"Of course, sir."

"You have a party to-night?"

"Yes, sir."

"Lady Boyington is here, then, and Miss B. and my sister?"

"Lor, no, sir."

The man's manner puzzled me; but, having held already too long an altercation with him, I resolved to wait further explanations from the lips of Sir George himself.

There were a great number of servants darting to and fro, and, at a sign from the porter, one important member of the household ushered me up the well-known stairs into that room from whence I had taken farewell of my sister and relatives, on the day I started on my wedding-tour, and left me to wait the new baronet's pleasure, and to communicate my name to him.

After a quarter of an hour had passed, Sir George Boyinging, with his thumbs in the pockets of his white vest, sauntered in, and nodding carelessly—as though he had seen me yesterday—crossed the room, and leaning against the mantel-shelf, drawled out—

"Well, Elmore!"

"I am sorry to trespass upon your time, Sir George, more especially on such a night as this; but I am desirous of Lady Boyington's address," I said, stiffly.

"She has apartments in Sloane Street, Chelsea—No. ——."

"I thank you."

I made a hasty movement to the door; I had had enough of Sir George Boyington. He had evidently no desire to continue my acquaintance; there was no more to be gained in my quarter, or to be got by my influence.

"Have you had a plea-sant trip, Elmore?"

"Very," I replied, curtly.

"Mrs. Elmore is well, I hope?" swinging an eye-glass I well remembered in his fingers.

"Very well."

"Pray pre-sent my res-pects."

I bowed, and Sir George rang for a servant to attend me. Biting my lip with suppressed rage, I went down the stairs and out of the house with a curse on the haughtiness of its possessor. I was soon driven to the house in Sloane Street, Chelsea, and a minute more saw me in the presence of Lady Boyington and her daughter Jane, who were occupying somewhat handsome apartments on the first floor.

They were both in deep mourning, and looked pale. Lady Boyington was a trifle thinner, and my cousin was not altered for the better in general appearance; there was a sharp, angular look about the face of both, indicative of mental harass and incertitude.

Lady Boyington began to moan as she embraced me.

"Oh! my dear nephew—my dear nephew! what a change since I saw you last!—what affliction and distress!"

I gave a wandering look round in search of Agnes, and replied—

"I regret it, and am sincerely grieved," I said. Then turning to my cousin, "Well, Jane!"

With a sorrowful, almost compassionate look, she advanced and saluted me. Lady Boyington was full of her own sorrows, and after spreading out her handkerchief across her knees, ready for any emergency or sudden weakness, she broke forth with—

"Oh! poor dear Sir John, my husband—my dear husband! You have heard of his untimely end!"

"I have, aunt. Let me not add to your distress by listening to its recapitulation," I said. "I am surprised to see you in Sloane Street!"

"Oh! that unnatural son!—that cruel young man!—that wicked, ungrateful boy!" sobbed my aunt. "See to what we are reduced!"

"Reduced, Lady Boyington!"

"Sir John died without a will, and his son has ground us down to the last penny law allows, and turned us out of Park

Lane, and given us the worst carriage and the ugliest horses, and shut his doors against us, and never comes to see us—oh! dear me, dear me!"

"These are but minor troubles, mamma," said Jane.

"You do not feel them as you ought to do—you do not feel them as you ought to do!" she cried, reproachfully.

No mention of Agnes's name—nay, even a studious avoidance of it, as if they were fearful of paining me, her brother, by its utterance.

"And my cousin Jack?" I said to Jane.

"Oh! my dear brother has had further promotion, and writes home in the gayest of spirits. That is a consolation—is it not, mamma?"

"Oh! dear me!" sighed Lady Boyington.

"But you tell me nothing of my sister Agnes," I said, anxiously. "Where is Agnes? Is she married, or——?"

I stopped short in my inquiries. Lady Boyington's face expressed astonishment and dismay, and Jane's eyes were filled with tears.

"What has happened? Why do you look at me so strangely?"

I glanced from one to the other hastily and inquiringly.

"My dear boy," cried Lady Boyington, "you never got my letter—you never heard?"

"I have heard nothing!"

"She has left us—she has gone from our protection—more than ten months. Oh! when shall our family be ever quit of the stigma of disgrace?"

It was some minutes before I could speak, or recover from a stunning sensation, as though I had received a heavy blow.

"Tell me all," I gasped out.

Kind cousin Jane, who thought the shock I was about to receive could be more gently dealt by her own lips, and had more faith in her powers of explanation than in those of her more worldly mother, said—

"It is a great sin and error into which my cousin Agnes has fallen, Luke, and which we all regret for your sake as much as for her own. Dazzled by a great temptation, weak in her own resolution, she has given way and forgotten her own self!"

I started from the chair I had taken near my aunt, and paced the room with rapid strides.

"Forgotten her own self!" The words were ringing in my

ears, and branding on my brain this fresh disgrace—this family's dishonour. My face was scarlet, as though I had inherited her shame, and had pandered to it by my long absence and continued silence in the stranger's land.

"Some one speak!" I cried at last, in a hoarse tone: "tell me more—how it happened—with whom she has fled—what were her motives? she who could have commanded an honest, lofty position, and yet chose degradation! It is fatality—it is God's curse upon us. There is no chance in all this—there cannot be. It was fore-ordained!"

"No, no, Luke!" cried Jane; "not the blame upon your Maker—not the worldling's ready subterfuge and vain excuse!"

"Go on—go on."

Lady Boyington, tired of being so long silent, broke in with heavy sighs—

"Jane, let me speak. You are so young, and it is, I think, unmaidenly in you—at least, it may be. Luke, my dear nephew, Agnes left us some time after your marriage—about a year afterwards, I think—and took up her residence in Darton House, and became the mistress of the Duke of ——."

"Where is she now?" I cried, fiercely.

"Still with him."

I snatched my hat from the table, and extended my hand.

"You will hear from me soon; I must go now—good-bye."

"Luke, be not rash. What do you intend doing?" cried Jane.

"I will see her."

"It is impossible."

"I will see her," said I, firmly; "it is my right—a duty delegated to me by my God—a duty speaking from the grave of that father who loved her so, and whose fears that her mother's fate, and his own disgrace, would have no warning for her, and would teach no lesson, have proved no visionary errors. I will see her!"

Lady Boyington shook her head.

"Good-bye; I shall see you to-morrow or the next day. I am going now to Darton House."

Making my hurried adieux, I hastened from Sloane Street, and was whirled in my carriage within a hundred yards of the Duke's mansion. I leaped out.

"You can go home, James," said I to the coachman; "I shall not require you again. Give that to your mistress on your return."

He took the hasty note I had scrawled on a leaf of my pocket-book to Ernestine—stating that strange circumstances, which would be explained when I saw her, compelled me to delay my return home—touched his hat, and drove away.

Another moment, and I was before Darton House. It was more of a palace than a mansion, and there was a broad gravelled space, hemmed in by lofty iron railings, before the stately residence. The gates were closed, and the house was dark in its exterior, save where two lamps shed a radiance on the great entrance-doors. All was still and silent.

After some deliberation, I walked swiftly along by the side walls and numerous offices, and went round to the back. There was more life going on in the street, upon which the back of the house opened, and servants in red livery were passing swiftly in and out, whilst one or two idlers loitered near the doors, and looked about them, open-mouthed.

Watching my opportunity, I intercepted one of the servants as he came from the house and crossed the pavement to his horse.

"Is the Duke within?" I asked, slipping a gold coin into his hand.

"No; but he will be home to-night, sir," he answered, touched to civility by the golden bribe.

"And—Miss Elmore?"

The man elevated his eyebrows, rounded his mouth, and stared at me.

"Where is she?"

"Miss Elmore is with him, sir."

He had mounted his horse by this time, and, after another lengthened stare of great perplexity, he rode away.

I retraced my steps to the front of the house, and took up my post a few yards distant from it. I had formed no settled purpose, save to see her by some means—to risk anything to see and speak with her.

Hour after hour passed—it was near midnight—the streets were deserted. I seemed alone on the watch. Presently, the entrance-doors were opened, and two men, in a kind of undress uniform, came out, walked across the gravelled drive, and, after opening the large, scrolled gates of iron, returned into the house.

They would be here shortly: every roll of the carriage wheels in the distance made my heart leap, and set it beating wildly, till the noise rumbled fainter and more faint.

The whirl of wheels once more—a rapidly-advancing noise. I gazed into the darkness of the long road, and beheld two fiery lamps gleaming and coming on. The doors were again opened. I could distinguish the figures of several servants in the hall. They were coming!

I directed my whole attention to the advancing equipage. I stood close in line with its intended passage, so that, if the blind was up, and a light were within, I might see the confirmation of my more than fears.

It was a dark green travelling-carriage, with no crest or sign of royalty upon its panels, and it whirled by and passed through the gates a blank.

Full of my project, unfearing and uncaring, I darted suddenly after the carriage, and, running by its side at my utmost speed, kept up with it, through the gates, across the drive before the house. The servants were too much engaged to note my dark figure standing by one of the bronzed lamps, and I kept my place, watching the lowering of the steps, and glaring at the opened carriage-door.

There was a sharp voice suddenly ringing through the night—a man was running across the fore-court, fearful of some attempted act of violence; but, ere his cry had roused the vigilance of the servants, the Duke had descended, and was handing Agnes out. Yes, Agnes—my own lost sister—so beautiful and so full of smiles for him in the splendour of her infamy! She was in full dress; and the diamonds—that fitting legacy!—were sparkling in her hair and on her neck, as they had shone out in her innocence; and she was full of pride, and the light, firm step with which she descended showed no indications of an aching heart or conscience tortured by remorse.

"Agnes!"

I started forward with the name upon my lips, and she gave a shriek, and clung to the Duke's arm. Half a dozen hands were instantly upon me, dragging me back; and the man, with royal blood within his veins, turned round and faced me with a bold, fierce look of supreme haughtiness.

"What man is this?"

"Agnes, I must speak to you—I will!"

"Remove him," cried the Duke, loftily.

As they moved into the house, and I was struggling with the servants, Agnes whispered a few words to her companion, and he halted on the door-step.

W

"Take him to the gates, and let him go."

Further resistance was unavailing, and I was led to the iron gates, and thrust forth like a beggar. I shook my clenched fist at the house in my impotence of rage; and, after a long gaze at the closed doors, turned on my heel and strode homewards, with a host of thoughts battling in my brain.

Ernestine, haggard with long watching, hastened to meet me as I entered.

"What has happened, dear Luke?" she asked, eagerly—"have our cares commenced so soon after our return to England?"

"The name of Elmore is doomed to disgrace," I said, gloomily, "and a sister's fall from honour has affixed a deeper stain upon it, and made it once more a mark for public scorn and common talk. It is well that her father died before such a night as this!"

CHAPTER XXXVIII.

AMBITION'S END.

And this was the end of all!—the conclusion to a father's tender care, Miss Osborne's studious watch upon her ward, a youth spent in a dull house by the sea-side, a family's love and pride, all ended thus—all proved to be nugatory and of no avail! Were there no warning voices bidding her "beware?"—no spirits whispering "look back?"

Oh, fatal hour in which she braved her father's dying wish, and left him in his mournful solitude—left him for what?

Through the early hours of the morning I brooded upon the strange events—many so small and trifling in themselves—that brought about this evil, and before me flitted the Agnes of the past: a little girl, a child with golden hair and thoughtful look; a woman, young, and beautiful, and vain; a reigning belle of a great city, with crowds of worshippers around her; a sister, capricious, wilful, determined, and yet loved.

Not in all her capriciousness, her wilfulness, her firm determinations bent upon wrong ends—not in her vanity, or in the dangerous attraction of her more than common beauty, did I think of this result.

Ernestine sat beside me at the breakfast-table, and was silent out of respect to my own fixed thoughts, which dwelt upon that one engrossing theme.

It was the more terrible to me because there was no backward step, no retrogression—not one hope. There was not a ray of light upon this worse than darkness—no hand could save her—no prayer avert the horror of her future life. I felt that she was lost to me for ever, that she was no longer my own sister, and that I was tied hand and foot, and had no power to aid her or avenge her.

Late in the morning a letter was brought to me. The superscription was in her handwriting, and eagerly I broke the seal.

"I will be in Kensington Gardens at three o'clock this afternoon. I shall expect you *alone*. "AGNES."

I passed the letter across to Ernestine, and resumed my old abandonment to thought. Ernestine read it, sighed, and returned it to me, saying—

"You will go?"

"Yes," I said, "I will go. Not for the good that I can do, or for any reason that I can urge, but to see her once again."

I waited impatiently for the hour stated in the letter by my sister, and set forth at last to the appointed place of rendezvous.

It was a bright afternoon, and there were many loiterers in the Gardens. Naturally imagining she would select one of the less-frequented walks, I sought those most deserted and free from visitors. A figure like my sister, followed at some distance by a servant, almost immediately caught my eye, and I hastened towards it. It was she.

"Agnes, I am here."

She took my arm, and we walked on the velvet grass, with the servant some paces in the rear. She was richly dressed, and on her face was a more patrician look—a haughty, disdainful expression that, though detracting from all airs of gentleness, added to her peculiar style of beauty.

"You have come home, Luke?"

"Yes," I answered, mournfully.

"You sought me out last night—for what good, or with what intent?"

"With what intent, indeed!"

"If you have met me in these gardens to-day to reproach

me, let our meeting end here. Reproaches are useless, and will not affect me."

"True."

"I have appointed this interview with the permission of His Royal Highness."

"He is aware that you have come hither to meet me?"

"He is."

"What have we met for? Why have I sought you out? What good to you or me can be derived from this appointment?"

"None."

"Agnes, are you happy?" I asked."

"I am resigned to the lot I have chosen for myself."

"Will you—it is my last request—fly from it? I, your brother, offer you a home—a refuge from this degradation."

"Folly, folly."

"Agnes," cried I, passionately; "it is more than folly; it is madness on your part, all this."

"No matter, now."

"Agnes, dear Agnes, if you will leave him, even at this eleventh hour, I will shield you from the world—I will love you as no brother ever loved. We will go far away to another land—you, and I, and Ernestine, and my child, and God will bless you in the late hour of your repentance."

No entreaty softened one deep line upon her face—the eyes were cold and steely, the lip curled; the voice unfaltering and calm with which she answered me.

"I followed not this path unreflectingly—no other than a king's son could have made me choose it. How many ready with their sneers and upturned eyes envy my position in their hearts!"

"Envy you," I cried; "and how many, vain-glorious girl, feel themselves like me, disgraced? Are you less guilty because a king's son points to the downward gulf, and leads you to it? Agnes, I know why I came hither to-day. It was with a last hope—a wavering, feeble hope, that some remnants of a true woman lingered, and some self-respect, and that I might have moulded them to some less sinful end. I find now that you seek to palliate your crime—a greater sin than all. Let us part here—I can do nothing but disown you!"

"I proposed this interview, and it was seconded by His Highness, for no other purpose. We are divided now for ever, and our meetings can bring but dissatisfaction to us both; so let us part—is it not best, Luke?"

"Yes—but, Agnes, I have this wrong to avenge," said I, gloomily.

"That were an act of madness," she said, hastily; "he is a royal duke, and beyond all vengeance."

"Not the vengeance of his God."

We strolled under the broad-spreading boughs of the great elms for a few moments in cold silence, and her gaze was ever directed straight before her, as though to some distant focus, from which she had no power to withdraw her eyes.

"Agnes, I can conjecture no reason for this wild line of action; my mind affords not one sufficient excuse for you—not one."

"My reasons will ever remain a mystery; they are buried within my own breast, and will die with me," she answered. "Think, Luke, if you like, that it was a dazzling temptation, and that I preferred it to Paul Redwin's wife, or to Sir George Boyington's young bride—think what you will," she added, recklessly.

"And you will not come with me?" I urged, in last entreaty; "you are resolved?"

"I am."

"God forgive you! strange, wilful girl, then—I have no more to say."

Without looking me in the face, she laid her hand in mine, passively and coldly, withdrew it after an instant, murmured some indistinct parting words, and glided from me.

I stood watching her figure—tall and queenly—vanishing in the distance, and thinking of what an end to her spring days of youth was this, and what mystery—for, was it not mystery?—had actuated her in her terrible selection? If there were any—and sometimes I am tempted to believe in some vile plot, or hideous snare, in which her vanity, perhaps, helped to entrap herself—it has ever been a secret unconstrued, and so will remain to the last days of my life.

There was no more for me to do—I had acted up to my own principle of duty—I knew there was no other course to adopt that would reclaim, or bring evidence of an atoning spirit. It was beyond my grasp—I could but sit down nerveless and disarmed, and listen to what the world said of her, and of what my heart accused her, even in its pity. I could but pity her as she went further down the winding path of sin—no voice or hand of mine could urge, or bring her back.

In the first moments of my indignation, I wrote a challenge to the royal villain, and received an answer from his secretary, formal, and yet scoffing. There was no meeting him face to face; shut up in his carriage, or hemmed around by guards, or seated with his peers in coronet and ermine, he was safe from man's vengeance, and above it, as poor Agnes had remarked; and so I left him to his God's!

CHAPTER XXXIX.

A WELCOME VISITOR.

One maxim of Jacques Vaudon's I could profit by, for all my detestation of his character and estimation of his motives. When he had said to me, that night on which I had refused to see the rector of Wharnby, "Brood not on irreparable misfortune—'tis the wisdom of the slave," he had sown the seeds of counsel from which, in this case, I had learned to profit; for there was a counterbalance to my sorrow and inward grief in my child and Ernestine; and in my love for them, and in the peace around my hearth, I could forget what a true child of her erring mother was Agnes Elmore.

I have said that we did not return to London to engage in the pleasures it presented, and we were more happy together in our own quiet home than in the crowd of fashion around us; and so we lived for each other, and were content.

We saw the invitations from old acquaintances, that had come thickly rushing in at first, grow less, and fade out entirely; we formed our own little circle; we chose our few friends by estimation of more sterling qualities than make up the aggregate sum of presentable people; we limited our feasting and revelry to a chosen few, and made home the first consideration, and were repaid for it by peace.

Lady Boyington and my cousin Jane were frequent guests at our house; and though my aunt's sighs and groans were not conducive to general entertainment, yet we allowed for them in her losses, and listened to her harrowing tales of Sir John's death and his son's ingratitude with grave attention and respect.

From my brother Edward—who had returned to "The

Rest,"* after mature deliberation over ways and means and probabilities of London turning out a fortune to him—I occasionally received a few lines; but they were all to one purpose, all set phrases, where common words of brotherly interest in me or mine were concerned, and he thought required; and full of small commissions for me, relative to his own interest, in one way or the other.

Of Vaudon I heard nothing, neither did I care to hear of him—our lives were separate and distinct.

The season was advancing to its conclusion, and the nights were growing longer. I was sitting alone in my favourite room—the room where I had told my love to Ernestine, and won her to myself—and reading the work of one of those enviable beings—a great author! Ernestine was busy in the nursery with little Luke, and my thoughts were left to their full occupation of one object.

I had in a great degree overcome the moody fits of reverie to which I had been subject from a child, and in my marriage felicity could forget the hours of gloom I had spent, or the misfortunes I had had; but they had never been entirely eradicated, and occasionally an unnatural despondency would fall upon and creep over me, and tinge everything with its own shadowy colouring.

Some such depression fell upon me in my solitude, and I gazed vacantly on the carpet at my feet.

And yet that night of all nights should have been symbolical of something less than misery to me; for one of the last gleams of perfect happiness that my life presented, shot across the darkening waste that lay before me.

As I sat oppressed, as it were, by stupor, I was unconscious of the door opening slowly, softly, and some one standing in the doorway, gazing in upon me. The watcher, after standing some minutes, regarding me observantly, entered the room, closed the door as silently as he had opened it, and moved towards me. When close to my side, he laid his hand upon my shoulder, and in deep, though cheerful tones, said, at the same moment—

"Brother Luke!"

"Gilbert!" I shouted, springing to my feet; "Gilbert, my own dear brother! Hold off a minute," I cried, clutching him by both arms, and gazing earnestly into his frank, manly face; "let me be sure I am not dreaming. It *is* you—it *is* you! At last!"

"At last," he answered, pressing me to his breast, as he would have done a child, and looking on me with his dark eyes, dim and swimming. "I told you we should meet again. I knew it the morning of our parting, if God would spare us both a few years longer. Dear Luke, I do not think even *you* can guess the full amount of pleasure at my heart, that I feel in grasping these honest, brotherly hands again."

He wrung them in his own, and standing facing each other, with our hands clasped in re-union, we looked upon the changes time had made, for better or for worse, since we parted at "The Rest."

For the better in Gilbert Elmore. Although he was pale—he was ever pale—there was a bright look in the face indicative of perfect health and peace of mind; and his form was well knit, and his chest broad and full. He had set his crutch aside to grasp my hand, and had evidently not so much need for its support as at Wharnby; for when he crossed to a chair, he but slightly limped in his progress, and touched lightly on the arm I had tendered for his assistance.

"What a host of things we have to ask of each other—what recapitulations of things past! I know not where to begin, or what inquiry to first suggest," I said, when we were seated.

"Patience, Luke," said my brother; "first, there is your own story. And there is a Mrs. Elmore I am curious concerning."

"Let me summon her hither to participate in my joy and——"

"A few moments," hastily cried Gilbert; "your story and my own would be tedious to Mrs. Elmore, and I would rather, without disrespect to my brother's wife, whom I long to see and claim relation with, listen to your tale of 'The Rest,' and my father, and——" he paused a moment—"and Agnes, and your own marriage, alone."

"You know of Agnes's fate?"

"Yes," he said, gloomily, "and have vainly tried to see her."

"And why have you been so long silent—so——"

"Patience, Luke," he said, holding up his finger; "to your tale—I am all attention."

Leaning forward with one arm upon my shoulder, he listened eagerly to those incidents of home that had happened since he left it, that have been chronicled herein, the records of "The Rest."

I told him of the changes that had gradually come upon our

father's house after his departure; of the infatuation of our father for Vaudon, which increased, and never knew a diminution; of my aunt's arrival at Wharnby, and the many sad events which her presence created and brought about; of the dawning of Agnes' future miserable life, in the severance of her plighted faith to Redwin—in the defiance of all counsel, and of a loving father's wish, and setting out to the city in which three out of four of that father's children were now dwellers. I told him of the sire's death, and spoke of the last words breathing his own name, and he listencd with the big tears of manly sorrow glistening on his cheeks. I told him all—of my own engagement to Celia—of the change brought about by Mrs. Silvernot, and my own pride, and Vaudon's silent hate—of my marriage—of my position to affluence once more—of my wedded bliss—of my boy, my son.

I did not mention the name of Miss Osborne, for fear of paining him by a recurrence to it, and he asked not one word concerning her.

Two hours had passed in the relation of my narrative—the servant had brought lights, and passed out unheeded—and we still sat absorbed in reminiscences of home.

"I have been to Wharnby once, Lukc," he said, at the conclusion of my long story, "a few weeks after my father's death—I heard of it even in London, for the world, I found, had not forgotten him—I paid one visit to his grave—it is the son's last duty to a father to pay many of them, but at that time necessity compelled my immediate return."

"And you never came to 'The Rest,' to solace me in my affliction?"

"In your excitement, you might have wished to follow me, and to join your fortunes unto mine, and I should but have marred thcm—I waited my own time, and I think I have chosen for the best. And now, let me have the pleasure of seeing my new sister."

"And your story?" I inquired.

"We will find a time for that; suppose you walk a little way homc with me, and hear thc humdrum, quiet existence I have passed—an existence with but little romance, and less interest—a life passed in fighting upwards, with 'Perseverance' for a constant watchword. Let me see my new sister now, and also, ere I leavc you, let me take a peep at my chubby nephew, through the curtains of his cot—you will not refuse me?"

In a few minutes Ernestine entered the room, and gracefully acknowledged the presence of the stranger.

"This is a very old friend of mine, Ernestine."

"He is doubly welcome, then," extending her hand.

"A friend that I have often spoken to you concerning, dear," I said, proud of my little mystery.

"Spoken to me," said my wife, wonderingly.

"No less a friend than my dear brother, Gilbert."

"A brother that had some difficulty in obtaining an entrance without some preliminary warning from the servants, Mrs. Elmore," said Gilbert; "some difficulty in startling him by an unexpected visit, claiming at the same time the right of relationship to you, fair sister mine."

There were fresh greetings after that, and we were all very happy, and had all so much to say.

Gilbert was a brother to Ernestine in a quarter of an hour; his genial open way, his manly frankness, his great heart, exemplified in his affection for me, so touching in its very minuteness and delicacy, charmed my bride to love him as a sister even in one meeting; and when before his departure he insisted on being escorted to the sleeping-room of our child, which was close unto our own chamber, and in which nurses were ever kept on watch, the delight of that never-forgotten evening reached its culminating point.

Reached, but did not begin to die off at its apex. It extended wide, and embraced everything around us. Ernestine's own hands drew aside the fairy drapery of curtain and held the waxen light, and we three stood and gazed upon the child in its deep, innocent sleep, with one tiny hand carelessly thrown over the coverlet. Gilbert stooped and kissed the baby almost reverently, and then stood up again and folded his hands upon his crutch, and looked long and wistfully at it.

"I will not say, God bless your first-born, Luke, for there is sure sign in that infant peacefulness of God's blessing resting on its head—I will say, God be ever with it! Mrs. Elmore, nay, if you will allow it, sister Ernestine," said he, turning to my wife, with a gayer look; "my brother was a lucky fellow when he was crossed in love at Wharnby."

"Does he think so?" she said, glancing smilingly at me.

"I think I am far from envying any man in England," I replied.

Dreamers! dreamers all by the bedside of that sleeping child!

CHAPTER XL.

HOME PEACE.

"Mrs. Elmore, I have formed a plan to rob you of your husband for a few hours," said Gilbert, upon our return to the parlour.

"He will be in good hands, and I can trust him," Ernestine replied.

"It is no less a plan than to take him home with me, and show him my diminutive house in the suburbs, and tell him my simple story as we journey on."

"Will you not take the carriage?"

"Thank you, sister, but if Luke objects not, I would prefer the walk."

"And I."

When we were in the lighted streets, he linked his disengaged arm in mine, and we walked, at a somewhat slow pace, in the direction of Paddington.

For some minutes he was silent.

"I am anxious for your narrative, Gilbert."

"You little think what a few words will tell my story when the one clue is given to the whole riddle, brother," he said; "the great secret is—I am an author."

"An author!"

"Not a famous one, Luke—not one whose name is heralded by pretentious announcement, or one that ever creeps into a dedicatory page, as mark of esteem or friendship from fellow-writers—I am not a novelist. To write a work of fiction was the first dream of my ambition, as it has been of many aspirants for fame before me. Well, I wrote one; and after months of hard labour, of toil—hard, unceasing mental toil, such as the careless readers and skimmers of books pay no consideration to—it had just sufficient talent in its composition to be received by a publisher—for nothing!"

"For nothing?"

"Ah! Luke, the world of books is a strange circle—a solar system, with one great sun in the centre—a few planets here and there—and innumerable nameless stars, some of which start from the heaven and are seen no more. The world of books to the amateur—to the unfledged authorling, who always dreams of eternal fame, of the top of the tree, not of its lower branches and boughs on which the *golden* fruit are so scarce and unripe —is the brightest of worlds, painted in colours the most brilliant and dazzling, while the fit lasts. There is no such temptation to the amateur as literary distinction; and yet there is no temptation that proves in the end so illusive and denying."

"You vilify your own craft, Gilbert," said I; "but your novel?"

"It had its day; it found a few kind reviews, one or two helping hands; it ran on an existence of some four months, was seen at circulating libraries and at marine bath-rooms, and then died a natural death. Publishers did not leap at me, or fight for me. I might have got, perhaps, thirty pounds for my second work's labour, if I had *begged* hard."

"But we read of writers receiving their thousands!"

"Suns in the solar system—there are few of them. For every amateur to build his hopes on such examples, is like every private soldier in the king's army to look forward to being a field-marshal; and, Luke, there is a greater chance for the soldier."

"But there *are* prizes amongst the blanks."

"There is the evil," said Gilbert; "one man by influence—great influence allied to great talent (both must co-operate to one end)—achieves an European reputation; and fifty thousand fools rush to their desk with the vain hope of reaching the same position, sacrificing time and valuable opportunities of other pursuits for the frail bubble that will burst before their eyes. But this is not my story."

"But you have succeeded?"

"Partly," continued he; "after my novel had been published, and the reviews had estimated me at my just worth, and brought me down to my fair level, I turned to the old study of essays, sketches, biographies, works that had occupied my time at 'The Rest.' Well acquainted with modern literature, I finally (for I will not harass you, Luke, with recounting all my rebuffs and disappointments) obtained the place of reviewer to a weekly newspaper, and this, added to chances now and then of furnishing dull articles on parliamentary topics and national grievances, is the life of Gilbert Elmore."

"I had hoped to have heard a fairer account of you, Gilbert," I said, mournfully; "I did not think such a struggle for daily bread compatible with the contented appearance you present."

"Was I not always contented, then, at home?" he asked.

"But the change from 'The Rest!'—from affluence to the monotonous existence of a poor writer!"

"I bore it with philosophic calmness," he replied. "I hoped on, and worked my way. The difficulties I encountered only nerved me to greater efforts at exertion. I thought not of sinking at the outposts, or giving up, faint-hearted, at the first barrier that crossed my path."

He then narrated to me the whole series of his attempts in literature, and his indomitable perseverance, month by month, and year by year—a narration tedious enough to the eyes that may dwell on these pages, but, ah! how precious to a brother who had lost him for so many years!

It was a pretty, tasteful little house, containing, probably, some five or six rooms, that we finally stood before, and to which he pointed as his home; but I could not look up at its diminutive proportions without sighing at the contrast it presented to my own mansion in the square, and to our father's great house looking on the sea.

He read my thoughts, and said, laughingly—

"You are dismayed at my Liliputian domicile, Luke! but it is a difference from my first lodgings, in the back streets near the Strand. I took this cottage with a very light heart, and have been happy in it with my housekeeper."

"Your housekeeper?"

"Ay!—the fairest, best of housekeepers!—you will like her at first sight."

He rattled cheerily at the brass knocker, and a spruce maid-servant answered to the summons. We entered the front parlour, and a lady rose to meet us.

I started back with surprise, exclaiming—

"Miss Osborne!"

"Miss Osborne no longer, brother," said Gilbert, as I warmly greeted her; "this lady is Mrs. Gilbert Elmore."

No wonder Gilbert was contented and happy now, or that he entered his cottage home with a light heart, when that cheering, pretty face was to be the comforter of his life, the spirit at his hearth.

"My congratulations come late," I said, kissing the sister that had so suddenly started up before me; "but they are none the less sincere—none the less full of my best wishes for your welfare."

"I am sure of that, dear brother," said she, in reply, as I recovered my first surprise.

"And now," said I, when we were seated, "there is a story to complete, deceitful Gilbert. How has this chain of fortunate events ended in accordance with the dearest hopes of your life? I did not think, Mrs. Elmore, when we took leave of each other at 'The Rest,' that I should welcome you as my brother's wife when we met once more."

"I did not think so myself, Luke."

"Now, Gilbert, the story; I am all impatience."

"When I obtained the reviewership to the weekly paper I have alluded to, I was thrown more into the society of literary men, and occasionally received invitations to *réunions* from some brother or sister of the order. I met with Miss Osborne one evening, at the house of one of our greatest living writers. It was a great surprise for both of us; for we had been in ignorance all our lives of the kindred pursuits we had followed."

"You are an authoress!" I exclaimed, turning to Mrs. Gilbert Elmore.

"I have been a small one all my life."

"Even at 'The Rest?'"

"Yes," she replied; "did I not regularly pay visits to Cliverton once a week? I was writing a serial tale for a journal at that time; and, upon our first meeting at Cliverton, you saw me coming from the office of a gentleman with whom I was commissioned by my publisher to transact all business that related to my poor profession."

"Might I inquire if you had any particular reasons for the retaining this secret so long from us?"

"My works were never popular, and I was almost ashamed of the weakness of my own productions," she said, modestly; "but writing was my chief consolation for long weary hours, and I followed it for the love of an old habit."

"But the secret was discovered at last?" I said.

"Yes," she replied, "and I was in a manner compelled to mix more with society; but it was society in which I could take an interest, and feel at home with: and so I bring my confessions round to Gilbert's story, for the interruption of which I hope to be forgiven."

"Forgiveness granted," said Gilbert; and continued—"It was an embarrassing meeting; for it reminded us of the last conversation we had had together—you remember Luke?"

"Well," I replied; "you were a disconsolate lover then, Gilbert, and were seriously thinking of dying of a broken heart."

"Rail on, brother," he said; "you have been more love-lorn than ever I have; but this narrative will never come to an end. When I was a rich man, or when hope held out to me the prospect of being one, this variable little lady could not murmur one word of encouragement; but when I was a poor scribe, who worked late into the night for a pittance I once should have scorned as derogatory on my part to accept—when I was one grade above actual poverty—I began to hope I might some day claim her for a bride. Nay, more, I discovered that it was not for want of love my first rejection at her hands brought me to despair. I found that out in its good time, when I learnt to love her more dearly than before—when I sought her hand a second time, and," proudly resting his hand on her shoulder, "won her for a wife."

"Is he not enough to make me vain, Luke?" said she, smiling.

"If he makes you happy, it is his duty, and what you deserve," I answered; "and, looking on you both, I do not augur much infelicity from the prospect set before me."

"We are contented, and so no misfortune can weigh heavily upon us," said Gilbert. "We married for love, and so, in this humble sphere, we jog on methodically enough, but still surely. By our united exertions we do not save much money; but we are free of the world's care, and have no envy for our neighbours."

"But you are enviable beings in yourselves," I said; "and the cares of a past life are forgotten in the present."

I stayed with them till a late hour, and listened to full recitals of the many struggles in their literary avocation they had gone through, and the waves of distrust and jealousy they had breasted, fighting always for one haven.

And they had found it. In the new life for them both, blest in the affection of the heart, they had found the only "Rest" on earth!

It was striking one when I entered Cavendish Square. A slight drizzling rain had begun to descend, and my few remaining steps were made sharply in the direction of my home.

A man, with a cigar in his mouth, was walking up and down before my house, and gazing curiously at its many windows. As I came up he advanced towards me.

"Whose house is this?" he asked, peremptorily.

"Mine, sir," I replied, laconically.

"Indeed!" he said, puffing at his cigar; "perhaps you can favour me by the information as to the locality of Mrs. Morton's?"

"Mrs. Morton's!"

"Yes; do you know her residence?"

"I know there is no Mrs. Morton, sir," I answered, knocking at my door.

"Is she dead, then? I never heard of that. That's strange news, at all events!"

Muttering to himself, the man gave one more look at the house, and sauntered leisurely away, turning round from time to time, and looking back at me—his lighted cigar a red spot in the darkness—until the door shut me from his sight.

CHAPTER XLI.

THE OPERA.

THE impression made upon me by the man I had seen watching the house in which I was a resident, faded not away, or became lost among those minor incidents which happen every day, and which live so short a time.

"Ernestine," said I, at the close of the following day, in which I had vainly endeavoured to exclude the man from my thoughts, "I have forgotten to mention a chance meeting with a friend of yours."

"Of mine, dear!" replied Ernestine; "who was he?"

"A gentleman, whom I met on the steps of this house about one in the morning, and who inquired after you by the name of Mrs. Morton."

"Inquired for me by *that* name!" she cried, "who could he have been?"

"The very question that puzzles and perplexes me, dearest," I said, "and try how I will, the man is ever before my eyes."

"What sort of a man was he?"

"A man of about my own height, with very sallow and sharply defined features, small dark eyes, and hair of considerable length, curling almost into ringlets, as I have seen a gipsy's."

"I do not know the man," she said, slowly.

"Not by one trait which I have represented?"

"Not by one. I can never have seen him. I *am sure* I have never seen him, Luke."

"It does not matter," I remarked; "only the lateness of the hour and the peculiarity of his questions, have more than a common effect upon my impressionable nature."

"Shall we ride over to your brother Gilbert's?" asked Ernestine, suddenly changing the topic of discourse; "you have promised me that visit."

"Willingly."

Ernestine was so long a time in her dressing-room, that, after waiting above an hour, I ascended the stairs in search of her. All was still within the room, and no answer being returned to my light tap on the panels of the door, I turned the handle and entered. She was praying!

"Ernestine, what is this?"

She started to her feet, and running towards me, flung her arms round my neck, and burying her head on my breast, gave way to a passionate outburst of tears.

"Ernestine, you are unnerved; this is childish. Why do you cry thus, dear?"

"Oh! Luke, I am——"

"You are what?"

She rested a white hand on each arm, and looked me long and anxiously in the face, so long, so anxiously, that I felt as if some horror were impending over me—as if her reason had received a temporary shock, or some alarming illness were about to strike her to the ground.

There seemed a struggle with her feelings, and then her natural look returned, and she murmured—

"I am fearful of that man. Suppose—suppose it were a plan to rob you, or this house, or that it is the beginning of some plot, concerning which we are at present ignorant—some dreadful plot that is to uproot our bliss of home!"

"And you have prayed for the averting of what dwells in your imagination alone, dear heart?" I said; "there, get on your bonnet—you have been too much in-doors, and a change will do you good."

I went towards the door, and she called me back.

"What is it, Ernestine?"

"Nothing—nothing. No matter. But a repetition of this nervous folly. I have shaken it off now. There!'

When we had entered the carriage, and had been driven from Cavendish Square, there were no appearances left of her recent agitation, and at my brother's house, she was the gay, witty, fascinating woman I had ever known.

We divided into two sections, after a few minutes' general conversation, and Gilbert and I left our wives to chat, and to become better acquainted with each other. Gilbert had that morning received a letter from Edward, to whom he had written a few days since, apprising him of his marriage, and his position in life, and this letter he passed to me, with a grave face.

"There is Vaudon's hand, and Vaudon's counsel in this," said he; "it is more cold and phlegmatic than I had anticipated. He is glad to hear I am well, and regrets that business, connected with some building shares at Cliverton and Wharnby, will compel him to decline seeing me in London for some time to come. Poor Edward! *In London* do you mark? He keeps me at arm's length from 'The Rest!'"

"More worldly and less brotherly, with every letter written by his hand," I said, refolding the letter after its perusal. "I have no doubt Jacques Vaudon's advice was asked, before this epistle was concocted."

"What influence this man has ever had—what a strange, mysterious, undermining life his has ever been!" said Gilbert. "Do you know, Luke, he proposed to my wife before she left Wharnby?"

"Proposed!"

"Yes; he told her he had loved her from the first few weeks she had gladdened 'The Rest' with her presence, he knelt at her feet, and implored her to accept him—this man of iron—this statue!"

"Then it was jealousy that engendered his vindictiveness towards you?"

"Well, I can forgive my disappointed rival's jealousy, although not the means he used to attain the end he sought—even to the lowering of the object of his own love in the eyes of the patron and the master. His enmity towards me has but brought about the very conclusion he fought hard to turn aside; he has gained a few more thousand pounds; and I, a richer legacy—a faithful, loving wife!"

Such friendly meetings as this occurred twice and thrice a week, either at my own house or my brother's; and the links of the family chain—those household ties between us that had been so long divided—were united more firmly together; the weight of the care that had set so long upon me, concerning him and his destiny, was removed for ever from my mind. Then, I had his works to read, and the forgotten novel, and Miss Osborne's, or Mrs. Elmore's, tales and her book of poems; and many were the hours they charmed me, and took me to ideal worlds and made me a dweller therein.

Ernestine and I became a little more fashionable, too; and, emerging from our hermitage, we took a greater part in the world. This was my own selection, and I did it for the sake of Ernestine, and with the desire of eradicating, by constant change of scene, the nervous demeanour she had of late assumed. I had cause to congratulate myself on this expedient, for, despite her reluctance to the revival of old associations, and her unwillingness to take part in festivities that once had charms for her, she became self-possessed, and more like the Mrs. Morton I had known at Cliverton, without the loss of one iota of her deep love for me—love which was expressed in so many thousand different ways—love which, by possession, knew no diminution—love which lasted all her life!

Our box at the opera was occupied more often by ourselves, and less by our friends; and, enshrined therein one evening at the end of the season, I saw from it another face that had long been missing in everything but my memory.

By a peculiar coincidence, that very evening, there entered the box opposite to ours, Agnes and her royal protector. There was no effort made to avoid the glances shot from myriads of *lorgnettes*—no shrinking behind the costly curtains—no drawing them before her. They both sat immediately in front, and paid great attention to the stage—the duke, from time to time, condescending to survey the house through his ivory-mounted opera-glass. I felt the tears of wounded pride swimming in my eyes—I felt what share of her shame I could not help participating in: for all the sole blame she had brought upon herself. She sat there like a beautiful statue, her white, rounded arm on the cushion before her, rich flowers in her hair, and a blaze of gems upon her neck; and beside her gleamed the star, glittering with a thousand hues, and scintillating with a thousand fires upon the black heart of its possessor.

She saw me, and her glance swerved quickly aside, and never more turned in the direction of her brother.

Studiously avoiding a look towards my box, she kept her face averted, and fidgeted with the bouquet of flowers by her side, with one restless gloved hand.

The music, the glowing scene enacted on the stage, the melody ringing throughout the house from the favourite prima donna of the season had no charms for me now, and I looked down into the crowded pit, and ground my teeth together with rage; for they were talking of her. There were six, seven, eight groups—I counted them—beneath me, and some were pointing towards her, and the opera-glasses were still turned upwards, and she sat there still, calm, and queenly, the pity of the virtuous, and the loud talk of the slanderous.

There were voices talking very high in the next box, and one, a woman's, said—

"To think the duke has not even a common respect for his own class, but must offer us this fresh insult."

"It is shameful and disgusting," was the reply; "but listen, you will much admire this trio."

Everywhere signs of her disgrace—signs which I hear by my side, which I see around me, in all parts of the house, and which is uncared for by the occupants of the box before me, and of which no consciousness is shown.

Ernestine saw my agitation, and whispered—

"Shall we go?"

"No," I answered, moodily; "if they can sit there in their infamy, we can remain here, knowing how little of their sinful inheritance descends to us. Let us not fly because Agnes Elmore's name is on more than our lips to-night."

Once again looking at the pit-stalls, my attention is directed to some late comers, who, with more noise than the *habitués* of the opera consider becoming in its aristocratic precincts, were making their way to some vacant seats. I started, and raised my glass. The three comers were Sir George Boyington, Lord Chilvers, and Paul Redwin.

Yes, Paul Redwin, with a bolder look upon his handsome face, a stamp upon it, that I had seen in many men's, that was apparent in his companions', but that I had never wished to see, or dreamt of seeing in his own, and usurping and destroying those finer attributes of soul which had shone out in his face. There was the old revived air of foppery about his dress, jewelled studs, meandering gold chain, embroidered vest, and cambric shirt-front with enormous frill, then the reigning fashion amongst town beaux, white gloved hands, one of which, as he leant carelessly on the back of his seat, served to support that curly head I knew so well. I felt a greater shock in seeing him there with these companions, than upon the entrance of my sister an hour before—I remembered the wild look in his dark eyes when he met me on the country road—the look of despair in his set features, rigid with the great convulsion that had shattered his one ambition, that she a few yards above his head had caused, choosing the darker path that set her by the side of the man with the star upon his breast.

After some whispering with his companions, he turned away from them, and the smile changed suddenly to a look of utter weariness, and he gazed languidly at the stage, his hand still supporting his head in the careless attitude he had at first assumed.

There was no keeping my eyes from Paul Redwin—he was a talisman that drew my attention from all beside, and fixed it on himself. The more I surveyed him, the more pain I felt at his appearance—the reckless air that demonstrated itself even as he sat there listening, or feigning to listen, to the opera. Lord Chilvers, lolling back in his seat, and running his hands through his hair, gave a careless stare round the boxes, and catching the eye of their occupants here and there, nodded familiarly. He would probably have bestowed his further attention on myself, had not Boyington suddenly caught his arm and whispered some communication. Chilvers immediately looked up towards the duke's box, and surveyed Agnes for several minutes. Presently he touched Paul Redwin's arm, without changing his own position. I sat and eagerly watched the effect upon my friend. So interested was I in all he did, that I leant forward in my box and held my breath with suspense. Paul looked up, looked full at Agnes Elmore, and I saw the colour leave his cheek, and the hand that had been buried in his hair, drop and clutch nervously the arm of his friend in the surprise of the moment; then he resumed the old attitude of apathetic indifference, and, after a laughing word with Chilvers, looked again at the stage, but with a heavy, gloomy frown darkening his face. Agnes saw him—saw the start and the feigned composure; and as I instinctively glanced across at her, I saw a quick red flush for a moment—for one poor moment—

pass across her face, like the shadow of a red hand, the last sign of the remembrance of the old love between them.

Paul and Agnes were both dwelling upon one theme then; the music sounded meaningless, the prima donna was but a mummer. They were living at Wharnby, and were engaged to be married!

To be married! Yes, erring sister, he might have been your husband, the sole comfort of your life, the protector of an honourable old age. Ye might both have been so happy; there was not one cloud to have darkened your lives, if ye had so willed it; not one dark spot on the sunny track you might have chosen! Is there no repentance now, Agnes Elmore?—not one sting of remorse, not one pang of contrition beneath that gently-heaving bosom—not one woman's wish that you had loved him better in old time? Remember the evenings at "The Rest," when he came night after night, when, in the young days of his courtship (before Wharnby saw your aunt and cousins on its cliff), you have run to greet him, open armed, as his tall form advanced towards his betrothed, and the fervour of his love shone out of his doting eyes. Remember the choice you have made; look down at him even now, wrecked as part of his better nature is; look at the well-known face and figure, and contrast him with the bloated piece of grossness in whose veins the blood of royalty stagnates! She raised her bouquet, but whether to inhale its fragrance, or to hide a weakness strange to her, God knows; but something told me, for once, there was a tear lingering amongst the flowers in her hand, and that one regret beat at her heart, and stabbed her with past memory.

I pointed out Paul Redwin to my wife.

"You have heard me speak of him?"

"I saw him at the Cliverton ball, but he was a very young man then. He was a great friend of yours, dear, was he not?"

"A very great friend, Ernestine," I replied; "and do you see with whom he is associated now?"

"Yes."

"Yet, Paul Redwin is the very soul of honour, and with a heart gentle as a woman's. They are not men to appreciate such qualities in him, and he is one to hide them beneath affectations and mannerisms, when aware of their unfitness to the friends he has selected," I said. "Ernestine, I must save him."

"Save him!"

"From those men—from himself," I said, quickly. "His is a nature not to be blasted and corrupted; but, by strong and repeated efforts, and a word of mine might turn him even yet. I will essay that word. It is the duty of a true friend. He might have been my brother once, and I feel a brother to him now."

"What can you do?"

"I can give him hope, and I will try it."

The opera was over--preparations for the ballet were going on behind the scenes—Agnes and the Duke of —— had retired, and Ernestine, leaning on my arm, proceeded to the carriage.

"Will you mind going home alone, dear?" I said; "I am desirous of intercepting Redwin at the entrance."

"No, Luke," she replied; "but you will not be late."

I saw her safe within the carriage, and then entered the Opera by the pit entrance, and took my post at the back, keeping them in sight. The ballet was a lengthy one, but they stayed till the act-drop fell upon the last scene, and a general departure had commenced.

Occupying a position which they were compelled to pass, I waited for their coming. Their voices warned me of a near approach.

"I don't ad—mire her da—a—ncing particu—larly, Chilvers."

"Oh! she is admirable. What do you say, Redwin?"

"She dances with much grace, it appears to me; but, then, I am no judge."

"Oh! I don't know that; I watched you narrowly, and you were absorbed in her *pas de* —— What was it?"

"I really do not know."

"We will go behind the scenes on Saturday, eh?"

"If you like—anything you like."

"Spoken like a—— Hollo, Elmore! this is a refreshing sight, by Jove! Glad to see you, man, and to congratulate you. Boyington, of course, you know this gentleman?"

Boyington and I bowed stiffly to each other.

"This is my particular friend, Mr. Redwin."

But Redwin had already recognised me, and had grasped me by the hand.

"I am glad to see you, Luke—this is an unexpected meeting; but the sight of an old friend does one's heart good."

"You are known to each other?" inquired Chilvers.

"We are old friends," answered Redwin. "I heard of your marriage from Boyington, this very evening, Luke. Indeed, I but returned from Paris with Lord Chilvers this morning, or should have made my congratulations earlier."

"When are you going to Wharnby?"

We were in the lobby leading to the doors that opened on the colonnade.

"Wharnby," he said, musingly—"oh! some day—not yet awhile."

"Will you turn in my direction, Paul?" I asked, when we were in the street.

"That be hanged!" cried Chilvers—"that be hanged for a shabby trick, Elmore—what! rob me of my friend? No, no! if you have given up late hours, like a prudent Benedict, that values his own ears, don't try to interfere with the time of the noble order of bachelors here assembled."

"Mr. Redwin can make good any breach of contract at another opportunity. Now, I am sure he will not refuse me so poor a favour. We are old friends, and have much to relate."

"Da—amon and Pythias," said Sir George, yawning.

"But, but—devil take it, man!" said Chilvers; "Mr. Redwin is going to sup with me to-night—I have his sacred promise."

"If you insist upon my compliance with that promise, I am your obedient servant, my lord," said Redwin, haughtily; "but, candidly, for this night, I give the preference to Mr. Elmore."

"Oh! If that's the case—so be it," said Chilvers; "it's of no consequence, so far as I'm concerned. But you will come to-morrow?" he asked, eagerly.

"If no peculiar circumstances should prevent me, Chilvers."

"Good night, then."

He turned away with Boyington.

"I am sorry, Paul, to see you with those men."

"Sorry, Elmore!" said he, linking his arm within my own. "What matters the company I seek, if excitement and pleasure be my object."

"Do you find much pleasure with them?"

"I find excitement, said he, heedlessly; "I see the world

with them; I gamble a little—just enough to keep my nerves strung and in play. I must have plenty to do, now—I must be here, there, everywhere—opera, ball, concert, race-course—whirling along bravely. That's life, old friend!"

"Not the life suitable for Paul Redwin."

"We differ there, Luke," replied he. "And, well, how prospers the Elmore of 'The Rest?'"

"Bravely."

"I am glad to hear it."

"Redwin," I asked, "how long have you known Lord Chilvers?"

"Oh! these nine months. He's a fine fellow, a trifle hasty, or so, and too impetuous even for me—but a fine fellow, as the world goes."

"Paul Redwin," said I, gravely, "may I speak of the past as to an old friend? May I set aside conventionalities, ceremonious forms, and speak as I would to a brother?"

"Speak on, Luke," he answered; "from you I can bear more than from any other man living."

"You left Wharnby with the intention of forgetting my sister Agnes," I said: "has the wound healed?"

"I do not know, Luke—truly, I do not know," he said. "I have tried to forget—I have plunged, as it were, into a host of things at once, and have buried my wrongs, if"—laughing hollowly—"ever I had any. My estimate of woman is not so high as formerly, that is all."

"Judging the whole sex by one," I said, "shallow reasoner!"

"I find them alike," he said, sternly.

"Those whom you have sought, perhaps so."

"My faith is shaken, Elmore, and will never more be firm."

"You saw *her* to-night."

"Yes," he said, sorrowfully; "and I would have rather seen her in her coffin. Luke, I found I had not forgotten her—for to-night I could have covered my face with my hands, and cried like a child. To see her thus—to see her thus, good God!"

"Paul, will you return to Wharnby?"

"No."

"Paul, will you throw aside these false friends, these heartless companions, and begin to think again for yourself, and to obey the promptings of your own impulse?"

"No, Elmore."

"Think of the mother of your own parent, poor, old, doting lady, who would die of grief if she heard you now; think of her in her loneliness—think how she loves you, Redwin!"

His lip quivered at this adjuration.

"Elmore, I thank you for this interest in me," he said, after a long silence, during which we had been walking rapidly, "and I value the noble heart that suggests the counsel, but to follow it is now impossible! What am I to go back for? To feel every pang again, that well-remembered scenes will recall to me—to live without an object in the great waste, with the mocking sea rolling its dreary waves to the arid sands—to be with a tortured heart in the seclusion of my own home! It would be maddening. Oh, Luke, if I had but one worthy object in life, one honourable ambition to which I might soar, and for which I might work—one spot of rest, to which by long effort, by arduous toil, and unflinching perseverance, I might attain! Give me a hope, and I will go," he cried, fiercely. "Show me a path, and I will follow it. I am sick of this loathsome life; when I am alone I feel it is a curse. I feel my soul is deadened, and the prayers learnt at the knees of my grandmother, forgotten and futile. Luke, I wish I were dead!"

He struck the pavement with his heel in his vehemence.

"At Wharnby or in London it is utter misery," he cried.

"Redwin, there *is* hope."

"How?"

"The hope of a wife—a faithful, devoted wife, such as you deserve—a wife that will love you for yourself, that will enoble every action you may do, and reward it with such tokens of affection as shall be balm and comfort even to your dying bed. Redwin, throw off the thoughts that have eaten like rust on the spotless brightness of your mind—look before you with a bold heart, have hope in God, and onwards."

"A wife—a wife! in whom?"

"In Celia Silvernot."

"In Celia! What do you mean?"

"It is she that is worthy of the offering of your love, who, I believe, will prize it, who will make you happy."

"Luke, to whom are you married?" he asked, sharply.

"To Mrs. Morton, the sister of Mr. Dartford, of Cliverton."

"Good Heaven!" he exclaimed; "when Boyington told me you were married, I did not think of any other bride for you but Celia. What happened after I left Wharnby?"

"No matter what, Paul," I said; "it is a long story, and reflects no blame on her, and attaches no discredit to her. Much of misconstruction, much of my own wilfulness, brought about the severance of our engagement. It has all happened for the best. I am content, and there is hope for you."

"Why, hope?"

"Redwin, I believe she never entirely forgot the first love of her girlhood. I believe that patient, respectful attention on your part—the earnest purpose of a ripened manhood—would win that love back once more, and make your life a heaven."

"I cannot—I dare not think so."

"Try it. Even in the prosecution of the purpose I have indicated, if it fail and bear no fruit, yet you will become more of the man, and less like its antithesis—the man of the world. But there *is* hope—there is more than hope for the man who has once had a claim upon her affections—a place in her heart."

"Luke, I know not what to say to this appeal—kind, urgent, and unselfish as it is. I thank you for it; but—but—I must think of it."

"If you will think of it, Paul, I have no fear for the result."

He was thinking of it even then; and to questions which I asked about Paris and his travels, he replied in monosyllables, and answered vaguely.

We parted at my own door, and I watched his tall figure moving with martial strides down the square.

"Oh, Agnes, Agnes! why did you not marry Paul Redwin?"

In the morning, Paul Redwin made his appearance at my house in the square.

"I am going to Wharnby, Luke," said he, with a flushed face and embarrassed air.

"Well spoken."

"I do not say what I am going for, or with what purpose," said he, affecting a light manner that sat ill upon him; "probably one of the wildest goose chases, eh, Elmore?"

"I hope not."

"Candidly, Luke," said he, more gravely, "I do *not* know what I am going home for. I should be sorry to say I am going in search of a wife in Celia Silvernot. I am not worthy of her; and, unless I loved her, I would not pay her the poor compliment of offering her *my hand* alone. I cannot say I love her now—my senses are in too conflicting a whirl to see anything very clearly—but, Luke, once more in Wharnby, I feel that I shall have a new ambition to strive for; and, in the hope of that ambition, I shall be a better man."

"When do you go?"

"This morning."

"This morning!" I repeated, smiling at his impetuosity.

"Why not this morning?" he asked.

"Oh! I do not advise you to prolong your stay. I am glad to see you availing yourself of the first opportunity to return."

"Truly, Luke Elmore, you have opened my eyes to the fool's life I have been leading, and for which I am not sparing in self-reproaches, be assured."

"Have you paid your farewell respects to Lord Chilvers?"

He laughed.

"I have sent him a thousand pounds—the sum of a silly wager I lost to him, and which will compensate for my non-appearance to his speculative lordship—I have paid for the honour of his acquaintance, and am quit of him."

"Quit of him for ever, Paul?"

"Yes," he answered, quickly; "friends are returning, and generous counsellors coming back."

"And Redwin is learning to look forward."

"I shall look forward to seeing you at Wharnby, Luke," he said, quickly; "to your return to 'The Rest'—to our old strolls—to our game at chess, by the red winter's fire."

I shook my head.

"I am apart from Wharnby, Redwin."

"Not for a lifetime."

"It is likely."

"Oh! nonsense," cried Paul; "why, it is almost your birth-place, and you will not desert it—and me."

"And Celia!" I added.

He forced a laugh, and hastened to change the topic of conversation.

After staying with me about an hour, during which time Ernestine looked in upon us, and welcomed him, he rose to take his leave.

Throughout the term of this farewell visit, I detected a feverish restlessness and excitability in his manner, the result of the sudden change in his wild resolutions, and the birth of the new and more honourable desire, which was the reaction of his heart. There was an alteration in his looks for the better in the short time that had intervened since I saw him at the opera : the face seemed clearer, the brow was open and unfurrowed, and amidst all the restlessness and excitability I have spoken of, there was a sparkling look, evidence of the Redwin I had known long ago.

He left me, fully assured of shortly seeing me at Wharnby, and confident of an early meeting between us. He could not reconcile himself to the fact that London was my home—I had been ever so associated with "The Rest" and Wharnby House, that to imagine it was a long parting we were taking, when our hands grasped warmly, and our lips spoke farewell, was to him inconceivable and irrational.

With my heartfelt wishes for the happiness of his future life, for the dawning of the star that was to shed lustre on his path, I parted with my dear friend—this tried companion, and staunch heart, and for ever after that good-bye, a yawning gulf increasing day by day, and hour by hour, kept us eternally asunder !

* * * * * *

Standing on the mountain-side, far down its winding path, I look back for one gone, and the figure threatens with its hand, and still points onwards, implying unto me, who read by signs mysterious and strange to others, "No more in life !"

The figure nods its head.

A path more wild, diverging from the steep ascent, more rugged and more fierce, falling, as it were, into darkness, worse than death.

"Not there, stern ruler of my fate—grim genius, that invisible at hours of content, or visible as now, art ever with me, controlling and yet prompting every impulse. Not there ! There are mocking voices yelling from the depths of those ebon shades ! voices that are calling me, shrieks as of a woman in wild agonies ! Not there !"

Still the figure points.

"Spare me !—I see the faces that were glaring at me in the streets of the great city, and I dare not meet them. The path is full of horrors, and—God of heaven !—red with blood !"

I dare not pause. Powerless beneath the will that bends my spirit like a reed, I pass into the darkness worse than death, and the marble hand upon my arm leads me to my destiny.

CHAPTER XLII.

THE CALM BEFORE THE STORM.

It is before me! This last section of my history—this section that comprises the deepening of the shades around me—the dread convulsion that has left me what I am. In every stage of these chronicles, written I know not with what reason, or for what shallow purpose, the crisis to which I have been slowly drifting has never left me for one instant. If any eyes but mine dwell at some time, when I am in my grave, on these records of my life, and of those with whom my life has been bound up, they will believe I could have written with no lighter heart, or cast no less a shadow of my undying thoughts upon this history.

One year has passed since Paul Redwin went to Wharnby. One year and a few days, and it is another summer, and the sun yet shines. I am happy still. Ernestine has recovered from her nervous weakness, and is as she has ever been. We have not sobered down into the man and wife, joined at God's altar three years since, and to whom the bloom of wedded life has been brushed away. In Ernestine there is ever that passionate demonstration of the affections, that studious solicitude concerning me or what I do, that never grows less, and that is exemplified each day. I can but love her with the same romantic fervour, and it seems as if it were but yesterday I made a bride of her. We have once more travelled, and have again returned to London, and our boy is two years old, and a well-spring of deep joy to us. He is a handsome child, with dark hair, like his mother's—a gentle, affectionate boy, who usurps all attention, and concentrates round himself all his fond parents' love. There is a strange attachment between us—he seeks me every hour, and sits at my feet, and prattles with his baby tongue about Uncle Gilbert and his aunt, and dear mamma. He is scarcely ever from my sight—he will not leave me even for Ernestine long together, and wanders about the house disconsolate and irritable, at times, when I am absent. Ernestine sighs at this sometimes, and wishes that he were more like other children, and loved the mother above all other ties, and sought more naturally the mother for a child's companion.

But it is a trifling antidote to all this bliss, and home is a palace of the heart.

I hear from Paul Redwin. He writes in the highest spirits,

and invites me to his marriage. He tells me of the patient earnestness with which he sought to gain her love, to bring back the affection she had had for him in her girlhood. He confides to me his entire story, and relates how, by sure proofs of his devotion, he won upon her sympathy at last, and revived the flame within her breast. There were many doubts in Celia —whether he loved her as he loved my sister—whether he had really forgotten Agnes—whether it was not another of those visionary whims that had played her falsely when she was younger by some years. But those doubts vanished in good time. Paul was a man now, with a man's set principles and firm mind; and in constant intercourse with his old love, he proved the strength of purpose with which he sought her for a wife. He had forgotten my sister. It had been a hard struggle; but, after weeks at Wharnby, with its old associations at evey step he took, after hours spent by Celia's side, or in calm discourse with the honest rector, coupled by the sense of the utter exclusion of hope in Agnes, and of her unworthiness, the true light came shining to his heaven, and never faded out.

I do not accept the invitation; I should suggest many unpleasant thoughts, and be a restraint, more or less, upon them. I wish them that prosperity they deserve—that contented bliss which they will attain—and so they marry; and the little rector joins their hands, in the old church where my father and his children — side by side, linked in one common bond — once sat; and there is an end to their sorrow, I believe, in the radiance of the life unfolding before them and around them.

"The Rest" at Wharnby is as it has ever been, and Vaudon, buried in its recesses, coiled like a snake, whose venom is exhausted with age, drones out his remaining years, and my brother Edward still remains with him, and keeps aloof from us. Vaudon contented with the injury bestowed, pauses at this youngest son, and having debased his nature, and narrowed his mind, takes him for the one companion of his life. And so that ill-assorted pair remain dwellers in my father's house, an anomaly of Nature. The deep thinker, the stern philosopher, a disciple of Voltaire, and a great scoffer, abides with my brother at "The Rest."

Gilbert and his wife remain inhabitants of the pretty, unpretending cottage at Paddington, and keep the even tenor of their fortunes. Pleasant writers, both—for they write from the heart, and without malice—their books and articles, if they make no great sensation, at least obtain a fair marketable price, and enable them, by united efforts, to live contentedly. If there is not that great genius exemplified which can raise a fortune by the pen, and can turn the eyes of the world upon the writer, there is that talent above mediocrity which commands attention, and they are spared the heart-burnings, and the bloodless, but bitter wars against honest, well-earned fame. I see them very often, and they exchange evenings with Ernestine and me. Gilbert and his wife are passionately attached to their nephew; and if there be one subject of regret between them—one alloy to their peace—it is that a boy like mine should have died at its birth, and not have shed the blessings of its presence round their home—that this frail bud should have been the first and the last!

And Agnes? she is with him yet; and the man himself is more a public mark. I hear his name fifty times a day; in every paper I take up, it is implied, and lurks beneath some covert meaning, and there are many who yell at him in the streets as he passes in his carriage—who point menacingly as he crosses the pavement to the entrance of the House of Peers; and one man has shot at his heart, and been imprisoned in a mad-house for the vain attempt. But his poor victim is gradually falling from him, despite the hold she strives to retain—there are whispers of other favourites—of fresher faces—and the time has come for this child of the night—the old end to an old story.

My aunt and cousin Jane are residents in Sloane Street, and have not changed. My aunt still cries over Sir John's fate and her step-son's ingratitude, and mourns her exclusion from aristocratic circles, and talks about my family with visage expressive of condolence. Jane is not dismayed at all by the dark pictures her mother is so partial to drawing, and, demurely prim and gentle as a child—and, perhaps, a trifle old-fashioned—she is as lovable a little woman, destined for old-maidism, as can be found in London itself; and though her mother is not one to appreciate the self-denying habits of her daughter, what a blank would she find in the world before her, if my cousin Jane were married or dead!

My aunt looks her old self for a few days, upon the long expected return of her son, Jack—no longer Jack to society, but Lieutenant Witherby—handsome Lieutenant Witherby, of H.M. ship, "The Thunderbolt," and true to the prophecy I had foretold on that night before he joined his ship.

He has grown a strapping young fellow, and his bronzed

whiskered face gives no indication of the boy features of a few years back, though he comes home with the same boy's heart.

Aunt Boyington gets accustomed to his presence, and takes to wiping her eyes, and indulging in sentiment and half-audible groans; but she is very proud to ride with him in the ugly carriage, drawn by the ugly horses Sir George has bestowed upon her, nevertheless; and to show to the friends who have cut her dead, what a fine fellow he is!

Lieutenant Witherby calls on Sir George, and they get quarrelling; and rumour asserts that the young sailor took unwarrantable liberties with the strikingly developed nose of the baronet upon an abrupt conclusion to their interview; but he came post-haste to me, and says nothing about so eccentric a finale; and Sir George must be of a timid disposition, or have great faith in Jack's habit of reserve, if it be a fact, for he lets the matter drop.

Lieutenant Witherby is Jack to me, although very proud of his naval cognomen for all that, and the house in Cavendish Square holds him within its walls for an hour or so each day. He takes a violent fancy to little Luke, and gives him his sword to play with, and suffers him to cling, for support, to his great red whiskers with the most perfect good humour, and brings him toys and large boxes of sweetmeats and books at every visit, and lowers his dignity and station in the navy by passing half the time on all-fours, for little Luke's sole delectation.

And the watcher in the streets! He comes once more. Late at night I find him before the house, as I had discovered him a year since. He is dressed in the height of fashion now, but his hair still curls in dark ringlets, and he puffs a cigar in a *nonchalant* manner. He waits not for my approach, but, with a start, crosses the road, and walks rapidly away. My impulse is to follow him; but a sense of its availing nothing restrains me, and I enter my house. I make no remark concerning the re-appearance of the stranger to Ernestine—I am fearful that the singularity of the occurrence may needlessly alarm her. I strive to convince myself that it is one of those peculiar coincidences that occur to all of us at odd seasons, and that have no meaning; and so the matter rests.

Presently young Witherby startles me with a recurrence to the subject. Three days after the recognition, the young lieutenant asks me, bluntly—

"Who's that fellow outside? Is he waiting for one of the servants?—not for you, is he?"

"For me—of course not."

"Confound his impertinence—how he stares."

A window in the front of the house admits light to the room in which this dialogue takes place, and I step to it, and look out into the square.

The man is there, and, unconscious of my observant eyes, makes quickly a sign towards some one at the windows above.

"He evidently knows an inmate of this house. Is he in love with any of the maid-servants, poor fellow?"

"It is mysterious, Jack," I reply; "but you may have given the right clue. *Yet*——"

"Yet what?"

"Nothing, Witherby. You must be right."

The man's small eyes meet mine, and for a moment we stand glaring at each other; then, with an air of affected *nonchalance*, he wheels gaily round, and saunters from our sight.

A sudden dizziness comes over me, and I reel from the window, and sink into a chair.

"What's the matter, Luke—do you feel ill?" cries Witherby, anxiously.

"No, no—a strange pain in my head," I answer: "a whirling sensation that has gone now." I felt, for the moment, as if some nerve or chord had snapped in my brain.

CHAPTER XLIII.

THE FIRST BLOW.

WHEN one seed of distrust, wafted on the wings of suspicion, falls upon the heart, and takes root therein, what a strong flower it becomes in its rank luxuriance!—what a hold its tendrils, mounting upwards, take upon the mind!—what branches from the parent stem shoot forth!—what blossoms, deadly as the nightshade, burst, with their distilling poison over every thought!

On me the seed had fallen, and had taken root. No matter that her love had endured so long, and been exhibited so tenderly—I could but connect the watcher in the streets with her. I could but remember, now, how I had found her praying in her dressing-room; and yet, remembering also her avowal, that, it was for my sake, I yet vaguely disbelieved it.

To whom was he making signs? I knew that Ernestine's room looked upon the square, and that she was in her room that moment. I knew that he had met me, and asked for Mrs. Morton's house, and that my wife had exhibited signs of great perplexity, and even agony when I had informed her of the meeting.

But, then, she had said, firmly and decisively, "I do not know the man: I am sure I have never seen him."

Ernestine could not have uttered a lie like that. No—away with such ungenerous suspicions! Why should I doubt her love when love was existent and before me?

Still the plant took deeper root. It was nourished by seeing him from time to time—by coming face to face with him in the street—by meeting him always in the precincts of the square, and in no other place. Was there some mystery from the past of which this man was cognisant, and which had power over Ernestine?

Fast sped the current of events — deeper and deeper ran the black waters to the sea.

One morning, the first blow from without broke down the outposts of the shrine, and startled me to something more than thought. It was a custom of mine to enter my library about an hour before Ernestine descended to the breakfast-room, and occupy myself with some favourite book until summoned to her presence. But of late I had spent the same period of time in pacing the floor, with hurried, disjointed steps, heedless of the offerings to the mind ranged, in their rich bindings, on all sides of me.

On the particular morning mentioned, I was striding to and fro, with my dressing-gown folded tightly round me, when a knock at the panel of the door without roused me from my cogitations of deep purport to listen.

The knock was repeated.

"Come in."

The door opened, and my valet cautiously entered.

He was a man I had ever had an undefinable repugnance to, although scrupulously exact in his duties and respectful in his demeanour; and this entrance, at a creeping pace, did not tend to allay any unsound objections of mine concerning him. He came in mincingly on tiptoe, his body inclined forwards, and a pair of little red eyes blinking at every step.

"What is it, Marks?" I asked, sharply.

"You will excuse me—you *will* excuse me, I am sure," said he, in a whispering tone of voice—"but the interest of my master is the interest—if I may so speak—of myself; and I cannot suffer so kind a benefactor to remain in total ignorance of all that is passing in this house."

This long speech was slowly and monotonously spoken, as if it had been carefully rehearsed beforehand.

Its effect disappointed him. Great as was the shock to my whole system—sharp as were the pangs at every heartstring—I maintained that cool, unmoved demeanour which I had shown at his entrance, although everything in the room, and he himself, was whirling round me.

"Will you oblige me by explaining?"

"Mr. Elmore, before I enter into explanation, it will be necessary for me to respectfully suggest that anything I make known to you must be made in strict confidence."

"Go on."

"Mr. Elmore, the honour of a master is the honour of a servant. It is the duty of the latter individual to guard over the interests of the one who places trust in him, and puts him in an important station in his household."

"I listen."

Every word I uttered seemed choking me, and the room, and books, and valet were whirling faster than before.

"Being of an observant nature, Mr. Elmore—indeed, I was brought up under observant eyes—any circumstance out of the common way immediately attracts me; consequently, when a gentleman lingers about this side of the square, day after day, my curiosity is aroused, and I am watchful."

I sank into a chair, and leant my head upon my hand, and glared at him.

"Proceed—proceed."

It would have been more creditable on my part to have dismissed this spy—to have expelled him from the room; but the wild craving for some confirmation of my own fear withheld me, and I could but listen greedily.

"This gentleman, watched in his turn, became more wary, and it was hide-and-seek between us, in which I"—with a self-sufficient air—"got the better game."

"Be quick with all you have to relate. Spare me comments, and give me facts."

"Yes, sir," with a dry cough. "Well, sir, three days since, after you had left the house, Annette——"

"Who is Annette?"

"Mrs. Elmore's lady's-maid, sir."

I was dumb. It was with an effort I could wave my hand as a sign for him to continue his relation.

"Annette, sir, left the house, and I followed her. She met the gentleman about half a mile from here, sir, and gave him a letter, which he opened, read, and returned an answer to by word of mouth. All this I saw with my own eyes, sir."

"Is this all?" I asked, my heart leaping with one hope—a hope that freed suspicion from my Ernestine.

"Not quite, sir," said he, chuckling. "Annette returned, and you came home, sir, and had dinner with my lady, and then went out to your brother's, sir, alone. Remember, sir?"

"Yes."

"Now, sir, what I am about to say, is with no intention of attributing injurious motives to Mrs. Elmore—I have more than a common respect for——"

"Well—well."

How the room whirled now!

"Half an hour after you had gone, sir, Mrs. Elmore left the house."

"You followed?" I asked, breathlessly.

"Yes, sir."

"And——?"

"And I saw her," sinking his voice to a still lower tone, "I saw her *meet the man with the ringlets in St. James's Park, take his arm, and walk towards Hyde Park Corner*, where I missed them."

"What more?" I cried, huskily.

"Since then, my lady has met the man once in the same place, but from good authority I have reason to believe their tactics are changed, and he will be here to-night."

"To-night!" I yelled.

"Yes, sir; Lieutenant Witherby and you are going to Lady Boyington's, I heard Annette say."

"True."

"If I can be of further use, sir, I am sure I am too much indebted to you, sir, not to make an offer of my services in any way that may be deemed most fitting—I am sure that my respect——"

"Enough of respect," I said, endeavouring to maintain a self-possession that was mocking me; "when the man leaves this house to-night, watch him to his residence. Here is your fee."

I snatched my purse from my pocket, and hurled it at his hands, motioning, at the same time, to the door.

"Thank you kindly, Mr. Elmore," said he, catching it adroitly; "I am sure this generosity, undeserved on my part, is so kind and so——"

I stamped with my foot impatiently, and stopping short in his protestations, and adopting the same silent, cat-like tread, he glided from the room and left me to myself.

For a moment I sat surveying the door that had closed upon the spy; then the horror of my position came with its full force—the utter misery of my future, the dupe that I had been all my life came with harrowing convictions there were no resisting, and I fell back in the cushion chair in a dull, death-like swoon, in which, deprived of power to move, to turn my head, to speak one word, I yet remained as in a trance, aware of the place wherein I was, and of the awful secrets I had become possessed of. I lay huddled in the chair, with a weight on body, mind, and limb, with stiffening fingers, and glazed eyes, and swollen tongue, a poor wrecked sufferer with a broken heart.

It was a wild scream that brought me to a sense of my position—it was the consciousness of Ernestine kneeling before me with a white face, convulsed with alarm, that made me, as by a giant force, upheave the load that bore me down and struck me helpless, and stand before her, shaking in every limb.

"Oh! Luke!—oh! dear, dear Luke!—what has happened? How ill you look—how strange! What is it?"

Something of the cunning of the madman came across me, and prompted my reply.

"Nothing, Ernestine, but a headache," said I, passing my hand across my forehead, and sweeping my hair back from it; "I think I must have been asleep."

"Oh! dearest husband!—you are ill—you *are* ill," she repeated with a wild, quivering note of woe.

"I may be a little weak," I said, for I could but totter to the door; "it is strange I should have been so suddenly attacked! But I can walk now. Thank you, Ernestine—thank you—I want no support—I can walk without assistance. *There*, see."

I made a bolder stride, and fell heavily to the floor, with shriek after shriek of Ernestine ringing in my ears.

* * * * * *

When my eyes opened to the light, I was in my bed, with Ernestine hanging over me, and a well-known physician by her side.

"What's all this, Elmore?" asked the physician, in a tone of assumed cheerfulness. "Come, come, man, we must have none of this."

"What time is it?"

"Never mind the hour, dear," entreated my wife, with my hand in hers.

"What time is it?" I persisted, struggling to withdraw my hand.

"About twelve," answered the physician.

"Call me at five; I am going out at five," said I, freeing myself from her clasp by a strong effort.

"Has he had any sudden shock, Mrs. Elmore?" asked the physician in a whisper.

"No—I hope not. I do not think he can have had," she said; then added, with suspended breath—"But there is no danger, sir?"

"No, I think not."

He drew her aside, and for some time they conferred together in a tone that was inaudible to me.

Presently I was left alone. This was the signal for me to rise and dress, and as I stood before the glass, I felt that an artificial strength was returning to me, and supporting me, though every vein in my body ran as with molten lead.

I descended to the parlour, and met Ernestine, who sprang towards me, crying reproachfully—"Oh! Luke!"

"I am quite well now," I said; "it was some sudden malady which has left me a little weak, but it is gone now—gone entirely!"

"Dr. —— said you were not to leave your bed, dear," said she, dubiously.

"But I am as strong as a lion; let me have some breakfast."

I could not take any refreshment when it was spread before me; my lips turned from the cup I affected to be drinking from with a sickening distaste; and my eyes dwelt upon one object, and that was Ernestine.

She sat by the window, glancing wistfully at me, and our boy lay at my feet, and played with his heap of toys on the carpet.

I looked at her glowing face, her matchless loveliness, her small, perfect form, seen to its full advantage in the blue velvet dressing-robe she wore, and thought—was all my happiness gone—crushed at one blow? Was it possible that she, who had demonstrated so much affection towards me, was false? was it a truth that killed everything but despair?

Then I was reminded of the part I had to play, and how I must dissemble more and more, or my strange manners would put her on her guard; I must unravel every thread that led to one end, coolly, cautiously, and with stern circumspection.

"Order the carriage, Ernestine."

"You will not go out, dear?"

"The ride will do me good."

In half an hour we were in the streets, and another half hour took us into the country, and the sweet summer air restored me more to myself. So well did I dissemble my inward agonies that Ernestine, quick and sensitive as she was, bceame convinced that my old manners had returned, and that it was but a passing indisposition.

My boy sat close to my side all the long ride, plying me with anxious questions, and wondering why I looked so pale.

The physician was awaiting us on our return.

"Upon my honour, Elmore," said he, "you have disobeyed orders in the most audacious manner. But you are better?"

"Yes, doctor."

"Mrs. E., will you leave this gentleman with me a moment?"

When we were alone he harassed me with embarrassing questions, to all of which I answered in the negative. He asked me about my sensations at the moment; he read the secret of my pains in body and mind correctly, but I denied them all, and persisted in maintaining to him my entire recovery.

Strangely bewildered and baffled, and yet inclined to believe me, knowing no grounds that could actuate me in so firm an assurance, he was borne to his next patient.

Despite Ernestine's entreaties, I started at the appointed time for my aunt's, with my cousin the lieutenant.

What torturing moments were they with my relatives!—what agony to me, in the endeavour to comprehend the subject of discourse, and to falter out some sentence not irrelevant to it! *He* was with her now, in my own house, and yet I was talking calmly about some common-place occurrence ! My agitation of nerve became above my command, and they all remarked it.

"Mrs. Elmore said you were unwell, but you would accompany me," said Witherby ; "come, I'll walk home with you. You must have had enough of our weary chatter for one evening. Come on, there's a good fellow."

"I said I would be home at eleven," I replied.

"My dear nephew, you cannot be well, your hand shakes so. Perhaps it *would* be better for you to go home with John," said my aunt.

"I shall go at eleven," said I, decisively.

And at eleven my carriage came for me, and, with heavy-clogged feet, I descended the steps, crossed the pavement, and entered. How my heart beat, how my temples throbbed, as I stood in the large hall of my own house, and the light of the great lamp fell full upon my haggard face. The valet, Marks, came bustling towards me, and took my hat from my extended hand.

"Thank you, sir."

"Has he been ?" I asked, in a low murmer.

"Yes, sir."

"Who admitted him ?"

"Annette watched her opportunity, and opened the door. It was a great risk, and very inconsiderate, I think. Bad policy —awful policy !"

I staggered to the door of the room, and Ernestine flew towards me, and kisssed me fondly on the threshold.

Will she tell me—will she tell me *he* has been ? Will she ease this load of misery, greater than I can bear, and save me from hours and days of bitter anguish ? Will she confide in me ? Oh ! God of mercy ! will she hide *all* beneath her smiles ?

No word ; no sign.

"Any one been, Ernestine ?"

"No, dear."

She changed colour as she spoke ; and as she crossed to the chair from which she had arisen, she pressed her hand upon her breast, as if to still its heaving.

Will she tell me yet ? Will not conscience urge her to the confession, no matter what it is ? will it not even now ? My love is strong, my heart is hers alone, and can bear much. Will not one angel from the many soften her iron will ?

I waited each moment—to every word, I leant forward, eager and expectant; but the time passed, and the night hastened, and we were alone in our bridal chamber.

Will she tell me now?

No word of confession, but signs of anxiety for me and my malady—nothing more.

She slept at last, and I lay awake and watched the grey morning come stealing on behind the blind, and drawing away the veil of mystery around me. I sat up in my fevered couch, and looked down upon her, so beautiful in her calm sleep, and prayed that she would wake up and tell me all.

But she slept on, and I bowed my head in silent agony, and wept a few bitter, scalding tears.

"They are the last," I muttered, with the sense of her deceit a greater weight than I had felt it yet. "The morrow has come, and I seek explanations for myself. The morrow is all dreariness and death; the yesterday that held my love, that charmed my soul, that told me of my happiness, is gone for ever! A few more hours—a few more hours," I cried, shaking my clenched hands in the air, "and *then!*"

CHAPTER XLIV.

THE RESULT!

At a late hour in the morning I left my house, unobserved by Ernestine. I had played the hypocrite before her, and enacted Judas well, and deceived her into the belief that all threatening aspects had vanished with the new day before me.

But my very nature had undergone a change, and I was full of distrust and malice. There was a secret kept from me—hidden from my sight; I was not thought to have sufficient love within me to guarantee its disclosure from her lips, or else it was the worst shame that could descend to me, and I was branded and disgraced.

I met the valet by appointment beneath the arched entrance to the Horse Guards. The last stroke of the bell had not announced twelve when he came, at his old creeping pace, from the direction of Parliament Street. He was to the minute, but I had arrived too early, and was maddened by impatience.

"What has detained you?" I cried, fiercely.

"It is twelve; did you not hear the bell strike, sir?"

"Yes, yes," I said, hastily; "but the man—you watched him last night, Marks?—you promised me you would."

"I did, sir."

"Where does he live? Quick!"

"If you follow me, I will show you the house, sir."

I turned back with the man, and he led the way across the road into Whitehall Yard, through a narrow passage into Whitehall Place and Great Scotland Yard, and then emerging into Northumberland Street, Strand, he pointed to a glass coach standing before a house some distance from me, on the left-hand side of the way, on the roof of which several trunks were being placed by the coachman and a maid-servant.

"He is going away. I am in time."

"That is the house, I am sure, sir."

"You can leave me, Marks."

"Leave you, sir?" he exclaimed, loth to be dismissed ere the sequel to the story was disclosed.

"Yes; go, now."

The man still lingered, until meeting my threatening visage bent upon him, he coughed and slunk away, leaving me watching the house and the preparations going on before it.

He came at last. From the house he jauntily stepped forth, the eternal cigar in his mouth, a coat flung across his arm, a tasselled cane in his right hand.

Ere he could enter the vehicle, as he stood one foot upon the steps, I made a rush forwards, and, griping his arm fiercely, flung him aside, and stood between him and the doorway.

He recoiled, as at the appearance of a phantom.

"I have tracked you at last," I cried; "I have discovered you, and I part no more until some elucidation of this hideous mystery be fully entered into."

"I do not know you. Let me pass."

"But I know you, and I will know further, man," I cried, passionately. "I will learn your reasons for entering my house like a thief, for playing the spy upon my actions, and watching my entrance and exit at all times of the day. I will unravel the mystery that connects you with my wife. Do you hear me?"

The man had turned pale, but was surveying me with flashing eyes.

"Will you let me go?"

"No."

"It will be better for you."

My answer was a scornful laugh.

"It will be better for you, and me, and Ernestine."

"Ernestine!" I shrieked; "do you dare to call her Ernestine? Does the mystery prove to be but my dishonour?"

"Come into the house with me," said the man, "and I will tell you all. It is your own seeking, so blame me not for what may follow."

We entered the house, and went up a narrow flight of stairs, and into a small and tawdrily-furnished room on the first floor. He waved his hand in the direction of a chair, but I made no movement to accept his offer, and stood a few yards from the door, keeping my gaze fixed on him alone.

"This is a damned unpleasant rencontre," said he, after the door was closed, "and will lead to much mischief and cross-purpose."

"No matter."

"Elmore," said he, in a conciliatory tone, "let us part as we have met. I give you my word that we shall never meet again."

"I have come to this room for explanation."

"Well, if it must be, it must be," said the man, shrugging his shoulders; "I wash my hands of all blame in the affair before us, and will promise, if required, to keep *your* secret."

He flung his cigar into the empty grate, and stared for some time at me.

"*My secret!*"

"Ay; it will be to your interest to keep it quiet, I take it," said the man; "and as for the affair itself, so far as it regards *me*, that for it."

He snapped his fingers in the air.

"Elmore," said he to me, "we are both men of the world, and need make no fuss about this droll affair. You will see it in this light, there is no doubt."

"There is no doubt that if this fencing round me continue much longer, sir, I shall tear the secret from your heart," I said, between my set teeth.

The small eyes flashed again, and an evil expression like that upon some grinning head I have seen carved round old cathedral doors, settled on his face.

"The secret is—that my name is Morton," said he, leaning

his back against the mantel-shelf, and swinging his cane in his right hand.

He started from his languid position at the unearthly cry that issued from my lips, and rang through the house. He made a hurried movement of alarm towards the door, but recoiled again at my menacing and defiant attitude.

"It is a lie—a hellish falsehood!" I cried, foaming at the mouth. "Morton—Morton—God—not her *husband* Morton!"

"Yes," said he, laconically.

I knew not what to do or say; my reason seemed deserting me with the shock of this new revelation, and twice I attempted to speak, and twice a hand appeared to grasp my throat, and choke my utterance.

"I am going from England directly," said he, quietly; "in a few hours I shall be at Southampton, waiting for my ship—so keep all quiet and you will find me safe, and true as steel."

The sharp tones of his voice recalled me more to myself, and I gasped forth—

"How long has she known of your existence?—no equivocation—the simple truth alone. There is much weighs upon this answer?"

"Oh! these many years—long before your marriage."

"*Before!*"

"Yes—what of it?"

"BEFORE!" I screamed again.

"To be sure. Many are the letters with acceptable remittances I have received in Sicily."

"Why did you report yourself dead?"

"That is irrelevant to the story—Ernestine did not remain in ignorance two years—it was a mercy to enlighten her, was it not?"

I made no answer, I felt that I was going mad!

"In my letters I had often made the declaration that I should never return to England, and that I left her free to act. Forsooth," with a scornful laugh, "she took me at my word!"

"Fiend, have you no compassion for my misery?"

"You would have the secret."

I pressed my hands to my forehead crying, "I shall go mad, I shall go mad!"

"Mad about what," said he, carelessly; "the woman fancied you, and you ought to feel obliged. If you wish to be quit of her, there is a grand opportunity for you, man. She was, and is a devil of a temper, and time must have frost-nipped all romance. Look on the bright side of everything—it is a motto worth emblazoning on the gates of every church in England. If you wish to keep all close, why, my tongue has been sealed with a golden key from the hands of your fair *wife*—ha! ha! and you may increase the obligation by——"

He advanced closer towards me, and was about to lay his hand familiarly on my shoulder, when I struck at him with all the violence of my hate, and he fell with a bleeding face to the ground, and with a heavy crash that shook the house.

Strangers came running up stairs, and forced their way into the room, and one man attempted to grapple with me, but I struck him off as though he were a child.

"See to him," I said, pointing to the prostrate form. Some one raised him, and he opened his eyes, and looked malignantly at me.

"I will remember this," he roared forth.

"Shall we secure him?" asked two of the lodgers from adjacent apartments, who stood blocking up the doorway.

"Let him go," he cried; "let him pass! I have a means of vengeance that will blanch his hair to the whiteness of old age; and I will do it, too, so help my God!"

"Do what you will," I muttered.

"Bring back my portmanteau and boxes from the coach, and send away the man," he cried, furiously; "I'll take my full vengeance for this! There is a word called 'Bigamy,' in 'The Newgate Calendar,' as well as 'Johnson's Dictionary.'"

I leaped towards him, but he shrunk behind the new comers, and baffled my approach.

"Coward!"

"You see the man, all of you," he raved, pointing towards me: "that man has robbed me of my wife; has married her, and yet I am alive and well! But there is law in England, and I will have it!"

His words thundered in my ears, and smote my heart with their appalling meaning. I felt all horror, all ignominy ended not with this day; and that on the name of Elmore still hovered Heaven's curse. My rage abated with the dread conviction of the power that man held within his hands; my reason was more calm, but my despair was more than human.

Breaking through the men and women round the door, I

forced my way down stairs to the street, and ran at a fierce speed homewards.

Homeward! There was no home for me—it was a blackened ruin, standing in its desolation, and speaking of the happiness that had died with its fall, and of the ashes so thickly strewn about my path. I had no home, no wife—my own loved child was marked with shame, and the best years of my life had been sacrificed in building a lasting monument to my own disgrace!

Running at a swift pace towards Cavendish Square, I formed my plan of action. I adopted the only course that it was right and honourable to do, and in all the turmoil of my excitement that one purpose was irrevocably fixed. Nothing shook it—old memories, past love, the passionate affection—guilty as it was—that had dared all this, I let them all accuse me in their impotence.

I stood within my own room, at last, with Ernestine before me. Whether the consciousness of her life-secret, kept so long and hidden so deeply, glowed upon my face, and spoke out of my lurid eyes, I know not; but she sank back into a chair and quailed from me, looking at me still, with dread, and love, and pity commingled in one glance.

The child was from the room, was out with its nurse, and I felt glad that we were alone in our blank misery.

"Ernestine," said I, in a hollow voice, "all is known by me!"

There was no passion in my voice—there was no passion in my heart; I spoke deep, distinct, and firm—there was a task before me, and it must be fulfilled.

Shrinking and cowering before me, she lay heaped upon the chair, with her hands covering her face.

"I have sought the man out, and wrenched the secret from him; and though it redounds but to my lasting shame, I feel that it has ended many years of future sin. Dare I regret it, Ernestine?"

Trembling within the chair, she made no answer to me.

"Woman! I can but love you even now, and——"

She dropped suddenly the hands from her death-like imprinted face with eagerness and hope, and half sprung up from the chair.

"Back, back!" I cried, shudderingly—"there is no hope for you or me in this world; our lives are separate. The tie is sundered with the revelation of our sin!"

"*You* cast me off like a dog. I care not for my after fate!"

"No, Ernestine—I cast you off as though I tore my bleeding heart from its seat—as though I consigned my soul to everlasting night. But I dare do this in preference. If there were one excuse—if there were but one thread left of poor extenuation, how gladly would I grasp it!"

Before I could restrain her, she was in my arms, her hands locked behind my neck—her whole form clinging to me in the abandonment of her grief. Her hair had fallen from its place, and showered in luxuriant disorder over her neck and shoulders to the waist; and the streaming eyes were fixed on mine, pleading and beseeching.

"Oh! Luke, dear husband!—for you are mine, you *must* be mine, even now—there is all excuse, there is all extenuation! I loved you madly—I loved you, I believe, as no woman loved before. My whole life was a barren desert without you; *his* life was spent in foreign lands, supported by my money—he was believed dead, and he *was dead* to me, and had ever blasted each young hope of mine. You came—you loved me, and I dared all for your love!"

I shook my head, and said—

"I have sinned unwillingly; but to look guilt boldly in the face, and know what laws I am breaking, and what divine commandments I am disregarding in my own cupidity, I cannot do it!"

"Luke! Luke! think again. Have I been less of the faithful wife—less true in a wife's duty, because there was an interdict from heaven on our marriage?" she said, frantically resisting my gentle efforts to disengage the arms twined round my neck. "Oh! forgive me, and let us seek another land together. Our sorrows will be all forgotten there. For you *are* my true husband—I have no other—and you have sworn to protect me at the altar."

"To protect my *wife*," I answered, gloomily.

"Think of our child—of its young life! Is there no father's love strong enough to alter the cruel determination you have formed?"

"My child must go with me—there is no other help."

"Luke!" she implored, with straining gaze.

"Let it rather share its father's sorrow than its mother's greater affliction and disgrace. Let it go with me where there are none to carp at our story, and bring the flush to his cheek —where, when he grows older, he may pursue some honourable avocation, without a slur upon his parents' history."

"Without a mother?"

"It is best."

"It is death! You leave me not one hope. In your anger you rend every tie from my hands."

"In my anger, Ernestine! I have none. I can forgive you —I do forgive you," pressing her for a moment to me; "but I would tell you that every minute is an object to your safety, Ernestine."

"Let me stay here and die!" she cried; "I have no hope, no wish to live. Let them imprison me for life in dungeon-walls—they have the power, and I—I——"

Her hands relaxed, unfastened, and she sank forwards, and would have fallen, but for my encircling arms. The eyes were closed, the breath seemed suspended, the shadow of death seemed casting that unnatural grey upon her face.

"Ernestine, dear Ernestine—my own, my wife!"

I clasped her to me, and she lay like the dead within my arms. I rang the bell violently, and bade the servants make *all* haste for the physician, and my own arms bore her light weight up the stairs to her room.

The physician came, and went away, and came again. I sat by the bed-side thinking of nothing but the past love revived now, and willing to dare all—to share her sin, and pass my guilty life with her. I called upon her name by old endearing titles, and the white lips made no reply; I brought her son, and placed him before her half-closed eyes, and there was no sign of recognition. More physicians—all the skill that money could command from men of science—and all in vain, for still the day went on, and still she lay there in a death-like stupor.

CHAPTER XLV.

THE END.

THE night has not passed away ere all is known concerning that poor silent marble figure in the bed, which faintly breathes, but speaks no word, and knows no familiar face. The servants whisper together about bigamy, and cite cases of the crime, and the sentences that have been passed upon it in their time and knowledge. The officers have been, and have stood within her chamber, looking suspiciously at the one accused, and for whose arrest they hold the warrant, and the head physician, a man of title, imperious and stern, says—

"Touch her at your peril! Her life hangs now upon a thread, and you shall answer for her death."

They bow to his assertion, and depart, although one man lurks about the servants' hall, and holds his place, and bides his opportunity. Morton keeps aloof from the house, but each hour brings a letter full of threats against me, defying me to touch anything within the house, which is his wife's and his. Each letter, torn into a hundred fragments, strews the floor—a silent mark of my disdain.

I have no thought for Mammon or for the change of life again for me—I care for nothing but to hear her voice, and say I have not been her murderer!

My sense of right is gone—my trust in God a void. I feel that I am bound to her—that she has loved me, and that her crime is love.

The long night sees me by her side, and there is no change from this likeness of the dead. Watchers by her, leaving her not a minute, keep me silent company.

In the first hours of the morning, I am persuaded to descend and see my child, who will not be pacified nor know no comfort, but cries incessantly for his dear mamma—his dear papa.

He runs towards me sobbing, "What is the matter with mamma? why do they talk of her so much, and will not let me see her?"

"Your mamma is very ill, Luke."

"When will she be better?"

"I do not know. Pray to the God she taught you dwelt above us, that the time may be soon, boy."

"Have you prayed, papa?"

The childish question strikes at me like an arrow. I have not prayed—I have not the courage. Is it right to pray for *that?* for the bringing of her back to ignominy—to disgrace eternal and indelible, that will live on in police records, and be registered in criminal reports—to the cells of Newgate—to the law's punishment!

I cannot think so, though I dare not wish her dead; though the thought of her passing from me, vanishing from my sight for ever, without one word of parting, is too horrible to contemplate.

"You will be a good boy, Luke, and not disturb mamma by crying for her?"

"If papa wishes it."

I snatch the child to my breast, and gaze long and mournfully at the beautiful expressive face—so like unto hers! and wonder what destiny this boy, so innocent in himself, is born to; and whether the sins of his parents will descend to him, and dishonour his manhood.

Too young to know what sin is yet; too free from guile to understand the mystery that has furrowed my face with those deep lines that will be with me to my grave; that has stretched his mother on a bed of sickness and of danger; I wonder if, when he grow old enough to comprehend the story strangers tell him, he will ever wish that he had died in the hour of his guilty birth.

But can I not hide all from him—cannot *we*?

Why dwell upon the future? there is no hope—the balance is between death and a prison servitude, for the fallen angel I have loved.

A prison life! I raise my hands in prayer, at last, above this child's fair hair, and murmur to myself, "If it be not wrong or impious to wish it, as I wish with broken heart, and every hope crushed at my feet, take her, in Thy mercy, Father of all!"

I think again—think of losing her—of her dying in her youth—and recoiling, I retract my prayer, to utter it again when I am by her bed-side.

Ever thus—one minute's reflection contradicting a second—no settled mind amidst this vortex in which I am engulfed.

There comes a change. She wakes from her long apathy to a weakness that cannot raise a hand to her head, or move that suffering head upon its weary pillow. She asks for me, but the physician interdicts the wish, and looks grave and decisive.

Day after day, and still I may not see her, and still I wander through the house benighted.

I meet the valet, Marks, and do not know him on the stairs—I pass into the library, and stare meaninglessly at the books piled upon the shelves—I descend into the parlour, and hearken to the noises in the house, and wait.

The physician comes twice and thrice a-day, and each time

he looks upon me in my grief, I start up with the eager question—

"How is she?"

"About the same, Mr. Elmore."

"Is there danger?"

"I cannot say," he replies, evasively; "her situation is critical in the extreme, but she is young."

"May I see her now?"

"Not yet."

Eternally, "Not yet," to the same question repeated every visit—to all my pleadings, this denial. I feel that I can comfort her, assuage her misery, cast a more brightening radiance on the heavy gloom enwrapping her; I tell him this, but he smiles sadly, and thinks not.

Dartford comes from Cliverton, and loads me with a thousand inquiries concerning his sister—about her property—if she has made her will—where Morton is, and what he is doing—and my spirit is more deadened in his presence.

Gilbert and his wife attempt to comfort me, but it is in vain; faces of old friends cluster round me, and come each day to learn the last report concerning her, and still she lies within the room, and still the door is barred against me.

I place my boy in Gilbert's hands, and beg him, until the crisis has passed over, to guard him for my sake; and Gilbert takes the precious prize with reverence, and bears him from the house of woe.

Day by day, no change for better or for worse, they say; but that affirmation tells me all is not well above, and that the shadows above the house-top are gathering in ominous intensity.

A servant stands before me, and rouses me to a sense of his intrusion by repeated coughs and shuffling of feet.

"What is it?"

"A woman wishes a moment's speech with you, sir."

"With me?"

"Yes, sir."

I forget the question until the man, after long silence, slowly repeats it in my ear.

"I can see no one; tell the woman so."

"Yes, sir."

Another day—Ernestine still denied my yearning heart. The physician answers, "Not yet," in deeper, graver tones, and leaves me hastily. At night, the servant summons me to present hours by saying—

"The woman's come again."

"What woman?"

"She who called last night, sir."

"Who is she?"

"A poor woman, sir."

"What does she want?"

"She will tell her business to no one but yourself, sir."

"I will not see her," I cry, passionately; "a week—a month hence. This is no time for strangers' sorrow and beggars' importunity."

One more day. The physician stays longer this time in the chamber of the sick, and I am jealous of him, and count each hour on my watch, until he comes to me in my lonely room.

"How is she, Sir ——?"

"Mr. Elmore, are you prepared to hear the worst?"

I read the worst upon his face, and stand before him benumbed and horror-stricken.

"I am prepared as man can be."

"Mr. Elmore, I am grieved to say, there is no hope. I am grieved to say that the weakness has been slowly, surely increasing every day since she recovered consciousness, and that no skill of mine can save her."

"No hope!"

He closes the door, and leads me to a seat, and takes another beside me, and says, kindly—

"The peculiar circumstances that have arisen, and have caused this sudden shock to Mrs. Elmore, must, in some degree, tend to reconcile you to the certainty of losing her. I do not say they do now, in the first bitter moments, my dear sir, but in the future they will be consolation to you. God has ordered it for the best."

"God has afflicted me all my life!"

"Hush! sir. It is man's passions, or man's weakness, that bring misfortune unto him—not his Maker."

I answer not.

"Yours is a strange story, and the end of it is better thus. Even now the conviction surely forces itself upon you," he continued. "Common reason will urge it is the lesser sorrow. Had God spared her, Mr. Elmore, it would have been an unbearable affliction for you both."

"May I see her now?"

He hesitates, and says, at last, "To-morrow she may be more composed."

"How long will—will this weakness last upon her?" I ask, tremblingly.

"It is uncertain. It may be a day—it may be a week."

"And yet, in this uncertainty, you will doom me to suspense? In one hour she may fade away, and my ears have not listened to one last injunction."

After some reflection, he says, "Come with me. I cannot leave you alone; but if you will bear my presence in the room, and abide by my commands, you may see her."

"I am in your hands, sir."

As we go up stairs, I ask, "Has she ever wished to see me?"

"Your name has seldom left her lips."

Bidding me wait without, he glides in to prepare her, and I stand with plunging heart upon the landing-place. The nurse comes rustling from the room, and whispers, "You may go in now, sir;" and, with leaden feet, I drag myself into the chamber of my poor dying wife. My wife before Heaven, and in His sight!

The air is thick and oppressive—there seems a vapour over everything; a pastile is burning on the dressing-table, and the physician, with his back towards me, stands leaning on his gold-mounted stick, and looks gravely at the carpet.

The curtains are drawn back, and she is there! So pale, so thin, so fragile in appearance, that when I meet the wan smile on her parched lips, and note the attenuated hand she with an effort draws from beneath the bed-clothes and extends towards me, I give a cry of anguish, and bury my face in the pillow by her side. The hand rests gently on my head.

"Dear Luke, am I forgiven now?"

"Ask not forgiveness of me," I groan; "this misery, this home-annihilation is my own work, and caused by me alone."

"Not so, dear husband," she says; "may I call you husband?" she asks, timidly.

I can but press her hand for my reply.

"He has prepared you?"

"Yes."

"I feel it is a mercy vouchsafed to me. I can bear to die, having no hope to live for."

"Live for me!"

She faintly smiles, and murmurs, "That is beyond my power, now!"

"If I had but said it on that morning!"

"No, no; you acted nobly, Luke, and God will bless you for it. This has saved years of sin for both of us."

"Dear wife!"

"Will you not look at me, Luke? Do you fear to meet my glance?"

I raise my head and look at her, retaining her fevered hand in mine.

"Luke, with the kind assistance of our friend," indicating the physician, by a motion of her head, "and of a legal gentleman well known to him, I have made my will."

"Ernestine!" I cry, fearfully.

"I have not wounded your sensitive nature, dearest. You will say I have acted well."

"Mrs. Elmore, I think this explanation may be deferred until the morrow," breaks in the man of medicine.

"No, no!" cries Ernestine, clutching my hand nervously; "he *must* hear all to-night. I wish it, sir, indeed, I do. You will let him stay?" she asks, imploringly.

"Five minutes," he replies.

"The illegality of our marriage being proved, has again made me the mistress of my own fortune, dearest," she continues, in a low voice, that long sickness has weakened, and rendered almost inaudible; "that fortune, had I died without a will, would have descended to my brother. I have adopted a wiser course, in making this good man and your brother Gilbert my executors, and in bequeathing all my possessions to my son—illegitimately born!"

A red flush sweeps across her face and passes.

"It is my atonement," she says; "is it just?"

I can but answer, "Yes."

"I must see my boy to-morrow, Luke. You have promised me," to the physician, "that he may come to morrow?"

"Yes, madam."

"May I see him to-night?" she cries, suddenly.

"The hour is late, and the excitement would be much too great," he answers.

"Luke," turning to me, with a wild light in her dark eyes, "I must see our dear boy to-night!"

"My dear madam," cries the doctor, interposing, "you will obey me, I am sure. It is impossible."

"Supposing I were to die to-night?" she cries—"to die without seeing him, my darling child!"

"Madam, I must beg of you to be calm," entreats he. "Mr. Elmore, will you oblige me by retiring? This interview has already lasted too long."

"If it be inconsistent with my safety—with a few short days of life—I will risk all to see him, sir."

"It cannot be. To-morrow."

"*Ah! to-morrow.*"

She heaves one long, quivering sigh, and says no more in intercession. The physician begs me once more to retire, and reminds me of my promise to him.

Reluctantly I bow my head in assent, and, stooping over the bed, press my lips to her hot face. Both arms are round me now, and she clings to me, and whispers, fearfully, "Do stay, *do* stay, dear Luke!"

"I dare not, Ernestine, my life," I say. "I cannot, to gratify my selfishness, prolong this interview."

"You will go?"

"I must!"

She kisses me long and passionately, and lets her arms relax, and murmurs, "Heaven bless you," and watches me from the room with an anxious, longing gaze.

In my solitary chamber I kneel before the invisible throne, on which He sits and ever watches, and pray for her till the morning comes again—pray for her till a violent knocking without convulses me in every limb, and I cry out, "Who is there?"

"Oh! sir—oh! sir—mistress is dead!"

"Oh! God—oh! mercy!"

I fling the door back, and stride out.

It is too late—it is too true! From her slumber by the fire, the nurse wakes to the presence of the dead—to find there is no need of longer watch! Without her son, without her erring husband, she has died, and by the white sculptured face it seems as if she left the world in peace, and breathed out her soul without a struggle in her awful loneliness.

Oh! wife, whose sin was love, whose idol was the erring sinner weeping over thine eternal sleep, may thy false step be blotted from the book by One who pardoned sins like thine, ere he died upon Mount Calvary!

CHAPTER XLVI.

UTTER DARKNESS.

FROM the hour I found her dead within her room, and knew that she had died alone, and, perhaps, had called my name and her dear son's in her last agony, in the final craving for one face beside her death-bed, my nature hardened into stone. Gloomy, morose, and full of enmity to fellow-man, day by day I sat in my room with its darkened windows, symbolical of my loss, and the night that lived for me, and shunned every solace that friends and brother came to give me.

I could not bear them, I could not listen to their well-meant advice, I could not comprehend of what they were discoursing. They came and went before me like figures in a dream, and yet I sat there in my grim reality.

She was dead, and I had killed her! There was no satisfaction for me in that which might have happened had she lived—there was no comforting assurance that I had sought to act in conformity with precepts dealt from Heaven—there was nothing but despair. I knew no one, I answered no one, I scarce touched food or moved from one position; I avoided my couch of rest at night, and companionship by day, until they laid her in her grave, and I mourned over it.

She was lost *then*—she was shut for ever from my sight. Her youth had ended where the placid joys of other youth begin, where life, divested of its gaudy hue of romance and fancy, sobers down to the calm reality, and is not less happy in content.

I grew more morose, and less capable of self-command. Every nerve was strung so tightly and so sensitively, that a word jarred upon it woke up a frenzy. Even a noise upon the stair—a foot-fall passing heavily without—the sudden entrance of a menial—the accidental contact with a stranger brushing by me in the street—for I had been persuaded to walk out from the house of mourning, and had suffered Gilbert or young Witherby to be the guides to the old age of my mind—unmanned me. I had not seen my child—I had not the courage to look upon him yet—he was so like his mother!

Young as I was, I had seen so much of sorrow, and the last blow had been so heavy in its strength—had struck down all that I had been rearing for so many years—that my face was shrivelled like that of an old man, and my hair was thickly streaked with white. No changes that I had read of in books on human form had altered man more than this calamity had transformed me; but then, what had I not lost?

Dartford, *her* brother, after following Ernestine to her last dwelling-place, took his cold departure, and went back to Cliverton, no richer man than he had come from it. Morton, baffled in his last stroke, had also gone to follow his old life, careless of the hour when to his Maker he should deliver up his stewardship.

He had been a bad man from his youth. He had married Ernestine from a wild caprice, as regarded her beauty—from a studied motive, as concerned her money; and when baffled in his wish to become the master of her wealth, he schemed to break her spirit and to crush out her life. In his dissipations he had endangered his own health, and medical advice had forced him to a milder climate. There, despairing of obtaining further means from Ernestine to keep him in his viciousness, and forming an intrigue with a wealthy widow in Sicily, he had promulgated a report of his death in England, and had found accomplices to write to Ernestine, acquainting her with the fact. He passed to Italy, married the widow, and saw her die one year after the evil union between them. Master of her wealth, he travelled through foreign cities in his wild course, until he had exhausted his illgotten legacy, and was on the verge of poverty. Then he wrote to Ernestine, and agreed to remain from England all his life, upon the annual payment of a sum of money sufficient to support him in his recklessness. This promise he had kept until the time I first met him in the Square. That time he had been bought off once more; but losing all by one stroke at a gaming-table in Paris, he had returned, had received a further bribe, and had brought about the end that had spread such devastation, and cast over all such fatal blight.

Three weeks after her death, I summoned courage to see my child, and at the first moment of our interview he clung to me, begging to be taken home to his mamma. He loved his uncle and aunt very dearly, and they were very kind, but he would rather go home with papa, and see his mother!

There is one tie yet to earth, one thing to love, and I take my boy home and make an idol of him. The affection between us becomes greater than before, and he is never from my sight.

She had been dead one month, one month to the day, when I sat in the room in which the physician had come to me and prepared me for the worst. The hour was nine at night, and my child had been taken smiling to his bed.

Oh! happy youth, envied childhood, that can so easily forget!

Whilst in my old brooding position, the servant entered.

"If you please, Mr. Elmore, that woman's come again."

"Come again!" I answered; "I do not understand you."

"There was a woman called when Mrs. Mor——Elmore was very ill, and you would not see her, sir, if you recollect."

"I have a faint remembrance."

"I told her you couldn't be disturbed by her now, sir; but still she persists, and says it is important."

"Let her be shown to this room."

"Yes, sir."

The servant retired, and in a few minutes returned, ushering in a tall, gaunt woman, with sunken eyes and wasted cheeks, whose dress was hidden by a large shawl, darned and patched in many places.

She took the seat indicated by a motion of my hand, and the servant withdrew, and left us alone together.

"You desire an interview with me?"

"Yes, sir," she answered, in a respectful tone.

"You require relief from my hands—you have some tale of misery and woe to tell me. Spare me it; my own sorrows are enough! I can believe all that your story has to tell by looking in your face, but I wish not to listen to its recital. Will that alleviate your distress, my good woman?"

I laid a guinea on the table, and she sat and glanced wistfully at it, but did not reach out her hand in its direction.

"I have hardly come with that object, Mr. Elmore."

"I am at a loss to guess it, then."

"I have come to ask you to accompany me some distance—it is imperative that you should do so."

"Imperative!"

"It is the request of an old friend of yours, who is in deep distress, and who requires your aid."

"His name?"

"I am forbidden to disclose the name, unless you positively refuse to come."

"Refuse to come! undoubtedly," I said; "how do I know that this story is not all a trick?"

I thought of Morton, and of some danger at his hands.

"You will not come?"

"Not till I know further," I answered; "be more explicit, and show less of this theatrical manner, woman."

"Theatrical!" she echoed, with a wan smile; "well, perhaps it is. Mr. Elmore," asked she, "if I tell you the name, will you promise to come?"

"If I see sufficient reason for the journey."

"I will tell you, then. You should have asked me some time ago '*her*' name, not 'his.'"

"Well."

"Her name is Elmore, like your own."

"Elmore! My sister—is it of my sister?"

"No sir—of your *mother!*"

The grave inflexibility with which I had listened to the woman gave way at that last name, and roused me to a passionate interest in all she said. Stunned by the shock, I could but repeat, "Mother!" and make signs for her to proceed.

"Your mother is in great distress, as I have already said, sir, and requires help and—money."

"I am ready to follow you," I said, rising from my seat.

When we were in the street, the woman, with her shawl tightly drawn over her shoulders, moved a few paces in advance, in the direction of Westminster Bridge.

Had there been a plan in all this, it could not have succeeded better in the desired object; the name of "mother" (hallowed name to all but me!) had been the loadstone to draw me from my calm reflection and lure me onwards. My mother in distress! There was no time to pause or to deliberate; guilty as she was. I felt it as a duty.

I followed the tall form of the woman along the streets, and over the dimly-lighted bridge.

What were the feelings that actuated me, and drew me from my apathy? Was I going to claim my mother, to fold her to my breast, or to reproach her, as I had a son's right to reproach?

Turning to the right, we wound along dark, narrow streets, through Bishop's Walk, and into a narrow lane, formed of grimy wharves, and warehouses, and factories.

"Here!" I cried, as she stopped at the entrance of a low street that turned in the direction of Lambeth.

"This is the street."

"Lead the way."

She halted at a house about half-way down the street, and, drawing a key from her pocket, proceeded to unlock the door.

There was a feeble light glimmering from an up-stairs window destitute of blind, and the figure of a woman came and stood close against the glass, and seemed endeavouring to peer through the darkness at us, as we stood beneath. The woman unlocked the door, and admitted me. After securing it on the inside, she preceded me up a flight of creaking stairs to the room-door above.

"This is a difference from Cavendish Square, sir," said she, insinuatingly.

"Open the door," I answered.

She complied with my request, and into the room we slowly entered.

It was a small, low ceilinged room, almost destitute of furniture, with rudely-plastered walls, and bare blackened floor, strewed with heaps of what appeared to me parti-coloured rags. Still standing by the blindless window, with the dark night for a background to her figure, was my mother—I felt it was my mother, although every feature was in itself unrecognised. Pale, haggard, wasted by sickness as it was, yet that frail slight figure reminded me of Agnes, and in the white, ghastly, seamed face I thought I could see a dim likeness to the daughter—an indistinct outline of what she herself had been once in her husband's home as well as in her pride of infamy.

She made no movement towards me; she even checked my own advance by a slight shrinking backwards, and instinctively I stopped. There was agitation in her face, but there was no *affection*—my jealous, watchful glance detected that. We had not met for any outpourings of soul; hers had been long deadened, and had little promptings of maternity; save the faint agitation—last instinct of nature—at knowing it was her son before her, she was cold and unimpassioned.

There was but one chair in the room, and the woman who had been my guide pushed it towards me. Declining its offer, I stood with straining gaze directed to my mother.

"You are Luke?"

A husky "yes" was my response.

"Divided as we have been so long, and knowing what has so long divided us, it has been a hard struggle to allow this meeting. But I am a beggar, and you are a rich man!"

She spoke with an unfaltering voice—a deep, ringing voice, that vibrated through me.

"Yet we have both been unfortunate," she continued. "A few years since I could have commanded thousands. When I was in Paris I was worshipped as a goddess!"

She said it proudly, even now; she mourned for her poverty—but not one word was there indicative of a just repentance.

"But a frightful sickness stretched me prostrate—changed me almost as horribly as I am now changed—caused all to desert me, and then my misfortunes began. From bad to worse—from bad to worse—until you see me in this den. And even this becomes too good for me. I have lost my engagement—we have both done so, and are starving!"

"Engagement?" I said, dreamily.

"Mrs. Elmore alludes to her stage life at the 'Coburg,'" explained the woman.

"Good God!"

"Under another name, mind," quickly said my mother. "I did not disgrace the name."

"You were politic," I answered, bitterly.

I could not master my rising indignation. This unnatural manner roused me to a sense of my position and her own—this selfish maundering only told me of what a mother I had reason to be proud of.

"So I have appealed to you, at last. I had hoped never to have done so; but circumstances, as you see, have forced me. When I left you all, I thought it was for ever, but that was not to be. And, Luke, from the time you met me in Park Lane, and called out my Christian name, I have looked to you as a last resource."

"Was it you?"

"Ah! you may well be surprised—and I was a lady born, too."

"Woman! have you met me but to speak like this?" I started, losing all control over my rising anger. "Is there not one expression of regret for others?—as if you had been unfortunate without a cause to make you, or without a sin wherewith to reproach yourself! Why do you not ask about my father, or mourn for the blight you cast around his life, and the grave you dug so early for him? Why not of Agnes, your own daughter, whose life has followed yours—whose feet have strayed down the same path, and profited by the same vile example? Has the mother no wish to hear of *them*, or of her sons, divided, disunited from her and from each other? Has she fallen to this misery, and has it taught no lesson?"

Startled by my vehemence, she yet looked at me defiantly.

"Speak, woman! unworthy of a mother's name—say something! Prove that there is one spark of a better nature in you—not all trodden out upon your guilty course!"

"My days of repentance are gone, Luke Elmore," she cried, fiercely. "At one time, I will own it even to you, I felt the sting, and writhed beneath it. At the time when he with whom I first fled deserted me in his turn, and left me in a foreign city, I felt it the most deeply. But I shook my cares off, I cast them all aside," she said, brandishing her arms in the air, as if she threw something from her—"I chose my life, and I was happy till that fatal illness."

"Happy!" I repeated.

"But, now!" she shrieked, without heeding my remark, "look at me now! Do I not make a good moral for a sentimental book?—what divines could not prate of me from cushioned pulpits! Do I not suffer in myself enough, without repentance or contrition? Have I not enough to bear, without ransacking my mind for fresh causes of self-torture?"

"What do you desire of me?" I asked, coldly.

"I wish to leave England. I wish to go to America with this friend of mine. There are great openings of life in America."

I did not ask her plans—I did not comment upon her talk of openings in life—she to whom life was fast fading out, and upon whose face the little time the world would be of interest to her was plainly evident.

"What money will suffice?"

"A hundred pounds."

The other woman came round, and stared greedily in my face to note the effect of the demand upon me.

"You shall have it. Give me the address of this place, and I will send the sum required in the morning."

The woman hurriedly laid before me a torn sheet of paper and the stump of a lead pencil, and I wrote the address to her dictation.

"There is nothing more to say," I said gravely. "The interview—how different from what I had expected!—is over, and I regret that it should have ever taken place. I would rather have died without meeting you—remembering you ever as the mother I had seen last in my childhood."

For the first time her lip quivered.

"I would have rather seen your tomb, or stood beside your dying bed than this," I said. "If you had come to me to-night —erring as you are, and full of crime as your path has been— if you had come to me truly penitent, I would have shielded you beneath my own roof, and shared my life with yours."

"You—*you* would have done this?"

"Without a moment's hesitation," I replied; "nay, more, you should have seen your eldest born, your Gilbert, and would have found in him a son, indeed! But there is no mother's heart with us."

"You may go now," she said, gloomily.

"There is time yet for repentance," I said; "if the conscience could but awake—no matter to what horrors—you might yet repent. Think of it—*mother!*"

"No," she answered, shuddering.

"Think of your husband—he died a wrecked man! From the night you fled, and tore from him all that love he had for you, you left his children a pale, careworn father, stern, wild, and mentally diseased."

She turned from me, and, looking into the narrow, loathsome street, said—

"Go, now—go! I want to hear no more."

I laid my hand upon the door, then said—

"There is one question to be asked. Concerning the man who first brought about this evil—who, defying God's sacred laws, strived hard (as he must have strived) to wean you from that devotion you once had for my father—what has become of that accursed villain?"

"I know not."

"Is there no clue by which I can track him, and revenge the evil he has brought about?"

"He can never be traced; and it is not your right."

"It is my right," said I, firmly. "I am commanded!"

"I do not understand."

"No matter. Is there not one thread, however broken, by which Sir William Ashford can——"

"What—what!" she shrieked, facing me again; "Sir William Ashford—did you say Sir William Ashford?"

"The name is not forgotten by either you or me."

"Is *his* name still spoken of as connected with my own in that elopement?" she cried; "has it never been known—never?"

"*What!*"

"It was not he, although the will was not lacking on his part. He was duped, too; he was the blind."

"The name—the name. I have a wild surmise, but I dare not give it utterance. Quick, quick!—the name, for Heaven's sake!"

"VAUDON!"

With a piercing cry, I flung my arms above my head, invoking God's curse on him, with an intensity of feeling that startled even the mother and her friend.

"The hour has come at last, and I am the avenger!" I cried; "it is the last drop in the cup—the last proof of the villain he has been. I will foil him; I will lay bare the long hypocrisy in its naked hideousness; I will revenge the wrongs of my poor father—wronged even in his grave. I swear it standing here before his victim!"

"Do you know where he is?" asked my mother, advancing towards me in her eagerness, and slightly resting a finger on my arm.

"I do."

"Is he well—prosperous?"

"Both."

She ground her teeth silently together.

"Do you wish to hear more of this man?" I hissed—"how he was my father's friend all his life, and how he eventually became my father's heir? But I will revenge him—I have sworn it in Wharnby's own churchyard!"

"His heir!" exclaimed my mother.

"The story is too long, and what avails its narration? I could not tell it if I had the will. I must go out; I must have air—I am stifling."

I dashed out of the room, and groped my way down the creaking stairs, opened the outer door, and stood in the narrow, dirty street.

Glaring up at the sky, which was blood-red towards the east, as if lit up with fire, I stood for some minutes on the door-step. My brain was burning—one terrible thought possessed it; I read it everywhere, on the dark warehouses before me, in the fiery sky above my head.

"Vaudon—Vaudon! the day of reparation has arrived!"

I strode into the roadway with my hands clenched, and my lips compressed.

The woman who had brought me to the place came stealing from the doorway.

"Mr. Elmore!"

"Well!"

"Your mother is not always thus, sir; you must not think her quite so callous. She sits sometimes and moans for hours by the empty fire-grate. To-night she has been hardly herself."

"She is an actress."

"It was to spare a scene, sir; and I think it was best. Are you going, sir?"

"I am. Take care of my mother; I shall never see her more."

"And, sir, you will not forget the money?"

"Ah! the money! No, I will not forget."

I hurried away, and the door closed softly on me.

I had seen her, more lost and more abandoned than ever I had dreamed—this fairy-like mother of my youth! Yet, in the whirl of brain that *one* revelation had brought about in this sad meeting, I could forget her, and it seemed as if before me, whilst I hastened homewards, I could see "The Rest" upon the cliffs, and my father beckoning unto me with that look upon his face which he had had when he died within my arms.

CHAPTER XLVII.

THE LAST SACRIFICE.

"It is the duty of a son to avenge a family's dishonour. The stain that rests upon the name of Elmore is still branding it, and a whole life's curse is covering it with shame. Seek not the quarrel, but abide the time. It will come one day to the father or the son, and then act. For the seducer and adulterer, there is but one atonement!"

No afflictions that had befallen me had had power to erase from my memory those words which he had written. Unprofitable and sinful as they were in their commands, they tallied with my own maddening wish, my own burning impulse to avenge his wrongs. He had said that it would come one day to the father or the son, and it had come to me. He had never thought that *his* life would bring the villain to the light—the first words of his stern exhortation were the proof—but he had trusted in his sons to act as he, with old, exploded notions of honour, would have acted had he lived. How much less did he think then that the man who had wronged him, bowed his head, dishonoured his name, shaken his reason, made a drunkard of him, was the man he met upon the sands when I was but a child.

"There is but one atonement!"—and that shall be. I swore it looking on his "Rest," the day I met Jacques Vaudon, and walked home with him. If he had known the settled purpose I had formed, the letter my father had written, in some hour when depressed beneath his shame, and which was within my breast, cold and deep as characterised his every action, he might have betrayed himself that morning.

I had found his secret: I had discovered that his hate extended further back than the children of his friend; and I had all this to have retaliation for. I would do it alone. Gilbert had a wife—was happy—had everything to live for; I had been afflicted with a curse all my life, and it mattered not to me if that life reached a premature conclusion, save that he would live after it, perhaps, and be safe from further vengeance.

Calmly, but resolutely, I set about the end I had in view; it seemed the last stroke I was destined to fulfil.

I weighed carefully all consequences, and looked my future in the face. If I fell, my child was provided for. If I shot him, as I believed I should, I must fly and become an exile from my home. Did *that* matter?

No, to me I felt that it would be relief—that I was but fit for a solitary life—that with every hope buried and all existence a blank, I should but cast the shadow of my own despair on the child left to me by Ernestine.

The child! There was the first and greatest shock. My love had grown with his, and to sacrifice it for his future peace, and to unselfishly part with him, and be quite alone, was a struggle which I engaged in, and came off a victor.

Yes, I would part with my boy—I would take him to his Uncle Gilbert, and leave him there, and go upon my way. He would be that blessing to them which I had dreamt he would have been to me; and I should be in my grave, or in a foreign land, with the mark of Cain upon me. I felt, in either case, we should be sundered, and for ever part. I felt that, with Gilbert, he would grow up generous, high-minded, and affectionate;

and that I should but mar his prospects if I took him with me to the wilderness. I would tell no one of my project—leave the child as for a day, and fly for ever.

It was a bitter resolution, but my courage did not fail me. It was but one more sorrow—the last. I could have none other after that! So I wrote a letter to Gilbert, which I intended to post at Wharnby, if I survived, and to remit by Edward, if I fell—a long letter, bidding him farewell, written with a shaking hand, but unstained with a single tear. My fount of grief was exhausted—I could give no outward sign of it, since *she* had left me—my eyes seemed burnt and dried up within my head, and glowed therein like heated coals. Yet it cost me hours and hours to write that letter—was put off till morning, and then again till night—was written line by line, and each sentence weighed as if it were the pronunciation of a doom. A few lines to Agnes—the transmission of double the sum required to my mother in her hovel near the water-side—the arrangement of my own small property—the transferring of the house in which I lived to my brother—and then all was ready and prepared; and fate was waiting for the sequel.

For one week I devoted myself entirely to my boy. It was an unwise act, and cost me many years of after-suffering—it was binding more closely bonds around my soul, which I was forced to burst through, and leave them torn and bleeding on the earth. It was loving the boy more ardently to lose him. But then my selfish heart told me it would be years before the impression of that week would fade away from this only son, and that he would bear in memory the remembrance of his father long after that father had been lost to him.

So the week passed—and one autumn evening, after one last struggle, I took him to his uncle, in the carriage. I had not been forgetful of the boy's future peace, in the week that I had spent with him; I had told him so much of Gilbert—spoken so warmly in his praise, and of his open heart, and taught my child to love him almost like a father. I knew that to Gilbert and his wife there could be no greater blessing than this boy; and that they would carefully treasure him for their sakes and my own.

It was nine in the evening; it had been a weary day for me—a day spent in final arrangements, in making calls (as if they were chance ones) on the Boyingtons and young Witherby, who were so unsuspecting of the final parting we were taking with each other.

By strong and repeated efforts I masked the conflicting and tumultuous war within by the dispirited manner now habitual to me; I wrestled with my passion of grief, and in their presence subdued it—compressed it, as it were, in the inner depths of my heart, too well aware of the rebound when the forced weight upon it was removed, and I was left alone.

"Gilbert, I have brought Luke to spend a few days with you."

Gilbert's face lighted up with satisfaction—and his wife had already seated my child upon her knee.

"No spring flower is more welcome," answered my brother.

"He will harass you, perhaps?" I asked, anxiously.

"Harass!" cried Gilbert—"I wish I were doomed to perpetual harass of such-like nature, brother."

It was a long evening I spent with him—we had much to say, and I had much to tell him.

For the first time I broke to him the interview with my mother, and he listened with a fearful interest. I did not tell him of Vaudon, and all that I had discovered concerning him, lest some untoward event should occur to frustrate my project, or he should assert his right to vindicate the name he bore with me. With trembling fingers he took down the address of the house I mentioned as having met my mother at, and spoke of his determination to proceed in search of her, early the next morning. I thought that it was useless, even if she were not already gone, and seeking mental trouble for no purpose, but he was resolved.

If she told him of Vaudon—it would be too late then, and I should be on my journey, and ere the night set in, at Wharnby. I prolonged my stay with Gilbert. I could not tear myself away; the carriage—sign of my old rank, that still abided with me—had been waiting without an hour; and though I had made two movements to depart, I had again fallen into my chair with a sinking heart. The child *must* be parted with—my stay was already engendering grave doubts—the hour was late, and I was there and lingering yet.

"Can I offer you a room to-night, Luke?" asked Gilbert, observing my reluctance to retire.

"No, no, I thank you," cried I, starting up and glancing at him with suspicion. "Why did you ask me, Gilbert?"

"I thought you might feel it dull, returning without the child, that is all, brother."

"Thank you—thank you, but I would rather go. Good-bye, good-night!"

I wrung his hand in mine, and took a last, earnest look at him, and then turning to his wife, I kissed her, and invoked a secret prayer for their life's happiness, and lasting peace.

Then came my boy! I snatched him from the ground, strained him in my arms, and held him to my breast as I felt assured I should never hold him more. He would grow up to be a man—years on years would drift by, each one cancelling some recollection of me, until some day, when he was married himself, and was happy in his home and wife, he would forget me entirely, and other cares, other objects of attention would obliterate, nay, annihilate all thought of me!

"I think I would rather go back with you, papa," he said, wistfully, as I still retained him in my embrace.

"No, you will be a good boy and stay with Uncle Gilbert, I am sure."

"But you are going home alone."

"Yes, and shall leave you here to love your aunt and uncle—you must try to love them," I said in a lower tone—"as well as you do me."

"Oh! that I can never do, papa."

"But you will try?"

"Why must I try?"

"Because they love you so."

"And when will you come and fetch me back?"

"Soon—soon."

"Three days—four days?" he prattled on, "papa will be so dull without me—oh! so very dull! In four days he will come for me?"

"To be sure—four days—what are four days? they are soon gone—gone ere we scarcely know they have been here."

"In four days then?"

"Ay!"

I set him down reluctantly, and pressed one last yearning kiss upon his lips. I shrunk from the boy's eyes—they seemed reading my thoughts, and deciphering the intention written on my furrowed brow.

It was the last link in the chain that riveted me to my fate, when I let the first-born pledge of my unhappy love pass from my arms, from my sight, from my hope.

A stern, momentary reverie, and then I tore myself away from him, and walked slowly and moodily to the carriage.

Ere I was within, Gilbert's hand was laid upon my arm.

"I do not like leaving you to-night, Luke," he said. "I am

not superstitious, brother, but I would rather you did not go home alone."

"Why, Gilbert?"

"I cannot tell why; it is an impression that will not bear a definition," said Gilbert: "perhaps your own manner has alarmed me."

"My manner is not different, I think, brother," I replied. "Life has cast too deep a pall upon me, to suggest anything but thoughts of the dead and the lost."

"But it struck me that there was a fresh secret—a——"

"Tush!" I exclaimed, hastily; "it is hallucination. Good night."

"You will not stay?"

"There is no danger in my going, Gilbert," I answered; "why continue this pleading? If there were danger—if I were going to die—I should still go home, relying on my child being in safe hands. God bless him and you! and—Good-bye!"

I leaped into my carriage, and was borne away.

Looking from the window, I could still see Gilbert standing on the spot where I had left him, with his gaze directed towards me—standing bareheaded and alone.

Could I but pray that in myself all sin, and shame, and misery were concentrated, and that his life might be eternal peace, and spared long to guard my child!

In his after life of tranquillity and happiness, chequered by but the lightest shadows of every-day occurrence—shadows that are here and gone—I can but believe that that prayer was heard, uttered as it was by sinful lips, and prompted by a withered heart like mine.

CHAPTER XLVIII.

THE MEETING AT "THE REST."

I STAND in Wharnby's green churchyard, with my father's grave at my feet and God's sky overhead. Looking from the first unto the last—from the rest of man to the dwelling-place of angels—I repeat a vow, made ere he who sleeps within had slumbered many days. My heart is troubled, and the holy calmness of the young morning reproves me as I make it, but still my heated brain urges the confirmation of the act, and it is sworn to be.

What a fair morning for so black a purpose! The rustling trees, dyed here and there with the first autumn flush of decay, are full of birds whose harmony disturbs the stillness of the early day—the graves are moss-grown, and some are thick with flowers, and there is beauty even in this charnel place.

Old remembered scenes are round me. The winding road by the cliffs, that leads to "The Rest," along which, years ago, I have so often come to this church I stand before, with my father—with Agnes, Gilbert, Edward—with Celia—with Redwin. The sea is still the same—it seems but yesterday I looked upon it on such a day as this with the sunlight tipping every gentle wave. Afar off, in the bold sweep of the coast—I can see the gleaming white cliffs, under whose rugged majesty I have so often strolled. Field on field to the right stretches away to the horizon, dotted here and there with clustering groves, or cottage-roofs, or farmhouse nestling in the valley. At a little distance is the rector's house, and the same white roses I had often plucked at, seem growing by the trellis work, and beneath the shady windows, and I can fancy that the hum of the bees around them comes to me in soft murmurings. The dark waving trees of the shrubbery belonging to my father's home are in the distance, and tell me of the end I have in view, and the rooks are floating over them—specks in the distance.

Wharnby town—a mass of house-roof—is piled together on my left, and Wharnby Harbour, full of shipping, and a forest of masts, breaks the vista of the sea.

Close unto me rises the old grey stone tower from which those giant bells peal out on Sabbath days, and grand in its old age it looks, with the blue heaven for its background.

There are ships with full-spread sails far out upon the waters—there is life in the field of labour—there are men and women moving near the harbour, and yet the sun has hardly risen.

I have not slept throughout the night, and the first beam of the coming day has been welcomed a relief. I have stolen from my hotel, and am prepared. Beneath the cloak I wear I clutch a case containing pistols, one of which will shortly be turned against my breast. My money, letters, are concealed about my person; and I wait in the churchyard—no fitter place for me to wait!—until the sun has risen higher from the east.

Vaudon is an early riser, and I shall meet him before all Wharnby is astir, and this bright morning is the last either he or I will see.

I wait one hour in solitary communion with my thoughts,

and then I move onwards to my destiny. A last look at the grave I shall never see again, but in which I may lie buried with my father, and then I pass through the swing-gate, and cross the chalky road, and move towards the winding path. I am not twenty paces down it, when I see the small figure of the rector coming from his house. I can but stand and watch as it emerges into the roadway, and hurries on a Christian mission to the sick or dying in some cottage home. I watch it out of sight, and move on once more.

As I near "The Rest," my heart bounds, and the blood mounts to my face—less of calm thought, and more of sinful wish—less of my hope in heaven, and more of my revenge on earth.

The lodge-windows are closed against the daylight, and no sign of waking life, save the noisy rooks cawing overhead, is near "The Rest."

"The Rest!"—my home!—the place where he who gave me birth died in his loneliness;—where I have been content—where I have planned and loved—where the best days of my youth were spent—where all lessons learnt in manhood were first taught—where Vaudon and my brother Edward live, usurping Gilbert's birthright. The gates are locked, but there is a wicket that opens with a spring, let into the park-paling a few yards aside, and it turns back slowly on its creaking hinges, and I stand ankle-deep in the long grass, thick with dew.

I strike for the sequestered portions of the park, intending to make my way to the back of the house and garden grounds, and the herds of deer fly before me wildly.

There are signs of neglect about the place—the green slopes are rankly luxuriant, and full of weeds—a sun-dial that I have often leant against and thought of Celia, is broken, and lies in many pieces—and a large vine, that crept along the garden-wall I am rapidly skirting, is trailing in the dust.

The side door is secured that admits me to the garden, but the lock is old and fragile, and one blow with a stone shatters it.

Into the garden, and advancing towards "The Rest."

As I near the house, I slacken my pace, and move more cautiously. The window of the old favourite parlour is unfastened, the blind is raised, and the folding glass doors are open.

He is up—he is there! I feel assured one minute will see me face to face with him.

I try to subdue, in some degree, the agitation that attacks me—I stand and seek to keep down the cry of vengeance that rises to my lips, and for some minutes I shake as with an ague.

Partly composed, I glide along the terrace before the window—pass into the room, and stand before him, like one risen from the dead.

For a moment he sits in the leathern chair—my father's chair—transfixed and wondering. Every line upon my face is so deeply graven now—care has so altered me, and made an old man of me—that the first great surprise comes not immediately upon him.

As I advance, the truth flashes to him; and, clutching each arm of the chair, he rises, with white face and glaring eyes, and the shadow of some fear passes for an instant over him.

Then, he is calm, and, with the hand upon his beard, stands silently regarding me, his tall form erect and still.

My tongue essays to break the bonds that hold it, but I make no sound, and he speaks first.

"I am glad to welcome you, Luke. Edward has not risen yet. He shall be summoned. I hope that you are well?"

He moves towards me with extended hand.

My tongue is free at last, and, recoiling from the proffered touch, I scream out, "Back!"

Again the shadow of some fear darkens his face, and, halting abruptly, he fixes on me those glittering, snake-like eyes.

"Back!" he repeats; "have you returned with hatred for me, Luke?"

"I have returned for vengeance, Jacques Vaudon," I say, sternly. "I have returned to cancel, by one stroke, the injuries you have for years heaped on us. You are unearthed!"

He takes a long breath, passes his hand across his face, and then is cold and placid, and a well-known curl of the upper lip betrays the ready sneer. It may be a natural recovery to his old demeanour—it may be forced, to hide an inward dread of something he knows not of; but he says, with his accustomed voice, and its deep intonation unfaltering in the least—

"You have returned a madman! Sorrow and affliction have diseased your understanding, and you take your friends for foes."

"I have taken foes for friends, years since," I answer; "now, the masks have fallen to the ground. Vaudon, I have come with but one purpose; and that is, to fight you to the death. There is no avoiding it—there is no backward step—there is a bloody retribution coming."

"Of what do you charge me, weak-minded friend?" sneers Vaudon. "You are ever ready with some slander. Let me hear the last."

"No slander, but the truth revealed at last!" I cried.

"The truth, then."

"Vaudon, I am not here to demand reparation for my own wrongs—for many cruel actions that have tended to blast the whole current of my life—they are known and past; but of deep villany, such as devil only could have planned, and followed out, I stand in this room the accuser—I have come to revenge my father!"

"Go on."

"To revenge my mother's shame brought about by you. *My mother!* Do you hear?"

He presses his hand across his face more slowly than before, then buries it in the drooping beard again.

"For what reason do you couple your mother's disgrace with any action of my own?"

"I have seen her!" I cry, maddened at his composure, which nothing seems to shake; "I have heard her own lips pronounce the name of the dastard who envied his friend's happiness, and tore it from him with his lustful hands—I have witnessed the wreck of a woman that she is, and that you have made her. If there be no accusations against you in these walls and beneath this roof, by the fireside, or at the grave in Wharnby's churchyard—as there cannot be to such a man as you—here am I with a more powerful means to aid me. I am here at *his* command—he spoke it from his coffin!"

I drew the case of pistols from beneath my cloak, and flung it on the table beside which I stood.

Vaudon begins to pace the room; his hands drop to his side, his calmness gradually forsakes him. Like a tiger caught in a snare, from which there is no escape, baffled at all points, he turns with a spring, at last.

"Well, why deny it to you above all men?" he cries, his broad chest heaving, and his hands clenched. "If you have found the secret, I am not the coward to disown it. Nay, more, I glory in the success of all that I have planned. By the God you pray to, I am glad that my revenge has swept across you all with such utter devastation! I have prosecuted it for a lifetime; I swore it years ago, when your father first married the only woman that I loved. Patience, patience—hear me out! Young as your mother was—but a child in other eyes—I loved her with such a passion as you, puling boy, have never known. Without one thing to love but her, there was no limit to my fondness. And she loved me till *he* came, my college friend—the one I thought I might have trusted with my secret. What did he do—what did he do, but rob me of my prize, but win her from me, and take her to his home, and give her his own name? I swore, upon his wedding day, to have a lasting revenge upon them *both*, that should never sleep, but follow them for ever, and wreak its hate even upon their children. I never forgot that vow. To them I was fair and open—I was their friend and confidant; but I had already begun to undermine. The time came. I won her love back after many years, and fled with her, and we fixed the shame upon another's head—that was a rare stratagem, that stood me in good stead. Well—I left her to the streets, and returned unsatiated and hungering for further prey. Mine was no English revenge—there was Italian spirit in it. I tracked you to this spot, and never quitted it until I had debased ye all. Was it not a glorious triumph, Luke Elmore, and did not your father reward me for it with his gold? What care I if it be known to all the world, now I have worked my schemes out? What should I fear from you, braggart, that I will shoot like a dog?"

"Your hours are numbered."

"Liar!" vociferated Vaudon; "it is your own doom that you have come to seek. If I have hated one of his children above all the rest, it has been you. Would that I had strangled you when we first met on the sands!"

"The time for words has gone—the hour for action has arrived—dare you follow me?"

I point towards the park.

"You require no seconds?" he asks.

"None."

"Your brother?"

"I would see him."

"And tell him all?"

"It matters not to *him*."

"I expect him every moment; if you are in no hurry, we will wait."

He is calm again, but every word is murmured through lips rigidly compressed.

It is not long before my brother breaks in upon our silent companionship, and cries out, "Luke!" with intense surprise.

"An unexpected visitor," I say, with a faint smile.

"Unexpected, indeed!" he answers—"but what has happened?"

He looks from me to Vaudon, and back again, and neither reply. At length I break the silence.

"What has transpired in this room, and on this morning, will, as I have said to *him*," pointing to Vaudon, "affect you but little. Let it suffice you to know we have met to settle an old quarrel, and that we thirst for one another's life. If you will come with us, so good; if you stay behind, I have one commission for you."

"But what folly is it?" he asks of Vaudon.

"He has found out the author of your mother's disgrace," answers Vaudon, boldly; "and that author is myself."

Edward starts, and his face flushes. A moment, and he is calm, and answers, "She is not worth fighting about. Come, come, men, shake hands with each other, and be friends. A quarrel, such as Luke threatens, would be unpleasant in the extreme."

"If you could guess half the hate with which I regard that man," I say, "you would spare me your commonplace effort to bring about a reconciliation. Reconciliation!" I repeat; "brother, have you no more honour in your heart, or shame within you, than to wish it?"

Edward, with more earnestness, turns to Vaudon.

"You will not accept this hot-headed challege, Vaudon? For my sake, give not way to such folly, or humour that of my brother. What should *I* do if you were killed?"

This solicitude in Vaudon's safety fires me to delirium.

"Will you come with us, Edward?"

Vaudon moves towards the open window.

"You are really going?" cries my brother to him.

"Yes; and if time has not palsied my hand, or weakened my sight, the Lord have mercy on him!"

I snatch the case of pistols on the table, and we three pass out of the cold room into the sunlight.

Vaudon leads the way; he walks slowly towards the gate I had broken to effect an entrance, and his hand gripes at his beard, and his high forehead is crossed by a hundred lines, and he pays no heed to the remonstrances that Edward urges.

How I hate him! I do not think of my own chances in the struggle now; I cannot but believe he will atone, so far as there is atonement unto man, for his long enmity to father, mother, sons, by a bloody death. I feel that he is going to his fate.

Into the deep recesses of the park we wind our way, and Vaudon halts in a wild glade, and, looking at me fixedly, says—

"Will this be secluded enough, think you?"

"It will do," I answer, hollowly.

"Then it will do for me," he says, shrugging his shoulders.

With one knee bent upon the grass, I seek to unlock the case I have brought with me.

"We are ill-matched, Luke Elmore," says Vaudon; "but you will have it, and your death will lic lightly on my conscience. I am a veteran in the art, and you a novice, and must pay dearly for the lesson I have to teach. Make your arrangements with your brother!"

Edward stands moodily regarding us. Unlocking the case, and rising, I say—

"I have but one arrangement to make; I have a letter to place in your hands, Edward. If I fall, you will send it to my brother Gilbert?"

"Yes," he answers, surlily.

"If I shall be destined for the avenger, still send it, or keep it for a time. It may be a proof required to exculpate you from any share in what may happen here this day."

Meanwhile, Vaudon has stooped and taken up the silver-mounted pistols in the case.

"A handsome pair," he mutters, sneeringly, "and new ones for the occasion. That is unwise."

A moment's pause.

"Are these loaded?"

"Yes."

"Who loaded them?"

"I had them loaded by the maker."

"I will take your word. Quick!" he cries, impatiently; "we tarry here too long."

"Will you choose?"

He carcfully examines them, and then passes one across to me.

Edward's cheek turns pale, and he murmurs a few last words of intercession; but with pain I note that they are all for Vaudon.

"Will you call, Edward?" asks Vaudon, weighing the pistol in his hand.

"Not I—not I!"

"Then the task devolves on me," he says. "Mr. Elmore, if you will stand where that sun-track marks the grass—a fair distance, I conjecture—and fire at the word 'Three,' you will oblige me."

There is an affectation in his calmness now, for I can see his teeth almost biting through his lip. My want of fear, my fixed determination, startles him for the first time.

I stride to the spot indicated, and he faces me at some distance with the silver-mounted pistol in his hand. Edward, with suspended breath, stands watching.

"Are you prepared?" he asks.

"I am."

My cloak has fallen to the ground, and I stand erect before him, without a quickening pulse or faltering hand.

"*One!*"

We raise our pistols; the sunlight gleams upon the polished barrel, but I see his heart behind it.

"*Two!*"

One look at my brother. If I fall I shall have seen him once again. The word "Three" remains unpronounced; he hesitates, and stands before me struggling with his speech. Does the shadow fall upon him now?

With his disengaged hand he sweeps back his hair from his brow, and, making one step forward, shouts—"*Three!*"

There is but one report, and loud and clear it rings from the pistol in my hand; there is but one man lying with a look of death upon his face, and that is Jacques Vaudon, the seducer of my mother.

Dropping the pistol in the long grass, I cross towards the prostrate form, convulsed with horror and alarm. Edward is hanging over him, but Vaudon resists his efforts to take his hand, or let a touch fall on him, and cries, as I advance—

"What juggling is this?"

"I know not. It is an awful mystery."

I stoop and take up the pistol beside Vaudon. It is unloaded!

"Good God! this is murder!" I exclaim.

"Treachery—treachery!" gasps Vaudon, with his hand to his breast.

"I knew it not; I sought not such revenge as this. I offered my own life for yours."

He replies not, but the bloody hand at his breast drops

powerless, and he murmurs, "You did not slay me with suc intent? Well, I must believe it—I will believe it. There ha been some mistake. Were—were——"

After a pause for breath, he goes on—"Were the pistol examined by you?"

"I told the man to load them; I was satisfied; I did no think, or care to test them."

"Fool—blind fool that I have been!"

He lies upon the grass, red with his life's blood, and pant like a dog. After a pause—

"If there be—if there be—a God," he says, his heavy lid closing over his glazed eyes—"there was his hand in this. Bu I do not—do not—think—that—if——"

He pauses, we stoop over him, he is dead.

Edward kneels beside him, and shrieks his name, and wring his hands in lamentation. I touch my brother, and he screams "Away, you have killed my only friend—my father—my sol comforter! Go on your course, murderer!"

I go. Stealing through the park, crouching by the garde wall, conscious that I have slain one of God's creatures, wh stood helplessly before me—conscious of how poor a gratifica tion is revenge, no matter the just cause of the avenger, feel that curse of blood upon me that no prayer can avert— the stain that no repentance can erase.

* * * * *

The figure never leaves me, although we are on the dark ened plain shadowed by the mountain, and there is no need c guidance more. The sun is set, the night is here, and yet th phantom waits; I cannot elude it, it is ever with me. Threaten ing, or imploring, it still abideth, and there is no rest for m The mountains, by which I am environed, have no charms i their rugged beauty, and I can but shun the hardy village who salute me as I cross their path.

In the bright morning comes the echoing horn, and I sta to despair and another day; and the eagle soars with flappin wings into the blue depths of the sky.

But the eagle has its young in the nest on the cliff, and m thoughts cannot soar to the heaven!

THE END.

CPSIA information can be obtained
at www.ICGtesting.com
Printed in the USA
LVHW101927170422
716440LV00004BA/304

9 783752 590265